Atlanta

The Veil: Book Two

J.N. Smith

To my mom, who made me read Nancy Drew and the Clue of the Whistling Bagpipes when I was a kid.
I love you.

One Week Earlier

KATIE SWALLOWED a groan as the throb beneath her skull turned into a drum solo, beating against the back of her eyeballs like John Bonham in a circa 1970 Led Zeppelin concert. Inhaling a mixture of fresh and burnt motor oil, she tilted her phone, then spun around slowly, praying she didn't throw up. Her tongue was a shag carpet in her mouth as Bonzo banged away at her temples and she tried to swallow. *Bonzo?* Her perfectly sculpted brows came together. And since when did she know anything about Led Zeppelin?

A vague, only *slightly* shameful memory from the night before surfaced. She'd been drunk and mostly naked in his bed. Not Bonzo's, some other guy's. She couldn't remember his name, but... he was young and single and the son of the largest RV manufacturer on the east coast. She forgot if there was anything more to him or not. But what she *did* remember was that he'd been boring her out of her mind with his collection of old rock videos and trivia while she petted his weirdly friendly Siamese cat named Fred, and his yacht rocked gently in the water off the south Georgia coast. The memory vanished, but the rocking remained as she blinked, and the task at hand came back into focus.

Making another turn, she lifted the phone a little higher. The right angle was the difference between her looking twenty-six and her actual age, which was a decade beyond that. It was difficult enough in good lighting, let alone in the gloomy garage. And her hangover wasn't helping a damn thing.

Walking toward the bay doors, but making sure she could still see Old Ray in the background, she panned her phone again and finally found it. *There!* Good light. Good background too. She simultaneously frowned and rubbed her forehead to relax the wrinkles creasing it.

Those damn worry lines were getting harder to hide.

Rolling her shoulders, she went through her checklist, starting with the top of her head, and working her way down to her feet. She learned early on that everyone in social media needed one, because once it was out there, that tree sticking out of your head like reindeer antlers, the booger in your nose, or your side boob–the gross kind that looked like an infant's fat little thigh—it was carved in proverbial stone, preserved for all eternity by the eidetic scribe of the modern era—the internet.

Her eyes dropped to the ample cleavage spilling out of the top of her white halter top. They were double D's and as perky as the barista at her favorite LA coffee shop. Boobs. Check.

The only thing in the mechanic's shop more valuable than the implants in her chest was the car that had landed her there. Both were top of the line, and the saying was true. *You get what you pay for*—she tugged the front of her top down just a fraction more—unless you were a social influencer, which she was. Then, as long as you maintained your popularity and got enough 'likes,' you got expensive things like breasts and vintage 1968 Chevy Corvette Stingray's, for free.

Well, technically, the car was a loaner until she got to New York, where they were holding a massive antique car auction for vehicles just like Old Ray, except with way fewer miles. She'd been elated when the auction house had contacted her and asked her to be their spokesperson. But the point was… The hangover gremlin in her head elbowed the back of her eyeballs, and she forgot what her point was.

Oh well.

Katie smiled brightly, revealing two rows of perfect, white teeth she hadn't paid for either, and hit the red record button.

She waved. "Hey!" Her annoyingly cheerful voice momentarily drowned out the throbbing against her eardrums. Faking an itch on the side of her nose, she sneaked her manicure into the shot. "Soooo... The bad news is, Old Ray overheated." She made her signature pouty face, which looked *much* cuter when she was eighteen, and invented it, and MySpace was still a thing. Oh well, again.

"Boo hoo," she said before flashing another brilliant smile. "*But*, the good news is that Mike, here..." She panned to the old man staring, mouth hanging open beneath his bushy, gray mustache like she'd just climbed down from the mother ship with a probe. "...at Mike's Auto Body in..." She drew a blank and her wrinkles gathered together in the middle of her forehead like annoying coworkers around a water cooler. *Fuck.*

With a sigh, Katie rolled her eyes and jabbed the stop button, dropping her arm as sweat dripped down her back. That was one of many reasons she hated the South. Too damn hot. Lifting it back up, she deleted the take. "Where are we again?" she asked, glancing at Mike over the top of her phone.

Mike blinked as if coming out of a trance. "Huh?"

"What is the name of this—"

"Hartford Creek."

Katie rolled her eyes again. Damn it. She *knew* that. The friendly redneck with a pickup that had towed Old Ray here from the lonesome stretch of highway where she'd broken down had told her his grandfather was *the* original Hartford. She wasn't as impressed by that fact now as she had been then. "Yes, that's right. Thanks." She wanted to rub her aching eyes, but refrained. It would take twenty minutes to redo her makeup if she smudged it. Turning back to the bay doors and the light, she got into position, went through her checks, flashed a smile, and began again.

"Hey!" she said, scratching her nose. "Soooo…"

The pounding in her head resumed, mixing with her voice as she spoke, and she deeply regretted the three-hundred-dollar bottle of Veuve Clicquot she'd purchased and consumed the night before. But ten-dollar shots of vodka were not worth the money or calories, and lover boy only drank scotch, so not wanting it to go to waste, she'd had no choice but to drink the entire bottle herself. "Mike here—" A wave of nausea rolled through her belly as she spun around and focused her phone on him. "At Mike's Auto Body in *Hartford Creek,* Georgia, has come to my rescue." She ducked into the shot and put her arm around his shoulders. With her heels on, he only came up to her chin, so she crouched down. Her face hurt from smiling, but she kept it in place. "My hero here has ordered a new…?"

"Er. Um. Th-thermostat."

She kissed his cheek, and they reddened on the screen of her phone. "Right. Thermostat. So as soon as that comes in, Mike will fix her up and—" Katie noticed the shadows under her eyes. They looked like twin hobo bags dangling from her face. Releasing Mike, she hurried back into the sunlight, practically tripping over her shoes, which reminded her she had to feature them. *Why do you do this to yourself?* An annoying voice asked. That question had been popping up a lot lately.

Lifting the phone higher so she could get her 'designer' shoes in the shot, she said, "Oh! I almost forgot. Check out these one-of-a-kind wedges from Caroline Banks."

As for why she did this to herself, well, what else was she supposed to do? She was a thirty-six-year-old high school dropout who had spent her entire adult life smiling in front of a camera. She did this because it was too late to start over and because, even if she wanted to, what she *wanted* now was completely out of reach. For a minute there, she'd had a chance with Matt, but then she'd gotten scared and…Well, as her mother would say, she'd dug her grave, and now she was lying in it.

Twisting her foot, she revealed the side of the wedge, which was carved out of some kind of sustainable wood. Multicolored pom-poms decorated the strap that covered her toes. They were literally the ugliest shoes she'd ever seen, and she'd almost died laughing when they'd arrived at her apartment.

"Aren't these wild?" She twisted her foot from side-to-side, not knowing why she bothered. They were unlovely from every angle, except maybe the bottom. "If I had to describe them in two words, I'd say—Hmm. Hip and…" Tapping her fingernail against her teeth, she skillfully showed off both as her stomach rocked and her brain, still hopped up on day-old alcohol, began offering suggestions.

Hideous?

No.

Repulsive?

No!

The unholy union of a rodeo clown and a tiki bar? She forced the corners of her mouth down. That was over two words. And, yes. But no. No funny stuff. *Why? It's fun—* "Fun!" She slapped her thigh. "Hip and *fun*."

That was close. She'd almost had to scrap the shot again. "Anyway, as soon as the new *thermostat* is put in Old Ray, I'll be back on my way up to NYC for the big auction. Come see me there! And also for the debut of Orlando Ventimiglia's winter collection—" she quickly positioned the phone back on her best angle "—which I'm *so* excited to be exclusively modeling for *again* this year."

The truth was, she was terrified. The 'real' models were in their teens, early twenties, with waists the size of toothpicks, making her look like a whale in comparison. And her breasts, while great for social media, were a nightmare on the runway. She'd been starving herself for the last month, and was still

5

afraid they'd have to rip the zippers out and sew her into the clothes. She'd lived through that humiliation before as a dozen wafer-thin girls stared on in horror, and she didn't want to do it again.

Katie flashed her nails again, then ran her fingers through her hair, getting the bright red tips in the shot. "Well, that's it for now. Until next time, keep living your perfect life, whatever that is! As you can see, I'm living mine! Love you!" She made kissy lips at the phone, then stopped the recording before she let her shoulders sag.

Perfect life.

"Pfft," she puffed, rolling her eyes. She didn't know what that was anymore. And the harder she tried to figure it out, the more elusive it became.

It reminded her of one summer when she was a kid. It was 107 degrees in south Florida, and while the other kids in her neighborhood were enjoying the sprinkler or popsicles, her mother had given her a bowl of ice cubes and locked her out of the house while she entertained a 'guest'.

Katie had sat with that bowl in her lap, shoulders pressed against the sharp edges of peeling paint in the thin seam of shade provided by the overhanging edge of the roof, sucking on the cubes and squeezing the cool blocks in her hands, trying to make them last. But the harder she tried to hold on to them, the quicker they disappeared, until there was nothing left but a bowl of hot water and a heat-stroked little girl crying to go inside.

Pulling her sunglasses over her eyes, she tagged the auction house that Old Ray belonged to, the department store that had gifted her the top and skirt, the aforementioned fledgling but wealthy shoe designer, the nail salon, Felix the hair stylist, Mike's Auto Body, and of course, Dr. Rayburn, L.A.'s premiere plastic surgeon. She hit 'post,' then sighed heavily.

The show was over. At least for the next hour.

Opening her transportation app, she went to hire a ride into Atlanta.

Zero appeared.

Turning to Mike, who was still staring at her like she was a fairy that had popped out of the red Georgia earth, she smiled. "Sorry about the video. It's just part of the job."

"Oh, that's—"

"Do you guys have Uber out here?"

Mike frowned. "A what?"

"Like a transportation service. Even a taxi would—"

"Nope. Ain't got nothin' like that around here."

His accent reminded Katie of her parents. It was a little heavier than your typical south Floridian, but it had the same cadence and drawl.

"Shit." She glanced down at her phone again. She hadn't seen the actual town, but if this little side street was any indication, she absolutely did not want to stay here until Old Ray was fixed.

Maybe she could hire a ride from the city? And... Scrolling through her contacts in Atlanta, she messaged a couple of high-end boutique hotels she'd stayed at a few years earlier, letting them know she was in town. Maybe she could score a suite. And there was that jewelry designer Zara, whom she'd partied with in Cabo, about a month back. She was a bitch, but then, mostly, they all were. She messaged her as well. Looking up, she asked, "Is there a bus? I need to get to Atlanta."

Mike shook his head. "No, ma'am. But I can have my guy take ya."

Although it happened all the time, and had for the past fifteen plus years, it still surprised Katie that anyone would go out of their way for her. Along with a chronic sensitivity to heat, it was an unshakable remnant of the pathetic girl she'd been before she was Katie Newman. "Really? Are you sure?" Atlanta was almost two hours away, as best she could tell.

The old man smiled, and she felt it, a good, wholesome, albeit semi-toothless, vibe. "Sure thing. No problem. I'll have my tow-truck driver take ya. He just went to luncheon."

Katie's perfectly sculpted brow went up. *Luncheon?*

Mike went on. "But as soon as—" he checked his watch. "Tell ya what. Go get a bite at the bar, and I'll have him come pick you up there when he gets back."

Katie smiled gratefully. "That would be perfect. Thank you so much, Mike. For everything." A bar was just what she needed. Dark and cool, and she could get a beer to take the edge off.

"It ain't nothing. Just doing my job."

Picking up her actual hobo bag, as opposed to the ones attached to her face, she took a step toward the door, then realized she didn't know where she was going. She turned back around. "Where is the bar? Is it in town?"

Mike laughed. "This is town."

Her brows went up again. Was he joking? Looking back toward the road, she squinted. There were a handful of what looked like abandoned old buildings, two houses, both with parched front yards, and a single old tire swing hanging from a towering oak tree between them.

That was it. There wasn't even a creek that she could see, so technically, it should have just been called Hartford. "I beg your pardon?"

Mike scratched the back of his head with a nervous chuckle. "Yep. Ain't much to her."

That was an understatement. Katie's bag slid off her shoulder, and she hoisted it back up. "Oh, um…Well, which one is the —" She squinted again, looking for a sign. None of the buildings were marked. Because why would they be? It didn't even look like anyone lived here besides Mike.

"It's the one ain't selling groceries or gas."

The corners of her mouth turned up. Ah, a funny guy.

A car rolled through the intersection and pulled to a stop in front of the middle building.

Mike pointed. "That there is Goebell's Grocery. The building on the right, at the corner..." Katie glanced at the blinking yellow light suspended above the crossroad. "...is the gas station. They also serve ice cream, if you're inclined." Katie hadn't had ice cream in over a decade. "And the one on the left, with the second floor—"

"The bar."

"Yep."

She sighed. Well, at least she didn't have to go far. "How will I know your driver?"

Mike pulled the greasy ball cap from his head and ran his fingers through his thinning gray hair. "Don't worry about that. He'll know you, I reckon."

Fair enough.

Hoisting her bag over her shoulder again, Katie carefully picked her way over the uneven concrete outside the shop, and across the pothole filled road. As she neared the buildings, she noticed the gravel lot out back, a handful of pickup trucks, beat up old cars that couldn't possibly still run, and a county sheriff's cruiser. Blinking, she made a slow three-sixty, noticing a handful of other decrepit houses back behind Mike's, and a pond, and finished the tour by looking up into the cloudless Georgia sky. "Congratulations," she whispered. If there was a middle of nowhere, she had found it.

Her gaze dropped to an old woman in a brightly colored floral printed shirt and black slacks struggling to get out of the car parked in front of the grocery store.

Katie tried not to roll an ankle as she hurried over to her, pom-poms bouncing. "Here, let me help you."

Pushing her hair back over her shoulder, she gently took the old woman's arm and pulled her to her feet.

"Thank you," the woman said, clutching the door, then

pushing her palms into her lower back as she stretched. "Oof." With closed eyes, she shook her head. "I'm gonna die in that car," she muttered. "One of these days I won't make it up outta that damn seat and Easton is gonna find me dead in my driveway, bloated and stinking to all hell…" Her voice trailed off as she finally opened her eyes. "Good lord," she whispered, staring at Katie's breasts, which were directly at eye level. Then she did a quick sweep from head to toe, her eyes widening as they landed on her shoes. "Oh, my. Aren't those…" Her eyes went back up to Katie's chest, and Katie's cheeks turned an even deeper shade of pink than the heat had managed on its own. She was not ashamed of the way she looked. Biting her lip, she looked down. Well, maybe the shoes…

"My apologies," the old woman said, her eyes crinkling at the corners as she met Katie's. "We just don't get many women like you around these parts." Katie guessed it was closer to none. "And you are just so…" The old woman's eyes fell to her breasts again. "…tall." Looking back up, she winked, making Katie laugh.

The old woman shuffled to the side. "Would you mind getting my purse? It's in the passenger's seat."

"Sure." Katie ducked into the sweltering car, wondering how the woman wasn't dead from heat stroke already, and pulled out a handbag so old that nearly all the black faux leather had rubbed off to reveal the white cotton fabric underneath.

"Thank you, darlin'," she said, as Katie handed it to her.

"Do you need help inside?" Katie asked, seriously doubting the woman would survive the next five minutes, let alone walking over the neglected concrete in the infernal heat.

"Oh no, love. I been navigating this damn town for eighty-one years. Ain't a stone on the ground I'm not acquainted with."

Katie stepped back, believing her, but still doubting she'd make it without falling. "Okay. Well, you have a nice…day."

The old woman slammed the door of the car and shuffled

toward the crumbling sidewalk that separated the buildings from the road. "You too, darlin'."

Katie made her way back toward the door of the bar, as the old woman paused at the decrepit curb, then heaved herself over it.

That will be you someday. Yes, she was aware. Pushing the morbid thought aside, she pulled open the door. A bell above her head jingled as she slid her sunglasses on top of her head and stepped into the gloomy bar.

It was just as she knew it would be. What she could see of it, anyway. Dingy bar, surrounded by a handful of old tables with vinyl chairs that looked very much like the purse she'd just handed off. A half-lit neon sign, filthy linoleum floors, a poster offering fifty-cent beers on 'ladies' night,' and a trio of ominous shadows sitting at the darkest end of the counter.

All of it reminded her of her dad and his friends.

"Great…" she whispered under her breath.

Her shoes clacked on the peeling tiles, and a chill raced down her spine as she pushed the memories back. Maybe she should do a quick social media post here. So when she went missing, they would know where to look for her body. *They who?*

Katie made her way to the bar top.

Matt would look for her. Even though she'd royally fucked everything up and he'd barely spoken to her in two years. He'd look for her because—*Do you honestly think he still loves you?* No, she didn't. That ship had sailed long ago. She didn't blame him, either. But he would still come. Because he was a good guy, the only one she'd ever know, and that was what good guys did. They showed up. Even when they didn't have to. Even for shitty ex-fiancés.

A toilet flushed somewhere down the dark hallway at the back, and a moment later, a small, tired-looking woman emerged from a dark hallway, wiping her hands on the grease-stained apron tied around her skeletal waist.

Katie had to *literally* starve herself to fit into a size eight, and here this woman was thin as a rail, and probably not even trying. She pushed the thought away, repeating the ever-so-deep mantra her therapist and current L.A. fuck-buddy, Hunter, told her to say when she tumbled down the rabbit hole of insecurity that seemed to plague her lately. *Let it be.* She was pretty sure he stole it from the Beatles, but when she asked him, he just sighed, accused her of using humor as a coping mechanism, and rolled her on her back.

The old woman passed behind the bar.

"Food'll be out shortly," she said to the men as she made her way down to Katie. "What can I get for ya?" she asked.

By the tone of her voice and the way she set her hands on her hips, Katie knew she was waiting for her to ask for something complicated and snobby. Like a skinny mojito or something. But she had been around places like this enough to know what she could and could not get. "A light beer and—Do you have coffee?"

The woman nodded.

"Coffee, black, please?"

"You want a menu?"

Heaving her bag onto the bar, she slid onto a sticky stool. "No, thanks." Small town bars always carried the same fare. And she couldn't eat any of it.

Apparently it was a one person show, because after pouring Katie a beer and a coffee, the woman hurried back into the kitchen.

Katie tested her coffee as the men at the end of the bar laughed. It was too hot, but tasted fantastic considering where she was. Or she was more hung over than she thought.

Her hands closed around the sweating pint glass next, and she took a swig. The beer was unremarkable and flat, and if the bar reminded her of her dad, the beer reminded her of her mom. "Cheers, mama," she said under her breath.

The smell of greasy fries made Katie's stomach rumble as the bartender set the men's food on the rail.

Pulling her phone out of her purse, Katie went to her photos. She must not have eaten at all last night. But she couldn't remember. Everything between the yacht leaving the harbor and waking up this morning in bed with… whatever his name was, was a blur except for Bonzo and the cat.

"Hey Barbie, you got any ketchup back there?" The tallest of the men wearing a sheriff's uniform asked as Katie's stomach growled again.

The seated man was the only one who thanked Barbie when she set the bottle in front of them, calling her Barb instead, as she hurried back into the kitchen.

From the photos Katie had taken, it didn't look like she'd eaten.

She checked her stats. Eight hundred likes on the mechanic post already. And about fifty offers for a ride. Katie scrolled through the names, recognizing most of them, knowing she would not accept a ride from any of them if her life depended on it.

The men at the bar laughed again, and the tall sheriff caught her eye. Built, buzzed, and blond, he was watching her.

Barb or Barbie reappeared. "You want another beer?"

Katie looked down, not even realizing she had finished the pint. She'd have to run an extra two miles if she had another one. Just the thought made her tired. "No, thanks. I'll stick with coffee for now."

Barb gave her a shrewd once-over. "Smart girl."

Katie harrumphed. That was debatable.

"Where you from?" Barb asked.

"Nowhere really."

The older woman pushed her gray, frizzy hair off her forehead and crossed her arms as she leaned back against the bar behind her. "Everyone's from somewhere."

Katie took another sip of her coffee. "South Florida originally, I guess."

"You guess?"

Katie had dropped out of high school her senior year, left Florida, and never looked back.

"I haven't been back there in a while." If one counted sixteen years 'a while.'

The bartender nodded in approval. "Where you headed?"

"New York for—"

"Hey there," a man's voice interrupted.

Katie turned. The sheriff stood beside her, smelling like cheap aftershave and a greasy burger. With bright blue eyes, he had a lanky-cowboy thing going on, and he was even more handsome up close, although something about him immediately set her on edge.

She smiled automatically. "Hello."

"What in the hell is a pretty little thing," Katie repressed the urge to roll her eyes. "...like you doing in a shitpot like Hartford Creek?"

Barb scowled. "Hey, now."

"Sorry Barbie, but you know it's true." The sheriff flashed Katie a swoon-worthy smile. "Name's Easton Barnes. I'm the law around here."

Katie covered her laugh with a cough. *And a grade-A asshole around here too,* she'd bet. "Oh, the law, huh?" She took his outstretched hand and went to shake it. Instead, he rolled it skyward and ran his lips across her palm.

Her brow went up. *Bold.* And smoothly executed. It was also completely wasted on her because she was not at all interested in men whose confidence exceeded their respect for women. And his clearly did. He'd probably call her baby-doll, and smack her ass if she'd let him.

Sheriff Easton eyed her like a meal he wanted to binge on as

14

she pulled her hand away and turned back toward the bar. "Nice to meet you."

"Looks like you could use some company," he said, placing his hand on her shoulder.

Slowly, she slid it off. Yes, his confidence definitely exceeded...most likely every other quality he had. "I'm fine, thanks."

"Nonsense," he insisted. "What kinda gentleman would I be if I let you eat—"

"But I'm not even eat—"

"Leave her alone, Easton." The voice at the end of the bar sounded tired.

Sheriff Barnes turned, and Katie squinted at the man seated at the end, hunched over a basket of fries and a burger. He did not look up.

"Shut up, Dayton," the sheriff said, turning back to Katie. "Barbie, bring my burger down here will ya?" He sat down. "As I was saying—"

It was Katie's turn to cut him off. "I appreciate the offer, sheriff—"

"Sergeant."

"Right. Sorry. But really, I'm just here to wait—"

Easton put a hand on her shoulder again. "It's my duty as an officer and a gentleman," he squeezed, "...to keep you—"

The screech of a barstool sliding back cut off the rest, and she turned as the voice from the end of the bar came again. "Didn't you hear her? She doesn't want your company. Just leave her alone."

Katie looked around the sheriff as the man who had been seated at the end came into the light.

He was a little over six feet tall, with broad shoulders. Despite being inside, he wore his ball cap low over his eyes. Barrel chested and solid, he had a rounder, diamond in the rough

15

physique than the sheriff, but that combined with his scruffy beard, and piercing brown eyes framed by thick lashes gave him a gritty, don't-give-a-shit sex appeal that the sheriff did not possess.

Normally she went for a six-pack over solid, smooth jaws and younger too, but the tattoos peeking out from under the sleeves of his T-shirt, and the fact that he didn't seem to be a self-righteous chauvinist prick more than made up for the lack of chiseled abs and a clean shave, and she found herself staring. Katie met his eyes, and to her surprise, she felt the elusive '*it*.' The trifecta of genuine attraction. It was different for everyone, but for her, it was shortness of breath. Check. Thumping heart. Check. Tingling everywhere, she liked to be touched. She bit her lip. *Definite* check.

The third man, who closely resembled the sheriff in stature and height, but older—probably his brother—put a hand on Dayton's arm for the same reason Sheriff Barnes had put one on hers. To intimidate him. Unlike her, however, Dayton shrugged it off and gave the other man a piece of his mind. "Don't fucking touch me, Wes." he warned.

The sheriff got up with a testosterone-soaked laugh that immediately set Katie on edge. She knew it well, and what followed usually ended badly for the person it was directed at. "Are you seriously trying to cut in?" he asked.

Dayton cast her a deadly look that she didn't understand and snorted. "No."

He wasn't lying. His disdain for her was coming across almost as strongly as his dislike of the sheriff, and she wondered if she'd met him before and pissed him off? She'd only been to Georgia once before. Or maybe he was a disgruntled fan? Katie racked her brain, trying to picture him as one of her followers, but couldn't. He looked like the kind of guy who didn't even know what social media was.

The sheriff laughed again. "You are."

Dayton ignored him and looked at her like she had some

kind of contagious disease he was trying to avoid. "If you want to eat in peace, you can sit with me. I'll leave you alone," he offered.

The sheriff snorted. "*You?* With *that?*" he asked.

That? She crossed her arms. "Excuse m—"

The sheriff cut her off. "In your fucking dreams, Day," he said, making her sound like an expensive watch.

Dayton took a step toward the sheriff, who took a step of his own while puffing up his chest like a rooster in a cockfight.

"Now, wait a second," Katie jumped up and stepped between them. Besides being cocky, the sheriff was a hothead. Her eyes darted to the brother. So was he. She met Dayton's eyes again. Not him so much. At least she didn't think so. But he *was* genuinely angry about something and out for blood, and she was pretty sure it wasn't because the sheriff was hitting on her. "Guys…"

While there was a time in her life when she would have been flattered to cause a bar brawl, she knew better now. Sensing imminent danger, Katie's hand shot out. She smiled at Dayton as her fingers curled around the sheriff's bicep, hoping he understood how much she appreciated the gesture he'd made on her behalf. "Thanks for the offer, but—" she looked up at the sheriff. As long as they remained in public, she could handle guys like him. It was only when they got her alone that they became dangerous. "On second thought, I'd love for you to join me for lunch, sheriff."

"Sergeant," he said, sitting back down.

She nodded. "Right."

Dayton saw right through her lie. "Don't let him intimidate you. You don't have to do anything you don't—"

She jumped as the sheriff slammed his fist on the bar. His stool skidded back as he stood up. "What is your fucking problem?" he demanded, his tanned cheeks turning red.

Someone had said something similar to her father, just before practically beating him to death with a pool cue in a place just like this.

Katie grabbed his arm. "Come on guys—"

Dayton took another step toward the sheriff, fist clenched, and she had no doubt he'd give the two men a run for their money. But eventually he'd get tired, and then they'd beat the shit out of him.

"Hey!" Katie grabbed a French fry out of the basket that Barb had set down and stepped between the men again. Coyly, she put it up to the sheriff's lips. Reaching behind her with her other hand, she pushed Dayton back the other way, very aware of his thumping heart against her palm. "I'm fine. I can take care of myself, thanks," she said over her shoulder, trying to ignore the tingling that shot down her arm as he stepped back.

Pulling her arm back around, she drew her fingers across the sheriff's chest and felt nothing but fabric and maybe the urge to throat punch him. She smiled. "Lunch with a handsome sheriff —" his frown faded, and a smile tugged at the corner of his mouth as he opened it "—sounds wonderful." She popped the French fry in and turned, giving Dayton a look that hopefully said, 'Get out while you still can,' as the sheriff grabbed her hand.

Dayton's eyes widened.

Hers did too, as she felt a moist tug on her index finger. *Oh god, no.* Katie squeezed her eyes shut.

The choking sound Dayton made confirmed her fear.

Trying not to gag, she opened her eyes and turned as the sheriff popped her thumb in his mouth and rolled his tongue over it, licking the salt from the french fry off. *Oh wow. Yep.* He was sucking on her fingers.

Katie pulled her hand away as Dayton huffed the incredulous laugh she was trying *very* hard to swallow and wiped her drool covered fingers on her skirt. She'd experienced some weird stuff with guys over the years, but that was a first. "Oh, that was..." She turned back to Dayton, "...interesting."

He looked disgusted. "Are you fucking—"

She cast him a warning glance. "Don't," she mouthed silently.

His jaw snapped shut. Then he shook his head. "Fine. Do what you want."

Turning, he went back to the end of the bar, leaving her with the sheriff and his brother. The sheriff's hand closed over her arm *again* as he guided her to her stool. "Now, where were we?"

As the sheriff droned on, Katie watched Dayton out of the corner of her eye. At one point, Barb said something to him, and he smiled, making her heart skip a beat. What could be funny enough to make *that* broody man grin? She wondered, biting her lip again and rubbing the tingly spot in the crook of her elbow. It had been a long time since she'd had that feeling.

Dayton realized he was being watched and turned. His smile faded as the tingles raced across her shoulder blades down to her fingertips, and she looked away.

After he went back to his meal, she watched him more discreetly in the mirror behind the bar. What was it about him that was so hard to ignore?

His eyes shot up and found hers in the mirror as a thrill raced across her skin. *That.* Katie bit her lip a third time. Yes, that.

———

JJ GRITTED HIS TEETH. Of all the fucked-up things Mike had asked him to do, this was the worst. "I'm not a goddamn chauffeur," he mumbled, pushing the door open and stepping back into the bar.

Easton looked over his shoulder, and rolled his eyes as he stood up. "Goddamn it, JJ. You don't know when to quit, do you?"

His 'fare' turned as JJ made his way toward them. Her eyes were like a match, and his blood turned to gasoline as they locked in his. Fire whooshed through his veins, and he tried to ignore it as she spun off her stool, almost falling over her *very* ugly shoes. He caught her arm.

"Shit," she mumbled, righting herself and pushing her delicious-smelling hair back off her shoulders.

He released her and stepped back as she held up her hand. "I'm fine, really," she insisted.

He rolled his eyes, barely able to get the words past his clenched teeth. "I'm not here to rescue you."

"Get the hell out of here, Jay." Wes said.

JJ ignored him. Wes was like the henchman in every terrible mob movie. Stupid, but innocent. His brother was the real asshole.

He met Ms. Newman's eyes again. "I'm your ride to the city, ma'am." He might have sneered that last word a bit.

Her mouth fell open. "*You're* Mike's driver?" He couldn't tell if she was happy about that or not.

He nodded. "Yep." He might have made the 'p' pop with a little too much contempt too, before pressing his lips together in what he hoped was a very fake smile and crossing his arms over his chest.

She squeezed her eyes shut in—he couldn't tell if it was relief or horror. Probably the latter. But when they flew open again, the smile that spread across her face almost knocked him flat on his ass. He glared at her as he grabbed the back of the nearest chair.

"Where you headed?" Easton asked.

"Atlanta," she said, her eyes never leaving JJ's.

God, she had beautiful eyes. A little heavy on the makeup, but the way the greenish edges faded to brown was... JJ frowned. Wait. Why was he even looking at her eyes?

He noticed Barb watching him from behind the bar and scowled at her.

The way she looked at him was exactly like his mom, making him feel like she could see straight into his brain. He did not like that feeling. His frown deepened. "What?"

Barb's brows went up, just like his mom's did, and then she held her hands up and shrugged innocently, mimicking his mom again. "Nothin," she said, but he knew that look. She was definitely thinking something. And whatever it was, he didn't like it.

"Well, shit. I can take you." Easton offered, dragging JJ back into the conversation. Ms. Newman was still staring at him.

He looked from her to Easton and nodded. "Sounds good. Disaster averted," he muttered the last part, turning to go. For some reason, as soon as Mike had told him he was Ms. Newman's ride, he hadn't been able to breathe right. But now—

"Wait!" The edge to her voice made him pause.

JJ turned as she grabbed her gigantic purse off the bar and fumbled for her wallet. "Hold on. Just a sec—"

Throwing a twenty on the counter, she grabbed his arm and shoved him toward the door. Just like before, when she'd pressed her fingers to his chest, he felt a jolt. And he knew exactly what that feeling was. It was a warning, a red flag, reminding him that if he didn't watch himself, he'd do something stupid and probably regret it daily for the rest of his life.

"It was nice to meet you guys!" she shouted over her shoulder, shoving her palm into his sweaty back as he stumbled toward the door. She was stronger than he expected. "Thank you...um, Barb. The coffee was amazing!"

The corner of his mouth tipped up briefly. At least she had good taste in coffee. *Maybe she has good taste in men too?* JJ pulled the door open, frowning. That was doubtful.

"Now hold up a second," Easton called from behind them. Then he said, "Barbie, how much do I owe you?"

"Let's go," she breathed against his shoulder as he tripped

over nothing, drunk on her very intoxicating perfume, which was a weird but enticing mixture of sugar cookies and mangoes.

As soon as they were outside, JJ yanked his arm away. The suffocating feeling returned as he headed across the road to get the truck, and Ms. Newman hurried behind him, clomping like a Budweiser Clydesdale in her ridiculous shoes.

"You sure you don't want a ride from the Sarge?" he asked, not bothering to turn around. "The a/c on the truck isn't working."

To his surprise, she hurried past him to the passenger's side door, yanked it open, and climbed in. "Yes."

By the time JJ got his door open, she was already buckled.

He frowned. What was the sudden rush? Was she late for a hot date? Or a spa appointment?

The bar door jingled, and Easton stepped outside. "Hey, hold up a sec," he called, fumbling for the sunglasses that were hooked over the pocket of his shirt. "I can take you," he shouted. "I'm headed to Decatur anyway."

Her heady perfume filled the cab, and JJ sighed as he stuck the key in the ignition. Jesus, how could anyone smell so damn good? "Are you sure you wouldn't rather—"

"Please—" she begged, digging her nails into the soft vinyl of the door handle. Red splotches that he hadn't noticed before dotted her neck and chest as it heaved, like suddenly *she* was the one who couldn't breathe.

His anger dissolved. "Are you—"

Easton appeared in the side view, making his way toward the passenger's side of the truck, as Ms. Newman jammed her finger on the button that should have rolled up her window. But only the control on his side worked. "What's the matter? What are you…?"

"Shit, shit," she whispered, punching the button.

"Hey. Take it—"

A weird sound erupted from her throat as Eason came to the

window. She ducked back like she was trying to hide, and a shiver raced down his spine. She was scared. Of Easton.

"Hold on." JJ threw the truck into first gear and punched the gas.

They screeched away just as Easton's hand found the sill. "Hey! Damn it, Jay. What the—" The rest of his words disappeared in the roar of the engine as they sped away.

Her bag slid off her lap to the floor, and she pressed her hand to her splotchy chest, gasping like she was somewhere between choking and throwing up.

"Hey, are you okay?" If she puked in the cab, he'd never get the smell out.

She stared at the glove compartment like she couldn't hear him, gripping the door handle as sweat dripped from her temples down the sides of her face.

JJ reached over and shook her shoulder, ignoring the thrill of her skin beneath his fingers. Women like her were off limits for guys like him. "Hey, miss? Are you okay?"

A deep breath wheezed into her lungs as she turned, looking surprised to see him sitting there. "W-what?"

"Are you okay?" he repeated.

She blinked and stared at him as his eyes darted between her and the road. As they bounced through a pothole in the road, she pressed the back of her hand to her forehead and sat up. "Oh! Sorry." She straightened her shoulders and scratched at her neck. "Sorry. I'm just—a little hungover."

He'd pulled his sunglasses down, his brows drawn together. "Are you sure?"

She forced a smile. He knew it was fake because he'd seen a real one only moments ago, and they were nothing alike. "Yes. I'm good." She glanced in the side-view mirror, back toward town.

Why was she afraid of Easton? Had he done something to her? It wouldn't surprise him, not after what Erica had told him.

Not that any of it was *his* problem, because Ms. Newman had made it very clear she could take care of herself. But still... He hesitated, then pushed the sunglasses back up over his eyes, shifted gears, and the truck accelerated.

Reaching into her purse, Ms. Newman pulled out a bottle of ibuprofen, dropped three pills into her hand, and swallowed them. "Thanks for what you said earlier in the bar," she offered a moment later, breaking the silence.

JJ's jaw tightened again. Did she mean when she insulted him and made him look like an idiot for trying to spare her from Easton? He shook his head, still unable to believe the bastard had actually sucked on her fingers. *Who the fuck does that?* Guys like Easton, that's who. They got away with it too. Case in point. She'd fucking sat and had lunch with him afterward, for Christ's sake.

"My name is Katie."

He didn't answer. That was why he'd sworn off women like her. No matter what they said, they couldn't help themselves when it came to men like Easton. Which was why men like him needed to steer clear.

Pulling her hair off her face, she wrestled it into a ponytail at the back of her head as they barreled down the road. She smelled wonderful. Like beautiful, delicious things, and he could only imagine how thick Easton must have laid it on. He probably offered her a good time in the back of his cruiser. Maybe that was why she was so anxious to get away. But again, if that was the case, then why in the hell did she sat with him in the first place?

"What is your name?" she asked when he didn't offer.

"JJ."

"What does—"

"Jensen James," he said, keeping his eyes on the road. "What the hell happened back there?"

"Nothing."

"Yeah, I know Easton. Did he—"

She shook her head. "It was nothing."

"Then why were you so scared?"

"I said it was nothing," she snapped, dismissing him and his good intentions once again.

And there it was. Her true self, the one she kept hidden behind her body, and long hair, and those goddamn eyes. Every attractive woman had one lurking somewhere, like a viper in an eye-catching basket, ready to strike idiots like him who were stupid enough to peek inside. It was his own fault. He knew better. He shouldn't have asked.

"I'm sorry," she apologized. "It's been a very stressful day."

Was that an invitation for him to ask why? Because he wasn't going to.

She sighed. "Look, I know you don't like me, and you think—"

"I don't think anything." *Oh, yes you do.* Of course he did. She was just like every other beautiful woman he'd known. A shallow, ruthless narcissist who used men like him when they needed something and threw them away afterward.

"Yes, you do. But you're wrong. I—"

He turned the radio on and cranked up the volume. An annoyingly twangy country song filled the cab, drowning out the rest of what she said.

Chapter One

JJ DROPPED his mom off at his sister's, then double checked the address Mike had sent him.

It came up as a Holiday Inn Express. And it was on the other side of town from where he'd dropped Katie Newman off last week, when he'd been forced to drive her all the fucking way to Atlanta. Then, she'd had him drop her off at a swanky downtown hotel, afterward insulting him by offering him a ten-dollar tip like he was a chauffeur, claiming it was all she had.

As if he'd believe that after seeing her car and her ridiculous but expensive-looking clothes. *She just reminds you a little too much of Erica.* Yes. They didn't look anything alike, but that didn't matter. As he'd reminded himself a dozen times over the past week, women like her were all the same; not to be trusted. *Then why are you on your way to get her, asshole?*

JJ signaled as he merged onto the freeway. He wouldn't be if his mom hadn't suddenly demanded he take her to his sister Sierra's for a mom/daughter 'night out.' He pressed his hand to the front pocket of his pants, making sure the precious item she had given him to hold on to was still there. But since he was already going, and Mike asked him and—*She's beautiful?*

He huffed as he glanced in the rearview mirror and switched lanes. That was a reason *against* driving her, not for it. Looks were the very last thing on his list of qualities—*Don't lie.* He sighed. Fine, very low on his list of qualities in a woman. Not that he was looking. *Of course not.* Because he wasn't. *Of course not.* He still hadn't recovered from his last bout of insanity when he *proposed* marriage to a beautiful woman just like Ms. Katie Newman, and actually thought she'd say yes. God, what an idiot.

The memory of that night still made him cringe. Him confessing to Erica how he felt. Her confessing how she didn't. He pulled his ball cap off and ran his fingers over his shaggy brown hair. The thought of Erica and Easton together still made his blood boil. But it wasn't their fault. It was his. Because he knew better, and he'd let himself get sucked in anyway.

JJ pulled his cap back on his head. "Fuck."

In July, it would be five years since they broke up. Erica had moved on. Actually, she had moved on *before* they'd even split up, apparently, which also made his blood boil, possibly even more so than the fact that it was Easton she was cheating with. So why couldn't he? Why couldn't he let it go? *You loved her.* No. He met his own eyes in the rear-view mirror. The person he loved never existed. The person he loved was a figment of his goddamn imagination. And the icing on the cake? She wasn't even with Easton anymore. No. They hadn't even lasted six months before she kicked him to the curb and left town. Not that he blamed her for that. But when she went, she took half of him with her, and he hadn't been the same since.

Signaling, he took the exit, then followed his phone's directions to the hotel.

He stopped in front of the lobby doors and hopped out. Cold air rushed past him as he pulled his sunglasses off and stepped into the dark, quiet lobby.

It only took him a second to find her, because that's all the time any man with eyes needed to spot Katie Newman living her 'perfect life.'

Yes, he'd looked her up on Instagram, found her 'vlog,' and browsed two years of posts, and no, he wasn't ashamed. *Hmmm.*

No, he wasn't. It was nothing more than idle curiosity. *You sure?* JJ frowned. The only reason he'd lied to his mom when she asked him what he was looking at on her phone—he didn't have social media on his—was because she wouldn't understand. *Understand what?*

He crossed the chipped marble lobby floor as a weird instrumental version of a Pussycat Dolls song filtered down from speakers in the ceiling.

His mom wouldn't understand that gorgeous women sang to men and lured them in despite their better judgment to run. He *had* to stalk her on social media to remind himself what he was dealing with. He *had* to stare for an hour at every ridiculously handsome, chiseled man she'd draped herself over in the last twenty-four months before she got to him with her wide hazel eyes and that damn smile and.... *And what?*

He hooked his sunglasses over the neck of his t-shirt and huffed. Stabbed him in the heart, cut it up into little pieces, and then ate it. That's what.

The Pussycat Dolls song ended, and another one came on as he approached the chairs where they were seated.

She was fire. He was a moth. End of story.

The man she was speaking to was a handsome doctor-y type guy in slacks and an ironed white shirt and tie.

JJ huffed again. If there was an opposite of him, it was that guy right there. From the top of his perfectly coiffed hair to the tip of his expensive-looking wing-tipped shoes. He was about as far on the other side of the man spectrum as he could get from JJ without falling off the other end.

JJ's brows came together as the man put a hand on the ripped knee of Katie's jeans. Her laugh was high and nervous as she pushed it away. Not taking the hint, the asshole put it right back as the scent of her perfume filled his nose. It smelled even better than he remembered.

"Fucking dick." JJ's heart thumped with anticipation as he stopped behind her and crossed his arms. "Get your hands off her, man."

Katie turned. Her hair was piled on top of her head in a loose bun, but strands had escaped and hovered around her face, framing her wide, greenish, relieved-looking eyes. "Oh!"

JJ sucked in a sharp breath. Katie Newman was pretty in pictures, but in real life, she was drop-dead gorgeous.

Doctor guy—who was wearing a fucking wedding ring by the way—had the nerve to look annoyed. "Who are you exactly?" he asked smugly.

JJ glared at him. "A repeller of assholes, apparently."

The other man's confident facade fell away, and JJ's shoulders sagged in disappointment, knowing what it meant. There would be no confrontation between him and the doctor man. "E-excuse me?" the man said with a wobbly smile.

JJ took a step. "You heard me. What the hell do you think you're—"

Katie leaped to her feet in another pair of certifiably hideous shoes and hoisted her enormous bag over her shoulder, smiling at him. "Mr. Dayton!"

Just as she had at Barb's, she threw a quick farewell over her shoulder and shoved him in the back toward the door.

"Say hi to your wife for me," he shouted over his shoulder as Katie shushed him and dragged him outside. "Thank god," she said under her breath as the automatic doors closed and the cool air disappeared. "That guy was…" She shook her head. "You have to be careful, though. He was a defense attorney. If you would have hit him, he would have sued you."

"Who said I wanted to hit him?"

Her eyes fell on his clenched fist, and he relaxed his hand.

JJ shook his head. A part of him wanted to feel sorry for her and all the seemingly unwanted attention she got, but it was her own fault. If she didn't like it, she wouldn't look the way she did. *Oh, really?* Yeah. The truth was, she craved attention, then pretended not to, to get even more. That had been the case with Erica, too. He'd learned that after the first couple of black eyes he got on her behalf.

A humid gust of wind rushed past them as he headed toward her door to open it for her, but she grabbed the handle and yanked it open before he could get there.

He stood back, unable to ignore her very form-fitting jeans as she climbed into the cab.

As a teenager, he'd had fantasies about a woman like her climbing up into his truck and heading off into a warm Georgia sunset with him. It was the stuff of every great country song ever written. Beautiful woman. Sexy jeans. A couple of cold beers and—

"Are you coming?"

JJ blinked. *"Shit."* His ears burned as he pulled his sunglasses over his eyes. "Fuck." Shaking his head, he went around the truck and climbed into the other side, reminding himself he hated country music.

"Thanks for coming—" she began.

"You can thank Mike. He's my boss and the *only* reason I'm here." *That was not nice.* JJ winced. Just because she annoyed him didn't mean he had to be a jerk. If his mom was here, she'd grab his ear and make him apologize.

"I know." She sounded sad, like he'd hurt her feelings.

"Well, still. And for back there too." She nodded her head back in the direction of the lobby as he pulled out of the parking lot. The embarrassment in her voice almost made him regret his rudeness. *Almost,* but not quite. Erica had manipulated him the same way, and—*Stop thinking about Erica!*

JJ's temples throbbed as he unclenched his jaw and sighed. He wouldn't have any teeth left by the time they got to Hartford

Creek if he didn't relax. And...goddamn it. "Sorry, and you're welcome," he muttered, unable to help himself as he reached for the dial and turned the radio on.

They got back on the freeway and rode in blessed silence for about ten minutes before she reached over and turned it off.

"Listen, I want to apologize for the other day."

JJ rolled his eyes. "You don't owe me an—"

"I hurt your feelings, and it's been bothering me all week, so yes, I do," she insisted.

Hurt his feelings? Was she kidding? "No—"

"I think you misinterpreted my actions in the bar the other —"

"Forget it."

"I can't." She turned in her seat and studied him, making him suddenly wish he wasn't wearing a grease covered pair of gray Dickies and a neon orange work shirt.

Dividing his attention between her and the road, he scowled. "What?"

"I *wanted* to sit with you when you offered, but...well, that doesn't matter. The thing is...what the sheriff...or sergeant, or whatever said about you not being my type. That wasn't true...I mean, I actually think you're much more attractive than he is. The only reason I sat with him was because—"

The temperature in the cab went up twenty degrees. "Just stop," JJ begged.

"No, I mean it," she insisted.

He shook his head. *This is not happening.*

She went on. "I mean, look at you. You're kinda broody, but it works for you, because deep down you're a nice guy. And between your eyes and killer dad-bod—"

JJ's cheeks burst into flames beneath his beard. That hadn't happened since middle school, when he'd gone to kiss Janet McElroy, and she turned her head and reminded him they were 'just friends.' Broody? Was that an insult? And *dad-bod?* What in the fuck was that? "Please, just—" The rest of the thought disappeared as a hazy sheen appeared across the road in the rearview mirror.

JJ rubbed his eyes under his sunglasses and glanced over his shoulder. "What the hell…?"

Chapter Two

KATIE CRINGED as JJ begged her to stop talking. *Dad-bod?* She groaned. Of all the stupid things to say. Of course, she'd meant it as a compliment, because he absolutely rocked it. Hard. But— *fuck.* She pressed her fingers into her forehead. She'd been hyperventilating—as quietly as she could—since she turned around and saw him standing there in the lobby, all tall, rough, and hot as hell, glaring at that asshole lawyer like he wanted to kill him. All of that oxygen had gone straight to her head and muddled her words.

JJ turned and looked over his shoulder as he switched lanes, mumbling to himself.

Taking a deep breath, she pinched the bridge of her nose and inhaled. Just because she'd been thinking about him non-stop since he dropped her off five days ago, was no reason to freak out. He didn't know she'd stalked his sister's Instagram account and his mom's Facebook, staring at the handful of pictures she had of him for hours last night while she polished off half a bottle of pinot grigio. There was no reason to panic, now that he was sitting beside her, in the flesh, making her entire body tingle. She was a grown woman. All she needed to do was calm down, curb the word vomit, and play it cool. "What I meant was—"

He held up a hand. "Please don't."

She shook her head. No. She needed to explain herself, get the misunderstanding between them off her chest, and start over.

Why? She didn't know why. There was just something about him. "I was just trying to avoid a confrontation, and I thought—"

"What the fuck?"

So, he *was* pissed? She knew it! "I know," she said, smacking her hands on the bench seat. "And I'm sorry. I'm sure you could have handled them. I should have just—"

Katie braced herself against the dash as JJ punched the brakes and signaled onto the shoulder. "What are you—"

"Shh," he snapped.

Her brows came together. Exactly how angry was he? She wished she could see his eyes through his sunglasses.

The truck came to a stop as a car whizzed by, going east-bound, and he stared into the rearview mirror. Was he angry enough to leave her here on the side of the highway? "Shit." Maybe she should have waited until *after* they were at the mechanic shop before apologizing. "Listen, I'm sorry. I made a mistake and—"

He threw the truck into park and unbuckled his seatbelt. "Will you just shut up?" he asked, looking over his shoulder.

Katie's jaw tightened. "Excuse me?" She crossed her arms. "There is no need to be rude. I was just trying to be…"

He pulled his sunglasses down, and the confusion in his eyes as he stared behind them, made her head turn. "What *are* you looking…?" The words died in her throat.

About fifty yards back, something hung across the road. It was transparent and sparkly, reminding her of a tulle skirt she'd wanted for her birthday when she was six. "What is—"

Boom!

The sound cracked against her eardrums, forcing Katie's arms over her head as she ducked. A weird, high-pitched whine filled her ears, making them feel like they were stuffed with screaming cotton balls as she pressed her hands over them and met JJ's surprised eyes. That only made the sound louder, so she put them down as she scanned the road for the source of the sound. "What was—"

Before she could get the sentence out, there was another explosion.

Boom!

JJ's head whipped around to the westbound side of the freeway, and Katie stared open-mouthed as a fireball erupted on the other side of the sparkly curtain.

Then two cars flew past them on their side, and—

BOOM!

JJ spun back around. Grabbing her head, he shoved it down onto the bench seat between them and threw himself over her as another explosion shattered the back window. Glass rained over them like confetti as the sound of brakes screamed through the truck.

Boom!

BOOM!

Katie clutched the seat in terror as JJ pressed himself down on top of her.

Boom!

Boom!

"What's happening?" she cried, throwing her arms over his lap, afraid that at any moment something would fling them apart. Was someone shooting at them?

Boom!

"Stay down." His voice rumbled against her ear.

Through the fog of adrenaline, she realized *this* was why she'd been obsessing over him like a teenager all week. Because he was like Matt. One of the good ones. And for those few minutes in the bar, just like now, he made her feel protected. And she'd lived almost her whole life without that—

BOOM!

The truck rattled, and she screamed.

His warm breath brushed against her side. "Stay down!" he yelled as she huddled beneath him. The sharp squeal of tires sliding across pavement echoed through the cab, followed by another boom that was closer than any of the others had been, and she screamed again as JJ's body jerked above hers. Katie's imagination immediately filled in all the gory details. Had he been hit? Or shot? Oh god, was he dead? Pushing him back, she scrambled to sit up, shoving her stupid hair that had come out of its bun out of her eyes. "Are you oka—"

Grabbing her arms, he forced her back down. "I'm okay. Stay down!" he yelled, pressing her head back into the seat.

More screeching filled the air, followed by the sickening sound of crumpling metal as JJ's weight against her back momentarily lifted. "What's happening?" she shrieked.

"Oh, shit!" He wrestled frantically beneath her for the seat belt and unbuckled it.

In one fluid motion, he pulled her back up to sit, dragged her legs over his, and threw her to the floor of the cab.

The breath rushed from her lungs in a cry as he fell on top of her.

"Sorry," he mumbled as his forearms closed on either side of her head, tucking it into his chest. He pressed his own head down onto the floor above hers just as a sharp snap echoed through her skull and the truck jerked, shoving her hip into the gear shifter and cracking JJ's head against the glove compartment. "Fuck," he hissed as she clung to him, gasping.

Several more bone-rattling explosions followed as the truck rocked back and forth. Were those bombs? "Oh, god. Oh, god," she choked. Had they been hit? Her vision darkened as she dug her nails into JJ's sides, unable to breathe. Holy shit. She was going to die. She was going to die in a tow truck, wearing the ugliest pair of shoes she had ever seen, and—

There was one more explosion, followed by a silence that turned the ringing in her ears into a shrill screech.

JJ shifted his weight onto his elbows, releasing some of the pressure on her chest as she dragged in a ragged, desperate breath.

"Are you okay?" he asked from somewhere above her.

She could barely see through the spots in her vision as she shook her head vigorously. "No." She was absolutely one hundred and ten percent *not* okay.

His heart thumped against the side of her face as hers banged in her chest. "I mean, are you hurt?" he clarified.

"No," she said as he shifted again, trying to get his weight off her legs, pressing her deeper into the gear shifter. The pain in her hip made her cry out.

He pushed himself back. "Sorry I—"

Terrified he'd get his head blown off, Katie grabbed his shirt and pulled him back down on top of her. "No! Don't—" The air rushed from her lungs again, and she gasped as JJ extracted himself from her frantic grasp.

"It stopped. Hey. It's okay." He smacked his back on the steering wheel as he rolled awkwardly up onto the seat, sat up, and looked out. "Holy shit."

"What?" she asked, not sure she really wanted to know.

He looked down at her, his eyes wide with disbelief. "Stay here. Don't move."

"Why? Where are you—?"

Grabbing the door handle, he pushed it open. "Stay here," he repeated, then disappeared.

"JJ!" Katie wrapped her fingers around the steering wheel and scrambled up onto the bench. Was he crazy? He was going to get—her mouth fell open. "Oh…oh…"

There were burning cars everywhere. On the opposite side of the freeway, a dozen vehicles sat smashed and askew to one another, smoke billowing from the hoods. The traffic behind had thankfully come to a halt. Her eyes scrolled to their side, where there were fewer cars and much less damage, and except for the vehicles that had pulled over like they had, the highway was empty as far as she could see. Frowning, she turned back to JJ in the middle of the road, screaming and waving his arms at the... Little chunks of glass fell onto the seat as she leaned against what was left of the back window and looked up. It glittered in the sunlight, like a roll of sheer iridescent fabric. Whatever it was, reached up into the sky and stretched in either direction as far as she could see. It was enormous, and—she looked back at JJ, who still stood in the road waving his arms at something on the other side. Leaning forward, she looked around the boom on the back of his truck and spotted the three cars that were rapidly approaching the wall, or whatever it was, from the other side.

She turned back to the handful of burning vehicles that had crashed into the median on their side of it, then looked back to JJ. "Oh, no." Sliding over, she grabbed at the door handle. Whatever that thing was, you couldn't go through it without wrecking on the other side.

Jumping out of the truck, she raced toward him in her ridiculous shoes. The hair on her arms and the back of her neck stood on end as she skidded to a stop beside him. The static in the air was so thick it made her entire body tingle.

"Hey!" JJ bellowed. His muffled voice sounded like he was shouting through a towel. "Stop! Hey! Stop!"

She joined him, waving, her voice extra loud in her head. "Stop! Hey!"

Thankfully, the approaching vehicles slowed as more appeared around the bend behind them. Katie dropped her arms. They were lucky traffic heading out of the city was light, otherwise...

She turned back to the other side of the freeway. The traffic into Atlanta had been far worse and was already backed up at least a mile. Dazed people were exiting their wrecked cars, and a school bus, that had been in the slow lane, heading onto the city, pulled over to the side of the road as a dozen faces stared at her from inside, their noses and cheeks pressed up to the glass, pointing. Past the wreck of cars, on their side of the wall, was another pile-up. A semi-truck trailer had overturned, and at least ten cars were on fire. She pushed her hair back. "Oh, god." What in the hell—

"Look out!" JJ shouted, shoving her out of the way as a red sports car flew through the wall—Katie stumbled, and he caught her—and the driver disappeared from the front seat.

Her mouth fell open and her head whipped around, following the car as it sped past them at about eighty miles an hour. There was another ear-shattering crash as it veered out of the fast lane and slid into the median about a hundred yards past JJ's truck. It continued, screeching against it for another fifty feet, as Katie covered her ears and stared before it crashed into an empty, burning minivan.

Katie started toward it. "Did you see that?" Her voice echoed in her head. "The guy in that car—"

JJ grabbed her arm, dragging her to a stop, and she almost fell out of her shoes. He said something, but her ears were still filled with cotton and she couldn't make it out. She scanned the back window of the car, swatting him away. Where was he? She tried to step around him. Where was the driver?

JJ stepped in front of her. "No," he said.

She blinked, looking from him to the car. One minute, the guy was there. The next…he was not. Did JJ see it? "But the man in that car, he—"

The inside of the car burst into flames and she ducked as JJ shielded her again. A second later, there was another explosion and Katie peeked over his shoulder as he pushed her backward, and the hood of the sports car flew into the air. It fell on top of a car parked on the other side of the median with a crash.

"We've got to get out of here." His muffled voice demanded as he spun around, grabbed her arm, and dashed across the empty highway. The lanes on the other side of the wall, on their side, were now backed up as far as she could see, and people everywhere were getting out of their cars, while the wrecked vehicles surrounding them continued to burn.

Katie followed dumbly behind JJ, tripping over her own feet, as she stared over her shoulder. This couldn't be happening. Could it? It looked like a scene from an apocalyptic video game. Acrid smoke filled her lungs, making her cough. This couldn't—

A flash of brown between two cars in the pileup on the other side of the median caught her eye, and if it wasn't for the adrenaline that had replaced the blood in her veins, she would have fainted. Instead, she jerked free of JJ's grasp and ran toward it, hoping it wasn't what she thought it was. "Hey!" She saw it again between two different cars and broke into a sprint, almost turning her ankle on a shredded piece of rubber.

"Ms. Newman, stop!" JJ called from behind her.

But she couldn't, and there wasn't time to explain. Cursing her heels, she kicked them off before scrambling up onto the median, which was much taller than it looked from a moving vehicle. Balancing on the top, she hopped across to the one beside it. "Hey! Stop! Stay back!" she yelled, choking on the combination of burning oil and rubber that smothered the sweltering highway like a toxic pillow.

"Katie!" JJ called as she hopped down to the other side. In addition to the trash, twisted bits of metal, and other normal roadside debris, there was glass everywhere, but there was no time for caution as she ran through the maze of vehicles. *Where did he go? Where*—her right foot landed on a burning piece of metal, and her flesh sizzled as she cried out, swatting at it until it fell away. A moment later something pierced the arch of the same foot as she hurried between the cars, toward the wall. "Fuck."

Katie spotted the young brown-haired boy just up ahead, making his way between two cars. Whatever she'd stepped on dug into her foot as she lunged, grabbing him by the hood of his sweater just before he touched it. "No!"

The air hummed and tickled Katie's palms and lips again as she dragged the boy backward away from the wall. He looked up at her with wide brown eyes.

"Where is your mother?" she demanded, dragging him back between the cars. There was another pop, and Katie glanced over her shoulder as another fireball erupted in the distance between the buildings. Turning back around, she collided with JJ, who appeared out of nowhere. "Oof. Sorry—"

He picked the boy up and grabbed her by the arm, only to release her a second later when the boy began screaming and hitting him.

"Help! Help!" the child cried.

"Shit," JJ hissed as he got clocked in the nose.

"Wait!" Katie grabbed the boy's arm as JJ set him down. She noticed the back of JJ's neck was bleeding. Pressing his shoulder, she tried to turn him to get a better look. "Are you okay?"

He jerked away. "Fine," he said as the boy struggled to get free.

"Stop!" Katie said. "We aren't going to hurt you. Where is your—"

"Hey, what's goin' on here?"

Katie spun around. A teenage boy with intelligent brown eyes, brown skin, and a backward Atlanta Braves ball cap on, stood glaring at them.

She loosened her grip on the little boy's arm, but did not let go.

The teenager took another step toward them, eyebrows drawn together. "I said—"

Katie interrupted him. "Do you know this boy?"

The kid huffed and crossed his arms. "Do you?"

Another explosion, from somewhere to the north, made them all pause.

"Is he yours?" Katie asked.

The teen scowled. "Not all of us black folks are related, lady."

Katie rolled her eyes. That was not what she was implying at all. "No, I just—"

The teen broke into a grin. "Just playing. No, he's not 'mine.' He got off that bus over there." He pointed to the bus she'd seen earlier. "I saw him from my Uber—"

"Well, where is the fucking bus driver?" JJ asked as Katie released the boy, and the teen grabbed him by the arm as he tried to escape again.

The teenager shook his head. "Language, dude. There are kids. And man, that is an interesting question. One I intended to solve as soon as I wrangled this little guy."

JJ looked at the little boy and apologized. "Sorry. What do you mean *'interesting'*?"

"I mean, the driver got off the bus screaming about Jesus and the Apocalypse or something, and ran right into whatever the eff that thing is, and just…" Pinching his fingers together, he opened them, like the blooming petals of a flower. "Poof."

JJ gave him a blank look. "Poof?"

The teenager shrugged. "He disappeared, man."

"What do you mean, he disappeared?" JJ asked, sounding skeptical, but Katie had seen it, too.

The little boy struggled free and took a step back toward the *thing.*

Katie grabbed his hood again. "No, you don't." She turned to JJ. "Do you have your phone?" Hers was in her purse in the truck.

He nodded.

"Call 911," she said.

"I'm sure someone has already—" he began.

"Tell them we have a bus full of kids without—" She grabbed the boy's hood again as he tried to escape. "… an adult."

Then she steered the little boy toward the bus, limping behind him as he scratched at his short black curls. Someone had to keep an eye on those kids until help arrived. Otherwise, they'd kill themselves.

"Hey!" JJ called after her. "What do you mean, *we*?"

Chapter Three

Day 1 // 10:10 a.m.

JJ STARED at Katie until she disappeared around the side of the bus as another explosion echoed in the distance. Whatever was happening, it was happening in more places than just where they were.

There was a low whistle from behind him and sweat dripped into his eyes as he turned back to the kid.

"Mm, mm," the boy said, staring at Katie's ass through the windshield of the bus. "What I wouldn't give for a piece of that."

JJ scowled as he reached into his pocket for his phone. "Cut it out." Dialing 911, he pressed it to his ear.

The kid laughed. "Man, unless you're gay—and I'm one hundred percent cool with that, by the way—then you're thinking the exact same thing I am. So don't act all chivalrous."

JJ's eyebrow went up. *Chivalrous?* Unsurprisingly, the line rang busy. He hung up and tried again. "I'm not chivalrous, I'm just not a disrespectful dick," he snapped.

"Hey, man. I didn't mean it like that. Chill," the kid said.

Chill? How in the hell was he supposed to do that when—JJ pulled his hat off, surveying the scene. Did this kid not realize they were standing in the middle of the freeway surrounded by burning cars? "Listen, kid—"

"Name's Sam. Wait, she's not *your* girl, is she?" he asked as the sound of approaching sirens echoed in the distance. JJ sighed. *Thank god.* Although…He turned, squinting through the barrier to the other side. It sounded like it was coming from over there, which would not be helpful.

He turned back to face the miles of stopped traffic behind him. Except for the pile-up right at the wall, there thankfully appeared to be very few accidents. Dozens of people stood beside their grid-locked cars, most of them either on their phones or taking pictures.

Shaking his head he turned back in time to see a young Asian woman in her early twenties start toward the sparkling screen of death. "Hey!" JJ shouted as the phone against his ear continued to beep. "Get away from there!"

She spun around. "What is this?" Her voice wobbled like she was going to cry. Or maybe she already was. "What's happening?"

JJ looked up at the wall, or whatever it was. One minute it wasn't there, the next minute it was. That was all he knew.

"*Is* she your girl?" Sam pressed on, giving JJ a once over as he hung up and dialed again. For a second, JJ had forgotten he was there. "What?" he asked, as it beeped again.

"Seems unlikely."

"Huh?" JJ hung up and dialed *again*. What were they supposed to do if they couldn't get a hold of the police?

Sam rolled his eyes and nodded in the bus's direction. "Hot pants. Is she your girl or not?"

JJ gave him what he hoped was an exasperated look. Why was this kid not freaking out? "Women are not property, asshole. She's not mine or anyone else's." JJ said, swiping at his brow again. It was one of the first lessons his mom had taught him when—he pulled the phone away from his ear and stared at the screen. "Mom. Shit."

Hanging up, he dialed his mom. Pulling his cap off, he wiped his forehead with his arm. She and Sierra were over there, on the other side of whatever that thing was. Looking north, then south, he tried to see if there was a way to get around it, but it went on as far as he could see in both directions, cutting right through buildings and continuing on.

Sam smirked. "So, no. I didn't think so."

The line was busy. JJ cursed under his breath as he dialed Sierra. Busy, too. "Damn it."

Sam started for the bus.

"Hey!" JJ called, waving him back. Katie had her hands full enough. The last thing she needed was an overconfident teenager hitting on her. "You stay with me."

Sam's brow went up. "Why? You worried I might swoop in on your girl while you're out here having your little..." He swirled his finger like he was stirring a glass of ice cubes. "...panic attack or whatever?"

JJ shook his head. *Cocky little bastard.* Actually, little was the wrong word, because the two of them were about the same height. But where JJ was solid, Sam was lanky and lean. "Shut up," he said, scowling.

Sam laughed. "Why? Can't handle a little competition?"

JJ dialed his mom again. Busy. He shook his head. Were they really having this conversation? Did this kid really not notice they were standing in the middle of fucking Armageddon? "Trust me. You're not her type," JJ offered. It was busy again.

Looking him up and down, Sam crossed his arms over his chest. "Well, no offense, bro, but I don't think you are either."

That was true. She liked guys like Easton and her doctor friend from the hotel lobby. *You don't know what she likes.* Oh, yes, he did. He saw them, *all* of her handsome, chiseled boy toys on Instagram.

He dialed Sierra again. Busy. "Damn it." The lines had to be jammed.

Someone else started toward the wall, and JJ waved his arm. "Hey!" he shouted. "Don't touch that!" The sirens grew louder as he dialed 911 again.

Turning to Sam, he said, "Make yourself useful. Don't let

anyone touch that thing." He pointed to the wall as he pressed the phone back to his ear.

Sam looked about to tell him to go to hell, but then, with a sigh, he strutted past him. "Hey!" he yelled at someone behind them. "Get back in your damn car! Yeah. I'm talking to you!"

JJ's phone rang busy *again*, as the young woman he'd seen earlier made her way between the cars, tucking her shiny black hair behind her shoulder. She stopped in front of him, teary-eyed and thoroughly terrified. "I-is your phone working?"

JJ shook his head as it continued to beep in his ear.

"My parents are on the other side. I can't..." She wiped her eyes. "What is all of this? What is happening?"

The sirens grew louder and JJ stared at the emergency vehicles as they wove between the wrecked vehicles on the other side of the wall. They were not slowing down. "Go to the bus," he said.

The girl sniffled. "What?"

"Hey!" JJ shouted, running toward the wall, waving his arms. "The school bus," he called over his shoulder. "There's a woman inside. Her name is Katie. She'll help you out—" Turning back toward the shimmering wall, he ran as close as he dared waving his arms.

The police cruiser screeched to a halt on the other side, followed by an emergency fire vehicle. Several uniformed men jumped out. They all stared at the wall, their expressions exactly how his had been, confused and filled with disbelief. The crackle of their radios reached his ears unhindered, and electricity tugged at the hair on his arms and chest as he came to a stop only feet away. Up close, it sparkled like a gray waterfall full of rainbow-colored glitter. If he hadn't seen what it could do, he would have said it was beautiful.

"Don't touch it," he warned.

A fire truck was the next to arrive. As soon as the sirens

stopped, firefighters jumped out and immediately began putting out the car fires.

For the first time, JJ noticed the overturned semi-trailer on the other side. That definitely accounted for at least one bang. Oddly, there were no bodies anywhere that he could see. He remembered what Sam had said. *Poof.*

"What the hell happened here?" one officer demanded. "What the fuck is this—" He waved his arm at the thing between them as if JJ were personally responsible for it.

He shook his head. "I don't know. It just—it just appeared."

"Appeared? How?"

JJ rubbed his eyes and shook his head again. *This can't happen.* He looked behind him at the grid-locked freeway as the sun beat down on the top of his head. *You're dreaming.* He had to be. Or maybe he was suffering from heatstroke. He should have fixed the a/c on the damn truck.

"Yeah. I don't know. It just—" He turned back around, just as the one officer reached his hand out and touched the wall.

"No! Don't—"

The officer's scream drowned JJ's voice out as four of his fingers disappeared with a sizzle. He stared in horror as the man fell to the ground, clutching what was left of his hand. His partner rushed over, dropping to his knees beside him. "What's wrong, Coop?" he cried. "What happened, man?" When his partner didn't answer, he turned to JJ. "What happened?"

JJ shook his head and stepped back. What had happened was the wall had chopped off the man's fingers like a knife. Only... His eyes fell to the ground where the missing digits should be. There was nothing there. Again, he was reminded of Sam's comment. *Poof.*

JJ pulled his hat off again. It had to be a dream. He turned to his truck. Or was he in a coma? *Wouldn't that be nice?* Yeah, being unconscious, tucked up in a warm bed in a safe hospital somewhere, was sounding very good at the moment.

The officer's screams quieted into agonizing moans as his partner helped him to his feet and led him away.

"Man," Sam's voice carried over the vehicles. "I said get back in your fucking car or I'll—" The sentence ended abruptly and JJ turned.

A burly giant of a man had Sam by the throat and was backing him into the side of a minivan.

JJ rolled his eyes as he turned and ran toward them.

"Hey!" This wasn't a dream, it was a goddamned nightmare. "Hey. Get your hands off him!" he shouted, wrenching the larger man's arm from Sam's throat, and shoving the boy back as he stepped between them. The man was huge. JJ only came up to his nose.

Without missing a beat, the man took a swing at him, but luckily JJ had been in enough fights to know exactly what was coming.

Deflecting the blow, he threw his hands up in a sign of peace and stepped back. "Hey. I don't want any trouble. He's just a kid. And I told him to—"

"I don't fucking care what you told him," Goliath said, shoving JJ in the chest. With a sigh, JJ took a step backward, not wanting to add a fist fight to the fucked-up menu the day was serving up on a silver platter. "Come on, man, relax."

Goliath laughed. "What? Are you scared?"

JJ sighed again. This guy was just like Easton and Wes and every other asshole he knew growing up. Too much testosterone and not enough brains. Luckily, he was an expert at handling idiots like that.

Goliath sneered. "What? The tough guy's suddenly not feeling so—"

Not waiting for him to finish, JJ popped him in the nose with a quick left jab. The man's head spun in surprise as Sam let out a hoot. "Oh shit…" he said as JJ, savoring the twist of his body, followed up quickly with a right hook, knowing his knuckles were at exactly the right angle to—His fist thudded against the man's jaw and Goliath's eyes rolled back in his head. Then he dropped to the ground like a stone.

JJ squeezed his eyes shut and exhaled. *God, that felt good.*

"Holy shit. You kicked his ass." Sam sounded thoroughly surprised.

JJ opened his eyes. "Yeah."

"You know I coulda handled that, though, right?"

JJ rubbed his knuckles and half laughed. "Yeah."

Katie's voice brought his head around. Stepping over the unconscious man, he made his way back through the cars over to the wall, where she stood arguing with the uniformed men on the other side.

"You have to do *something,*" she demanded, with her hands on her hips. "They are just kids. I mean—"

JJ came up beside her.

Three new officers stood on the other side and stared at Katie as she mopped the sweat that dripped from her temples and between her—JJ finally noticed she wasn't wearing a bra, and his eyes latched onto her chest. *Dear god.* They were perfect.

"Did you get through?"

Much too late, he realized she was speaking to him and JJ's eyes flew to hers. "Huh? W-what?"

She scowled, crossing her arms. "To the real police? Because apparently, these guys can't do shit."

"No."

JJ looked up at the men, still blatantly staring at Katie. To be fair, she was a sight to behold, those curves, and her long wild red-tipped hair, standing tall and oh-so perky in the middle of all the wreckage, barefoot no less. The officer with a wedding ring collected himself first and spoke up. "There's a precinct about three miles back that way. On McClintock and Second. Take them there."

Katie turned and looked over the miles of trapped vehicles. "How? How are we supposed to—"

The crackle of their radios cut her off, as a voice rattled off something he couldn't understand. Both of the officers' eyes widened as they looked at each other. "Shit," they exclaimed before turning and running back to their squad car.

"Hey!" Katie yelled as they hopped in. "Come back here!" she demanded as they flipped their siren back on and sped away.

"Shit," she hissed, turning to him and throwing her hands in the air. "What are we supposed to do now?"

What they needed to do was get out of there. It was a hundred degrees on the road, and—JJ looked over his shoulder—Goliath was going to wake up any minute and be really pissed.

He eyed his truck and the mostly open stretch of highway that led away from the city. They had a clear shot out of town. Under the circumstances, wouldn't it be okay to just go home and let the cops deal with—

"No," Katie said, reading his mind.

"No?" he said with a sinking feeling.

"We can't leave these kids here."

He looked at her. "Can you drive a school bus?" he asked.

She gave him a stern look that reminded him of his mom when she was about to give his dad the what-for. "No. But I'm guessing you can."

He shook his head. *Technically*, yes, he could, but— "No, no, no." She put her hands on her hips, as he continued "First of all, there are kids on that bus...*kids*. They hate me. I don't like them either. Second, you needed a license to drive a bus. Third, what if—"

"You have to," she insisted.

"Why don't we put them in the truck?"

Katie shook her head. "There's fifteen of them, mostly little ones. And they have head lice. And where would we even—"

"They have *what*?"

51

"That's why they were on the road and not in school. They were on their way home. It's not a big deal."

Just thinking about it made his head itch. "Yes, it is. And I can't leave the truck here," he said.

"Fine. I'll drive it," she countered.

Was she joking? "You're not driving my truck."

"JJ, please—"

He pressed the heels of his hands into his eyes, not knowing why he was bothering to argue with her. His dad never won the argument when his mom got like this, and besides, deep down, he knew he couldn't leave a bunch of kids stranded on the side of the road during a terrorist attack, or whatever the hell this was, any more than she could. Even if they did have fucking bugs in their hair. "Fine. I—"

Holding her hand up, she silenced him. "Shh. Do you hear that?" she asked, spinning around.

JJ turned and scanned the horizon. It had been several minutes since the last explosion. Except for the firefighters on the other side, everything had come to a stop, and the highway was weirdly quiet. "Hear what?"

She spun around again, wincing as she turned. "I thought I heard something."

JJ squinted in the blinding sun. People were out of their cars. Most of them appeared to be paralyzed with shock as they stared up at the shimmery death trap. It was deceivingly beautiful as it twinkled and sparkled like a five-year-old girl's unicorn-crusted fantasy. No wonder the little brown-haired boy had wanted to touch it.

Katie pulled her hair back, shaking her head. "I thought—"

He looked up at the blue sky, which was empty, when a muffled cry finally penetrated his brain. His eyes fell to a crumpled gray sedan, two cars back in the pileup, and then to the little girl crying in the back seat. "Shit—Over there!"

Racing to it, he threw the door open. Heat poured from the

car as Katie ran around the other side and pulled the driver's side door open. The slumped woman in the driver's seat tumbled out of the car, knocking Katie over as JJ unbuckled the sweaty little girl and scooped her up. She threw her arms around his neck as he stood up. "Shh. It's okay, kiddo. I got ya. Ms. Newman?" He patted the girl's back. "Are you alright?"

Katie's eyes were wide and sad when, a moment later, they met his over the roof of the car. She shook her head.

"Shit," he said again as the girl wailed for her mother. "I've got you. I've got you, munchkin."

There was another explosion somewhere far away, and his sense of urgency returned. "Check the rest of the cars over there to make sure they're empty, and then we need to get out of here."

"But what about…" Katie looked down at the body he couldn't see.

They couldn't take it with them. He shook his head. "We can't."

"But—"

"We can't, Katie!" he said, bouncing the girl, petting her head as she wailed. He would not traumatize her anymore by dragging her dead mother along with them.

Katy quickly peeked in the windows of the surrounding vehicles, as he searched the ones nearest to him. Only one vehicle in his search area still had a driver. It was a younger man in a pickup. But from the giant radiating crack in the windshield above the steering wheel and the way his eyes stared vacantly up toward the sky from his twisted neck, JJ knew it was too late to do anything for him. Like the driver in the little girl's car, the man had not been wearing his seatbelt.

"Anything?" he called to Katie as she limped over to him. She shook her head. He frowned. "What's the matter with your foot?"

"Nothing. It's fine. Come on, let's get out of here."

The sticky little girl continued to cry in his arms as they

started for the bus, and he wished he had a doll or something to distract her with. He spun around and Katie crashed into them as he pushed the girl back, so he could see her face. "Hey, do you have a teddy or a blanket or something?" he asked.

The girl looked at him tearfully. "Like Beaver?"

"Yeah. Like Beaver." Katie's brow went up, and he ignored her questioning look. "Is he in the car?"

"She," the girl corrected.

JJ rolled his eyes. "Right, sorry. Is *she* in the car?" he corrected.

The girl nodded. "Yeah."

He met Katie's eyes. "Grab it, and see if there's a bag…with ID." Meaning the mother's purse, so they could at least identify the girl. Katie nodded and limped back to the car, as he carried the little girl, who'd resumed crying, to the bus.

Katie reappeared a moment later and handed the stuffed beaver to the girl.

"Okay, you sit—" JJ tried to set her down, but she clung to him like a baby opossum. "It's okay…"

"No!" she wailed, squeezing his neck.

He gently extracted himself. "You're okay, munchkin. I'll be right here, okay? But I need you to sit, so I can drive, okay?"

She nodded. "O-okay."

He met Katie's eyes. "Okay. You take the truck. Meet me—"

"Kids love you," she accused.

He ignored her. "Meet me at the next exit. Second gear sticks. So you have to—"

"It's manual?" she asked, sounding surprised as she stepped back toward the door.

JJ's eyes narrowed as he followed her. "Yeah. It's a fucking *tow* truck."

Smiling sweetly, she turned and stepped down into the weeds on the side of the road. "Oh. Okay."

"Is that a problem?" he called.

She shook her head, making her way around the front of the bus.

Sam tried to scoot past him, but JJ grabbed the back of his shirt. "I don't think so."

"Come on, man. You heard her. The kids have the creepy crawlies. I don't want to ride in here. And just because she doesn't like you doesn't mean—"

"Get back on the fucking bus, kid."

"I'm not a kid. And I told you, my name is Sam."

"Fine. Are you coming with us, Sam?"

He nodded.

"Then get on the fucking bus."

JJ shooed him back up the steps.

Luckily, it wasn't one of the super long buses. It could hold maybe thirty kids. He hadn't been on one since high school, and there wasn't a moment of those three miserable years he wanted to remember, yet they all came back in a rush as he glanced at the handful of kids huddled in the back.

He counted one, two, three, four, five little girls. Two little boys. Four...medium aged girls and three boys and one angsty-looking teenage boy with a black eye, and the young woman from outside. Half of them were scratching their heads. JJ resisted the urge to run. "I'm taking you guys to the police station, okay?"

"It's alright. We're gonna help you," Sam said, reassuring the kids as he slid onto the bench behind the driver's seat, next to the little orphan and her beaver.

JJ sat down and buckled his seatbelt. Thankfully, the keys were still in the ignition. He took a quick inventory of the dash, closed the doors, and turned the key. "Here goes nothing," he muttered.

He planned to back down the shoulder onto the on-ramp about two hundred feet behind him and make his way back onto the surface roads.

Glancing in the side view mirrors, he checked to make sure none of the people abandoning their cars were behind him, then shifted into reverse. Slowly, the bus began to roll backward.

"What the hell…?" Sam said.

JJ punched the brakes. "What? he asked, looking up in the giant rear-view mirror above his head. Sam was staring out the window toward the other side of the freeway where Katie and his truck…*Oh, no.*

His head spun around as his truck jerked, then stopped, then jerked again. "What the *fuck?*" he whispered.

The truck lunged again, as the sickening sound of grinding gears penetrated the thin windows of the bus.

"Yeah, I don't think she can drive—" Sam began.

JJ threw the bus into park, and it rocked. "Goddamn it!" he shouted, fumbling with his seatbelt. "She said she could drive it!" He unclipped it and jumped up, reaching for the door release. Fuck. She was going to burn out his transmission.

Sam leaped to his feet too and grabbed JJ's arm as he yanked on the lever. "Language, and I got this man. Really. *I* can drive it," he said.

JJ stared at him. Language? *Language?* There were more important things than fucking language at the moment, namely the destruction of the hundred- and twenty-thousand-dollar truck he'd *just* paid off.

JJ punched the lever for the doors again, as the little girl leaped off her seat and attached herself to his leg like a frightened koala. He looked down at her little tear-stained face, as she squeezed him and her beaver, then jiggled the lever again, but the door wouldn't open. Fuck his life, and why couldn't he get the door open?

Reaching down, he picked up the sobbing girl as his truck lurched *again* and the lid on the cool he'd been keeping blew off.

It was too much. The exploding cars, the sparkly death curtain, the fact that he was now somehow responsible for one orphan, and the lives of fifteen flea-infested children while Katie slowly destroyed his truck before his eyes. "No. No…" Pressing the girl's head to his shoulder and covering her ear, he hissed, "Fucking no!"

"Seriously. I can—" Sam began.

"No!" JJ roared into the beaver that was covering his face as the little girl gripped his neck like a boa constrictor. He jiggled the door lever again, spitting out brown fuzz.

It finally opened. "Thank—"

"Hey!" Sam stepped in front of him. Lowering his voice, he pushed the beaver out of the way and pulled their heads together. "You can't leave these kids here, man." He met JJ's eyes. "I can't drive this bus. But I'm telling you, I can drive your damn truck."

JJ tugged at the girl's arms as her shoulder dug into his throat. "No!" he choked.

Sam crossed his arms. "Why? Is it because I'm black? You think I'm gonna—"

JJ rolled his eyes as his truck rolled a couple more feet and ground to a halt again. He spun away, struggling to inhale. The girl was surprisingly strong for being so little. "No. It's not because you're *black*." Pulling her arms free, he gasped. "It's because you're fucking *twelve* and—" She got a hold of him again, redoubling her effort.

"I'm eighteen, and I'm telling you—"

A kid in the back began to cry, and the Asian girl JJ had met outside slid across the aisle to comfort her.

"You're scaring the kids," Sam accused, as more wails erupted.

"Well, they should be scared," he hissed. "*You* should too! What in the hell is the matter with you? Did you not see—"

"I'm just tryin' to keep my cool man, until I know the facts."

JJ pushed the beaver away from his face again. "Facts? What *facts?*"

"Calm down."

"I am calm!" he choked, about three seconds away from asphyxiation.

"No, you're not," the little girl offered helpfully, loosening her grip as she leaned back to study him.

Gasping for much-needed air, he tried to set her in a seat. She immediately latched onto him again like a little octopus.

"Nu-uh," she said, shaking her head. Her hair got caught in his beard, and he pushed it away as he dragged his hand over his face and stood back up. "Eff my—"

"I'll meet you at the next exit," Sam said.

JJ looked up at the ceiling as the little girl pressed her head against his neck. Once again, he didn't know why he was arguing. Sam was right. "Fine." His shoulders sagged as Sam brushed past him and out the door.

"Don't forget second—"

Sam turned and saluted him, looking like he didn't have a care in the world. "Second gear sticks. Got it." He ran through the cars, hopped the median like a hurdle jumper, and raced to the truck, shouting and waving his arms.

JJ held his breath as Katie slid over and Sam hopped in. A second later, his truck pulled smoothly off the shoulder and headed down the road. JJ squeezed his eyes shut, praying he saw it again, as he pulled the girl from his neck again. "What's your name?"

"Amelia."

"Okay, Amelia. I'm JJ. Didn't your mom ever teach you it's not nice to choke people?"

She frowned. "I don't want you to go."

He pulled a smile out of his ass and plastered it on his face. "I'm not going anywhere. I'm staying right here with you, kiddo, but I do have to drive now. So you have to go sit down."

Nodding, she let go of his neck as another kid started crying. JJ looked back at his passengers as Amelia took her seat. "Sorry guys. I'm…" The crying stopped as he dragged his hands over his face again. "Everything is fine. I just got a little…" Fifteen sets of wide, trusting eyes met his and his gut twisted at the memories their faces unearthed. "I'm fine. We're going to go now." That part of his life was over. In the past.

"Are you sure you want to come with us?" he asked the older girl from outside.

She looked over his shoulder to her SUV locked in the middle of the road, then back. "Yeah…If that's okay?"

"Yeah. Of course. What's your name?" he asked over the crying.

"Jinn."

He nodded. "I'm JJ." Looking at all the kids, and little Amelia, he said again. "I'm JJ. Everything is going to be fine." That was probably a lie, but what was he supposed to do? Tell them the truth? He didn't even know what that was.

Getting back in his seat, he caught his reflection in the mirror as the crying resumed. "Keep it together, Jensen," he mumbled.

"Hey, JJ?" Amelia asked from behind him, sounding much perkier than before.

"Yeah?"

"Didn't your mom ever teach you inside voices?"

Squeezing his eyes closed, he sighed. "Yes, she did. I'd be in big trouble right now if she was here."

"You said a swear too, I think."

"He said three," someone offered from the back, making JJ cringe.

He took one more look at the deadly barrier.

"Wait, is goddamn a swear too?" another little voice asked, as he shifted into reverse.

"Yeah, I think so," someone else replied.

"Then it was four," the first kid said as JJ slowly backed down the shoulder.

Chapter Four

KATIE'S TOES felt like ice cubes, while the bottoms of her feet, specifically her right one, throbbed as she stood barefoot on the worn tile floor of the sheriff's office. JJ stood beside her, holding the little girl Amelia in his arms, looking as dumbfounded as she felt.

"What do you mean, you can't take them?" he asked. "You're the police. If you won't take them who—"

The woman behind the desk, Deputy Montgomery, her name tag said, looked apologetic, but she held her ground. "I understand. But I am the only one here. Everyone, *everyone* else is out on calls. The governor has declared a state of emergency. The Coast Guard has been called in. They are—It's happening all over, not just here," she whispered the last part, so the kids huddled with Sam and Jinn against the wall wouldn't hear.

"What is *it*?" JJ cried, sounding about two seconds away from losing his shit. To be honest, it surprised her he'd held it together this long, literally *holding* a child no less. "What in the hell is that thing out there?" he demanded.

Officer Montgomery shrugged. "No one knows. But it has completely surrounded the city."

Surrounded? "What? Why?" Katie asked.

"And Atlanta is not the only one," Deputy Montgomery whispered again.

The hair on Katie's arms stood on end. "What do you mean?"

The deputy turned the small TV behind the counter so they

could see it, and Katie stared at the headline. "Oh, my god," she whispered, pushing the hair off her sweaty forehead.

L.A, New York. Paris. Moscow. Dozens of cities around the world were similarly cut off.

"Holy shit," JJ said beside her.

"You said a swear again." Amelia piped up.

Katie's voice sounded funny in her ears as she spoke. "I don't—I don't understand. The whole *world* is under attack? By whom? Why?" She locked eyes with Deputy Montgomery. "*What* is going on?"

"Damn'd if I know. Nobody knows."

"But..."

"Can I watch cartoons?" Amelia interrupted.

There was something in JJ's voice that warmed Katie's heart as he said, "No, munchkin. Not right now. Hold your beaver."

"I'm sorry." Deputy Montgomery said. "I can't do my job if I'm trying to watch a bunch of—And they have *lice?*" She made a face. "Nuh-uh. No. No thank you."

JJ slammed his fist on the counter. "Well, what the hell are we supposed to do with them?" His voice was thick with restraint. "We can't just—These are people's *children.* If we leave here with them—Isn't that... I don't know, kidnapping or something? I mean, we could be *eff-ing* serial killers—" he hissed.

"Can I have some cereal?" Amelia asked as JJ tried to set her down, but she wouldn't release him. "I'm hungry."

With a sigh, he lifted her back up, shifting her into his other arm as she adjusted her beaver in hers and Katie caught the wide eyes of a girl about ten who had been listening to their conversation. The last thing they needed was for the kids to think they were going to be murdered. She smacked JJ's arm. "We are *not* serial—we are good people." She met the eyes of the other kids. "We are good people. I promise."

The doors banged open as another deputy, about sixty, with a flushed face, rushed in. "Allison," he gasped. "We're up. There's an eighteen-car pile-up on the 78/Ten interchange. Multiple injuries and fatalities."

Deputy Montgomery jumped up. "But I'm the only one—"

"There is no one else. We gotta go."

"What? We can't just close—"

"Everyone else is already dispatched. There is no one left. All the precincts are closing. It's a full-blown four-alarm fire out there. Everyone's ordered to head out."

"Wait!" Katie shouted.

The older deputy stopped and stared at her like she'd appeared out of thin air.

"What about these kids?" she demanded.

His eyes widened as he finally noticed the band of children huddled together in the hall. "What about them? Whose are they?" He turned to Deputy Montgomery. "Why are they scratching—"

"Their bus driver is... no longer with us and—someone needs to take them," Katie said. "Find their families." She pointed to Amelia. "Her's too."

"Well, we can't do it," the deputy said, making it sound like that should be obvious.

Katie finally made out the name on his shirt. Rochelle.

"Yes, you can," JJ roared. "You're the goddamn police. It's your job to defend and protect!"

"You said another—" One of the boys by the wall began.

JJ spun around. "I know it's a swear! I'm sorry. *Damn it!*" He pulled his hat off with his free hand, raked his fingers through his hair, then slammed it back on his head.

Deputy Rochelle mopped his brow and chewed his lip, looking between Katie, JJ, and the kids. "No, you're right. You're right. We gotta keep 'em safe. You ever been convicted of a felony?" he asked JJ.

"What? No," he snapped, sounding offended.

The officer turned to her. "You?"

Katie's brows came together, not understanding what that had to do with anything. "No. I've never even—"

"Good. You can take them then." He turned to Deputy Montgomery. "Let's go."

The room rocked, and JJ caught her arm as the edges of Katie's vision darkened.

"Excuse me?" JJ's voice was incredulous, as he dragged her back to her feet and planted her firmly beside him. "We can't— Don't we have to be...deputized or something? This is *insane*."

"Naw," Rochelle said, waving his hand in their direction. "Civilians do good things every day. Besides, you seem like nice folks." He looked at Deputy Montgomery, who nodded in agreement.

Nice folks? Katie looked at JJ. Were they serious?

He looked about ready to pass out, and to be fair, she wasn't far behind him. There was no way they were leaving here with those kids.

"Get them to an office further from the city, where someone can take them." Deputy Rochelle said before rushing off into the other room. Katie gripped JJ's arm. "But—they are not puppies we found on the side of the road. They're *children!*" she shouted after him.

"I'll issue you a temporary permit to drive the bus," Officer Montgomery interrupted.

They both spun around to face her as she pulled a sheet of paper from one of the cubbies behind her. "But I guarantee no one will try to stop you."

Katie shook her head in disbelief. They were serious. They were bloody fucking serious. "No—" She shook her head again. "We can't—don't we need to take an oath or *something*? You can't seriously just give us—"

"Would it make you feel better to take a little oath?" Deputy Montgomery asked, giving Katie an exasperated look.

Katie glanced at JJ, who looked as flabbergasted as she felt, and her anger surged as she raised her right arm. "Yes. Yes, it would. Because I cannot believe I live in a country where the police hand kids over to complete strangers!"

JJ pushed her hand down. "What are you doing?" he hissed. "Don't piss them off."

"Piss *them* off?" Katie glared. "I'm not the one not doing my job!"

"Fine. Raise your right hand." Officer Montgomery said, crossing her arms.

Katie stuck out her chin and raised her right hand as JJ hesitated beside her, and Amelia held up her left one.

"Have you lost your goddamn mind?" he whispered, pulling it down again, as if it made any difference.

Amelia gasped but kept her mouth shut.

"Come on, you too," Deputy Montgomery said.

Katie elbowed him in the stomach and met his eyes.

This is all your fault, JJ's angry, beautiful brown eyes said.

This most certainly was *not* her fault. And if he thought she had any interest in taking a bunch of *kids* anywhere, then he was sorely mistaken. She was just trying to do the right thing. "Raise your hand," she demanded.

"Fuck," he growled, raising his hand as Amelia gasped again, and JJ rolled his eyes. "Sorry, munchkin."

Katie lifted hers again.

"I—state your name…" the deputy began.

"I, state your name," Amelia repeated dutifully.

———

THE NEXT THING SHE KNEW, Katie was ushering the kids, *all* of them, down the walkway toward the bus, loaded down with plastic grocery bags full of chips and bottled water. The deputies had shoved them at her as a consolation prize before throwing them out, locking the doors, and taking off with sirens wailing.

She looked over the heads of the kids, then at the school bus. The Veil, as the news was calling it, rose in the distance behind them. It was a perfect social media shot.

Her brain composed a caption without her even trying. *On a mission from the Sheriff's Office, to deliver school children home after terrorist attack. Wish me luck!* The situation was so unbelievable, so utterly ridiculous she had almost asked for a uniform, because she was ninety-nine percent certain she was dreaming and they would have given her one.

The concrete was hot on her bare feet as she rubbed her dripping brow with her weighted-down arms. As the kids climbed back into the bus, her brain went through all the poses that would have accompanied the caption. Peeking under the brim of the Stetson, cleavage showing just right. Check. Glancing over the top of a pair of aviators, with the school bus in the background. Check.

Her sweat-soaked, fifty-dollar tank top—what the kids in high school used to call a wife-beater. It was a horrible name for a shirt, but surprisingly accurate. Because it was exactly what her father wore when he beat—*Forget about it.* Check. The fabric clung to her, and she felt the itchy beginning of a heat rash forming between her breasts.

"What are we going to do with them?" JJ hissed in her ear, drawing her back to the sweltering heat and impending crisis.

Amelia was walking beside him, her little hand in his huge one, and Katie absently wondered what her life might have been like if she'd had a hand like that to hold when she was growing up.

The Veil caught her eye again, standing over the buildings like something from outer space. The impossibility of everything that was happening hit her again, and again she was almost sure she was dreaming. Two hours ago, she had the world at her feet and her biggest responsibility in life was posting pretty pictures of herself on the internet. Now she was *barefoot* and playing Mary Poppins to a bunch of freaked-out toddlers and second graders...or were they in third? She had never hung around kids of any age in her adult life, and couldn't tell.

"Hey." JJ snapped his fingers in front of her face. It took her a second to remember what they were talking about. "I don't know. But we can't leave them here," she whispered back.

"Goddamn it." He looked like he wanted to punch something. Maybe her.

She understood why he was upset. She was too. And she'd shave her head before living with head lice again. But this wasn't her fault. *She* wasn't the one that did this.

Jinn stood at the door of the bus. The girl had been staring at Katie's chest since she stepped on the bus, making her wish she'd worn a bra.

Grabbing JJ's arm, Katie pulled him aside. "We need to stay calm and think."

"Stay calm? Stay—"

Katie shushed him. "Please. You're scaring the kids."

JJ squeezed his eyes shut and ran his hands over his face, mumbling to himself.

"What?"

"What if we take them back to their school? Someone there will—"

Katie's heart leaped. Yes! That was a good idea. The name printed on the side of the bus in black letters said Carlton Christian School. "Sam!" she called. He was dragging Leo, the boy Katie had caught trying to touch the Veil, back to the bus. "Do you know where this school is?"

"No," he said, wrestling Leo as the boy tried to wiggle free. "I don't live around here. And normally don't come out this far."

Jinn spoke up. "I think it's off Belvedere Drive."

"It is," the angsty teen said, uttering his first words. "But I'm not going back there."

"Do you know where it is?" Katie asked.

The boy shook his head. "Between Darnell and Kingsly, but I don't know which way that is from here. Not without getting back on the freeway."

They were definitely not doing that.

Sam hoisted Leo over his shoulder. "If you give me lice, I swear to god—" Leo squealed with laughter and pounded on Sam's back as they climbed onto the bus.

Katie turned back to JJ. "Okay, well, I know we passed Belvedere on the way here. I remember seeing it."

"Okay, so we drive up and down the road until we find the streets or the kids see something familiar?" he asked.

"Yeah." It wasn't a great plan, but what else could they do? None of their phones were working. Katie had tried a dozen times to make calls, and get on her pages. Everything was jammed up. She couldn't even access a map, and without one, they were practically blind. "Yeah?" she repeated.

"Yeah. Okay." JJ said hopefully as he paced in front of her. "We'll drop the kids off, and then head back to Hartford Creek, and figure out—" he turned and looked back toward the Veil. "We figure out what in the hell *that* thing is, and how to get around it. Because I need to get my mom and sister out of there."

She followed his eyes. To the north, it ran into a metal tower and turned. There was no top to it that she could see. It just went up several hundred feet and ended, like a giant fence around the city.

"We'll go in front," Katie said, handing him the bag of snacks. "Are you okay?"

JJ's lips were tight as he nodded.

"Are you sure?"

Leo dashed off the bus again, followed by Sam. "Get back

67

here, you little monster!" Sam yelled, grabbing the boy, and wrestling him back toward the doors.

JJ nodded. "Go hop on the bus," he told Amelia. To her, he said, "Fuck this day," then headed for the bus, extracting Leo from Sam. The boy wiggled again as JJ picked him up and tucked him under his arm like a football.

"Hey!" she called, suddenly overwhelmed by how glad she was that fate had paired them together for this crisis. She could have been anywhere, with anyone, right now. But thank god, she wasn't.

Leo squealed with delight at being spun as JJ turned. Katie's breath paused in her throat and she gave him a small grateful smile, as the trifecta worked its magic on her insides again. "Drive safe," she said.

A smile tugged at his mouth, and if the world hadn't been ending, Katie might have swooned. She almost did anyway. His tan forearms, calloused hands, scruffy beard, and piercing brown eyes had been steadily growing on her since they met. But it was the heart beating beneath all that, making it hard to breathe now. A heart that threw itself over a stranger's body to protect her. A heart that held a little girl *and* her stuffed toy while she cried. A heart that agreed to drive a school bus full of lice-infested kids away from danger.

JJ was the whole package. She'd sensed it from the start. *That* is what she should have said to him earlier in the truck, instead of that stupid dad-bod comment. JJ was all man, and every decent thing a man could be on the *inside,* rolled into one. And at that very moment, she couldn't imagine a sexier combination.

"What?"

She shook her head. "Nothing." Now was not the time.

He shook his head, gave her another quick penetrating glance, sending a jolt of electricity down her spine, then disappeared into the bus, closing the doors behind him.

Katie limped back to the truck. Brushing more glass off the seat, she climbed in next to Sam and sighed. "Go out here and take a left," she directed. "Belvedere is back that way."

He shifted gears and pulled out of the parking lot.

As they headed up the road, Katie kept glancing behind her. Every time she caught JJ's eyes, she felt it. The pull, the pulse, the—

"You like him, don't you?" Sam asked, interrupting her thoughts.

She turned back around, blushing. "What? No."

"Pshh. Don't lie."

"I-I'm not." She pointed. "Turn here."

Sam expertly turned the big rig. "So.... How'd you two meet, anyway? What's your story?"

"What?"

"How do you two know each other?"

"I don't. He's... He's just my tow truck driver. My car is in the shop and —"

Sam burst out laughing. "Are you serious?"

Katie frowned. "What?"

"Him being all offended, acting like you were his girl. I knew it!" He slammed his palm against the steering wheel. "F.Y.I. You are *way* out of his league."

That was absolutely not true. "No, I'm not—"

Sam changed the subject before she could set the record straight. "Hey, what's the chick's name on the bus? The Asian girl."

Chick? She rolled her eyes. "What?"

"The shorty we picked up? The one dressed like my grandma."

Katie pulled her sunglasses on the top of her head and glared at him. "That's not nice. She just dresses conservatively—"

"Like my grandma."

"And her name is Jinn."

Sam frowned. "Gin? Like the booze?"

"No. Jinn, like—I don't know. She's from China. Her parents immigrated here when she was eight."

Sam's jaw dropped. "Really? She speaks perfect English. I thought she was American."

"She is, now. She said her parents sent her to an all-English-speaking school, and she's scared. We all are, so don't give her a hard time, okay?" Katie spotted the sign for Belvedere. "There! We'll try right first. If we don't find it, we'll go back the other way."

Sam signaled and turned. "Yeah, yeah, I got you. I don't usually go for strait-laced, skinny girls like her, you know, I like a few more curves, but those eyes. Man," he whistled. "You think I could score a chick like her?"

Katie didn't bother to hide her disapproval as she turned and scowled at him. He clearly was not picking up what she was putting down. "Score her? She's not a pinball game. She's not a—"

Sam held up his hand. "Women are not property. I know. I know. He already told me. Sorry, that was just a figure of speech. What I meant was—"

"Who told you?"

"Indiana Solo, back there." He thrust his thumb in the direction behind them.

Katie turned and looked over her shoulder. "Who?"

"I put Indiana Jones and Han Solo together because he's acting all the hero-y, and he seriously needs a haircut. Your dumb-ass boyfriend. And—"

"He's not a dumb ass. And he *is* a hero." She looked at JJ in the rearview. "He told you women aren't property?"

"Yeah, right before he called me an asshole.... Or maybe it was after?" Sam held up his hand. "Which, to be fair, is true. That's why my mama sent me to Christian school like those little gremlins back there. But she wasted her money, because not only am I still an ass, I'm an atheist and a man of science. Just like my daddy."

Man of science?

"What I meant was," His voice was deep and scholarly as he continued. "Do you think she—Jinn—might be interested in pursuing a romantic relationship with someone like…moi?" Sitting up, he waved his hand over his body like a game show model.

Katie looked over her shoulder again.

JJ had lectured Sam about respecting women? She shook her head in amazement as he steered the bus behind her, while Amelia's beaver danced back and forth across his shoulders. He wasn't a good guy. He was a *saint*, one of those mythical wonderful men that women dreamed of but most never found. She owed him an even bigger apology than she thought for the other day at the bar, for being such a bitch when he was trying to defend what she should have been.

Sam misinterpreted her silence. "No? Really? Why not? She's hot in a librarian sort of way. And I dig books… if you know what I mean—"

"There is more to women than looks."

"Pfft. Says you, sitting beside me, looking like that."

Katie sighed. "It's my job."

Sam laughed. "It's your job to look hot?"

"I—" she leaned her arm against the window and pushed the hair back off her forehead. She didn't want to go into it. "Do you see anything?"

Sam shook his head. "No. And don't change the subject."

"I'm what is called a social influencer. I—"

"I know what a social influencer is. I'm not stupid."

"I didn't say you were."

"But you were thinking it."

Katie knew exactly how he felt. "Sam. I wasn't. Trust me. If there is anything I've learned in my life, and my line of work, it is not to stereotype and judge, because all it will do is expose *you* as a fool. And I am a lot of things, but thank god, a fool is not one of them any—"

The truck jerked to a stop as the car in front of them braked.

She braced herself as he said, "My Gran says the same thing. Do you know I got a scholarship to go to the University of Georgia?"

"That's great. What do you study?" She looked ahead as the road curved to the left, out of sight. A car honked from somewhere behind them as Sam shifted back into gear, and they moved forward slowly.

"Space, baby," he said, smiling.

Space? Did he want to be an astronaut then? He seemed kind of old for that sort of thing.

She looked out his window at the Veil in the distance. Even from far away, it was otherworldly. "Do you think it could be aliens that did this?"

He laughed as if that was a silly question.

"What?" she asked. "You don't believe in aliens?"

"Well, I do…theoretically, but this isn't aliens. No way."

"How do you know?"

He glanced at the Veil and frowned. "Because the only aliens that would ever land here would either be too smart to give a shit about us, or too stupid to know we're even here."

She didn't know what that meant, but his certainty was comforting. "So, you want to be an astronaut?"

He laughed again. Oh, hell no. No, no…I'm a math man. Astrophysicist, technically, and up until about two hours ago, I really liked being on Earth."

"Oh." She didn't know what any of that meant.

They crawled around a bend in the road, and Katie fanned herself as he braked again. It was bumper to bumper for a mile and at the end was a red light. Traffic was getting worse by the minute.

Tugging at his shirt, Sam said, "But deep space is looking pretty good right about now. Fuck it's hot."

She huffed a laugh.

"I'm getting a degree in literature, too. But that's for my mama. Couldn't do the church thing, so I figured the least I could do was quote her Shakespeare. She loves Shakespeare." Resuming his scholarly voice, he raised his arm and said, "*Let heaven and men and devils, let them all, all, all, cry shame against me, yet I'll speak. I kissed thee ere I killed thee: no way but this, killing myself, to die upon a kiss!*" The couple in the van next to them stared as Katie clapped and smiled, forgetting for just a moment they were in the middle of a nightmare.

She studied Sam. "Are your mom and dad on the inside?"

He pressed his hand to his stomach and bent over in a bow. "Thank you." Traffic moved slightly, and he shifted back into gear. "And only my mom. My dad passed a few years back."

"I'm sorry. Have you been able to get through to her?"

"No. But I know she's okay. She's got a boyfriend now. He's cool. And her sisters, my aunties, and grandma live just next door. And my uncle Jim lives a half mile away. I'm the only one who's not there." He paused, then laughed. "And she has Jesus. Lord, does that woman have Jesus. How about you?"

Katie heard more honking. It was coming from up ahead. If her parents were even still alive—and she highly doubted that—they might be trapped behind the south Veil in Miami but to keep things simple, she said, "Nope."

Cars from the side streets were trying to merge onto Belvedere, quickly making it impossible for the vehicles already on the road to move forward.

"This is going to take for fucking ever," Sam said, slumping back.

Fanning herself in the sweltering cab, Katie couldn't help but agree.

She looked back at JJ again and shrugged, raising her arms. "What do we do?" she mouthed.

He stared at her a moment, then the doors of the bus opened, and he hopped out.

Katie's heart skipped a beat as she watched him in the side-view mirror pull his cap lower over his eyes, and made his way to her door. He leaned on her window and looked at Sam, and again she couldn't help but notice his arms and the golden hairs covering them.

"Any of this ringing a bell to anyone back there?" she asked.

He shook his head. "The older boy refuses to speak, so I'm stuck with the little ones. 'Maybe, yes, but... not really'," he said, rolling his eyes. "Those are their exact words every time I ask. I mean, they've only gone there five days a week for the last nine months. Why would they know how to get there?" he asked sarcastically. Pulling his cap off, he swiped at his forehead. "The one older girl, Gracie or Grace, said she thought we were getting close, though. She said there's a white house with a giraffe in the front yard on the way, and a 7-11, which we passed, but all 7-11's all look alike, so I don't fucking know."

"What should we do? Split up?" she asked.

JJ shook his head again. "What good does that do without our phones?"

He had a point.

He looked ahead at the traffic that had barely moved and shook his head, and sighed. "They're saying it's a terrorist attack. The cities are completely cut off. People everywhere are flipping out. And I don't blame them. Look at that fucking thing."

Despite the heat in the cab, goosebumps rolled over Katie's body. "Terrorists? What terrorists? Who is saying that?"

"The news."

"News?" She stared at him dumbly. "Is your phone working?"

"The fucking radio, Katie."

So she was Katie now? Since the Veil went up, she'd been trying to get online. It had never occurred to her to listen to the *radio* for the news. "Oh, right."

"What do you mean, walled off? Can't they just go over the top?" Sam asked.

JJ shook his head. "The Wall, or Veil, or whatever they are calling it, has a lid. We just couldn't see it because it's flat. Nothing can get in or out of the city."

"But my mom—" For the first time, Katie heard worry in Sam's voice as he fumbled for his phone. "That doesn't make any sense. What do the terrorists want? Why would they hold the whole *world* ...Shit."

Shaking his head again, JJ shrugged. "They don't know yet. They just keep repeating the same things over and over."

Katie's throat went dry. "Which is what?"

"That they are everywhere. Fucking Jakarta, Beijing, Chicago, you name it, to stay away from it, which we already know. And to go home and stay there until someone figures out what the hell they want."

"That's it?"

"That's it."

"Fuck." Sam pulled the phone away from his ear, pushed more buttons, and pulled it back up. Katie made out the faint sound of a busy signal before he swore again. "It's not going through. The signals must be jammed."

"Are you serious?" JJ asked. "We've been saying that for the last hour."

Katie looked over her shoulder at the 7-11. JJ was right, they all looked alike. The one at the end of her street, when she was a girl, looked exactly the same. Her mother used to use the payphone outside to call her boyfriends, so her father wouldn't know. Katie stared at the pay phone that hung on the wall outside next to a window advertising two-for-one energy drinks. Why did the radios still work, if the phones didn't?

"Get out and go check up ahead," JJ said to Sam, interrupting her thoughts.

"What?" Katie and Sam's voices overlapped.

"Get out and check ahead," JJ repeated. "You'll be faster on foot."

Katie looked at the grid-locked traffic. He was right. They'd make much better time on foot. She turned to Sam. "He's right."

"Why do I have to go? And what about the truck?"

"We're going slow enough that I can drive both." JJ argued. "You can't drive the bus, and she doesn't have shoes."

They all looked at Katie's filthy feet and bright pink toes as she crossed them and tucked them as far under the seat as she could.

JJ stepped back. "Let me just go tell…"

"Jinn." Katie and Sam's voices overlapped again.

"Right. Go," he said to Sam. "I'll be right back."

JJ went back to the bus as Sam unbuckled his seatbelt and opened the door. He paused before getting out.

"What?" she asked.

"You're not going to leave me—"

The seriousness of their situation had finally penetrated his teenage brain, and he was scared. She got it. They all were. Katie covered his hand with hers and squeezed it. "If we won't leave flea-infested kids, we certainly won't leave you. We'll stick together until everyone is safe. I promise."

The corner of his mouth turned up as he nodded. "Okay. Cool." He got out, made his way to the sidewalk, then disappeared into the sea of traffic.

A minute later, the driver's side door opened again and JJ hopped in. They stared out the window for a moment in silence.

Katie raked her fingers across her sweaty scalp. "This is crazy."

"Yeah."

"How are you holding up?" She asked, scratching at the rash forming in the hollows of her elbows.

"I'm fine. But my mom and sister...They are in there. On the inside."

Katie's heart dropped. "Are you sure?"

"Yeah. And I can't get either of them on the phone—"

"Oh, god. JJ, I'm so sorry..." *She* didn't have anyone on the inside, thank god. But JJ, and those poor little kids...their *families,* the people they loved, were in there, being held hostage.

"I'm so sorry for everything."

He rubbed his temples. "Why? It's not your fault."

"But I—the kids, and the bus and all of this. I didn't even think about the fact that...you might have other things on your mind. I didn't mean to drag you into this mess."

"We both know I wouldn't have left those kids there." He shook his head. "I just... Kids and I don't get along."

Katie smiled. Children were excellent judges of character, savvy little lie detectors who could spot bullshit—*and kindness* —a mile away without even realizing it. "Little Amelia would disagree, I think."

She turned and waved at her as the girl, clutching her bored-looking beaver, watched them from the front window of the bus. The stuffie had been a lifesaver. "And I would too. How did you know to ask her if she had a special toy in the car?"

"All kids have one."

Katie didn't know that. "Did you?" she asked. Because she didn't. Or if she did, it was long lost before she was old enough to remember.

"Yeah." The corner of his mouth turned up. "It was a duck."

They were quiet for a moment as she studied his profile. "I think they scare *you*," she said.

JJ met her eyes through his sunglasses and huffed a laugh. "Yeah, well, you scare me too."

Katie's brow went up. "What?"

He looked away. "Nothing. Never mind."

"No. What—"

"Look!" He pointed. Sam was already making his way back, weaving between the cars. They hadn't even moved an inch.

Breathlessly, he climbed up onto the running board and hung his arms over Katie's door. "Good news is, the ugly-ass giraffe is just up ahead on the right, and the school is about four blocks that way, and then a block down," he said breathlessly.

"The bad news?"

"It's closed."

"Closed? How can that be?" Katie looked at her phone. It was only a little after noon.

"I tried to go in, but the doors were locked."

"No. No." JJ slammed his hand on the steering wheel. "No! Someone has got to still be there."

Katie put her hand on his arm, and something more than heat spread through her palm. "Okay. We'll just have to think of something else."

"Like fucking what, Katie?" JJ demanded. "We are stuck in the middle of fucking—" He punched the steering wheel again.

"Let's just go there anyway and see. Maybe the school is on lockdown or something. Maybe when we pull up with a bus with their name on the side, they'll let us in."

That seemed to calm him a little. The car ahead rolled forward about three feet, and JJ pulled forward as Katie returned to her earlier thought.

"Why do the radios work, but not the phones?"

Sam frowned at her. "They use different technology and different frequencies. Cell phones use microwaves to send and receive large quantities of information and rely on a network of base stations, whereas radio towers just broadcast, usually at much lower frequencies, and our radios are just simple receivers that—"

JJ sighed. "Who cares why they don't work? They just don't."

Katie looked over her shoulder at the 7-11. "Because if it's just the cell phone *signals* that are jamming, then..." The guys turned and followed her eyes to the decrepit payphone attached to the brick wall. "Maybe the land-lines still—"

Sam cut her off. "You're a fucking genius! Any of you guys got any change?"

Katie rummaged around in her bag for her coin purse and handed it to him.

He took off running.

They sat for a moment in silence before JJ spoke up. "That was... a really good idea," he said, sounding surprised.

Katie turned and smiled. Now was not the time to take things personally. They were all having a bit of an off day. "We don't know if it's right, though."

"But it's a good thought." He studied her again from behind his sunglasses, and she thought about his earlier statement. What about her scared him, exactly? "Why did you say I—"

Jinn appeared behind JJ at the window. "Guys, I know we have much bigger problems, but the kids—I don't know what to do. The girls are crying, one of the boy's scalps is bleeding..."

JJ blanched. "Oh, god."

Katie bit her lip. "Okay. Um...I'll figure something out. Can you go back and keep an eye on them?"

Jinn nodded and left as Sam ran back up to the truck.

"That phone doesn't work." He said, beads of sweat dripping down his forehead as he leaned against JJ's window. "They just never took it down."

"Do the kids know their addresses? Can't we just take them home?" JJ asked.

"No," Sam said, wiping his brow and trying again to dial his phone.

"Why not?" JJ asked, sounding frustrated again.

"Because they all live on the inside."

"What? How do you know that?" JJ asked.

"That's why they were on the fuckin' freeway, dumb-ass."

"Don't call him—" Katie began.

JJ's voice drowned her out. "Do not call me that. And I'm sorry if my thoughts are a little muddled right now. This is my first terrorist attack. I'm not good with *children*, and I hate being stuck in traffic, which is why I live out in the middle of nowhere. God. I could *really* use a stiff drink right now..." he mumbled to himself.

"Hey, man. Chill. And I am not a child."

"Yes, you—"

Katie held up her hand and looked between them. "Both of you, shut up." She looked at Sam. "You are not a child." Then she turned to JJ. "And you're not a dumb-ass. But even if both of you were, I wouldn't care because we have larger concerns right now." She turned back to Sam. "Maybe we can just get someone to let us use their phone? Do you have any friends or family on this side of the..."

"Veil." JJ supplied.

"Yeah. Veil. Anyone at all you know, who you could stay with until—"

He shook his head. "I told you, my whole life is in Atlanta. My grandma, aunts, friends."

"Then why were you way the fuck out—" JJ began.

"Because I go to school in Athens! Because my mama asked me to be home by ten-thirty this morning to go to church with my grandma, who turned eighty today. And because nobody disobeys my mama, that's why!" He looked like he was about to cry.

"Okay. Everybody calm down." Katie scratched at her stomach. They were all hot, tired, and overwhelmed. "Let's just get to the school."

Sam shot her an aggravated look. "You plan to just dump them off there?"

"No. Of course not."

"Then what good is it to go there? I told you it's fucking closed."

"Don't talk to her like that." JJ snapped. "She's trying to help your sorry ass—"

"My sorry ass? What's that supposed to mean?"

"Stop!" Katie shouted. "Just...stop. We have to work together! We have to..."

By some miracle, the cars suddenly began moving.

"Quick, let's go!" she said.

JJ threw the door open and hopped out, and Sam hopped back in.

"One thing at a time," she said. "Let's just get to the school."

———

THE GOOD NEWS WAS, the school was not empty after all, just closed. After a lot of banging, someone finally came and let them in. The principal, a Mrs. Felicity Driver, had the nerve to look annoyed when Katie and JJ ushered the fifteen little ones safely back inside. As they passed the classrooms on the way to the gym, she saw kids waiting at their desks.

"I was hoping they'd made it home," Principal Driver said tersely as her heels clacked down the hall. "We have over a hundred and eighty students, half of which live on the other side of that thing out there, and we are trying to figure out how to get a hold of their parents or someone to take them, which is nearly impossible with all the phones down."

"Even the land lines?" Sam asked.

"I don't know. We've got landlines on our end, but most of the parents have cell phones. We have gotten through to a few though. Maybe that's why."

Entering the gym, there were several small groups of older kids sitting quietly together. As they walked by, Katie heard snickers directed at the teenage boy with the black eye, followed by smug laughter.

Principal Driver led them to a folding table set up near the middle of the room. On top was some kind of camo-printed fire-proof box.

"Line up." Principal Driver said as the kids formed a line and she reached into it and pulled out a bunch of...Katie didn't know what they were. Little silver wires, with a single oval metal bead attached to them. Then, grabbing something that looked like a video game controller, she began pushing buttons on it.

"Leo, you first," she said as the boy obediently came forward. Taking one of the bands, she looped it around his wrist and adjusted it, then locked it in place. "Okay. Go sit down," she said, pointing to an empty space on the floor. Then she called the next child up.

"What is that?" Katie asked.

"I haven't a clue," the principal said, shaking her head. "All I can tell you is this box has been sitting in my office closet for five years, and as soon as that thing outside went up, I received an executive order, from the Office of the President of the United States, to open it and follow the instructions."

Katie felt her eyes bulge. "The president?"

"What were the instructions?" Sam asked, stepping forward.

"To tag each of the kids with one of these, and to enter their names, and the corresponding bracelet numbers in here," she held up the controller, "and then try to get them home as quickly as possible. Sophia!" The next little girl came up, scratching her head. "I can tell you right now, I can't keep all these kids," Principal Driver said, strapping the bracelet on the girl's tiny wrist.

"What?" Katie asked, praying she'd misheard.

"I'll keep the ones I know have family close by. But the others..."

JJ groaned. "Jesus Christ. You've got to be fucking—"

The principal gasped. "Excuse me, this is a Christian school, and we do not allow—"

"He swears *a lot*." Amelia interrupted. "And did you know goddamnit is a swear word?" She asked innocently, still clutching JJ's hand, making Katie strangely jealous.

Principal Driver gasped again, then her eyes narrowed on JJ, who had the decency to blush. "I apologize. I—" he began.

"Who is she?" Principal Driver interrupted, pointing to Amelia. "She's not one of ours."

"We found her on the road," Katie said. "She's been... orphaned."

"What's orphaned mean?" Amelia asked, tilting her head.

Raising her eyes skyward, the principal crossed herself. "I pray for these children, Lord, for all the children who have suffered."

Katie knew she shouldn't, but she couldn't help herself. "How about you just keep them instead?"

Principal Driver glared at Katie. "I told you, I'll keep the ones I can, but you're going to have to take the rest," she said again.

"What is it with everyone today?" JJ mumbled. "Just handing off kids like they're Halloween candy."

"As of right now, each teacher at this school is responsible for *all* the children in their classes." Principal Driver snapped. "That means, if we can't get a hold of someone to take them, we are each taking thirty kids home with us today. Some only live in apartments, some lived on the other side of that—" She waved her hand in the general direction that Atlanta lay.

"The Veil."

"Yes, so they themselves have nowhere to go. And you went out of your way to bring these kids all the way here, which means you're decent people. So I am not just 'handing them off.' I know they'll be looked after. And there are two of you. Surely you can manage a couple of children for a few days?"

"But—" Katie scratched at the raised, irritated skin on the back of her neck. *Few days?* Was it possible this whole thing would only last that long? Oh god, she hoped not.

"I'll take the ones I can," Principal Driver repeated. "And we will track the rest. If anyone shows up looking for them, I'll send them your way. That's all I can do." She looked up. "Parker, you're next."

———

LESS THAN THIRTY MINUTES LATER, they were back outside, standing in the shade of the bus.

"So what do we do?" Jinn asked, staring at Katie's chest again. "When are they going to take the Veils down? What are we supposed to do with them until then?" She pointed to the remaining children sitting on the bus, who were now apparently theirs until further notice.

Katie dug the heels of her hands into her eyes.

"And how are we gonna get through to our people inside?" Sam asked. "My mom's gotta be flipping out."

"Mine too." Jinn agreed.

"And what about food? I'm hungry."

They all turned. It was the teenage boy with the black eye, speaking up for only the second time. He was about as tall as Katie, thin, with saggy skinny jeans and a band hoodie over his uniform. His straight dark brown hair, sticking out from a black beanie, hung over his eyes. "Are the stores even open?"

"Man, we got more important problems than food," Sam said.

"Actually, no we don't." The boy retorted.

"What's your name?" Katie asked.

"Parker."

"Well, *Parker,* if you hadn't noticed, there's been a terrorist attack—" Sam said.

"Yeah. I'm not blind, asshole."

"Don't you call me an—"

"Hey! Cut it out!" JJ's voice boomed.

"Well, we can't just stand here all day," Parker said, stating the obvious.

"So what do we do?" Jinn asked again as Parker and Sam got into it again and JJ took off running after Leo, who'd made a downright diabolical game of trying to escape the bus.

The truth was, Katie didn't know what to do. Not without a phone, anyway. It was almost literally the first step to solving every problem in the modern world. Tears filled her eyes as JJ dragged the boy back again, football-style, and Amelia cried to be picked up.

The last week had been bad enough. Not that anything *quite* compared to what they faced now. But the boutique hotels had shunned her, forcing her to stay at the noisy inn where she'd barely slept because she was so hungry and worried about that stupid runway show. Then Zara had humiliated her by claiming she was out of town when she wasn't. After Katie posted her regrets about not being able to catch up with her "friend," Zara posted photos of herself partying at the club just down the street from the one Katie had gone to Saturday night, *alone* because she needed to look like she was living her fucking 'perfect' life. She swiped at the tears gathering in the corners of her eyes. And now this.

LA was behind a Veil too, which meant she was homeless, and since the internet wasn't working, she had no access to her money, which meant she was also penniless. "Hey. Are you—" JJ began.

"No! I'm not okay!" she cried. "Terrorists are taking over the world if you haven't heard. My stupid phone doesn't work!" She resisted the urge to throw it against the bus. "I am melting in that damn truck. I desperately need a shower. I don't have any *fucking* shoes, and I'm probably going to die of tetanus!" She raked her fingers across the hives on the back of her neck that she'd been trying to ignore. "So no. No, I'm not okay. No, I'm not—"

"Well, what are we—" Jinn began again, sounding like a broken record.

"We're going home," JJ said, cutting her off.

"Home?" Sam asked, eyeing Katie warily as she wiped her eyes on the back of her hand again. A black smudge appeared on it and she knew exactly what manner of shit she resembled. *Fuck.* Pressing her ring fingers under her eyes, she attempted to wipe the running mascara away.

"Hartford Creek," JJ said.

"Where in the hell is that?" Parker asked.

JJ ignored him. "We'll go to Hartford Creek until—"

"Until what?" Sam asked.

"I don't know. But it's where I live. And while it's not much—"

Katie rolled her eyes. That was an understatement.

JJ went on. "It's better than getting stuck here, with all these people, waiting for whatever is going to happen. At least we have somewhere safe to stay."

He had a point there.

"And you're gonna drive that bus all the way there? For only four kids?" Parker asked.

It was four kids, plus Parker, Jinn, and JJ, and they had no choice. They couldn't all fit in the truck.

"Unless you'd rather walk?" JJ offered. When Parker didn't answer, he went on. "Then, once everything goes back online—"

"What if it never does?" Sam asked.

Panic blossomed in Katie's chest. Without the internet she had nothing. Without the internet, she *was* nothing. How would she support herself? What would she do?

"We'll worry about that later. Let's just get these kids to Hartford Creek. One thing at a time."

"Okay. Yeah." Sam said.

Jinn nodded in agreement and climbed on the bus, as Sam made his way around to the driver's side of the truck, leaving Katie and JJ standing together.

"I don't know anything about kids," she confessed, wiping her eyes again with the heels of her hands. And there was nothing in Hartford Creek, certainly not for her.

"It will be okay," he said. "They're all basically the same. We'll take care of them together."

"How are we supposed to do that when we don't even know what's happened? What if we can't?"

"I'll figure it out," JJ said.

Katie pulled her hands through her hair. She wasn't cut out for this. She should be soaking in a bathtub right now, in—she gasped quietly as it finally occurred to her that if Old Ray hadn't broken down, she would be in New York right now, behind a Veil.

"What?" JJ asked.

"Nothing," she mumbled.

"I'll figure it out," JJ repeated.

She wasn't one to fantasize about white knights and being rescued because she knew better. But still, his leadership right then was welcome. Because she was out of ideas, didn't have a penny to her name, and had no idea where they were.

There was one thing she could do, though. She squared her shoulders. "If you take care of the kids, I can handle the lice."

JJ's brow went up again, and she had the feeling she'd surprised him again.

"Deal," he said. "Let's roll."

Chapter Five

Day 1 // 7:44 p.m.

I'LL FIGURE IT OUT. JJ shook his head as he glanced at his truck behind him in the side view. Why had he said that? Why had he promised them that? *You know why.* Because it was what his dad would have done.

He sighed.

But he wasn't his dad, and he had no fucking clue what to do with a bunch of kids. And it wasn't because he hadn't had plenty of time to think about it. He had. *Hours,* in fact, because that was how long it had taken them to get out of town and go the hundred and forty-five miles back home.

They were down to a thankfully potty-trained three-year-old, two five-year-olds, a terrified eleven-year-old, and one moody, beat-up teenager. Even though that was less than a third of their original group, he'd still about had a coronary. But Principal Driver had not budged. "Deal with it," she said, before taking down their useless phone numbers, JJ's address, and dismissing them.

JJ ground his teeth together as he looked in the rearview. Amelia was curled up on the bench behind him, asleep.

He knew the principal was probably just as overwhelmed as they were…But damn it. He didn't do kids. Not anymore. Not since… Spinning the steering wheel, he turned onto the county road that he knew like the back of his hand and pushed the name and the adorable little face that went with it back into the shadows of his past. This was not the day to go down that rabbit hole.

Home was two miles away. They were almost there. Between the traffic and an obscene number of "emergency" bathroom breaks, most of which had occurred on the side of the road, he was surprised they'd made it at all. Unfortunately, all the time to think hadn't helped him come up with a plan. At least Katie had offered to deal with the lice. He wouldn't have even known where to begin with that. That wasn't the first time she'd surprised him today, either. To tell the truth, she was turning out to be nothing at all like he imagined when she strolled into Barb's, looking like a spoiled Barbie doll.

Glancing out the side-view mirror, he saw the headlights of his truck behind him. He huffed a laugh. That was some shit, Sam riding all the way back with her while he played bus driver. But then, maybe it was for the best.

Either way, he was rolling into town with a bus full of kids—he looked in the rearview mirror at the mostly empty seats—Well, not *full*, but still he had no clue what to do with them. Pinching the bridge of his nose, he sighed and stretched his back, selfishly wishing his mom was there, like she normally was when he got home from work. Rolling his wrist, he looked at his watch. She'd be watching Jeopardy in her living room next door right now, waiting for JJ to shower and come over for dinner. She made the best meatloaf and fried chicken. His stomach rumbled.

But then he thought about Sierra and was glad his mom was there with her. Not that his sister couldn't take care of herself. She was a capable, confident woman. But she was also twenty-four and there was a deadly virus on the loose in the city. At least that was what the president had said as JJ steered the bus through the hilly Georgia countryside.

When they made the announcement on the radio that the president was going to address the nation, he yelled at the kids to shut up and turned up the volume. A minute later, President Rodriguez's familiar voice filled the bus, and JJ's jaw dropped as he confessed that *he* was responsible for the Veils and that there was some super contagious X-Virus on the loose.

"Here is what we know about the X-virus so far." The president had said. *"Like other viruses, for example, the pneumonic plague or, more recently, COVID-19, the X-virus is transmissible through the air. I repeat, it is airborne. Unlike those other viruses, however, it does not favor a particular age or demographic."*

JJ had glanced in the rearview mirror as Parker pulled the earbud out of his ear, wondering if maybe the kids shouldn't be listening, but he needed to know what was going on. So he had left it on.

"At present, the mortality rate of the X-virus is an unheard-of one hundred percent, which means everyone we know that had been infected has now died. The virus affects us all equally —adults and children alike. Therefore, until the origin is revealed, and a cure is discovered, the quarantine of the affected cities is not only the best but also the only solution we have. The problem we face, my fellow Americans, and citizens of the world, is not another typhoid or Covid scare. It is much, much worse. It is the annihilation of our species."

"Jesus Christ," JJ breathed, shaking his head.

"Our very existence hangs in the balance."

While he tried to figure out if that was better or worse than terrorists, the president had gone on to explain the quarantine protocols for those inside the Veil.

"Any physical contact outside of your household is strictly prohibited. Since the X-Virus is airborne and extremely contagious, all businesses are to remain closed until further notice. There will be a zero-tolerance for gatherings of any kind. Only essential workers will be allowed to leave their homes, and they will be required to wear PAPRs or a higher-grade mask when

out in public. These masks are already in route to the cities. Anyone on the streets without authorization or proper protection will be arrested. I cannot emphasize enough how crucial it is to follow this order. This is not a joke. You cannot bend these rules. Your lives depend on it. Your children's lives depend on it."

The rules for the outside were much more relaxed: go home and stay home until the quarantine was lifted. JJ listened for a few more minutes, only turning it off when Grace started crying.

So, if Sierra was stuck in the middle of all that—JJ sighed again. His mom would want to be there with her. Pressing his phone to his ear, he tried calling her again for the hundredth time. For the hundredth time, it beeped busy. Setting the phone back on his knee, he pinched the bridge of his nose again. He couldn't imagine how terrified they must be.

In addition to the kids, he'd been wracking his brain trying to figure out a way to get them out. But after the president mentioned the *'devastation in Beijing and Moscow,'* whatever that meant, his confidence that there was anything he could do had begun to fade. Maybe there still was a solution, a way out, but like with the kids, either it wasn't obvious or he was too stupid to see it.

He passed Ms. Michelle's house and knew he had about three minutes to come up with a plan.

Thumping his thumbs on the steering wheel, he glanced at the kids. All three of the little ones and Jinn were asleep. Poor Grace was scratching her head, looking miserable, and Parker was slouched in the back, listening to music, staring at his own reflection in the window.

He passed the sign welcoming visitors to Hartford Creek. At least it used to. Now it was just a weathered piece of plywood with a bunch of weeds growing around it. Two and a half minutes.

JJ sighed. Maybe he was going about this the wrong way.

Maybe he needed to start with a smaller problem than getting the kids home to their families, or rescuing his mom and sister, and work his way up from there. *What do they need?* Besides their heads shaved, they needed food, water, and sleep. Probably in that order. He had no food at his house, and whatever leftovers his mom had would not be enough to feed eight people, so...

"Barbs." Assuming there was electricity—there had been in the city—they'd have dinner there if she was willing to quarantine with them. If not, he'd order takeout. "Done. Boom."

Next? Next would probably be the lice. At one of their numerous bathroom stops, Katie had informed him she was going to get what she needed to take care of that. As she headed toward the shopping center, barefoot, he reminded her everything was closed. Ten minutes later she returned with a bloody arm, a pair of cheap flip-flops on her feet, and, according to her, everything she needed to conquer head lice. When he'd asked her what happened to her arm, she'd winked at him and said, 'You don't want to know.'

His smile faded as the final task came into focus. Where in the hell were they going to sleep? Especially the infested ones? The thought of bugs in his house sent a shiver down his spine.

There was no hotel in town. And even if they took them to the Sheriff's office, which was in the next town over, there was nowhere for them to sleep besides a cell, and they'd been through enough. He hated to do it, but sleeping on the floor at his place was the only thing that came to mind. He'd probably have to burn his house down after, but... It would get them through the night, anyway. Then in the morning, they'd head over to the Sheriff's office and figure out a way to contact the rest of the families.

Jinn, looking tired, made her way up and sat on the edge of the seat behind Amelia.

"Were you able to get through to your parents?" he asked.

Jinn shook her head, looking like she might burst into tears. "We don't have a landline at our house."

He glanced over his shoulder at her. "Hey, listen. I really appreciate all you've done today for those kids. I couldn't have done this, them, without you."

"Sure, of-of course."

"I know you probably miss your folks and you're scared. But you're safe with us, okay? You're not...alone."

She nodded. "Did you know I've never spent a night away from my parents?" she asked with an embarrassed smile. "I know it's stupid, but we were a close-knit family, and...my mom was pretty protective, so..."

JJ smiled. "Do you mind if I ask how old you are?"

"Nineteen. Twenty in August."

He remembered when his sister was nineteen. It was right about then that she stopped acting like a spoiled brat and actually became pretty cool. He nodded. "It's a good age."

Toothbrushes. The kids needed toothbrushes. He'd check at his mom's. After Covid, she always stashed stuff like that around the house.

Leo's voice piped up from the back. "Goddamn it, Saffi."

JJ looked in the mirror. Both of the twins were awake. "What's going on back there?"

"Saffi peed her pants. Eww. Goddamn it. It's on the seat!"

JJ blanched as he met Jinn's eyes, and she shrugged. "You do swear a lot."

"We'll be there in a minute," he called back, handing her the roll of paper towels from the metal basket under the dash.

"Goddamn it," he whispered as she went back to her seat.

He coasted into town, and couldn't remember ever being more relieved to see the yellow blinking light over the crossroads.

He was home, and he had a plan. It would only get them

through till morning, but according to the president, it was more than most people had.

Slowing down just before his house, he turned the bus into the empty lot beside it, noticing the gas gauge was on empty. They'd barely made it. Almost immediately after the Veil went up, all the gas stations closed as the result of a direct order made by the president. He'd nationalized gas, along with a bunch of other stuff. Banks had been frozen, and services, like water and electricity, had been taken over by the government. The bus bounced over the uneven, overgrown ground. Too bad his mom wasn't here to see this. She wouldn't believe it.

He shifted the bus into park and cut the engine. Taking a deep breath, he turned. Five pairs of eyes stared back. *It's just dinner and bedtime.* Exactly. JJ exhaled. How hard could that be?

———

"OH MY FUCKING GOD," he said, falling onto the step beside her. Despite the late hour, the air was still warm and dry as it blew up from the south.

Katie scooted over, making more room for him. "Shh," she whispered, rubbing her temples. "If you wake up those kids, I swear to god, I'm going to drown myself in the bathtub."

He huffed a laugh, and handed her a beer, then leaned back against the post beside him and closed his eyes.

"I am not joking," she said, sounding quite serious.

She was right. Between the bathroom 'accident' on the bus, the crying, the impossible task of trying to watch the news while simultaneously being talked to by three over-tired kids who wouldn't sit down and eat their fucking dinner, and the lice—god, *so* much lice—The last four hours had passed in a frustrating, disgusting, painfully noisy blur.

"I feel like we've died and stepped into hell," she said.

"They're just kids," he said, opening his eyes. It was what he'd been repeating to himself over and over all night.

She was watching him in the dark. "I know. I know... And I don't mean them, specifically. I mean all of it. How's your neck?"

A piece of debris from one of the explosions had fallen through the open window and burned his neck. He ran his fingers through his hair and took a long pull of his beer. "It's nothing. Just a scratch. How's your foot?"

"Same," she said. "You are really great with them," she said.

He glanced at her out of the corner of his eye, and his heart flip-flopped at the way she was looking at him, making him feel like a teenager again.

"I'm not, so much," she confessed.

He huffed another laugh. That was obvious when she had asked Sophia if she still wore diapers. *I'm five,* the girl had answered. Confused, Katie had then looked at him. *They're in kindergarten,* he'd replied, as she continued to frown at him like he was being unhelpful.

"Thank you." Her voice wavered, making him turn.

Lightning shot through his chest as their eyes met, and he tried again to ignore the way she was looking at him. "For what?"

"For saving my life."

He laughed again. "I didn't—"

"Yeah, you did," she insisted. "Back on the freeway. You tried to protect me...again."

He shook his head and took another swig of his beer. About six more of those, and he'd be in good shape. Beers, not sips.

"I know what you think of me. I know you think I'm just a shallow, stupid—"

He held his hand up. "No." He *had* thought that. But he didn't anymore. Not after she'd thrown her shoes off and chased after a little boy she didn't know through a pile of burning cars.

Not after she'd raised her hand and solemnly swore to protect the kids sleeping on his living room floor, and spent the last three hours helping bathe them, combing fucking *bugs* out of their hair, and putting them to bed. "Listen, I owe you an apology—" he began.

Katie held up her hand. "Just let me finish, okay?"

He sighed and took another long pull of his beer. "Fine."

"I still don't understand how the president can justify what he's done. And I don't know what the hell we are going to do with these kids tomorrow—" She put her hand over his and squeezed. "But I do know one thing."

His heart skipped as he looked down, but he didn't pull his hand away. "What's that?"

"I am *so* glad I'm going through this with *you*."

He repressed a snort. *Right.* She sounded just like Erica had. This is where girls like her sucked guys like him in and—he jerked his hand away.

Katie folded her fingers around her beer. "Sorry." She tucked her hair behind her ear and turned. "I know I don't know you, JJ. But I know what kind of man you are. I learned to tell the difference between good men and bad ones a long time ago. And even if I hadn't, seeing you with the kids today was—you are..." She huffed a laugh. "Contrary to what the sheriff or anyone else might think, it's me who doesn't deserve a guy like you. I know it. *You* clearly know it. So, I get it, and that's okay. I'm not looking for—" She shook her head. "My point is, you're a decent man, and I'm so grateful..." Her voice broke. "I'm just glad you're you and I'm not alone right now. Because I'm really scared. I...feel like this is some crazy dream that I don't know how to wake up from."

It only took ten seconds of listening to her cry quietly before his arm raised on its own, and he tucked Katie against his side. She sniffled against his chest as he stroked her hair. *Sucker.* JJ rolled his eyes. He didn't *like*, like her. He didn't totally believe her, either. All he was doing was comforting a frightened woman. *Sure.* It was the decent thing to do.

"What is going to happen to us? To those kids? To everyone on the inside?" Her arm reached up, and she wrapped it around his neck. "I keep thinking about Amelia's mother—"

"That wasn't her mom."

Kaie stilled. "What?"

"Amelia said it wasn't her mom. I-I think she was a sitter. So…"

That made Katie cry harder, and he totally got it. Relief sometimes did that.

Setting his empty bottle down, JJ covered her bandaged hand with his and hugged her, surprised by her empathy for the little girl. "Shh. You're gonna be alright." More lies. It seemed to be all he was capable of today.

"No. I'm not. I feel like I'm falling and I don't… there's nothing to grab onto."

"You're just tired. And we've had an impossibly long, surreal day."

To be honest, he was kind of feeling the same way. Like the world had been pulled out from under his feet and he was free falling into oblivion. He looked down at Katie nestled beside him. She was right. There was something comforting about being together. At least he was falling with her. *You mean for her?*

JJ shook his head. He wasn't even going to go there. *Too late.* No, it wasn't. *Yes, it is.* No, it wasn't. They were just…crisis buddies. A team tasked to look after a handful of kids until someone else could take them. They would go see Easton in the morning, and figure out what to do with them. And then it would be over. "What happened this afternoon when you went to get the stuff for the kids?" he asked. "Why is your hand all cut to hell?"

She sniffled, then shrugged against him. "Lice is *really* easy to get rid of if you have the right tools. It's *really* hard if you don't." She shrugged. "So, I broke a window at a CVS with an empty kombucha bottle I found in the trash and shoplifted what I needed."

The laugh came out before he could stop it. "Are you serious?"

Katie sniffled. "Yep. You're harboring a fugitive, as we speak. And since I left the bags with you, technically, you drove the get-away vehicle."

"Which was a school bus full of kids."

She laughed as she scratched at the rash that covered her skin in patches. She'd said it was from the heat when one of the kids had asked her about it at dinner.

"So, you really shoplifted?"

"Yeah. Desperate times, you know. Why? Does it surprise you?"

"A little. And how did you even know what to do with the kids and the lice?"

She blew out her breath. "That story is not as funny."

He waited.

She sighed, scratching her arm again, then tucked her arm against his chest as he took another pull from his beer. "The first time I had lice, I was five, like Sophia and Leo, I guess. The school called and my mom sent my dad—who was drunk—to pick me up. He took me straight to his 'best friend' Uncle Dylan," she said, bending her uninjured fingers in air quotes, "who was also a loser and a drinker and a drug dealer. They shaved my head with dull clippers that pulled more of my hair out than cut it."

JJ winced.

"I begged them not to, but they just… laughed like it was the funniest thing in the world. I was mortified, of course. I'd always had beautiful long hair." Absently, she twisted a lock of hair around her finger. "Even now… Anyway, mom had to physically drag me to school the next day, kicking and screaming. And I almost died of humiliation when my teacher made me take off the beanie I'd worn to hide it. No hats in school, you know. My scalp was covered in scabs. To be fair, it was disgusting. But…"

"Shit."

"Yeah. It pretty much killed any chance I had of ever having friends." Katie covered her mouth and yawned. "I got lice twice after that. Both times in second grade. Needless to say, I did *not* tell my parents. I figured out how to get rid of them myself." She wiped her nose on her uninjured hand. "Krusty Kathy, spelled with two K's was my nickname until the day I dropped out of high school."

JJ snickered. His nickname, *Jerkoff,* had been less clever. "Kathy?" he asked. He'd assumed her name was Catherine. *You assume a lot of things.*

Katie laughed. "Kathleen Lewandowski."

"You're kidding."

"Nope." She yawned again. "I changed it when I was eighteen to Katie Newman, and I'm glad I did."

"Why?"

"That other girl was…weak. And she was dying anyway. I just…. put her out of her…."

Katie's arm slipped from his neck to his chest, and she sagged against him.

"Hey, we better head inside," he said, shaking her shoulder. He'd let her sleep in his bed with Jinn and he'd sleep in the… in the bathtub. It was the only place left.

She didn't answer.

JJ leaned his head to the side. "Katie?" Her eyes were closed, and her lips were parted just enough to let her breath through. "Fuck." She was asleep.

Carefully, he lifted the mostly full beer out of her hand and sighed. Taking a swig, he settled back against the post as Katie shifted in his arms, then snuggled up to his chest. He smoothed her hair back off her face. It was like silk beneath his calloused palms. He knew he shouldn't, knew it was a bad idea. But she was asleep, and...after that sad story about her shitty childhood... Just this once. *Just this once, what?*

JJ breathed in Katie's expensive perfume as the full moon illuminated the front yard.

Just this once, he wouldn't push her away, like he knew he should. He would break the rules like he knew he shouldn't.

The tire swing he'd hung with his dad rocked gently in the breeze. It was quiet except for the crickets, the bullfrogs in the pond behind Mike's, and the papery rustle of leaves as they hung from the giant oaks that surrounded the shabby buildings and reminded him of being a little boy. It sounded like it always had. Like home.

Maybe that's why he stayed. Because Hartford Creek wasn't much to brag about, and neither was he. They fit together. *That's not what she thinks.*

At least his parents hadn't been assholes. But the kids at school had been the same for a different reason. He thought about Easton, Wes, and Erica, and their obnoxious little clique. They had lived to torment him, going out of their way to be assholes.

JJ looked down at Katie's adorable upturned nose and perfectly sculpted brows and realized what a fool he was being.

He pulled his hand away. She was just like Erica. *What if she's not?* He couldn't take that chance because the first time almost broke him and his heart wouldn't survive being wrong again.

Chapter Six

Day 2 // 6:55 a.m.

"KATIE?" JJ whispered against her ear. She smiled as her shoulder shook and she snuggled back against him.

"Katie," he said, shaking her a little harder.

Rolling over, she pressed her ear to his chest and threw her arm around him. His heart thumped quickly beneath her ear, and she groaned. "Whatever time it is, it's too early—"

"I want my mom," a child's voice said, dunking Katie into ice-cold consciousness.

Her eyes flew open. She was lying on the floor, staring at JJ's chest, as his beard tickled her forehead.

"Oh!" Shoving herself back, she bolted upright and blinked, as scalding heat rushed to her cheeks. "Oh—" Blinded by sunlight, she threw her arm up squinting. Bits of red dust hovered in the sherbet glow. Her eyes caught and held on the blanket over her lap.

JJ was lying on the floor beside her, under the other half of the blanket, looking paralyzed with embarrassment while three sets of little eyes stared at them from behind the screen door.

"Wh-what?" What the hell happened? She met JJ's eyes and then looked back at the girls as she shoved her wild hair back.

"I want to go home. And I want my mom and I want Floppy and Rainbow Sunshine." The girl that was not Amelia demanded.

Katie couldn't remember her name. "Rainbow what?" Katie dragged her hands over her face.

"Why does she get her stuffy, and I don't?"

"Why don't you have any toys?" Amelia asked JJ.

The events from the day before rushed through Katie's head like a tidal wave, and she swayed. The destruction and the ... Veil. The bus... She turned and sure enough, there it was, parked in the grass. The kids. She groaned. And the lice. And then the president, on the news, saying there was a virus. A bad one. "Oh, god."

JJ sat up and put a hand on her arm. "You alright?"

Katie pushed her hair back again, not believing she'd actually fallen asleep. "What..." She fingered the blanket that was still over both of them. "What happened?"

"You fell asleep, and I didn't want you to wake up out here alone in the middle of the night."

Katie rubbed her eyes. Her mascara crumbled into bits beneath her fingers. She'd slept *outside*? On the porch? Thank god for the blanket or she would have been covered in bug bites. A bead of sweat dripped down her back as she scratched her neck and a memory surfaced. She had been sitting on the step, talking—*crying like a baby*—with JJ.

"Oh, geez," she began.

"I didn't mean to..." He scratched his neck, looking uncomfortable. "I didn't—*we* didn't—"

Katie set her hand on his leg. "Relax. It's okay, JJ. Thank you. I'm surprised we weren't eaten alive."

"I sprayed the blanket with—"

She spied the can of bug spray and remembered the girl's name at the same time as Sophia stomped her foot. "I want my mommy!"

She was going to wake up the other kids, namely that little hellion, Leo, who was half cheetah, half Harry fucking Houdini. Scrambling to her knees, Katie pulled the door open. "Shh. Come...Come out here—" she said, ushering the girls out "—so you don't wake up everyone else."

"I don't care about everyone else," Sophia wailed.

Katie met JJ's eyes, and heat flooded her cheeks again as the dream she'd been in the middle of sparked in her consciousness. They had been...together. Not naked in bed or anything, but close, intimate—Her insides tingling as Sophia said, "I. Want. My. *Mommy!*"

Katie stared at the girls, then JJ. Her eyes went to the blankets on the floor before settling on pathetic downtown Hartford Creek. The gears in her head jammed.

"Katie? Are you—" JJ began. She couldn't hear the rest over the pounding in her ears. The underside of her breasts itched like crazy, as the beads of sweat turned into a river down her back.

"I want my mom," the girl repeated as Katie pulled her sweat-soaked hair up and tied it in a knot on top of her head, feeling like she couldn't breathe. "Oh god." It was too early and too *hot* to deal with any of this. And what was she supposed to say to this little girl, anyway? The poor thing had been dragged out in the middle of nowhere by strangers. Of course she wanted her mother and her Rainbow Sun-whatever. *You're the grown-up here, Katie.* "Oh, god." That was probably the most terrifying thought of all.

"Are you—" The rest of JJ's words were lost, as she buried her face in her hands. She needed a coffee, maybe three, and a shower and a massage, a doctor for her aching foot, and a nap—

"I. Want. My—".

"Ice cream," JJ said before she could finish.

Katie's eyes popped open, and they all turned to him. "What?" she asked.

"There's ice cream...at the corner store." He glanced at her, shrugging slightly, then back at the girls. "You want ice cream?"

The girls looked at each other in confusion, as Katie's brain recovered from its stupor and sputtered back to life, and she sucked in a much-needed breath. Looking at her watch again, she confirmed the time. "But it's seven a.m."

JJ pushed the blanket back and gave her an impatient smile. "Well, *Katie*, I think we have bigger problems than that, don't you?"

He had a point. She nodded.

Waving his hand toward the door, he said, "Go shower…or whatever you need to do."

"What about you?"

"We'll get ice cream. And I'll get some coffee. And then we'll…" He scratched his beard. "We'll make a plan."

"To go home?" Sophia asked hopefully.

"First, we have to let your parents know where you are," he said. "Then we'll figure the rest out. Okay?"

She frowned, looking doubtful. "I guess so."

A shower sounded like heaven, but Katie hesitated. "Are you sure?"

"Yeah. There are towels in the hall closet. Do whatever you —" He waved his hand around in her general direction again, then groaned as he got to his feet. To the girls, he said, "Come on. I know where Don keeps the spare key."

Katie took his hand as he helped her up and squeezed it gratefully. "Thank you. And coffee would be great."

As soon as she was on her feet, he jerked his hand out of hers and looked away. She couldn't tell if he was embarrassed or—

He scratched the back of his neck. "Yeah. No problem."

Mike pulled up to his shop across the street and waved JJ over as Katie retreated into the house.

"Come on, kiddos," she heard him say. "I need to talk to Mr. Mike for a second and then we'll go get…" His voice faded away as she crept around the sleeping kids, grabbed a towel and her bag, and made her way down the hall to the bathroom at the end.

Katie's suspicions about her appearance were confirmed in the mirror as she stripped and scratched at the hives on her stomach and then at the bumps on her ankle. The bugs, it appeared, had gotten her after all.

Turning on the water, she waited until it was warm, then stepped into the mint green bathtub. It surprised her that there was running water at all. They had electricity too. She had just assumed when Armageddon came, society would grind to a halt, the infrastructure would collapse and they'd all find themselves in a wasteland on the verge of death, eating each other or something. But that wasn't the case at all. There was a quarantine issued for everyone on the outside, gas was unavailable, and their cell phones still didn't work, but other than that...It was weirdly normal.

Hot water cascaded over Katie's face and down her sticky body. A pleasure-filled groan fell from her lips as she rinsed the sweat away. She would give a million dollars to forget the last twenty-four hours and stay there, under the stream of water, forever.

You can't.

Pressing her forehead to the cool matching mint-green tiles, she sighed. She wished it would go away, the paralyzing exhaustion that brought her brain to a grinding halt every time she tried to wrap it around what was happening. But it remained. Each time she tried to make sense of what the president had done, it just gave up before she even started and said, 'Nope. Too crazy. Too much.' And wanted to quit on her.

Katie squeezed a dollop of her custom-scented shampoo onto her palm, then massaged it into her scalp. After what the president said the night before—things were probably going to get a lot worse before they got better. And she could not keep falling apart like she had last night, crying and blubbering like a baby in JJ's arms. That was not who she was, even though sometimes she wished she could be. Katie Newman was tougher than that. She was a fighter. A survivor. She would not let *anything* defeat her. That was the promise she made to herself when she changed her name. She hadn't broken it yet, and she wasn't about to start now.

One thing appeared clear, though. With the internet down and no access to her normal amenities, her career was on hold indefinitely. Rinsing her hair, she laughed, realizing it wasn't her wrinkles that had done her in after all. Instead, it was a deadly virus, straight out of a bad sci-fi movie. Who would have thought? Either way, she was essentially without any money or worldly possessions besides what she'd stuffed in the trunk of Old Ray. That made her laugh again because she was not nearly as worried about it as she should be. She had her health. And she wasn't trapped inside the Veil. She had a safe place to stay. Barb at the bar promised meals for all of them until she ran out, and the grocery store had enough food to feed the small community for at least a month. Maybe more. Hopefully, the crisis would be over by then and everything would go back to normal. And if she was being honest, the contents of Old Ray's trunk were half of what she owned, anyway.

And lastly, Katie had her past. A shitty childhood that taught her how to live through bad while expecting the worst, including head lice. That was exactly what was happening now, and she could handle it. She just couldn't overthink it, or try to understand what the hell the president was doing. If she just kept her nose down and focused on what was right in front of her, she would be fine.

As she lathered the conditioner into her long locks, her thoughts went back to JJ. She had meant what she said the night before. She was lucky it was *his* truck she was in when the Veil went up, lucky that he was the one fate had paired her with to go through this. The kids were too. Because if he'd been like any of the other men she'd met over the past two years, they'd all still be sitting on the side of the road.

For as great as he was, though, he was just as confusing. He made no secret of the fact that he didn't like her. From the moment they met, she sensed his disgust. As if she were some sort of...criminal or something. It was there *before* she blew him off and sat with the sheriff. Even after her apology yesterday, there was *still* tension between them. She couldn't tell if it was disapproval, or distrust or what, but every time she touched him, or looked at him, she got the feeling he wanted to run far, far away and never return.

But then yesterday, when he'd complimented her, she felt something else from him. Something good. And when he'd stood in the door of that bus, holding Leo, and smiled, she'd felt something good then too. Something real and *magnetic*. And last night...after their hellish experience of trying to get the kids to sleep, he'd been so kind and comforting. He'd almost acted like he liked her as much as she liked him. And maybe she'd misread that, but then...if he hated her so much, why did he sleep on the damn floor next to her last night? He could have gone inside and left her out there by herself. He could have woken her up. Instead, he'd gone inside, gotten a blanket, laid back down beside her, and slept. Why did he do that?

Katie rinsed her hair and sighed, knowing the nightmare she faced on the other side of the bathroom door. Maybe now was not the time to contemplate her attraction to JJ. They had larger concerns.

Turning the water off, she got out and toweled off. First things first were the kids. She needed to go through their hair again with the comb, and they needed more than ice cream for breakfast. Second, JJ insisted they *needed* to get word to the families that their kids were safe, and it had to happen *today*. She was no parent, and she never would be, but for a single guy, he seemed unusually empathetic to the suffering of the families. It occurred to her to ask him about it, but something made her stop, so she didn't. Third, after they contacted the parents, they needed to see if any of the kids had any friends or relatives on the outside to take—

"I need to pee!" a small voice called.

Blinking, Katie realized she had taken too long. *Shit.* Pulling the towel off, she rummaged through her bag for a clean set of under—

"I have to go now! I can't hold it!" The desperation in Amelia's voice drove Katie into action.

Flinging the towel back around her, she threw everything back in her bag, dragged it off the toilet seat, and pulled the door open as Amelia rushed by, crunching Katie's toes as she shoved her shorts down. Katie hurried out of the bathroom and slammed the door just as the little girl hoisted herself on the toilet.

Heart thumping, she stood in the darkened hallway, pushing her wet hair back off her shoulders.

Someone coughed behind her, and she turned.

JJ and Sam were standing in the living room staring at her. Sam looked away, while JJ met her eyes, looking utterly confused, like he suddenly didn't know who she was. Looking down, she made sure none of her lady parts were showing. They weren't. Had he never seen a woman in a towel before?

Pointing to the bathroom door, she said, "She had to—" She peeked into his bedroom. "Is it okay if I get dressed in there?"

His eyes clouded, and he stared at her for a moment. "Yeah. hold on. Let me just…" Hurrying past her, he ducked into the room, leaving her standing half-naked as Sam scratched his head and stared at the coffee table. There was a scraping sound from inside the bedroom, and then the opening and closing of a drawer. JJ reemerged a second later, walked past her without meeting her eyes, and headed for the kitchen. "Go ahead."

Katie stepped into his room and shut the door. Putting her bag on his bed, she sat down and looked around. She'd been in a lot of men's bedrooms. Too many, probably, but none of them had felt this—she glanced at the pine bookshelf, the low, broad dresser to match. A TV sat on the top, and behind it was a large mirror. The walls were a relaxing shade of sage, and the bedspread and curtain were both white and almost glowed in the sunlight that poured in the window. None of them had felt this *normal*. It was homey and unpretentious, and something about that felt good. Like he did.

Getting up, she ran her fingers over the marks in the dust on the dresser. Pictures, that was what JJ was hiding. Why didn't he want her to see them? *When Erica left you...* Sheriff Easton's words echoed in her head. Katie's hand flew to her mouth. "Oh..." Was JJ still hung up on his ex? Was that why he was so distant? Because he was still in love with her? An unfamiliar and very uncomfortable jealousy reared its ugly head as her eyes fell to the drawers, and she touched one of the knobs.

But as she met her gaze again in the mirror and knew she couldn't. He had opened his home to them. She could not invade his privacy, even if he would never know. It wouldn't be right.

Katie pushed her wet hair back off her shoulders, wondering what Erica looked like, if she was as beautiful as she was imagining. Without make-up on Katie looked like a completely different person. Especially her eyes. With liner and mascara and shadow, they were mysterious, sexy. She blinked. Like this... well, like this, she looked shy and forgettable. Shaking her head, she huffed a laugh. No wonder JJ had stared at her in the hall. He probably really hadn't recognized her.

She quickly got dressed, knowing the shredded jeans and skin-tight, black cropped cami she wore were probably not appropriate for the circumstances, but nothing else she had was any better. The little boy, Leo, had already destroyed her flip-flops in a fit of rage the evening before, but thankfully she'd remembered she had her running shoes in the trunk of Old Ray. Sliding her foot in, she immediately regretted it and pulled it out. While the arch support was great when she was pounding the pavement, it unfortunately pressed in just the wrong way on the burn on her foot. "Shit."

Her eyes darted between the lace-up stilettos, and a second

slightly different, but just as hideous, pair of Caroline Banks tiki wedges on the floor beside her bag. She should have taken the yellow clogs from the pharmacy instead of the flip-flops. They were still ugly as sin, but at least they would have been comfortable. Oh well. She also wished she wouldn't have forgotten her workout clothes in the dryer at home. Those would have come in handy right about then. Oh well, again.

Opting to go barefoot, at least in the house, she quickly applied her minimal 'beach' makeup, leaving her hair down to air dry. Standing back, she surveyed the finished product. Her eyes were tired, her neck ached, and compared to normal, she looked like shit, but at least the rash had subsided, *and* she was clean. Katie squared her shoulders and put on her game face.

Pushing her hair back off her shoulders, she took a deep breath and opened the door. It was time to get down to business. Making her way down the hall, she paused as it opened into the living room, taking in JJ's home for the first time in the daylight. It was a small two-bedroom, one-bath ranch, and much like his bedroom, simply and cleanly furnished except for the guest room, which was piled with boxes.

In the living room, Grace sat on the white leather couch, playing checkers with Sophia, while Amelia sat on the edge of the light oak coffee table, watching them. Parker was sitting in the matching recliner, still looking just as he had the day before, which was constipated and pissed off at the world. At least the swelling around his eye had gone down.

Jinn was sitting on the tan, carpeted floor with her back to the coffee table, watching the news on mute, and Sam was sitting on the kitchen counter, with his back against the light oak cabinets, eating a bowl of cereal.

There is one missing. Katie spun around, scanning the rooms again until she spotted Leo under the kitchen table, playing on the ugly but clean green 'tiled' linoleum floor.

"Morning," she said to Sam.

He nodded to the Styrofoam cup on the round oak dining table, tucked in the corner against the wall. "JJ left that for you."

"Left?"

"He had to go. He and the guy from the garage across the street. I guess the Army or someone called. It was an emergency. They need tow truck drivers to help in the city. Look for survivors or whatever."

"Shit." She wished she could have at least said goodbye. "Did he say when he was coming back?"

He shook her head.

Worry crept into Katie's heart. She didn't know why. It wasn't like she wasn't used to being on her own.

You're not worried about yourself. That was true. For once, she was worried about everyone else.

A crow landed on the rail of the back porch and cawed at her as she stared at it through the window on the kitchen door. She was worried about JJ and the kids. If something happened to him, she didn't know what she'd do. She didn't know children like he did, didn't own a house to take them to. Clearly, she didn't know how to drive a bus. And she didn't know the people in this community the way he did... Assuming there were more than the ten she'd already met.

Grabbing the Styrofoam cup, Katie took a sip of her coffee and read JJ's note on the table beside it. **Had to go. Find a way to contact parents if you can. Ask Barb if you need anything.** He must have been in some hurry, because he didn't even sign it.

Katie went into the living room, careful not to rub the bottom of her foot on the carpet, and read the headline on the TV as she took another sip of her coffee. *1.28 million deaths confirmed in Beijing.* She shook her head. Everyone was still reeling from the shock. Last night they'd watched footage of people with heavy machines trying to destroy the towers there. Half the city had been vaporized. Moscow too. Entire sections of the city just gone as the Veil reestablished connection with the next nearest tower

and continued to hold the cities hostage. It was so crazy it felt...
fake. Like the leaders of the free world were playing some kind
of ill-humored joke on humanity. "Have they said anything new
since last night?" she asked, sitting on the edge of the coffee
table.

Jinn shook her head. "Nothing about the Veils, but look." She
unmuted the TV.

The scene switched to footage on the westside of Atlanta
where firefighters were battling a blaze that broke out in an
apartment complex. *"Fires continue to rage through portions of
Smyrna, Marietta and Kennesaw, Tucker and Lilburn, over-
whelming firefighters who have been battling the blazes since
late last night, with little to no success,"* the news anchor said.
*"Fire teams have been brought in from as far as Chattanooga
to assist, but to little avail. Officials have yet to disclose the
initial cause of the fires but say the combination of high winds
and lack of rain has contributed to the rapid spread, as have
the numerous wooded areas that surround many westside
communities. In a brief press conference held only moments
ago, fire officials stated that it was 'an ongoing investigation.'
However, when asked if the Veil may have had anything to do
with the initiation of the fires, Fire Chief Silas Dunner said,
quote, 'Preliminary reports indicate that at least in some cases,
particularly in Smyrna, the fires appear to have begun at or
near the time of the activation of the Veil around the city of
Atlanta.' He went on to add, 'But until the reports are
complete, we cannot rule out foul play.' Deaths from the fires
are estimated to be at an astonishing twelve hundred, with over
ten thousand more reported missing."* The scene switched to an
aerial view of a wealthy neighborhood. Half of it was on fire, the
other half charred and smoking and covered in ash.

*"For this reason, the president has recommended each
state issue a curfew until further notice, and continues to urge*

the American people to stay vigilant, stay at home, and report
any unusual behavior to authorities immediately."

"In response to this call by the President, Governer
Williams has issued a statewide curfew effective immediately.
Anyone caught on the road without official documentation
between eight p.m. and six a.m. will be arrested and questioned
and added to a watch list. Government officials are urging resi-
dents to stay off the streets and be vigilant. If anyone notices
any suspicious behavior or has any information regarding the
fires, they are encouraged to contact their local emergency
services or dial 911."

The report switched back to the destruction in Moscow, and
Jinn muted it again.

"Sophia, it's your turn," Grace said.

"Saffi," the girl corrected, as Katie turned to the girls. Saffi's
face, and adorable springy dark curls, were covered in what
Katie hoped was chocolate ice cream. There was a spot on her t-
shirt and a drip on the heart-printed leggings Katie had hand
washed only the night before because the girl had peed in them.
That had been a first. Washing pee out of clothes.

Grace nodded. "Right, sorry. Saffi."

Katie got up and went back into the kitchen with a sigh. Not
only did they have an infectious disease to worry about, and the
Veil, but now fires, too. Katie looked out the kitchen window
past JJ's mom's house, to the sprawling countryside that lay
beyond the pile of buildings that made up Hartford Creek,
suddenly very glad there as one of the girls started yelling.

A minute later, Grace stormed in. She had ice cream all down
the front of her shirt, too. Katie rolled her eyes. Did they not
know where their mouths were? "What happened to your shirt?"

"Leo happened. And Sophia is cheating!" she huffed angrily.
Her stringy blond hair that had been in braids yesterday, hanging
over her shoulders.

Katie sighed. "They're little. They probably just don't understand."

"I understand fine!" Saffi shouted unhelpfully from the other room.

"See!" Grace waved a skinny arm toward the living room. The girl was tall for eleven, but as thin as a rail. "They're cheating and—"

Saffi came around the corner. "You're just a poor loser."

"I am not!"

"Yes, you are!"

"No. I'm—"

"Hey!" Katie held up her hand. "I haven't even finished my coffee yet. Can you just give me five—"

"The little one cheated," Parker called from the living room.

"No, I didn't!" Saffi crossed her arms, giving Grace what would someday be a killer death stare. "I don't want to play with you anymore," she snapped.

"Well, I don't want to play with *you* either!" Grace retorted.

"Fine! I'm just going to take the checkers and play somewhere—"

"No! I found it in the junk room," Grace said, blocking her path.

"Junk room" was apparently what they were calling JJ's spare bedroom, and it was an accurate description. There was so much stuff on the bed she hadn't even noticed there was one there at first. Amelia appeared in the doorway. "It's my turn! I wanna play!" she said.

Saffi scowled at her. "No. You're too little."

Grace huffed. "You are the one that's too little," she said under her breath.

Saffi lunged, and Katie slid between them before she could hit Grace. "Okay, okay. Take it easy," she said as Saffi hit her arm and coffee sloshed onto her hand, and onto her jeans. Amelia gasped, and they all stared at her with wide eyes, waiting

to see what she'd do. She knew what *her* parents had done, but…
She was not about to smack a little kid around. Still, she needed
to establish her authority as the only adult in the house, otherwise they'd run all over her. "You made me spill my coffee," she
said, pointing a finger at Saffi.

Saffi crossed her arms defiantly. "No, I didn't."

Katie crossed hers too, and her brow went up. "Oh, really?
Then who did?"

"You did it by getting in my way. And she did it by being
stupid." She pointed to Grace.

"I'm not—" Grace began.

Katie held up her hand. "Eh." Then, smiling, set her coffee
on the table. Maybe she didn't know anything about taking care
of kids, but she remembered *being* one. And one lie deserved
another, did it not? "Do you know what happens to naughty kids
in this town?"

Saffi smugly shook her head as Katie crouched down.

"The night leeches come—you know what those are,
right?" She scrunched her nose. "Little black, slimy, wormy
things with teeth—and they suck the blood out of the bodies of
little liars when they're sleeping. They enjoy toes in
particular."

Katie could practically hear the wheels in Saffi's head
turning as she stared into Katie's eyes. Finally, the girl crossed
her arms. "No, they don't," she said as Leo climbed out from
under the table, looking *very* concerned and Amelia quietly
stared at her toes in horror.

"Oh yes, they do," Katie said, calling the girl's bluff. "Ever
wonder why sometimes you go to bed with socks on and then
they're off in the morning?"

Leo gasped. "That happens to me all the time," he whispered.

Katie tried not to smile. "That does not surprise me," she said
solemnly. Turning back to Saffi, she sat in the chair beside the
table and continued. "Look." Lifting her foot, she exposed the

raw red flesh on the arch of her foot. "They got me good last night."

It was Amelia's turn to gasp. "What did you do?"

"I lied and said there were only good kids in this house."

Sam snorted, and she shot him a look that hopefully said 'keep your mouth shut' as her eyes darted between the kids. Leo and Amelia were sold. Saffi was a tough little nut to crack, though, and still on the fence. "I don't—"

Tilting her head, and thinking fast, Katie said, "That's why JJ and I slept outside. To protect *you.*"

Saffi's facade cracked. "What?" she whispered.

"Why else would two grownups who don't know each other sleep on the floor outside? On the *ground?*"

Saffi didn't have an answer for that.

"No, we *had* to. It was the only way to block the door."

Amelia's eyes widened and if JJ wasn't already her hero, he certainly would be now.

Katie shook her head and sighed. "But we can't hold them off forever. And my neck hurts, and I've lost too much blood to sleep out there again."

"I-I don't believe you," Saffi said, clearly believing every word.

It was time to go in for the kill. Katie inhaled deeply, got up, and shrugged, holding out her hand. "Fine. Come on. I'll show you where they live." Saffi's eyes widened, and Katie pursed her lips together to hide her smile. *Checkmate, you little shit.* Waving her arm, she said, "Come on. They're in the pond out back of Mike's over there, just past the quicksand." Saffi's fear turned to terror at that last word, and Katie would have felt bad, but…eh, she didn't. "I saw them squiggling back there this morning. Let's go. I'll hold on to you, so don't get sucked in and you can check it out for yourself."

"No, I—" Saffi backed away from her.

Katie took the girl by the arm. "No. Seriously. You don't

believe me? That's fine. All you have to do is dip your toes in and they'll come swimming right up. Especially if you've been naughty."

Leo started crying, and Amelia looked about two seconds away from bursting into tears herself.

Wrestling her arm free, Saffi took another step back. "No, I—"

"Or…" Katie paused for effect. "Or you could just say you're sorry and promise not to lie anymore and go play. Then they'd leave us alone, and JJ and I can go back to sleeping in beds and no one has to get hurt. It's up to you."

For dramatic effect, Katie limped back to the chair, wincing in pain. She wasn't faking the last part. It hurt like a bitch.

"Sorry." The words rushed out of Saffi's mouth as she rushed out of the room.

Katie smiled.

"Sorry." Leo cried, grabbing her leg with his sticky little fingers.

Her smile fell as she looked down at him. "What are *you* sorry for?"

"For breaking your shoes and…" His eyes fell to the floor.

"And…?"

He pointed under the table, and it took a minute, but then she saw it. The tube for her custom Yves Saint Laurent lipstick. It was on the floor, and empty. "What in the…" Crouching down, she looked under the table. "Goddamnit," she whispered under her breath as Amelia gasped beside her. He'd used it to paint a picture on the underside of the table. And it wasn't even a good one. Grabbing the tube, she turned. "Where did you get this?" she demanded.

"F-from your bag."

"That was a one-of-a-kind lip shade created especially for me, to match my skin tone. Do you understand?"

He shook his head. "I-I thought it was a-a paint…" he said.

To be fair, it had a small brush. Pinching her nose, she inhaled, then exhaled deeply. *Let it be.* "Did you take anything else out of my purse?"

He nodded.

Of course he did. The little fucker. "What—"

Scrambling under the table, he dragged something off the seat of the chair that was wedged between the table and the wall and dropped it into her hands. Two bottles of nail polish, the lip liner that went with her custom lipstick, her liquid eyeliner, and a hundred and eighty dollar tube of mascara. "Jesus Christ." She squeezed her eyes shut. *Let it be.* The boy was only five and her makeup was just...*irreplaceable now that the Veil had gone up.* Fuck. She inhaled, imagining punching Hunter and his little mantra in the face, then exhaled. That actually worked better at calming her, and she almost smiled. *Almost.*

Setting everything on the table, Katie grabbed the edge and added pick-pocketing to Leo's list of nefarious skills as she stood back up.

Amelia watched with bated breath to see what would happen, as Sam tried not to laugh.

Pushing her hair back, she took another deep breath and looked down at the forlorn little boy. *"Let it be"*, she said, mentally decking Hunter's tanned, square jaw one more time as she met Leo's eyes. "Okay. Do not take anything out of *any* of my bags again, or the leeches will eat you alive and spit out your bones. Do you understand?" She probably could have skipped the 'spit out your bones' part, but...eh, this kid needed the fear of Katie Newman put into him before he destroyed everything she owned.

Staring at her injured foot, Leo nodded.

"Good. Now all of you, go play...nice." It was the first thing she'd said all morning that sounded adult. She smiled. Maybe she wasn't so bad with kids after all.

The kids ran off, followed by Grace, as Sam dropped his bowl in the sink. "Wow."

Her smile faded as she turned, and he leaned back against the sink crossing his arms.

"What?" she asked.

"I'm not sure if you are aware of this, but for the last several *decades,*" he paused for effect. "...the APA has frowned upon the use of fear and intimidation to control children."

Katie's frown deepened as she downed half her lukewarm coffee in one gulp. "APA?"

"American Psychological Assoc—"

Katie held up her hand. Okay. She got it. "Yeah, well, maybe the president should have consulted with them before initiating the Veils."

"True. But still. They're just kids."

She winced. "Was the quicksand part too much?"

"No, I'd say the leeches sucking them dry in their sleep was."

"Well, they started it."

Sam pushed off the counter, pointing a finger at her as he laughed. "And you definitely ended it. There's no doubt about that."

"Which is what grownups are supposed to do, right?"

"Yeah...." he shrugged, looking unconvinced.

She sighed, slumping into a chair. "The truth is, I don't know anything about kids."

Sam laughed again. "I'm just giving you a hard time. And that was obvious when you made them wear clothes in the bathtub."

JJ had looked at her like she was crazy when she wrapped her tube top around each kid and secured it with a hair tie before they stepped out of their underclothes and into the tub.

"Well, I don't know the rules, and... they aren't ours. I was trying to respect their privacy. I've never even held a baby, so how in the hell should I know?"

"First of all, privacy and five-year-olds are like fermions. Second, what do you mean, you've never held a baby? *Everyone* has held a baby."

"Not me, and what is a fermion?"

"You ever heard of the Pauli Exclusion principle?"

Katie shook her head, draining the rest of her coffee.

"Well, in physics, you got fermions and bosons—"

Great. The only thing she knew less about than kids was physics.

"—and the Pauli Exclusion Principle states that two identical fermions cannot occupy the same..." He paused. "You know what, never mind. Now that I have to explain it, it's not funny anymore."

Thank god. Katie pinched the bridge of her nose. "Okay. Coffee break is over. What does JJ have to eat around here?"

"Cereal and beer. No wonder he's...thick."

Katie got up and poked her head in the living room. "Who wants cereal?"

The kids all cheered.

After she set them up at the table, she turned to Grace. "How's your head feeling today?"

"Not as itchy."

"Good. Let's just get you in a clean shirt, and I'll comb it again, and then I'll do the little girls, okay?"

Grace sighed dramatically. "Fine."

Katie passed Jinn in the hall on her way back to JJ's room and grabbed a cropped tank top from her bag. She'd have to tie the straps up, but it would work, at least until she was able to wash and dry the other one. Halfway back down the hall, she stopped. Sam was in the living room, talking in a low voice.

"I know what he said. I'm trying to keep them out of her hair. You could help, you know."

"Help?" Jinn whispered back, sounding angry. "I was just in the bathroom wiping a little girl's butt—"

Katie turned the corner. They were standing, heads together, in front of the TV. "What's going on?"

Sam's eyes widened as he and Jinn backed away from each other. "Nothing," he said.

"Who are you talking about?"

"No one," Sam insisted.

Jinn blushed, avoiding Katie's eyes.

Katie put her hands on her hips. *Bullshit.* "Who is 'he'?"

Jinn and Sam looked at each other, then back at her. "No one. Nothing." Sam repeated.

"It's nothing. Really." Jinn confirmed.

But it wasn't nothing. "JJ told you to keep the kids out of my way, didn't he?" Neither of them moved, as heat rushed to her cheeks. "Because he doesn't think I can handle it."

"He just said you were a little...overwhelmed last night, and he was concerned about the kids..." Sam began.

Jinn smacked him in the stomach. "Shut up."

"I'm just trying to help—"

"Well, you're not," she snapped.

Overwhelmed? No. That wasn't it. JJ didn't think she could handle the kids, just like he hadn't thought she could handle the sheriff and why he was so surprised by her all day yesterday. For some reason, it hurt that he thought of her as a child he needed to take care of. Yes, she'd cried...a little, but... Damn it, she thought they were a team. Katie rolled her eyes. But no. He *still* didn't trust her. Not even to take care of the kids.

She stormed past them into the kitchen, the wheels in her head turning furiously. Dropping back into her chair, she flipped JJ's note over and started a list on the back, finishing her coffee, wishing she had about four more to chase it with.

"He didn't mean anything by it," Sam said, leaning against the sink.

Katie tucked her hair behind her ear and didn't answer. Yes, he did. She could see it in his eyes every time he looked at her. She thought after he apologized yesterday, maybe he'd changed his mind, but that clearly was not the case.

Well, she would show JJ Dayton *exactly* what she was capable of. She was going to take control of this shit show. Katie took another sip of her coffee, forgetting it was empty.

The first thing on the list was to get a hold of the remaining kid's families. That was the thing that him the most, letting them know they were safe.

She tapped the pen on the table. She had used her socials many times to help people find things. A dog once. A wedding ring. How to do that without the internet? Katie took another sip of her coffee. She couldn't get online, but still had loads of connections and their phone numbers. If she could get the kids' faces to the right people—*How about just their names?* Names? She tapped the pen against her lip. Yes. That would work, too.

Chapter Seven

Day 2 // 10:20 a.m.

THE AREA outside the Veil was crawling with military personnel, and as they made their way to the next wreck site on the list he'd been given, JJ wondered if it was like that everywhere or if there was a specific reason they were patrolling so many of the streets east of Atlanta. He could see the smoke from the fires that had broken out to the north and west of the city. Maybe that had something to do with it?

His phone rang in his pocket, and the truck jerked as he jumped. "Sorry," he said to Mike. With one eye on the road, he fished it out of his pocket and pressed the button. "Mom?"

"Oh, thank god!" The relief in her voice matched his own. "Where are you?"

"I'm—"

"Are you inside or out?"

"Out," he said. He didn't know why he felt so guilty when it hadn't been a choice, but he did.

There was a heavy sigh on the other end of the line. "Oh, thank god," she said again.

"Are you alright? Is Sei okay?" he asked.

"We're fine. Everything is—"

"What's going on in there?" he asked before she could finish.

"Nothing. I've never seen the city so quiet. We haven't left the apartment, but from what I can see from the window, all the businesses below us are closed. A few are even boarded up."

"You haven't seen any...sick people?"

"No. But, like I said, we've just been inside."

JJ signaled and turned onto a boulevard, passing a convoy of military vehicles. "And everything is working? You guys have water and—"

"Yep. TV, air conditioning. It's so weird. I would have thought... I don't know, everything would have gone crazy. But everything is still working. I even had your sister take a long hot bath last night to calm her nerves."

"How's she taking it?"

"How we all are, I imagine. Half in shock, half...not believing it's really happened. We can't see the Veil from here, but we've seen it on the news. It's...something."

JJ looked out his window at it rising up beyond the buildings in front of him. Yes, it certainly was that. "How about you?" she asked. "How are you holding up, sweetie?"

"I'm actually just outside the Veil now. Mike and I were called in to help clear the wreckage."

"No," her voice hardened. "You need to go home. It's not safe—"

"We're not getting close to anyone else. They're being really strict about that, just dragging vehicles. Looking for survivors."

"But still—"

"There isn't room for me at home, anyway."

His mom paused. "What do you mean?"

"Yesterday when the Veil went up, we inherited a bus-load of kids. Thankfully, we got rid of most of them but—"

"We?"

JJ blushed, avoiding Mike's stare. "Ms. Newman is... She was with me when the Veil went up, and now she's staying at the house with the kids until we figure out—"

"Katie Newman?" his mom interrupted. He pictured her eyebrow going up the way it always did when her voice took on that tone. "You mean to tell me the woman you haven't been able to shut up about for a *week* is staying at your house?"

"Mom." JJ rolled his eyes behind his sunglasses. It wasn't like that. *And haven't been able to shut up about?* What was that supposed to mean? "It's not like—"

"Where did she sleep?" she asked.

His blush deepened. "Well, actually—"

But before he could answer, she spoke again. "Wait, kids? What kids?"

"They were on a bus, heading into the city, and their driver went…I guess he disappeared into the Veil."

"Oh, shoot." She paused. "How many are there?"

"Three little ones and two older."

"And their families are…"

"In there with you."

"Oh, no." The devastation in her voice was clear.

Mike pointed to the right at the road coming up, and JJ turned. "Yeah. It sucks."

"Oh, that's so… That's terrible. How are you handling it?"

"What do you mean?" He knew exactly what she meant.

"Having kids around again… Are you—"

"I'm fine." And he was. Mostly.

She paused. "Well, at least they are with you and *Katie.*"

He frowned. "Ms. Newman."

"Uh huh. Sure. Going back to my original question, where did *Ms. Newman* sleep last night?"

JJ winced, knowing he was about to get in trouble. "On the front porch?" Why he said it like a question, he didn't know. But moms had that effect on their sons.

She gasped. "Jensen James Dayton. You made her sleep on the porch? What is the matter with—"

"She fell asleep!" he cried. "And there was nowhere for us inside, anyway! I-I stayed out there with her."

"You did?" His mom's voice softened as heat crept into his cheeks.

He glanced at Mike. "Yeah…"

"Why didn't you take her to my house?"

He wasn't about to do that. "Mom, it was no big—"

"Don't sabotage yourself, JJ."

"What?"

"I've got a feeling about you and her. Don't blow it because you're scared."

JJ prayed Mike couldn't hear her. "I'm not—"

"Yes, you are."

He was just playing by the rules. Rule. There was only one, and it was his; do not get mixed up with beautiful women who were out of his league.

"It's there." Mike said, pointing to the delivery truck blocking two lanes.

"Mom, I've got to go. I'm glad the phones are working. I'll call you back when I get a chance."

"Listen to your mother."

He grunted.

"And stay safe, sweetie."

"I will. I love you."

"I love you too."

Chapter Eight

Day 2 // 8:35 p.m.

KATIE SLUMPED BACK into the recliner, utterly exhausted as Jinn flipped on the TV and Sam and Parker sat on either side of her on the couch.

She pushed her hair back and closed her eyes. The little kids were finally asleep. It had only taken three stories, three trips to the bathroom, two glasses of water and one really shitty rendition of Rock-a-bye Baby, that she wasn't sure she'd sung correctly, to get them down. If the words were what the kids said they were, it was a pretty fucked up song about putting a baby in a tree, then watching it fall and die.

It was after eight, and JJ still wasn't back. Her phone wasn't working either, although they'd said earlier on the news that some people were reporting service. Katie stared at the TV. They were showing aerial footage of the dozens of pile-ups around the city. That had to be why he was taking so long.

"Turn it up," she said.

Jinn turned up the volume.

"Crews continue to clear the wreckage from around the Veil, searching for survivors amid the pileups of vehicles, and clearing the roads to allow emergency vehicles and utilities crews to safely travel the roads, while firefighters in areas to the north and west of the city continue to battle the wildfires sweeping through and devastating the small communities to the north and west of the city. In a press conference earlier this

afternoon the governor called the devastation caused by the fires as 'unprecedented in Georgia's history' as the numbers of dead and missing persons soars to over fourteen thousand souls. Fire officials have released a statement claiming the initial cause of the fires appears to be sparks from power line transformer fuses that were blown when the Veil was activated. The ongoing drought and high winds have exacerbated the situation, providing both fuel and momentum, creating what Fire Chief Dunner called 'a perfect storm.'"

Deciding she needed a coffee and a minute with an actual grown up, Katie decided to head to the bar. Hopefully Barb was still up.

Dragging her aching body to its feet, she whispered. "I'm going to head over to the bar. See if there's any coffee—"

Parker snorted. "Yeah right."

He was definitely the most difficult of the kids. It had only been a day, but his hostility and attitude were grating on her nerves. He was also the one that reminded Katie the most of herself. He was hurting. And not just because the school and his family, which the school had contacted, had turned him away. There was something else going on.

"I'm serious. Just coffee. I'll be back in a few. Just run over if you need anything."

Sam nodded.

"Hey, look!" Jinn said excitedly.

Katie paused by the door as the segment ended and the scene switched back to the studio. *"Also during his press conference today, Governor Williams issued a statement concerning the displaced families, particularly children, outlining a temporary plan to help connect families torn apart by the Veil. We urge anyone with a rescued child to call into their local radio station. Every hour, the names of the children will be aired and passed along to us here at the Network. If you hear your child's name, you are requested to call the radio station. They will provide a direct number..."*

The names of children began scrolling across the bottom of the screen, and Katie stared as Sophia and Leo's names rolled across amid dozens of others.

"It was a good idea," Sam said. "And...pretty cool how you made it all happen. You've helped a lot of kids and scared parents today. We all think so."

Jinn nodded, and even Parker's face softened for a fraction of a second before hardening back into a scowl.

Katie smiled. The truth was all she'd done was make a phone call that thankfully went through. "We all have to help each other. "

The segment switched again. "Don't watch too much of that," she said, reading the headline. "It's not..." She tried to find the right words. "Some of it is true, but a lot of it probably isn't."

Parker huffed. "Yeah. We know. We're not stupid."

Katie let it slide and slipped out into the twilight.

The bar was only two doors down from JJ's house, so it was only a minute until she passed through the door with the closed sign on it and was back inside. She sighed as she sat down at the bar top. The world was in crisis, yet somehow there was still air conditioning. Amazing. The sound of dishes being washed came from the kitchen where the light was still on.

"Hey Barb," she called, announcing herself.

Since Katie, JJ and the kids had all been together when the quarantine went into effect, and Barb had been here serving dinner to most of the older, single, local people who were not going anywhere *and* had enough food to feed them all, they decided it made sense to act as a 'family unit.' So she, JJ, Barb, the kids, Mike, the old woman she'd met in front of the grocery, Michelle, and two other people whose names she'd been too tired to remember were allowed to come and go in all four of the town's businesses.

They had agreed that if any of them broke the circle, they'd stay away until the quarantine was over, which was two weeks. Otherwise, for the time being, they were one big, weird family.

"Be there in a sec," Barb said, peeking her head out of the kitchen.

"I just want coffee if you have it." Katie called.

"You know where it is. Go ahead, help yourself."

Katie went around the bar, and poured herself a cup from the carafe, and stared out over the empty dining room, which now felt like a sanctuary. A week ago she had never set eyes on this place and now she was helping herself to drinks, behind the bar. *A lot can change in a week.* Yes, it could.

"How you holding up?" Barb asked as Katie reclaimed her seat.

She sighed. "Well, I'm tired, but..." She took a sip of her coffee. "I'm good, all things considered. Better than a lot of people are."

"Easton said you moved some pretty tall mountains today."

"Easton? How does he know—"

Barb huffed. "News travels fast in these small towns. What little of it there is. You best remember that. It'll save you a lot of trouble."

Katie nodded. "Good to know."

"He was pretty impressed, though. Said you got the governor onboard and everything."

"Well, *I* didn't talk to him."

"But someone did. On your behalf."

Katie smiled. "Yeah. A designer I've known for a long time. I remembered they were friends."

"Well, having people call into the radio stations with the names of lost kids was a good idea. They aired the statement at six. And I was just in the back listening to the radio. There are already hundreds of them on it—"

"They're on the news now, too." Katie interjected.

Barb nodded. "Luckily, most of them were in school and accounted for, but still. There are a *lot* of displaced children out there. And those are only the ones that people *are* reporting. There have to be some that…"

It was a terrible thought, but it had crossed Katie's mind too. Kids had a hard enough time as it was and they were so vulnerable. It made her angry that the president had put them at such risk, practically handing them off to predators on a silver platter. Katie slammed her mug on the bar. "It's unethical, inhumane! How could he do any of this?"

"Who? The president?"

"Yes. How could the virus kill any more people that have already been taken by the Veil? *Thousands* of people have died, millions of families have been torn apart. It doesn't make sense. There is no way that—"

Barb shrugged. "Maybe it's worse than you think it is."

"I was there when the Veil went up, Barb. Literally *right* there. It was like being in the middle of a war zone. I saw people *vaporized* before my very eyes. How could it get any worse?"

"I don't know, then. But I do know you done good today, girl." She patted Katie's hand.

Katie took another sip. "Anyway, you were right. Michelle had kids' clothes. Some were already cut for her quilts, but there were enough left over to outfit all the kids. So once they're dry, the kids will at least have clean clothes. And I went to Mr. Gobbel's and picked up groceries. Oh, that reminds me. I have a thought."

"About?"

"Well, I don't know exactly how things are going to work once the quarantine is over, but…. Maybe we should be more careful with the food. I don't think things are going to go back to normal anytime soon, and from what they are saying on the news, all the relief efforts are headed to the cities. I'm worried that… I just think, with the kids to feed, we should be cautious."

"Like ration, you mean?"

"No, well, sort of. Now that everything is closed, all the produce at Goebbel's—I don't know how much of that will go bad. And I don't know when we'll get more. Maybe we should try to use it up, not waste it?" With a sigh, she pressed the fly-aways off her forehead. "To be honest, I don't even know what I'm talking about. This is my first world crisis. Half the time I feel like I'm overreacting, the other half…I feel like we're all going to die."

"I see. Like cook it up here before it goes bad?"

"Yeah, maybe? Have everyone in our group meet here for meals or something?"

"It's not a bad idea. I know the old folks would appreciate that."

Katie sipped her coffee, wondering if she should mention to Barb she didn't know how to cook.

Barb laughed. "I about died when I saw JJ tromp by this morning with those kids like a mama duck and her ducklings."

Katie smiled.

Barb shook her head. "I never thought I'd see that side of him again."

That caught Katie's attention. "What do you mean?"

Barb hesitated, then shrugged, looking guilty, like she'd divulged a secret she shouldn't have. "I think it's best you ask him about that."

Katie frowned. "Why?"

The old woman shrugged again. "Because this is a small town, and while we ain't much, the folks here are the closest thing I got to family. That's includin' them damn Barnes boys. And like I told you, news travels fast and I don't want anyone thinkin' I'm talking behind their back. I thought you already knew, is the only reason I said anything."

That was fair. Katie let it go. "Barnes boys? Sheriff Easton, you mean? What is his deal?" she asked.

Barb laughed. "Yep. Easton and Weston. Those boys have been…a handful all their lives, but deep down—"

Katie choked on her coffee. "What? Really? Wes's name is Weston?"

Barb chuckled again. "Yep, their mother was always one screw loose of a nuthouse. And their daddy was the one that made her that way. Those boys have had a rough go of it."

That actually explained a lot. "Easton and Weston, huh?"

"Yep." Barb looked up. "Speak of the—"

The door jingled, and the sheriff walked in. He was wearing a mask, which he pulled off his face, and stuffed in his pocket.

"The usual?" Barb asked, not mentioning his breach of protocol.

He nodded, and she headed for the kitchen as he removed his Stetson and took a seat next to Katie.

"Ms. Newman," he said.

Katie slid off her bar stool and backed away. "What are you doing? The quarantine—"

His hand shot out and closed around her arm. "Where's your guard dog?" he asked, pulling her back down onto the stool beside him.

"We really shouldn't be—"

"I'm not infected. Are you?"

"That depends on if you're wrong or not." Katie pulled her arm away, slid two seats down and took an angry sip of her coffee.

"Come on, I'm just messing with you. I haven't broken the quarantine yet. Just been around Barbie and Dave at the station, and they're both in your little group. So I'm clean. Come sit by me."

Katie shook her head.

Easton's jaw tightened. "I said, come sit by me."

Her brow went up. Was he serious? She shook her head again. Fuck him because there was no way—

He got up and before she could slide away again, his hand closed over her arm, *again*. She tried to snatch it away as he sat down beside her, but that made him squeeze her harder.

"You're hurting me."

He smiled at her, calmly, as if he wasn't totally violating her space. "Don't be scared."

"I'm not scared." That was a lie, and he seemed to know it.

"Oh, please," he said with a laugh. "Of course you are. And you should be."

He gave off so many mixed signals it made her dizzy.

"Not of me, of course," he added coyly. "But that virus... New York is fucked. That's where you were headed, right?"

Katie huffed a laugh. "You've been stalking my social media?"

"Just getting a little background is all. And I must say... I was surprised."

"Why is that?"

He touched her hair, sliding it back over her shoulder, as she tried again to push him away. He squeezed her arm again. "You didn't strike me as a bad girl at first."

That brought her head up. "What are you talking about?"

He turned her chair and set a giant palm on her thigh, like he had the first day they met. "I told you. I'm the law around here. Nothing happens that I don't know about. No one has secrets from me."

He sounded like a mob boss. "You don't know me." She tried to pull away again, but he held her in place.

"I did some digging. I saw the police reports." The hair on the back of her neck stood up in warning. "There was more than one, and they seemed to have a common theme."

If by common theme he meant they had almost all been

defamation complaints, then yes. Men were assholes to her, especially when she'd been young and stupid.

He leaned closer and whispered in her ear, "You're a bad girl, aren't you? You like to do bad things with bad boys."

Katie's heart banged in her chest, and she tried to pull away. "No." She didn't. It was just—

"I saw the videos, *Kathy*," Easton said, his eyes slowly, looking her up and down.

Fuck.

"You were quite the promiscuous young lady," he continued.

No, she'd been a stupid, naïve, young lady who got herself into a bad situation. She tried to pull away again. "Leave me—"

"I'd hate for it to get out that you're a porn star," he said through his teeth.

Katie looked over his shoulder. Where was Barb? "I'm not —"

"Don't get me wrong. *I* love it," he interrupted. "But JJ, that's exactly the kind of thing that would turn him off, you understand? He's…old fashioned that way."

Her eyes widened. Was he trying to blackmail her? "Are you seriously threatening me?"

"Admit it, Kathy, I am exactly your type. JJ is too…white picket fence for you. You need someone—."

"My name is Katie, and you don't know anything—"

"It's just you and me here now." He interrupted. "We can both be honest." He set his hand on her shoulder and she shrugged it off. "About what?"

"Men like him jerk off to photos of you, but you like to fuck men like me, which is perfect because then we can skip the foreplay and get right down to—"

Katie shoved her chair back and jumped up. It clattered to the floor with a bang. "Get away from me."

Barb poked her head out of the kitchen as Easton bent down

to retrieve it. "Everything okay out there?" she asked as Katie backed toward the door.

"Everything is fine, Barbie. I was just telling Ms. *Newman,* we received a message down at the station for her from the grandparents of the twins she's got."

Katie stopped. "You did?"

Easton nodded. "They heard the radio announcement, and they will be at the station in the morning to pick them up."

Katie's heart soared as Easton continued. "You will have to be fitted with one of these." He wore the same bracelet the kids did. She nodded.

Barb smiled. "That's great news." Barb looked at Katie. "See. I told you, you done good, girl," she said before ducking back into the kitchen.

"Come on. Sit with me while I eat." Easton's voice was friendly, but the hunger in his eyes wasn't.

Katie shook her head. "Sorry. I need to get back to the kids. Thanks for the coffee!" she shouted to Barb.

Easton nodded slowly. "To be continued," he drawled as Katie hurried out the door.

Cutting across the yard, she ran back to JJ's house, heart thumping and the bottom of her foot on fire as it rubbed against the arch of her shoe, bringing tears to her eyes.

The TV was off and the house was dark. The older kids must have gone to sleep. She glanced over her shoulder at the mechanic shop. JJ's truck still wasn't back.

Katie sat down on the front steps, just as she had with JJ the night before. It felt totally different without him there.

Resting her elbows on her knees, she inhaled and exhaled deeply. She couldn't let Sheriff Easton rattle her. He wasn't the first to discover those videos, and he wouldn't be the last. And who cared, anyway? *You do.* Yeah, she did, and she didn't want JJ to find out.

The moonlight lit the front yard like a porch light, and Katie noticed the remnants of a white picket fence that must have surrounded the front yard at some point. Was that what Easton was referring to with his comment about JJ? She could almost imagine a green grass inside it and wondered if Hartford Creek had ever had a heyday. It didn't seem like it. With only a dozen houses and three buildings, it was hard to imagine it was ever anything more than a dumpy back-country shithole. But maybe. It gave her an idea, and she spent the next ten minutes wrestling with the hose that sat curled up on the side of the house.

The jingle of a bell split the quiet evening and Katie slid back into the shadow of the house as Easton emerged from the bar with a plastic bag, and got into his cruiser.

She dashed up the steps and through the front door as he backed up, hoping he hadn't seen her.

"Is everything okay?" Sam asked sleepily from the couch.

"Yeah. Just...bugs."

"Maybe you ought to sleep inside tonight," he said dryly, rolling over.

Katie crept into the kitchen and poured herself a glass of water. Glancing at the clock, she gulped it down. It was almost ten. Where was JJ?

Pulling her phone out of her pocket, she sat down at the table. Not knowing why, she thumbed through her useless apps. It had been two days. Since she started her accounts, she'd never gone longer than twenty-four hours without posting. Katie glanced at the clock ticking quietly on the wall above her head, then looked out into the darkened living room where Sam and Parker slept on the couch and recliner respectively, while the twins slept on the floor.

The distance from her life, even a mere forty-eight hours, was affording her an uncomfortable amount of clarity about her life choices. It had been a long, stressful day, but it had also been filled with something she had never felt before, except on very rare occasion. Purpose. Like what she was doing really mattered.

Like what those kids needed was more important than her. And it was such a… Her mouth curled up in a sad smile. *Relief.* She squeezed her eyes shut. Oh, god, it felt so good to just take a break from her own life and her own head with its relentless worries and doubts.

Katie stared at her phone. She had spent the last twenty years thinking *only* about herself. She'd never paused, never stepped away from her own drama, as stupid and unimportant as it was, to care for someone else's, and she'd lost all perspective on how small her problems really were compared to what others faced.

And what a strange freedom there was in taking a break from herself. Tears filled her eyes, and she wiped them away. She was *so* tired of trying to make herself happy and never succeeding. Today, something inside her had come alive, and she'd done amazing things that actually mattered. She'd found clothes for the kids, and a few games and toys for them to play with. She had washed two loads of laundry and cleaned out JJ's guest room and turned it back into a bedroom. Families were even being reunited because of her.

Katie caught her disheveled reflection in the door of JJ's ancient microwave. She *looked* like shit, but for the first time in a long time, her body and mind felt like a fortress instead of a ticking time bomb waiting to destroy her and dump her on a curb. It was good. It was all good.

After finishing her water, she brushed her teeth, poured more alcohol on her inflamed foot, then stood in the doorway of JJ's bedroom, eyeing his bed. It was the only place left to sleep, and he wasn't even there, so it made sense to crash there but…

Katie chewed on her lip and peeked into the next bedroom. The lamp illuminated Jinn and Amelia's heads in the bed, and Grace's body curled up in a ball asleep on the floor. She supposed she could squeeze into bed with the girls, but… She stepped back and eyed JJ's empty bed again.

Katie rolled her eyes. *Oh, for the love of god.* Why was she making such a big deal out of this? He wasn't even there.

Slipping into the room, she noticed the nightstand on the right. That must be the side JJ slept on, so she went and sat down on the left. Then, dropping onto the pillow, she promptly fell asleep.

Chapter Nine

Day 3 // 4:24 a.m.

JJ CUT the engine on the truck and sighed.

"It's a hell of a thing, ain't it?" Mike asked wearily beside him.

JJ leaned his head back against the seat and closed his eyes. That was putting it mildly. The destruction caused by the Veil was unlike anything he had ever seen. *Thousands* of people had been killed or injured when it went up. NPR confirmed more than a million deaths so far from Veil-related accidents. A *million.* Meanwhile, only New York was suffering from a notable outbreak of the supposedly 'deadly' virus. How could whatever was behind the Veil possibly be worse than the carnage he'd seen over the past twenty-odd hours?

"Yeah." He had discovered two bodies himself, for Christ's sake, as he and Mike dragged one car after another off the pile-ups that were scattered around the Veil like a halo. JJ didn't have a sensitive stomach, but the mangled flesh, the vacant stares from soulless eyes covered in flies, the *smell...* He'd lost his lunch a couple times.

The passenger's side door creaked open. "You ought to get some shut-eye," Mike suggested, before climbing down and slamming the door.

JJ pulled the keys out of the ignition and pushed his door open. The moon had set and the porch light was off, swallowing his house in darkness. There was a weird sound somewhere he didn't recognize, but otherwise, the night was quiet. He locked the truck, then crossed the empty street.

Halfway up the front walk, he was caught in a deluge. Icy drops of water splashed on his arms and shoulders. Shielding his head, he ducked, then peeked between his arms at the *clear,* starry sky. "What the fuck—"

He ran for the front porch as a familiar sputtering sound filled the night. *The sprinkler.* Someone had turned it on. Changing course, he ran around the side of the house and turned it off.

One of the kids must have messed with the sprinkler. And what did he expect? Katie was clearly in over her head. He could only imagine what it looked like inside.

Clenching his exhausted jaw, he headed back to the house.

Fumbling with his keys, he slid what he hoped was the right one into the lock and twisted the knob. The door opened, and he stepped inside.

The light above the kitchen sink was on, gently illuminating the living room. JJ's heart thumped at the sight of the bodies strewn across the couch and floor. *They are asleep, not dead.* He pressed a hand to his chest. "Right," he muttered.

Making his way into the kitchen, he noticed it was much cleaner than it had been when he left. There was a note on the table and he read it as he wiped his wet arms with a kitchen towel.

Turn off the sprinkler when you get home. There is a ham sandwich in the fridge. -K

JJ opened the fridge and blinked. It was full of food. "What in the…?" Baggies filled with cut up fruit and veggies, all from Goebbel's he guessed. Containers of pasta salad and… he didn't know what. On the top shelf was a plate with a sandwich on it, wrapped in plastic. He turned and looked over his shoulder at the sleeping forms in the living room.

This was not what he expected. At all.

Grabbing the sandwich and a beer, he quietly tore off the plastic and gulped his dinner down in six bites. Then drained an entire beer in a single thirst-quenching sip.

Utterly exhausted, he quietly set his dish in the sink and headed down the hall, doing a double-take when he passed the 'guest' bedroom. All the junk had been removed and a small lamp he had never seen before cast a soft glow over the walls, revealing the double bed he'd always assumed was still there, but hadn't seen in at least a couple of years. Jinn and Amelia lay nestled together in the middle of the bed, while Grace slept on the floor. One of them was snoring. He rubbed his eyes. Katie had cleaned the guest room?

JJ took two more steps and his breath paused in his throat as he fell against the door frame. Katie was asleep in *his* bed? His heart skipped again, just as it had when she walked into Barb's and pulled her sunglasses up on her head, just as it had in the hotel lobby the day before yesterday, just as it had this morning when he saw her standing in the hall.

Katie jerked, but her eyes didn't open as her face contorted into a grimace and she shifted. A small cry broke the quiet, and her shoulders twitched again. She was probably having the same nightmare he'd had the night before of crumpling metal and heart-stopping explosions. A second later, her face relaxed, and her breathing steadied once again. He stared at her in the semi-darkness, her dark hair spread across his pillow. She looked like someone else. She looked... He couldn't think of the word, but he could feel it. It was like someone was squeezing the air out of his lungs and he didn't want them to stop.

JJ rolled his eyes and pushed himself away from the door as his insides erupted in civil war.

No. As nice as she appeared to be so far, Katie was off limits. He had to remember that.

His brows came together. Which was going to be very hard to do with her sleeping a foot away from him in his own goddamn bed. Where in the hell was *he* supposed to sleep now? His jaw tightened. He knew there was nowhere else for her to go, but even so, it was presumptuous of her to assume—*she's not assuming anything, asshole. She's still dressed and dead asleep.* JJ ground his teeth together. Yeah right. If you counted skintight jeans and a barely there top 'dressed.' *On top of the covers.* Well, that was true. His eyes swept over her hair, across her shoulder, up and down the curve of her hip to her... He frowned again he got to the bottom of her right foot. "What the hell?" She'd said it was just a scratch.

He came into the room and bent closer to inspect it. Red, raw flesh covered the arch of her foot. Turning to the chair beside him, he saw two pairs of insanely ugly heeled shoes on the floor and a pair of sneakers. There was a bloody stain inside the right one.

At the Veil, she had been barefoot and limping. Touching the side of his neck, where the burn still ached when it rubbed the collar of his shirt, he tried to imagine how it would feel on the bottom of his foot. "Shit."

She twitched again with a small gasp as he got up and went back to the door, intending to go into the bathroom, but he turned around instead.

She really was turning out to be much tougher than he expected.

He leaned against the door frame as her head turned on the pillow.

He just didn't want to think about that, because then he'd start to like her. And there was nothing wrong with liking her... as long as he didn't break the rule. Unfortunately, he knew himself well enough to know he would. Or want to anyway. *That* was why he had to keep his distance, because he'd sabotage himself and all hell would break loose. *What do you want from her?* He wanted her to apologize for crashing into his life, confusing the hell out of him, and making him feel things he didn't want to feel. As soon as he thought it, he knew he was being a dick, acting like a stupid kid.

JJ shook his head and headed into the bathroom. Flipping the light, he found his eyes in the mirror. He didn't hate Katie. He just had way too much baggage to like her without… *Without what?* Falling for her, pushing her away, projecting his insecurities on her, despite every attempt not to. Take your pick. He was fucked up. Ruined. There were a couple of nice girls who would testify to that, and it was the reason he'd limited his relationships to one-night stands. It was better that way for everyone. It was better for *Katie* if he didn't like her, he told his reflection. *You make no sense.*

JJ sighed again, too tired to argue with himself any longer. He needed to brush his teeth and go to bed before he fell asleep standing up.

Two minutes later, JJ dropped onto the covers in his sweaty, filthy work clothes. He left his socks on too, just to prove to himself how uninterested he was in impressing her. His body vibrated with fatigue as he laid down on his side and pulled the pillow over his head. He would do his best to be nice to her. But he would also stay as far away from her as possible.

Two seconds later, social influencer Katie Newman, with her million and a half followers mostly made up of middle-aged men like him, turned and curled up beside him, throwing her arm across his chest.

Fucking hell.

A terrible, wonderful moment later, he passed out.

Chapter Ten

Day 4 // 10:13 a.m.

A SQUEALING noise roused him from sleep. Rubbing his eyes, he turned his head toward the door. It sounded like a pig was running around his living room. He groaned and rolled over, dragging the pillow back over his head to block the daylight pouring in through the window. There was another squeal, followed by the maniacal laughter of a five-year-old.

"No. No, no…" JJ squeezed the pillow over his ears as a sound like stampeding elephants shook his bed.

Everything went quiet for a moment.

Then he heard a muffled giggle. Lifting the pillow, he opened one eye and found himself staring at Amelia, who was tucked between the nightstand and the closet door. She put her finger to her lips. "Shh."

A voice from the door yelled, "I see you! I see you!" as JJ covered his face, wondering if it would be possible for him to smother himself. "Fuck my life," he whispers into the pillow as his head pounded.

"Huh?" a voice above him asked.

He pulled the pillow back and jumped. "Holy sh—"

Grace and Amelia stood beside the bed, staring at him with two pairs of big eyes.

He looked down frantically and was relieved to find himself dressed. He didn't even remember going to bed. JJ glanced at the clock on the nightstand and groaned. It was after ten?

"Where is Katie?" he asked, rolling to the other side of the bed and sitting up.

"She went to take Saffi and Leo to their grandma, I think."

JJ squeezed his eyes shut, then reopened them. Then who was watching the kids while he slept? "Where is everyone else?" he asked, sitting up.

"Everyone?"

JJ sighed, feeling like he'd been run over a dozen times by his tow truck. He turned as the girls came around the bed. Grace was wearing a pair of overalls he didn't remember seeing on her before. "Who's watching you?" he asked.

Amelia frowned. "You are."

He squeezed his eyes shut for a moment. "No, not at this very moment, I mean—"

Jinn appeared in the doorway. "Amelia, girls, I told you this room was off limits." She turned to JJ. "Sorry. Katie asked me to keep them out of here, but…" She ushered them out of the room. "They don't listen," she said quietly, so they wouldn't hear.

JJ huffed a laugh as she shut the door. He stared at his feet and his smile faded as he remembered the day before. The devastation, the death. For a second, for *one* brief second, he'd forgotten. But it was back now.

Pressing the heels of his palms into his eyes, he inhaled heavily, then exhaled. And now he had to deal with a houseful of kids before heading back to Atlanta for another day of hauling. The desire to smother himself resurfaced. With closed eyes, he got up, shuffled into the bathroom, and leaned heavily on the sink. Turning the water on, he rinsed his face and—he caught movement out of the corner of his eye and froze. *Oh, dear god, no.*

"Whacha doin?"

Slowly, he turned. Amelia sat propped up on the toilet, with her pants around her ankles, staring at him.

JJ bolted, almost knocking himself out as his forehead hit the edge of the bathroom door. Stars hovered in his vision as he hurried into the hall, slammed it shut behind him, and pressed his weight into it like there was a grizzly bear, and not a toddler on the other side. "What the fuck?" he whispered to himself before banging on the door. "Hey! We've got rules around here," he shouted. "And rule number one is close the door when you're in the bathroom!"

Turning around, he leaned back against it, raking his fingers through his hair. "For Christ's sake." He hadn't even had a cup of coffee yet—

The door opened, and he stumbled backward, almost falling over as Amelia hopped out of the way and walked past him. "We don't close the door at our house," she informed him.

"Well, newsflash, this isn't your house." He followed her down the hall. "And..." He looked back toward the bathroom. "Hey. Wait a second. Did you even flush?"

The girl turned and put her hands on her hips. "Yes."

JJ shook his head and pointed a finger at her. "No, you didn't."

"Yes, I—"

"I can smell it. You didn't wash your hands either."

Amelia tucked both hands behind her back. "I don't want to."

JJ threw his hands up. "What's the matter with you? Were you raised by wolves?"

The girl looked confused. "No. By my mom and Nana."

"Were your mom and Nana raised by wolves?"

The girl's frown deepened. "What?"

"Never mind. Go flush the toilet. And wash your hands."

Amelia eyed him, and JJ puffed up his chest, trying to look confident and intimidating.

Her shoulders sagged. "Fine," she sighed.

She went back into the bathroom and shut the door. A second later, the toilet flushed, and a second after that, she pulled the door back open. His eyes narrowed. "Did you wash your hands?"

She nodded.

Little shit. No, she didn't. He shook his head and leaned down so they were face to face. "My mom buys me very fancy, expensive hand soap," he said. "*If* you washed your hands, they *should* smell like a pina colada, which is exactly what I wish I was drunk on right now on an island far, far away from here."

"What?"

"Never mind, the point is, I don't smell coconut, which makes me think you're lying. And you know what happens to little girls who lie—"

The girl's eyes widened. "Oh! I forgot! The leeches!" She quickly retreated into the bathroom, slamming the door in his face as he stood back and frowned. "The what?"

She didn't answer, but the water went on as he leaned against the wall, dragging his hands over his face. He was too tired to deal with this shit.

The door opened again and Amelia held up her hands as she stepped out.

He sniffed. Pina colada. "Okay good. Now go play."

Amelia took a step, then paused again. "Are you a grownup?" she asked.

JJ frowned. "Yeah."

"Then why does your mom buy your soap for you?"

"Because I'm a single guy, and that's what moms do."

She tilted her head to the side, like a puppy hearing a new sound. "What does 'single' mean?"

JJ sighed. "It means I don't have a partner."

"Like a wife?"

"Yeah." He turned to the bathroom.

"Why not?"

He sighed and turned back around. "Honestly? I don't know. Probably because I fall for the wrong kind of girls."

Amelia shook her head. "No. That's not it."

JJ smirked and crossed his arms. "Oh really? Then what is it?"

She bit her lip, then said, "I think it's because you say a lot of swears, and you sleep in your clothes and you smell like…" She shrugged as if at a loss for words. "Like garbage or something."

Wow. Okay. "Thanks for your insight. Now go play." Lifting his arm, he gestured down the hall, and gagged on his own stink.

Amelia took a step, then paused. "What about Miss Katie?"

"What about her?"

She tilted her head. "Is she the right kind of girl for you?"

"Nooo." He shook his head. "Not even close."

"So she is the wrong kind of girl for you, then?"

"Yep. Exactly." That was *exactly* what she was.

"So, you don't want to marry her someday?" Amelia asked, looking skeptical.

He crossed his arms. "Nope."

Amelia studied him again, her eyes narrowing. "Do the leeches bite your toes a lot?"

JJ frowned. *"What?* What leeches?"

She ignored his question." I bet they do." Then her black little eyebrows came together. "Why?"

"Why what?"

"Why is Miss Katie wrong?"

JJ sighed. "I guess she's not *wrong,* really. She's just… trouble," he said, more to himself than her.

"Like Leo?"

"No, not like—"

"I don't get it."

He tried to think in terms she'd understand. "Have you ever seen a princess fall in love with a guy that looks like me?"

She thought about that for a moment. "But Miss Katie's not a princess."

"But she looks like one."

"Belle fell in love with the Beast," Amelia argued. "And *he* was ugly, too."

JJ huffed. "Thanks."

"Oh, but then he turned into a prince," she said. "You can't do that."

No, the sad truth was he could not. "Nope."

"Well anyways, if I grow up and marry a girl like my Aunt Vikki did, then I think Miss Katie would be the right kind of girl for me."

Leaning against the door, JJ folded his arms, the corner of his mouth turning up. "Why is that?"

"Because she's nice and has pretty hair and funny shoes, and she made me Mickey Mouse pancakes for breakfast. And she got me a doll and some games to play. And she read me *three* stories last night before bed. Mama only reads me one. *And* she made me chocolate milk at Miss Barbie's, even though it wasn't a special-a-cashen."

JJ's brow went up. "You mean special occasion?"

"Yes. That's what I said."

"She did all that?"

"Yeah, and she got me new clothes because...because I had an accident, like Saffi on the bus."

"That's a lot."

"Yeah. And when I talked to mama yesterday, she said that I am a very lucky girl that I have someone as wonderful as Miss Katie to take care of me."

"You talked to your mom?"

Amelia nodded. "Yep, Miss Katie called her." Tears filled the little girl's and JJ couldn't help himself. Kneeling down, he hugged her.

"I know I'm lucky, but I miss my mom and Nana," the girl confessed, as she threw her arms around his neck and sobbed against his shirt.

JJ patted her back. "I know, kiddo. Miss Katie and I *both* promise to do what we can to help you get home."

"JJ?" she sniffled after a moment.

"Yeah?"

"I like the Beast better," she said quietly. "The prince was s-scary."

He looked up at the ceiling. Goddamn it, if that wasn't the sweetest thing anyone had ever said to him. He gave her a squeeze. "Thanks."

She was quiet for a moment, then she leaned back and asked, "Did you fall in a garbage can? Or—"

A laugh lurched up his throat as he pushed her away and stood back up. "Okay. I'll take a shower."

Amelia's nose scrunched. "Maybe you should take two."

JJ laughed again as he retreated into the bathroom. "Fucking kids," he said under his breath. They sure were honest little bastards. But when he looked in the mirror, he was smiling.

———

HIS SHOWER only lasted about three minutes, because someone else needed to use the restroom. JJ quickly got dressed, then ran the towel over his hair and dropped it on the bed. At least he didn't smell like a dumpster anymore.

The second-oldest boy was sitting at the kitchen table. "Hey," he said, going to the refrigerator.

"There are pancakes in the microwave," the boy said.

There wasn't much that was more awkward than having a conversation with a kid you didn't know in your own damn kitchen. *Except maybe having the same conversation with a kid on a toilet.*

JJ opened the microwave, and sure enough, a stack of pancakes was there waiting.

He poured himself a cup of cold coffee and threw the mug in the microwave with the pancakes as they warmed.

"What's your name again?" he asked.

"Parker."

JJ leaned back against the counter, studying Parker and his

emo vibes. It was so surreal, all the strangers in his house. "I'm JJ."

Parker rolled his eyes. "Yeah. I know."

The microwave dinged as the screen on the front door squeaked open.

"We're back," Katie called. A second later, she rounded the corner into the kitchen, hair up in a ponytail, tank-top, jeans and sneakers on. She stopped when she saw him. "Oh. Um...Hi."

She limped to the coffeemaker as he studied her sneakers. Those were probably not the best shoes for an injury like hers. It needed to breathe.

"Is there any coffee left?" she asked.

JJ nodded, taking his plate and sitting beside Parker at the table. He watched out of the corner of his eye as Katie poured the rest of the coffee in a mug and put it into the microwave. "I don't know where you guys get your coffee from, but it's amazing."

He grunted, then swallowed a bite of pancakes. "You dropped off the twins?"

Her eyebrow went up. "Yeah. Didn't you notice?"

He met her eyes, and they were filled with laughter. "Ha, ha," he deadpanned.

Katie pushed the button on the microwave. "Two down, so only two more to—"

He looked at Parker, scowling quietly beside him. She was off by one. *"Three* left," he corrected.

"No," Katie began, as Parker's chair screeched back, and he jumped up.

"Wait!" Katie called as the boy raced from the room. "Shit," she whispered under her breath, running after him. "Parker! He didn't mean—"

JJ heard a door slam, and a moment later Katie reappeared, looking sad and frustrated.

She grabbed her coffee, sat down in Parker's vacated chair,

and pulled her feet up onto the seat, resting her mug on her knees. She made it look so easy, but if he tried to sit like that, he'd probably fall off the chair and kill himself.

Even tired, which she clearly was, she was beautiful. How was that possible? JJ swallowed the thought and another bite, then asked. "What was that all about?"

She shook her head as she leaned forward and pulled her phone out of her pocket. Her brows furrowed as she tapped and scrolled.

"Your phone's working?"

"On and off. Mostly off, but I got a hold of Amelia's mom. Jinn spoke to her parents too for a minute before getting disconnected last night."

"How are you getting a hold of the families then, to reunite the kids?"

Sam came in and went to the fridge. "Because she's a fucking genius, man." He whistled. "Looks and brains."

Katie rolled her eyes as Jinn came in and cast her an odd glance. "I'm not a genius." She turned to JJ. "I just had an idea that worked out."

"What?"

"She went old school, and got the damn governor on board…"

JJ's brow went up. Katie knew the governor? He repressed an eye roll. Of course she did. *"What?"*

"Radio, man. Every hour they're broadcasting the names of kids who have been separated from their families."

JJ looked at Katie, and she shrugged. "Most of them were in school and accounted for. But kids like Amelia… Or parents that nobody could get a hold of because of their phones…It's an easy way to reach a lot of people and let parents know their kids are okay."

Sam took a bite of an apple. "And now, thanks to Ms. Katie Newman, every radio station surrounding Atlanta is doing it, listing kids' names, and the local precincts where family members can go to claim them."

JJ looked from Sam to her. "They are?"

She shrugged. "Yeah—"

"Come on now." Sam said, patting her shoulder. "Don't be modest. You're a fucking hero." He turned to JJ. "We heard on the way back. Over thirty kids have been reunited so far, including Leo and Saffi. And a shit-ton more are scheduled to be picked up."

Katie took a sip of her coffee, and JJ reminded himself she was off limits, a 'no-no' as Amelia would say as Sam went on. "And the radio dude said other cities are copying us. Taking her idea and doing the same thing."

That was...*incredible.* "Really? But what about the quarantine?"

Katie held up her wrist, revealing the same bracelet the kids at the school had been fitted with. Sam had one too. "Kids being reunited with family are exempt as long as everyone at the exchange is fitted with a tracker, and agrees to resume the quarantine once they return home. When I dropped the kids off, we were told to stay on opposite sides of the parking lot, and the kids walked between us. The sheriff's office recorded everything and got everyone's information, and then we all left."

JJ stared at her. "What was Parker's deal, then?"

Katie rolled her eyes and slammed her mug on the table, burying her head in her hands.

"His family on the outside doesn't want to take him," Sam said.

JJ turned. "*What?*"

Katie sighed. "That's probably why the principal sent him with us. She knew they wouldn't. So, he's with us until the Veil comes down."

"Great." That was all they needed. "What the fuck is wrong with people?"

Katie glanced over her shoulder. "He's got issues."

JJ huffed. "So what, now?"

Katie dropped her feet to the floor. "For now, he stays with us. Amelia too. I spoke with her mom yesterday. She's got a brother in Mexico and her parents are in Texas, but no one here. She's trying to get a hold of her folks to see if they can make the trip to come get her. Jinn has decided to stay with us—"

"Me too," Sam said.

Katie nodded. "Grace has an aunt and uncle on the west side of the city. They contacted the sheriff's office. They'll be here as soon as they can."

"I have to go back to the city," JJ said, dreading the thought of another day sifting through the wreckage.

"Again?"

"The Army and Coast Guard need us back until everything is cleared."

"And then what?"

"Hey—" Jinn interrupted, staring at the TV in the living room. "You guys need to see this."

Katie gave him a worried look as he followed her into the living room. The headline on the TV read '**A million dead in New York.**'

JJ stared as the news anchor continued. *"Despite the warning from the president, thousands of New Yorkers have ignored the quarantine, and are congregating outside the hospitals within the Veil, demanding access and medical attention for loved ones who have been exposed to the virus."*

Video footage, from a drone, showed a mob of people outside the emergency department of the closed Manhattan General Hospital.

"Law enforcement officials have been alerted and..." The anchor paused as a small explosion ripped through the awning that covered the entrance to the hospital. The anchor pressed her fingers over the speaker in her ear as police cars screeched to a

halt before the building. *"It appears the mob has gained access..."* Several officers jumped out. They were heavily masked and began firing at the crowd. *"Oh, oh...I...oh my god."*

Katie's fingers were ice as they gripped his arm. "Oh, my god..." she whispered, as one by one the panicked people began to drop.

JJ stared. "They are *executing* them?"

"Wh-what's happening?" Grace asked from behind him. "Why are they—"

The video feed was cut, and the news anchor appeared on screen again, looking as horrified as JJ felt. *"All citizens within the Veil are reminded to stay...Stay home. Please."* She paused, and looked off screen, then sat up and blinked as if coming out of a trance. *"I'm sorry. I...The ICPH believes the acceleration of the X-Virus in New York is due to the fact that it was already circulating in several populations throughout the city when the Veil was activated. They have also confirmed the virus has spread to Philadelphia and San Diego as numbers continue to rise in Atlanta and Dallas, which reported their first cases the day the Veils were activated."* The video switched to a graph showing the list of other affected cities and their death tolls. Although the bar was a hundred times smaller, Atlanta was second behind New York, with over ten thousand unconfirmed dead from the virus. *"Death tolls in New York have reached an astonishing million fatalities, with another two million reporting symptoms, and the numbers keep climbing, while other cities, like Detroit and Chicago, are still reporting none —"*

"Turn it off," Kate said.

JJ turned. A thousand deaths in Atlanta? How could that be? They hadn't seen a single person, besides the police on the first day, out on the streets inside.

"Turn it off," she repeated, looking over her shoulder. The kids were all on the couch, staring at the TV. "Now."

JJ swung around and hit the button on the TV.

"Is it in Atlanta too?" Grace asked. "The virus? Is it—are my mom and dad going to die? Are *we* going to die?"

He was wondering the same thing, and was just as terrified by the answer. "Um...well..."

"No one is going to die," Katie interrupted.

JJ shook his head. "Katie, don't—" Lying to the kids was not going to help anything.

She met his eyes. "No one is going to—"

"Excuse us," JJ said, dragging her into the kitchen.

She shook her arm free. "What?"

"Do not lie to those kids," he said, as his worry for his mom and sister grew. Was Atlanta going to turn into New York in a couple of days? Overrun with sick people, and cops shooting everyone?

She stared at him. "What are you—"

"Whatever this is, it's bad."

"But—"

JJ shook his head. "I've been asking myself what could be worth the death of a million casualties, and now we know."

She stared at him.

"A *million* people have already died in New York, Katie."

"I know, but—"

"It's only been four days." JJ pressed his fingers into his forehead. "Only *four* fucking days."

"I know but—"

JJ knew he was no genius, but he wasn't stupid either. If the NYPD was executing people on national television... "Shit." His mom and Sierra were going to die. He'd been putting the thought off, skirting around it, trying to stay busy, hoping he was wrong, but now... "They're all going to die."

Katie put a hand on his arm. "We don't know that. The president said—"

JJ jerked it free. "I know what the president said!" he shouted. Glancing over his shoulder at the kids, he lowered his voice. "But what else is he going to say? *'Everyone inside the Veil will be dead in a week?'* Goddamn it. Why did they even bother putting it up to begin with? Clearly, it's not helping anyone in New York. Why didn't they just get it over with, murder everyone—"

There was a gasp behind him, and he turned. Grace stood in the doorway wide eyed and pale.

"Grace..." Katie began.

The girl spun around and ran for the front door as Katie dashed past him. "Grace! Wait! He didn't mean it! He was just..." her voice drowned out as the screen door slammed with a thwack. It opened and closed again, as Katie shouted from outside. "Grace! Wait!"

"Damn it!" JJ punched the wall. The clock above the phone crashed to the ground, the glass splintering into a thousand pieces at his feet.

"Hey, man, take it easy." It was Sam's turn to occupy the doorway.

JJ looked up. "Fuck!" He hit the wall again. "How am I supposed to take it easy when the goddamn President of the United States has...They're gonna die. They are going to die if I don't get them out of there."

"We all got someone inside. We're all..." Sam's voice wavered. "But we need... Man, *I* need you to keep it together."

JJ pressed his head to the wall, feeling like it was going to explode.

Sam continued. "Because I'm scared too. And I don't know what to do either."

JJ turned as tears ran down Sam's cheeks. "Sam, I'm sorry. I shouldn't have—"

"But, you're right. They are gonna die if they stay in there. So, w-what do we do, JJ? How do we get them out? I need you to help me. Because... I can't." He shook his head. "What kind of man, what kind of *son* would I be, if I just let her die?"

JJ stared at him, wondering the same thing.

For the first time since meeting Sam, he seemed like a boy. Not a teenager even, but a frightened little boy who was on the verge of losing his entire family.

JJ's father appeared in his mind again, like he always did when he faced a seemingly insurmountable crisis. JJ never knew what to do in tough situations, but somehow he always knew what his father would do. He would hug the boy.

JJ pulled Sam in for a hug, ignoring the awkwardness he felt. His dad wouldn't have thought twice about comforting a kid who was afraid. And he would tell him... "Maybe...maybe if we help the people we can out here...others will help the people we can't, in there. And if we all do that..." He patted Sam on the back and noticed Jinn standing in the doorway. Her eyes were full of tears. *Fuck.* JJ waved her over, and she collapsed against them, sobbing.

JJ blinked back tears of his own, ashamed of letting his own emotions get the better of him. His jaw tightened. It would not happen again. Not until the kids were back where they belonged.

After a minute, he gently pushed them back. "Here's what we are going to do. I have to go back to the Veil. Sam, you can come with me." He paused, remembering the dead bodies. "If you want—"

"Yes."

"Jinn, Katie needs help with the girls and—Just in case anything happens, I'll feel better knowing the two of you are together. Does that make sense?"

She nodded as Amelia came into the kitchen, clutching Beaver and a Barbie doll.

"I know you miss your families," he said. "And I know

you're afraid for them, and maybe a little for yourself too, but I promise you. We are here for you. Katie and I. You are not alone out here. You have us. We will be your family until you are reunited with your own."

Sam wiped his eyes, and looked at Jinn, then Amelia, then JJ, and smiled weakly. "We're one weird-ass lookin' family."

"Damn right," JJ said, hoping he sounded more confident than he felt. "Now, we've got to get moving. We're already late. I'll go see if Mike is up, and we'll head out."

Katie was at the front door when he pulled it open. "I can't find her."

JJ frowned. "Grace?"

"Or Parker. I don't know where either of them went."

JJ looked at his watch. "I have to go. I'm already…I was supposed to report in an hour ago—"

Jinn appeared beside him, only her red eyes letting on that she'd been crying. "We got this. You go. We'll find them." She turned. "Amelia. Come on."

JJ looked from Katie to Jinn. "Are you sure?"

Katie nodded. "Yeah. We'll see you tonight."

Chapter Eleven

Day 4 // 4:47 p.m.

IT WAS Parker who found Grace, hiding underneath an abandoned car in the lot behind the bar and grocery. It had taken all of Katie's negotiating skills to get her to come out and go back into the house, and then the girl just cried until it was time to go to meet up with her aunt and uncle.

Jinn had stayed behind with Amelia, while Parker and Grace squeezed in the passenger seat of Old Ray. For reasons she didn't understand, Parker had insisted on coming. It was the first time he'd shown any interest in anything at all, which was half the reason she'd said yes. The other half was that something about his presence seemed to soothe Grace, and she'd calmed down once she knew he was coming.

By the time they pulled into the parking lot, Grace's relatives were already there waiting. Relative. There was only one. An unremarkable man in his early thirties, with blond clipped hair, in jeans and a red and yellow striped t-shirt. "Is that your uncle?" Katie asked.

Grace nodded, looking like she might cry.

Katie cut the engine and chewed her lip. Something just didn't feel right, but she didn't know what it was. "You really don't want to go with him?"

"No. I want to stay with you," Grace burst into tears.

"Why?"

"I-I barely know him! A-and my cousin April said...he's a-a

c-creep." She grabbed Katie's arm and squeezed. "Please, I want to stay with you and JJ."

Parker's eyes flicked to Katie's. "Creep? What does that mean?"

Grace shook her head. "I don't know."

Katie looked out the windshield, a warning growing in her belly. She'd known plenty of creeps, and *she* knew exactly what it meant. "How old is April?"

"I don't know. But she's in college."

April does too. Yep. "Okay." Katie didn't know how JJ would feel about what she was about to do, but there was no time to ask him. "Okay, Grace. I hear you." She pulled the girl in for a hug, smoothing her blonde hair against her chest as more tears leaked from the corners of her eyes. How many times as a young girl had she longed for someone to say those words to her, to help her when she was too afraid to ask for it or tell the truth? "You're not going anywhere." The relief in Grace's eyes broke her heart for the little girl she had been. "Stay here. I'll be right back."

Katie opened the door and got out. An officer she had never seen before started toward her. She met him on the sidewalk and stopped when they were about ten feet apart. His lapel read Witherspoon, and like her, he was unmasked. "We're all set to go. That there is Brandon Walden, Grace's father's brother. Step-brother, I guess. All the papers have been signed, and she has been released into his custody."

Katie nodded at the man across the lot. He nodded back. "What if she doesn't want to go?"

Deputy Witherspoon turned, squinting at Grace inside the car. "What do you mean?"

"Can we hurry this up?" her uncle called. "We've got to drive all the way around those damn fires to get home—"

"She doesn't want to go with him."

"Why not?" The deputy looked perplexed.

"I thought his wife would be here?"

"They are separated."

All the more reason not to let her go. "Yeah. No." She shook her head. "He's not taking her."

"Ms. Newman, you can't arbitrarily decide—"

Oh yes, she could. That man was not taking Grace *anywhere*.

"Hey," Walden called. "What's going on? Are we doing this or what? I got shit to do."

"She's not going anywhere with you," Katie yelled across the lot.

"What?" He started toward them.

"Stay back," the deputy said, taking several steps toward him and holding his hands up. "I'll handle this." Turning back at her, he said, "It's not your choice. You have to let her go."

Katie shook her head as Grace's uncle hurled obscenities at her. *Nope.* "He." She pointed her finger at Walden. "Is. Not. Taking. Her. Anywhere."

Witherspoon took a step toward her, then stopped. Whether it was his own intuition that suddenly kicked in or her glare, he spun around. "Get back," he shouted to Walden, who paused in the middle of the parking lot for only a fraction of a second before continuing. The deputy pulled out his gun. "I said stop!" He turned to Katie as she backed toward the car. "You too. Now, what the hell is going on? What's wrong?"

"We've changed our minds," she said. "Grace wants to stay with us."

Her uncle laughed. "You can't change your mind. She ain't a cat. She doesn't belong to you."

"No, she doesn't. But she belongs *with* us." Again, Katie wished JJ was there, but for a totally different reason. What would he do? Would he run for it?

Witherspoon shook his head, looking confused and apologetic. "He's right. You can't—I'm sorry but, you can't keep her. Not when there is a willing family member."

Katie glanced over her shoulder, found Parker's eyes, and tilted her head toward the exit. Hopefully. he understood. "She's already been with me for four days, and she's fine," she said.

No, JJ wouldn't run.

The deputy shook his head again. "Her mother—"

"Her mother doesn't know this man," Katie interrupted. "And if she is worth a damn, she'd never send Grace anywhere with him."

The deputy took another step toward them as the second officer put a hand on her gun. "I'm sorry, but it doesn't work like that. She needs to—"

Katie turned as Old Ray rocked, and Parker settled into the driver's seat. *JJ would stay and fight.*

"Go!" she yelled as Witherspoon turned.

Parker tried to shift it into reverse, and the tires spun.

"Hey! Stop. Come back here!" Witherspoon shouted, running toward them.

Katie sprinted toward Deputy Witherspoon, and for the first time in her life, tackled a man. They fell to the ground in a heap, as Old Ray's tires squealed on the freshly laid asphalt.

It only took a few seconds for the deputy to subdue her, but it was long enough for Parker and Grace to escape. The masked deputy aimed her gun at Katie while Deputy Witherspoon, with a grunt, rolled her onto her chest. The black asphalt burned her chest and shoulders and he dragged her hands behind her back and cuffed her hands together. "That was really stupid," he huffed, dragging her to her feet.

"Not as stupid as letting that man take that little girl," she shot back.

"What are you talking about?" the masked deputy, Green, asked, looking over her shoulder at Grace's uncle, who was pacing the sidewalk, shouting obscenities at her.

"I know men like him."

"What do you mean?"

"Grace was afraid of him." A chill raced down Katie's spine. And she'd almost made her go.

Deputy Witherspoon shook his head. "We have instructions to do a background check on all relatives. His record is clean. He checked out. He's an accountant, for Christ's sake, got a wife and three kids, and a house in the burbs."

The creepiest creeps were always the unsuspecting, unremarkable men. That's how they got away with it. "That just means he's smart and hasn't been caught," Katie snapped.

"Well, you have," Witherspoon glared at her. "And now you've fucked everything up, and neither of us is going anywhere."

Katie frowned. "What?"

"You broke the damn quarantine."

Shit. She'd totally forgotten about that. "What does that mean?" Was she going to have to stay away from everyone for two weeks? It was a dire thought. Where would she even go?

"It means that you are under arrest, and neither of us can go anywhere for forty-eight hours."

Katie frowned. *Forty-eight hours?* That wasn't so bad. "I thought the quarantine was for two weeks?"

"For the general population it is because they haven't been tagged yet, and they don't want people moving around until they are." He held up his arm, revealing his bracelet. "But all of law enforcement and military have already been issued bracelets, so the rules are different for us."

"Well, I have one too, so can't we just—"

"We've been issued very strict guidelines by the CDC and ICPH, and I'm not putting my family at risk because of your stupidity. That virus is no fucking joke."

Katie sighed. "So if we are clear in 48 hours?"

"Then we don't have it and we're free to go home." Deputy Witherspoon pushed her. "Now move it."

Deputy Green put a hand on Katie's arm as she walked by. "How do you know…?" she nodded toward Grace's uncle.

"I don't. But I have a feeling that I've learned to trust. Grace has it too, and she didn't want to go," Katie said, as Deputy Witherspoon shoved her again toward the entrance to the building.

"Do I go after them? The kids?" Deputy Green called.

Deputy Witherspoon looked at Katie and then at Grace's uncle.

"Please," she begged. "Let them go."

He sighed. "No," he said, as his eyes remained locked on Katie's. "Tell Mr. Carson to go home. We'll be in touch… *if* we find them."

Katie sighed in relief. "Thank you."

He pointed a finger at her. "Shut up."

Fair enough. "Do I get a phone call?" She'd never been to jail before and wasn't sure if that was a real thing or something fabricated by television.

Officer Witherspoon huffed a laugh. "Sure, why not? What's the number?"

She didn't know, but she was pretty sure he did. "Do you know the bar in Hartford Creek?"

His brows came together. "Barb's?"

Katie refrained from rolling her eyes. "Yeah." Of course he did. And that was good, because she had to let them know she wouldn't be back tonight, and to warn them about Grace's uncle.

If her instincts were good—and they usually were—he was nothing but trouble.

Chapter Twelve

Day 5 // 2:15 a.m.

THE FIRST THING JJ noticed on arriving home was that the sprinkler was off. Had Katie given up on the lawn already? Not that he blamed her. He turned the key in the lock, but oddly, the door didn't open.

He juggled the handle. "What the hell?" Then shoved his shoulder into the door, but it wouldn't budge. He turned to Sam. "Something is blocking it."

"Blocking it?" Sam tried the handle. "Like what?"

"I don't know. Come on. Let's try the back."

JJ led the way around the side of the house to the kitchen door. The lock turned, and it opened. He and Sam crept through the kitchen to the living room.

Through the darkness, he saw the dining chair propped under the knob of the front door.

"What the hell?" JJ said, as they exchanged perplexed glances. He looked over the back of the recliner. Parker was there, asleep. "Parker is here," he said in a hushed voice as Sam went down the hall.

He paused in front of the girl's room. "The girls are in here, too."

JJ shrugged. "Okay." Katie must have been feeling extra cautious.

His stomach growled. They hadn't eaten all day, and he was starving. "Come on." He nodded toward the kitchen. "Let's eat."

He went to the table, but to his surprise, there was no note from Katie. Not that he expected her to leave him a note every night, but... He turned, listening to the quiet house. Something wasn't right. The refrigerator light blinded him as he pulled it open. No sandwich. "What's the matter?" Sam asked.

JJ shut the door, his worry returning. "I don't know. I'll be right back."

He went down the hall, saw Jinn and the two girls asleep in the guest room, then went to his room and pushed the door open. His bed was empty. "Shit." *Where is Katie?* Had she ditched him, left him with all the kids?

JJ turned back toward the guest room. "Jinn?"

It was Parker who answered from the living room. "Shh. Don't wake the girls—"

"Where is Katie?" he said, making his way back through the dark.

"I don't know. In jail...I think," Parker answered in a loud whisper.

JJ stopped. "*What?*"

"Shh. It's a long—"

"Damn it." JJ pinched the bridge of his nose. "I knew something like this would happen. What did she—"

"Don't talk about her like that." The edge in Parker's voice made him stop.

"Like what?"

"She saved Grace."

JJ was either too tired or too stupid to understand. "Saved her from what? Where is she now?"

"From her shady-ass uncle. We had to make a run for it, because the cops were going to make her go with him. I left her at the sheriff's office—I brought Grace back here and we barricaded the door... Katie told us to wait for you."

JJ pulled the chair away from the door. "Fuck. Alright, I'll be —what was the matter with her uncle?"

"I don't know. It was just...vibes. Grace seemed scared of him, and then Katie just... changed her mind."

JJ stared at Parker through the dim light, remembering what Katie said about being able to tell the good guys from the bad ones. "Fuck." He knew exactly what had happened. He met Sam's eyes. "You're in charge until I get back."

Sam nodded. He turned to Parker. "You did good."

"So did Katie." Parker said.

JJ huffed and went to leave. If by good he meant getting herself locked out of their quarantine group, then yeah, she did great.

"I don't know what your problem is, but you need to quit treating her like shit. She's not the enemy," Parker said.

JJ shook his head. "I didn't mean—"

Parker grabbed his arm. "I mean it. Fucking lay off. She's a good person. Better than you'll ever be."

JJ wasn't sure which surprised him more, that Parker could actually speak in complete sentences, or that he was defending Katie. "Get your hands off me. And I don't think she's the enemy." He pulled the door open. "What did she do that made you such a fan, anyway?"

Parker met his eyes. "She *listened* to Grace. What has she done that made you *not* one?"

———

JJ WENT over to the bar and banged on the back door, which led upstairs to Barb's apartment. A moment later, the lock turned, and the door opened. "Katie's been—" he began.

She held up her hand, then tied her bathrobe around her waist and ushered him inside. "I know. I talked to Easton and her. Come on. You just getting back? I got a half a club sandwich in the fridge."

"I don't want to eat—"

She flipped on the lights over the bar top and ushered him into his seat at the end. "There's nothing you can do for the next couple of days. She's in quarantine lockup."

"Quarantine?"

Barb shrugged. "She assaulted an officer, and neither was properly protected. According to Easton, the ICP-whatever has fifty pages of procedures for law enforcement that must be followed to the letter, since they're movin' around so much." She disappeared into the kitchen, but continued their conversation, shouting through the open door. "One of which is, if they come in contact with another person, they gotta be held together for forty-eight-hours."

"Why together? Why forty-eight-hours?"

Barb reemerged and set the sandwich in front of him. She shrugged again. "You'd have to ask Easton about that. You want some coffee?"

JJ shook his head, pulling his cap off and raking his hands through his hair.

"How you holding up?" Barb asked, sounding like his mom. It made him miss her even more than he already did.

"The truth?"

"Why not?"

"I still can't believe it's happening."

Barb laughed.

"I spent all day sifting through crumpled metal and unearthing dead bodies. I'm a fucking tow-truck driver. How did my life come to this? And now, I'm supposed to believe that there's some virus that is going to kill..." He shook his head. "It's insane." He slammed his fists on the bar. "It's got to be a dream. None of this... is possible. Is it?"

Barb patted his hand. "Hell if I know. You get through to your ma, or Sierra?"

JJ sighed. "Yeah, for a bit. They're fine."

"Good. I saw on the news that the government has taken over

cell phone coverage and is trying to get everything back up ASAP. And Michelle got a call from her granddaughter last night. She's in L.A."

"Yeah. I think everything is working, just overloaded."

"Eat your sandwich and then get yourself to bed. You won't be good to no one if you fall asleep behind the wheel."

"So you think Katie is alright?"

"She's at the sheriff's office. She'll be okay. But…"

"But what?"

"When she called, she asked me to relay a message to you."

"Which was what?"

"Don't let Grace's uncle take her."

"You think he would have hurt her?"

Barb shook her head. "I dunno. Katie seemed to think so, though. And she seemed pretty sure. She said Grace was scared of him."

JJ swallowed the last of his sandwich around the lump in his throat. "I'm not ready for any of this, Barb."

"None of us are. But it's like they say in AA, *'God grant me the serenity to accept the things I cannot change, and the courage to change the things I can.'*"

"You went to AA?"

Barb smiled. "For twenty-five years."

JJ's brow went up. "Really? But you drink. I've seen…"

"People change, JJ. I'm not the same person I was forty years ago." She laughed, "Thank god too, because I was a bitch. You can ask your mother."

JJ's smile faded. "What can I change Barb? What can I possibly do to…fix any of this? The whole world is on fire."

"You can start by protecting that little girl from her uncle."

"And then what?"

"One thing at a time, Jensen."

"What about my mom? Sierra?"

Barb came around the bar and put a bony hand on his cheek.

"There is nothing you can do for them, honey. Not to protect them from the virus, anyway." Tears filled JJ's eyes as she went on. "And in your heart you know that."

He did know it, but he couldn't *accept* it. The whole virus-Veil thing felt like a shitty movie plot, and in the movies, the good guys *always* found a way out. They always found a way to save the day, because the hero didn't give up, because he was smarter than—he squeezed his eyes shut, wishing he was something more than a stupid truck driver who barely finished high school. "But I—"

"Call them. Tell them you love them."

"What is that going to solve?"

She shrugged. "Maybe they won't get the virus. Maybe...I don't know, they'll find a cure."

"It took over a year with Covid, Barb. These cities won't last two weeks if the virus takes hold."

"Then all we can do is pray."

JJ looked at her, wondering if he'd ever really known her. "You believe in God?"

"No, but like I said, people change. And I can believe whatever I want *when*ever I want. So can you."

JJ shook his head. He knew better than to hope any of this was going to end well. The president himself had said it. The fate of humanity hung in the balance. If the Veil was the best idea anyone had, they were all fucked.

"Get some sleep," Barb said, leading him to the back door.

"Hey, Barb." He paused at the door.

"Yeah?"

"Thanks."

Chapter Thirteen

Day 7 // 6:01 p.m.

THE GOOD NEWS was neither Katie nor Deputy Peter Witherspoon showed signs of the virus, not that she thought either of them actually had it. The bad news was there was nothing to do but watch the news, and she'd been doing it for two days straight. It was terrifying, as was the idea of the kids being at JJ's without either of them there. Jinn assured her she and Parker could handle Amelia and Grace, but after talking to JJ who had shown up first thing the following morning to see her, he had insisted that Sam stay back too, just in case Grace's uncle somehow found out where she was.

Easton was making a nuisance of himself, but hadn't attempted anything like he had at the bar, probably because Peter was sitting ten feet away. So, all there was for Katie to do was sit in the uncomfortable chairs they'd dragged into the conference room where they were camped out, and watch TV.

According to the news reports, things in New York were beyond hope, and she couldn't help but agree as she stared at the bodies being dumped into garbage trucks and then vaporized in the Veil. At first the networks had tried to avoid showing the devastation, the bodies of the children, the horror, but now there was no way to even show a video of Manhattan or Brooklyn or Queens without seeing it piled on every curb. Over and over it reminded Katie that if it hadn't been for Old Ray, she'd be there now, dying too. It was a sobering thought that both haunted and relieved her at the same time.

"Dinner." Deputy Green announced, swinging the door open. She had been issued a special quarantine mask that covered her entire face, and she smiled through it as she dropped two bags on the table. Katie sat up and opened her mouth as the deputy inserted the thermometer. "Any symptoms?" she asked.

Katie shook her head. Peter sat up next, and she asked him the same question as she slid a new sleeve on the thermometer and put it in his mouth.

"Good. You have another thirty minutes and then you are both free to go."

Katie opened the bag. Ham sandwiches and Coke. Two things she hadn't had in years until two days ago.

Guiltily, she opened the bag of potato chips and took a bite of the soft bread smothered in mayo. She had nothing to starve herself for now. It was divine. The news segment switched to local news.

"The scene in Scarborough as firefighters battled a devastating apartment fire that broke out earlier this morning. According to reports there were no survivors, and local police have issued warnings to all of those within the Veil to be on the lookout for suspicious behavior, stating that in the aftermath of the wildfires that ripped through the nearby cities earlier in the week, the cases of arson have gone up and astonishing thirty percent, and reported thefts, primarily of local businesses, is up twenty..."

Katie shook her head. Why did people have to be like that? As if things weren't bad enough. The news anchor went on.

"...while the list of missing persons continues to grow, with over seventeen thousand unaccounted for men, women and children."

Katie shook her head again. If the internet was working, this could never have happened. But with it down, and the phones being so spotty... She took another bite of her sandwich. Now anything could happen and no one would ever know. If it wasn't for the local news… they'd all be blind, lost to what was happening in the world. It was a helpless and terrifying thought.

"City officials urge citizens both inside and outside the Veil to remain at home, and follow the quarantine. In a statement made to Channel 4 News by Police Chief Sandra Polanski, she acknowledged the uptick in violence, saying quote 'We are aware of the situation, and doing our best to mitigate the situation.' However, she went on to remind frightened citizens that although there has been more violence, what there have not been are any cases of the virus. "The quarantine is working, and we'd like to keep it that way. And the best way to do that and keep your families safe is to stay home."

JJ was picking her up on his way back from Atlanta, but she didn't know how long it would be until his shift ended. Once she was out of here, it was back to veggies and water, but for now… Katie slumped in her seat, propping her knees up on the edge of the table, and grabbing a handful of chips before setting her bag on her stomach.

"And now we go to our Network affiliate in New York where the horror of the deadly X-Virus continues to unfold…"

"I'll be glad to get home," Pete said, unwrapping his sandwich. "This whole thing is…" He ended the sentence the way most people seemed to lately, with a shake of his head.

She leaned forward and grabbed the soda off the table. Popping the tab on her Coke, she took a cold sugary sip. It tingled as it slid down her throat, sending a shiver down her spine. Katie looked up at the TV and her smile faded, and guilt stabbed at her heart. People were dying, and she was sitting there, enjoying a Coca-Cola. The view of the trucks and the suited workers hauling bodies was devastating.

"As the chaos in the streets continues to accelerate, sources within the NYPD have confirmed that they no longer have the manpower to—" The news anchor vanished in a flash of white, that shook the camera before it turned to static. Katie stared at

the ticker still scrolling across the bottom, declaring 'New York overrun with angry mobs, deaths exceed four million.'

Another anchor appeared, smiling apologetically. *"We seem to be experiencing technical—"* Gasping, he pressed his fingers to his ear as the color drained from his tanned face. *"What?"* he cried, swinging his head around and looking off camera.

The screen blinked twice as the feed switched back to static, then became more of a billowing cloud rather than fuzzy lines. *"Oh-Oh…Oh…god. Oh, god,"* the news anchor repeated over and over as fear pricked at Katie's skin and she sat up. "Wh-what's happening? What are we looking at?"

Pete just stared open-mouthed at the TV.

Katie jumped up, spilling her chips on the floor. She ran around the table to the TV and stupidly wiped at it with her fingers, as if she could clear away the smoke, because that was what it was. Smoke.

"I-I…I…Oh my god. What just…Wh-what just…" The news anchor fumbled over his words, unable to get them out as it billowed into the sky like a giant gray cauliflower.

"Oh, my god. New York is gone." The last word came out as a choked whisper, like he was being strangled.

Gone? Katie swayed with dizziness, as the headline appeared on the screen **New York rocked by massive explosion.** *Rocked?* What in the hell did that mean? By whom? She turned in the direction that Atlanta lay. Was it just New York? Or had all the Veiled cities… "JJ," she whispered, falling against the table. Was he… The cloud of ash on the screen continued to billow, obstructing any view of the city. If Atlanta had exploded too…"He's too close." He wouldn't survive. She ran to the door, pounding on it. "JJ!"

She knew he wasn't at the station, but there was so much adrenaline in her veins she couldn't remember the deputy's name. All she could think or see in her mind was him beside the Veil, and Atlanta disappearing in a cloud of— "JJ!" she screamed, beating her hands against the door. She could not do this without him. "Let me out of here! J—"

The door swung open, and Easton was there, looking annoyed behind his mask. "What the hell—"

She rushed past him.

"Hey! You can't—"

Like hell she couldn't. "JJ!" She rounded the corner of the hall, ready to run all the way back to Atlanta if she had to, when she collided with someone. Falling backward onto her butt, she quickly reached for the hand, offering to pull her back to her feet. "Sorry about that," Mike began.

"Mike?" Her eyes flew up, then over his shoulder. JJ stood behind him, staring.

A sob burst from her throat as she ran to him and threw her arms around his neck.

He grunted. "What the—"

"Oh god. I thought…I th-thought…" She squeezed him, then pulled back and cupped his surprised face in her hands as every emotion in her head unraveled around her like a ball of yarn. "You're okay, right?"

"Yeah," he said slowly, trying to extract himself from her embrace.

Squeezing her eyes shut, she pressed her forehead to his, her relief so fierce it stole her balance

She swayed and he caught her around the waist. "Hey, what's—"

She shook her head, crying and laughing at the same time. "Oh, thank god."

"Katie?" He steadied her again as her knees wobbled.

She pressed her palm to his cheek and leaned closer, squeezing her eyes shut again. *He's not dead.* His beard tickled her cheek, and his breath, stuttering across her lips, sent a jolt of lightning through her to all the right places as her heart took off again in her chest and she quickly became aware that she wasn't either.

"Katie?" His voice was hoarse as he gently pushed her back. "Are you okay?"

She blinked as he stared at her. "Yes." She laugh-sobbed again, pulling him back in for a hug, knowing she should let him go, but not wanting to. The ten seconds she'd thought he might be dead and facing whatever lay ahead without him was enough to confirm the suspicion that had been brewing in her heart over the last few days. She cared about him. *A lot.*

Her knees buckled again, and suddenly she couldn't breathe. Stumbling back, she clutched at her throat with shaking hands, trying to inhale, but the air refused to fill her lungs. She doubled over, gasping, her insides feeling like they'd been turned into a shivering liquid.

JJ pulled her back into his arms. "Okay. Okay. Just breathe. I've got you. Just breathe." He rubbed his rough hand across her shoulders in a circle until she remembered how to inhale again. "You're okay," he said, which felt debatable just then.

She buried her head against his chest, and his heart pounded wildly against her forehead. He smelled like motor oil and sweat, and she'd never smelled anything sweeter. Her lips curled up in a smile, but then she remembered the reason for her fear, and it fell.

Her head flew up. Were all the cities gone now? L.A. Paris? London? Or was it just New York? She glanced over JJ's shoulder out the door, toward Atlanta. What about JJ's mom and his sister, and the kid's parents? Were they gone too? Would they have heard the blast from there?

"It's gone." She mumbled against his shirt. "It's—"

"What's gone?"

"New York. It's gone. All those people—" It finally sunk in, hitting her all at once. Orlando was gone, the auto auction house was gone, everyone she knew in Manhattan and Brooklyn were gone, vanished off the face of the earth, and if it wouldn't have been for a faulty thermostat, she would be too.

JJ's hand stilled against her back. "What do you mean, gone?"

"I don't know. It exploded or—I thought Atlanta..." She shook her head. "I thought you—"

JJ pushed her back, his eyes darting between hers. "What do you mean, *gone?*" he demanded.

Katie shook her head. She didn't know "I don't—It just happened. It's on the TV," she pointed down the hall.

JJ practically dragged her down past Easton, who was sitting on the desk, on some kind of short-wave radio or something, and pushed Deputy Green and Mike aside as the news anchor, who had finally regained his composure, continued to speak. *"...no official statement has been made, but eyewitness reports... There appears to have been a massive explosion originating near Central Park that has leveled all of Manhattan, Newark, and half of Long Island..."*

"Oh, no," JJ said beside her, finally understanding her worry and wondering the same thing she had. "Did they say anything about Atlanta?"

Peter shook his head. "No."

He spun around toward Easton. "Atlanta?" he shouted.

Easton clicked the button on his radio and shook his head. "No. Thank god. Not yet, anyway."

"I've got to go," JJ said, spinning around. Katie was about to grab his arm, but Mike got to him first.

"No, Jay," the old man said.

"I have to."

Mike held his arm. "We spent the last week down there. You know there's nothin' you can do for your mom or Sierra. You can't get through it. No one can."

JJ ripped his hat off his head and threw it at the wall. "Well, I have to try! I have to do something. Damn it."

Katie picked up his hat. "Call your mom. Right–right now, JJ. Maybe the lines aren't jammed yet…"

He met her eyes, and they were wild, like on the first day she met him, full of grief and sorrow, and again her relief that he was alive and okay threatened to draw her under. She had been in some awful situations before and never fainted, so why she felt so near to passing out when everything was actually alright was a mystery. Maybe it was because her past nightmares, while terrible, were short-lived and there was no risk of anyone dying while this one had dragged on for days and was threatening to kill everyone.

Katie looked around the room, at the stunned, pale faces staring at the TV, which continued to show nothing but gray, smokey clouds. The stress was taking its toll on all of them. And if New York was any indication, things were about to get a *lot* worse.

"Mom?" JJ's voice brought her back to the present. "Oh, thank god."

He stepped away from the group, whispering quietly into his phone as he headed down the hall toward the front doors.

"Dear lord…" Mike gasped.

Katie turned. The smoke was finally clearing, and where the infamous Manhattan skyline once stood, there was nothing but a giant hole, rapidly filling with water. Katie watched in horror as a blurry camera zoomed in. A massive wave rushed over Liberty Island. It was only seconds before the Statue herself leaned and crashed into the water. Then the east shore of Jersey city began to crumble and sink, like a scene from a science-fiction movie, disappearing into the waves as they slipped over the edge of the massive sinkhole.

Katie fell against the wall and slid to the ground, burying her head in her hands. She knew she should be frightened, but suddenly all her fear was gone, replaced by a weird numbness, and the sneaking suspicion that she had lost her mind. She looked up at the TV. The headline had changed. It now read **'Unidentified explosion in New York, over 12 million confirmed dead.'** That had to be it, didn't it? She had to be crazy, because this could not happen in the world she lived in. In the world *she* lived in, there were rules, and the Veil, that kind of technology, didn't exist. And no one would ever blow up twelve *million* people, especially the President of the United States. It was ludicrous. It was…

Katie pulled her fingers through her hair. It made her want to crawl into bed, hide under the covers and never come out.

"Hey."

She lifted her head. JJ's boots were toe-to-toe with her bare feet. She looked up at his outstretched hand and took it. He pulled her to his feet, and she fell against him as he hugged her. All his hostility was gone, all the distance he'd been putting between them from the first day they'd met had vanished. She hugged him back, never having felt safer in her life, as the news anchor continued on. *"The Coast Guard has been deployed, but… As you can clearly see, the chance of finding survivors is…"*

"Turn it off." JJ said against her hair.

She heard the click of the TV switching off. "You get through?"

"Yeah, for a minute."

"Are they okay?"

"Yeah, for now." he swallowed hard. "Scared but okay."

Katie heard Easton's voice behind her and her arms tightened around JJ.

"Atlanta is still there. For now, at least," he said. "The offices inside are reporting quiet streets. Seems most folks are following the quarantine."

Katie pulled back and frowned. "Then why are the numbers climbing?"

JJ looked at her. "What do you mean?"

"I just saw the report on CNN. The numbers in Atlanta are skyrocketing. They're saying people are ignoring the quarantine."

JJ shook his head. "No. That's not true. I haven't seen a single person on the inside that wasn't masked and my mom says the streets are empty."

"Yeah, those are the reports we're getting too," Easton confirmed.

Katie looked between Easton and JJ. "But that doesn't make any sense. How can that be? Is it spreading some other way?"

JJ sighed, taking her hand. "I don't know. Come on. Let's get you home."

Easton snorted at that. "Are you playing house again, Jay? How cute." JJ's grip tightened around Katie's fingers, as Easton, being the idiot he was, went on. "Have you forgotten what happened last time—"

JJ spun around, and the fire in his eyes would have burned Katie to the ground, but Easton just laughed.

"Please don't," she begged, tugging on his arm

JJ stared at Easton for a moment, then glared at her, sending lightning down her spine. Then his angry brown eyes flicked back to the sheriff. "Fuck off, Easton," he said, pulling Katie away and heading for the doors. She heard the clunk of Mike's boots as he following them.

"Hope you enjoyed your stay, Ms. Newman." Easton called after them. "See you soon."

JJ's grip on her hand tightened again as they headed out into the east-Georgia sunset.

Chapter Fourteen

Day 7 // 10:01 p.m.

"YOU CAN'T GO BACK to the city. It isn't safe." Katie said, lying down, pulling the covers over her.

JJ sat on his side of the bed. He would sleep on top of them. Just in case. *Just in case what?* The hell if he knew. But something had happened tonight. He could feel it. Sometime between when Katie had thrown her arms around him in the hall and when his mom said "You really care about her," and he didn't ask who she was talking about or argue, something inside him had shifted. It was like—*like what?* He didn't know. But whatever it was, he'd never felt anything like it before. And the way her hands shook as she inspected his face. He'd never had anyone look at him the way she had, with such utter relief, like he was the most important person in her world. Well, maybe his mom, but thank god, she didn't make him feel like he was going to have a coronary when she touched him.

"You can't go back," Katie repeated.

He sighed. "I have to. I have a federal issued order."

"I don't care!" There it was, that tone in her voice again, like she was genuinely worried about him. It tugged at his heartstrings. And scared the absolute shit out of him.

"And I have to find a way to help my mom and Sierra." Because his dad wasn't here to do it, and JJ had promised him when he was ten that he'd look after his mom and baby sister if anything should happen to him.

"There's nothing you can do. Mike knows it. I know it. Everybody but you—"

"I have to help them!" Damn it. Why didn't anyone understand that? It wasn't a choice. He couldn't give up on his own mother and sister. What kind of man would he be? What kind of son and brother?

"Who do you think you are, JJ?"

Heat rushed up his neck at those words, replacing the warm fuzzies, or whatever the fuck he'd felt before. "Oh, I see. You think because I'm a stupid tow truck driver, I can't do anything, is that it?"

She sat up and met his eyes. "What? No. I think you can't help them because you can't."

"I may not have gone to college or have a business degree or whatever the fuck the guys you normally share a bed with have, but I am not an idiot." *Debatable at the moment,* his inner voice whispered.

Katie squeezed her eyes shut in what looked like an attempt to ward off a string of expletives and sighed. "I'm not insulting your intelligence. I just mean, whoever made the Veil *knew* people would try to bring it down. New York is proof. You heard what they said on the news. The people tried to take it down, that's why it…erupted. You get anywhere near the Veil and best-case scenario, you kill yourself, worst case, you'll wipe out the whole damn city. I don't want either of those things to happen."

A part of him knew she was right, and just worried. It gave another part of him the warm fuzzies again, which made the rest of him want to pick a fight with her so he'd have a reason to yell and hate her instead of liking her, like he wanted to. Shoving his feet back into his boots, he stood up.

"Where are you going?" she asked, jumping up and following him down the hall.

"Anywhere you are not," he whispered, before storming out of the house.

It was only twenty steps to the door of his childhood home. Feeling along the top of the window, he found the spare key and let himself in.

The house was dark, but he made out his mom's sweater thrown over the back of the couch and picked it up. Pressing it to his nose, he inhaled. It smelled like her, a mix of cheap laundry detergent and the same Estee Lauder perfume she had worn his whole life. His dad had bought it for her on their second anniversary, and in forty years, she'd never worn anything else.

JJ dropped on the couch and stared at her crossword book, opened and flipped over to save her page, waiting for her to return.

"Jesus, mom." He shook his head before burying his head in his hands.

The grandfather clock in the hall chimed, reminding him of when his family was intact and mean old Mr. Fogarty was the one who lived in the house next door. Glancing at his watch, he sighed. It was midnight, and he was supposed to be back at the Veil by seven.

Chapter Fifteen

Day 9 // 9:01 a.m.

JJ PUSHED THE LEVER, and the chain moved. A moment later, the screech of metal against pavement pierced the quiet morning as the cargo van they were dragging slid toward his truck.

"Keep 'er steady," Mike called.

JJ nodded. They'd been at it for days, but the wrecks continued to devastate him.

"Ho! Wait!" Mike cried in a half-strangled voice. JJ winced, and stopped the chains, as the smell hit him. "Where is it?" he asked, walking toward Mike.

They had stopped looking for survivors days ago.

Mike pointed. "There. In that gray Civic…"

Now they were recovering bodies. JJ spotted the bloated remains behind the windshield, unable to tell if it was even a man or a woman. At that point, it was neither, he supposed. It was nothing more than a balloon of flesh around a decaying skeleton. At least that was what he tried to tell himself.

"Sam!" he called.

Sam poked his head out the window of the truck. "We need a recovery team."

"On it," the boy said, ducking back into the cab for the radio.

Sam seemed unphased by the death, but poor old Mike. Every time they found another one, his eyes became a little more haunted. JJ patted him on the back. "We'll get this one loaded and then take a break."

Mike nodded silently as Sam jogged over.

"No one can come out right now. They said just to flag the car and someone will come when they can."

Shaking his head, JJ tried not to think about the family that was wondering where this person was. With a heavy heart, he made a giant X on the front window with the red spray paint he'd been given, then went back to the truck and started up the winch. The grinding wail resumed.

A few minutes later, they pulled away from the pileup. Everyone was silent.

"Come on, let's take a breather." JJ said, about to turn onto the thoroughfare.

About a mile away from the Veil was a park, and he spied a picnic table beneath a stand of tall Georgia pines. Pulling over, he parked, grabbed his cooler, and headed toward it. As he sat down, the phone in his pocket rang, scaring the living hell out of him. The table rocked as he jumped up and fumbled in his pocket for it.

It was his mom. "Mom? Are you alright? Is everything—"

"We're fine, Jay."

Pulling the phone away from his ear, he was surprised to see his signal was strong. He turned to Sam and Mike, pointing at his phone, then giving a thumbs up before walking away.

"How are things? How are you and Sierra?"

His mom huffed a laugh. "It's been... Interesting." JJ heard his sister giggle in the background.

"Interesting?"

"Well, the end of the world brings out a lot of honesty and truthfulness..." Sierra laughed again as his mom continued. "But it's been good. I'm glad to get to know my daughter once again." He could just imagine his mom patting his sister's knee.

"I'm glad. You guys have enough food and stuff?"

"Yes. They've been delivering food. Twice now, I think. And they gave us tracking bracelets."

He looked at the band around his wrist. "We have them out here, too."

"We haven't gone anywhere. Haven't stepped foot out of the house."

"Good. Don't. Stay inside."

"But..."

He didn't like that tone at all. "But what?"

"I don't want to worry you."

"Too late."

"I just feel you should know. We saw a woman yesterday. She was walking down the street, and then she just... she started screaming all kinds of crazy things and then...she fell, and just lay there on the ground, convulsing. I've never seen anything like it." His mom's voice trailed off. "They came and got her. I think she was already dead by then but... It is here, Jay."

"I know." Pressing his fingers into his eyes, he rubbed them.

She continued. "I keep thinking there has to be a way out of this. That there has to—But whatever this is, the president is right. It cannot get out. If it hasn't already."

"But—"

"Your sister and I agree, Jay, based on the little we've seen. It was the right thing to do if it works."

"And if it doesn't?"

"So far, so good, right? Everyone in here has been following the quarantine, as far as we can tell."

"Yeah, but then why are the numbers still climbing?"

"Enough about us, honey. How are you?"

"Fine."

"Are you and Kate still together?"

JJ's brows came together. "We are not together."

"Hold on. I'm putting you on speakerphone. Your sister wants to hear this."

"Jesus, mom." He rolled his eyes.

"So, spill it." His sister's voice came through the speaker. "Have you slept with her yet? How was it?"

JJ blushed despite being alone. "What the hell, Sei?"

"What? We are all adults here. Besides, except for the virus, it's all mom, and I have talked about for days."

Ignoring his sister's question, he said, "She is fine, the kids... we've got three left, not counting Sam and Jinn, they are all fine."

"And what about you?" his mom asked.

He was barely holding it together. "I'm fine."

"No, you're not."

JJ sighed. She'd always been a bit of a mind reader. "Yes, I —"

"Have you forgotten who I am? You came from my *loins*."

He pressed his fingers to his forehead. The *very* last thing he wanted just then was to think about his mother's loins.

She went on. "I *know* everything."

Well, that was true, he thought, remembering all the times when he was a boy and got caught doing something he shouldn't, like sneaking ice cream in the middle of the night, or playing in the creek when he wasn't supposed to. He'd lie, and his mom would stand there with her hands on her hips and say, *'Don't lie to me, Jensen James. I am your mother. I know everything.'*

He sighed. "Fine."

"What is the matter, honey?"

It was nothing. At least that's what he kept telling himself, but there had always been something about his mom that forced the truth out of him. "I don't know," he said, opening a can of worms he shouldn't.

Glancing over his shoulder, he looked to make sure Sam and Mike were far enough away to not hear him.

"What don't you know, sweetie?"

Sweetie? JJ huffed a laugh, swiping at his beard. He was a thirty-five-year-old man, for crying out loud.

Before he could answer, his mom sent Sierra away to go make tea. "It's just us now," she said a moment later. "Spill it."

Two squirrels chased each other around a tree as he shook his head. "There's nothing to spill." That was true. At least for the moment. But...

"There's plenty," she said. "Starting with, you like her."

He laughed, damn she saw right through him. It was comforting to know she loved him, anyway. "Yeah, me and every other guy with eyes."

"I don't care about every other guy, I only care about you. And...?"

"Never—"

"Jensen James." Her tone made him wince. "Don't you dare never mind me. Is this about your *'rules'*?"

Rule. Singular. "Sort of."

"Rules are made to be broken."

That was a little ironic coming from the queen of grounding when he and Sierra were kids. "Actually, no, they are not. They are made to be kept."

"Not stupid ones."

Wow. "I'm not her type, ma. I'm not the kind of guy she's used to."

"So what?"

"So..." So, he was wasting his time. Wasn't he? But he couldn't get the words out.

"Is this about her or you?"

"I don't know. Me, I guess. You know how I am, how I get."

She sighed. "You're right. You're not like the other guys. Because you're *better*. I bet you are the best she's ever met. She knows it too, which is why she's stuck around."

"She has nowhere else to go."

"If you believe that, you're dumber than you look. If that girl didn't want to be with *you*, she'd have been long gone by now."

Leave it to his mom to make him feel better. "Thanks mom."

"I'm serious, Jay. Do not get stuck in that head of yours."

Too late, he thought as she went on. "You are just like your father, and men like you two make the best partners, *if* you can learn to control all those big feelings you have." There was a pause. "I know they all hit you the same, but you have to learn how to…weed out the good from the bad and focus on those."

"And how do I do that?"

"I don't know. But I suggest you figure it out fast."

"Gee, thanks—"

"And you can start by *not* assuming you know what that girl wants or is thinking. I taught you better than that."

Yes, she had. How many times had he stared at the ceiling in the kitchen while she waved a wooden spoon covered in spaghetti sauce around and gone on about stupid, misogynistic men? "I know, but—"

"No buts. I saw a difference in you the minute she walked into your life. The way you couldn't stop talking about her."

Talking was a nice way of putting what he'd done, which was storm into his mom's kitchen and go on a thirty-minute rant about how absurd and entitled Katie was. Only she wasn't. She *looked* the part, but she'd never acted that way toward him. Not on that first day, certainly not on any day since.

"Trust your instincts. Give her a chance."

"My instincts? Yeah, I think we can both agree—"

"You have good instincts. You just made *one* mistake. One. That's it. And you got hurt, and now you're scared. But you've got to push past it."

He sighed. She was right about one thing. The thought of making a move on Katie, or letting her know how he felt, made him so nervous he could piss himself. He shook his head. "Who the hell cares anyway with all this shit going on?"

"I care. You need to live again, Jay. Take a few chances. Otherwise, what's the point of *any* of this? Of trying to save humanity at all? Talk to her."

"I-I want to." His brow went up at his unexpected confession, as he removed his ball cap and ran his hands through his hair. "But I'm afraid I'll...mess it up."

"You probably will, but that's what apologies are for."

"Gee, thanks again—"

"Your father was a train wreck when we met. Brawling and hot tempered, because he took and felt everything ten times harder than everyone else did. But *I* hung in there, because I knew—"

"Katie is nothing like you, mom."

"Good. Because that would be weird." Her voice softened. "But you are just like him, Jay. And he turned into the most loving man I've ever known."

"I-I don't think—"

"You are the kind of man that would go to war and die for the people he cares about," she said. "But you are also the kind of man who is afraid to do anything with his feelings but pick fights, because you got burned once. And being that way won't get you what you want."

"I don't know what I want."

"Yes, you do. Deep down you do. I know you like her. And now I know just how much, otherwise we wouldn't be having this conversation. You think she could be..." She let the sentence hang, but he knew her well enough to know what she hadn't said. *The one.*

He shook his head. "No, I don't."

His mom's voice and the one inside his head answered in unison. "Yes, you do."

"But—" They hardly even knew each other. If anything, it was too soon to tell.

"She's not Erica."

He sighed. "I know, Ma."

"Do you? Because I'm not so sure."

"It's complicated." He knew that she wasn't Erica, but he felt the same as when they first started dating, like he'd met a girl that was a little too amazing, like he'd awakened in a dream that felt just a little too good to be true.

"It's not, sweetie." He could hear her smile in her voice. "You just tell her how you feel."

"I feel confused. I feel like I don't want to like her. I feel like I have rules for a reason and if I break them, then..."

"Tell her that, Jay. See what she says."

"She'll think I'm crazy."

"I'm pretty sure she already does with the way you've been acting."

It was true. He was his own worst enemy. He hadn't realized his dad had been the same way. By the time he was born, his dad was... everything JJ wasn't now. But it had taken his mom... He shook his head. "I don't want to talk about this anymore."

"Fine. But for the record. I like her," she said, making him laugh,

"You've never met her."

"I looked her up on the internet."

JJ called her bluff. "The internet doesn't exist anymore."

"Before all this, when you wouldn't shut up about her." She paused. "Well, actually I had your sister do it, because you know how I am with these things."

Yes, he did. She couldn't log onto her online banking without his help. "Great. So, you guys *stalked* her?"

"No, we *'followed'* her. Well, again, Sierra did."

JJ sighed. "Then you saw all the fancy clothes and rich men?"

"I saw a woman who was searching for happiness in all the wrong places."

"She looked pretty happy to..." His voice trailed off. *Shit.* He'd just confessed that he'd been stalking her, too.

If his mom caught his admission, she didn't act like it. "I feel sorry for her," she said.

"*What? Why?*"

"Call it a mother's intuition. I think you're just what she needs." She paused again. "And I think she knows it, too."

He laughed. "What exactly do you think she needs? An overweight truck driver who lives next door to his mom?"

"First of all, you're not overweight, you're husky," she said, sounding offended.

"No, that's a breed of dog—"

"Second. There is nothing wrong with living next door to your mother."

"I know. I just meant—"

"You are a handsome, kind, caring, thoughtful man who is interested in more than just getting in her pants."

JJ pressed his palm to his forehead before dragging it across his face. "Jesus, mom." There was nothing more awkward—the image of Amelia propped on the toilet popped into his head. Scratch that. There were, but discussing his sex life with his mom was still pretty high up there on the list, and he wasn't in the mood. "I'm not discussing my personal life—"

"Good. Because I don't want to hear it." She paused. "Just talk to her, Jay."

"But—"

"Promise me."

"I—"

"Promise me."

He groaned. It was impossible to say no to her when she got like that. "Fine."

"That's my boy. I just want you to be happy."

"I—"

"You still have my ring, right?"

He'd forgotten about that. It was in the top drawer of his dresser. "Yes, it's—"

"Good. keep it safe. I'm glad we had this conversation. I love you, sweetie."

He sighed. *Conversation?* Did it even count as one if she was the only one talking?

Sam shouted. "We gotta go!"

He turned and nodded. "Listen, I gotta go. I love you too. Don't go outside."

"We won't."

"Wait!" He thought of something. "Would it be okay if I borrow a pair of your slippers?"

His mom laughed. "Dare I ask why?"

"Ha ha. They're for Katie."

"Of course. Anything you need from the house, just take it."

"All I need is a pair of slippers."

"I love you Jay."

"I love you too, mom."

Chapter Sixteen

Day 9 // 9:58 a.m.

MR. GOEBELL SHUFFLED to the back door of the grocery, in his faded plaid shirt and threadbare suspenders, and pulled an enormous set of keys from his pocket of his worn-out jeans and fitted one into the lock. The store was nestled between the bar, which it shared a wall with and an alleyway that separated it from Dave's Gas-n-Go.

With a twist, he pushed open the door and waved her inside the small office in the back, with a Parkinson's riddled hand.

The scent of rotting produce hit her nose as she waited for him to flip the light switch. That wasn't a good sign.

The lights went on and he waved at her again, before scratching his nearly bald head. "Come on in. Let me show you what we've got."

Passing through another door, they entered the store, which was small, but surprisingly complete, and the rotten smell grew stronger.

The back wall nearest the office and the lot out back held the dairy items. The one to her left on the gas station side held all the produce, and the meat counter and register were at the front. There were two rows of pantry items in the middle of the store, and the fourth wall that he shared with Barb held everything else, from cough medicine to toilet paper.

Shaking her head, she eyed the cheese and milk as she rounded the corner. Unfortunately, there wasn't much she could do with those.

"This is what we got left. I been tossin' stuff out daily, or feeding it to Michele's chickens, figuring we'll be eating them soon enough. But, I ain't no cook, and since the missus passed... Well, I'm afraid I won't be much help."

"You've already been a help. You *are* helping, donating all this food to the town."

He scratched the back of his head, looking just like his cousin, Mike. "Yeah, well, what would I do with it all, anyways?"

"Do you know what time Mike and JJ left this morning?" she asked.

Mr. Goebell shook his head. "Early, though. I heard the truck take off."

She looked down at her t-shirt and then at her feet. She hadn't seen JJ this morning, but he'd left her some clothes and a pair of house slippers on the dresser that were much more comfortable than the sneakers she'd been wearing. After a week of misery, maybe her foot would finally heal.

They headed up front to the meat. It was in a small case, but even so, there was too much. If she cooked all day for two weeks, maybe she'd be able to get through it all, but...even if they temporarily froze what they could—picking up a package of chicken breast, she checked the expiration. Tomorrow—half of this would go to waste.

Katie's instinct had been to freeze everything, but Michelle had vetoed that idea, when she, Barb and Katie had sat together at the bar, trying to come up with a plan for the food after Mr. Goebell had agreed to share it. "We don't have near enough freezers, and as soon as the power goes, we'll be in the same boat, anyway, "Barb had said.

"Then what do we do?"

"We can it all. Or as much as we can, anyway." Michelle had replied, like it was the natural solution. Like it was something everyone should know how to do. And maybe they did, fifty years ago, when she was Katie's age. "It'll last a couple years then, and if we keep the jars in the cellar, the weather won't bother 'em."

Katie set the chicken breast down and picked up a package of ground beef. But the only thing she knew less about than kids and physics was canning. And meat. She'd been a vegetarian most of her life. Just the sight of plastic wrapped flesh made her nose wrinkle. But she wasn't doing this for herself. She was doing it for the kids, and for the people in town who were so generously taking all of them under their wing.

She stared at the red ropy strands of meat. Could ground beef be canned? And what would she make, anyway? Little jar sized hamburgers and stack them up inside? And what did one season hamburgers with besides salt and pepper? She hadn't eaten one in a decade unless the single bite of a bacon burger she'd consumed for the sake of a photo, to promote a sea-side burger shack in Pismo Beach three years ago counted.

Starting at the left, she counted, giving up when she reached one hundred. Over one hundred cellophane wrapped packages of chicken, beef, pork. Thank god there was no fish.

"Whaddaya think?" Mr. Goebell asked.

She was thinking she had never canned anything in her life. She was thinking she didn't have enough jars or time to save it all, and even if she did, she didn't know how to *cook* without the internet to guide her. But why worry the poor old man? "This is great," she said.

"Mike said it's gettin' worse."

Katie turned. "What?"

"Seems more folks on the inside is catching it."

Had Mr. Goebel heard something she hadn't? "Have you got news about JJ's mom and sister?"

Mr. Goebell's brow went up. "Ain't you seen JJ?"

She blushed. "I-we don't really—he seems to be avoiding me, although I don't know why."

Mr. Goebell laughed.

Katie's forehead wrinkled in a frown, but she wasn't half as worried about those creases as she had been a week ago. "What?" she asked, putting her hands on her hips.

"Nothin." His face turned as red as a beet as he wheezed.

Crossing her arms, Katie scowled. "What's so funny?"

"That boy is scared shitless..." the old man laughed, shaking his head as he backed away. "I guarantee it."

She sighed. "Scared of *what*?"

He eyed her, nodding his head like he'd just figured out one of life's great mysteries. "Of his own demons, I reckon."

"What?" She crossed her arms.

"Don't worry. He'll come around. He just needs a little time."

"To what?"

"To see what the rest of us do."

Katie bit her lip. "Which is what?"

Mr. Goebell blushed. "Well, beggin' your pardon, miss." He hesitated, looking for a second like a young boy as he stared at his feet. "Well, that yer inside is just as...nice as yer outside."

It was Katie's turn to blush.

He met her eyes. "And there ain't no devil hidden in you."

Devil?

He slapped his thighs. "Whelp, I'm headed home," he said before she could ask what he meant. "Lock up when you leave and let yourself in as you will." Then he was gone.

Katie stood alone in the store, staring at the wall of rotting produce. Beets, apples, cauliflower, radishes, peppers...She grimaced at the pile of rotten bananas. "One thing at a time."

Chapter Seventeen

Day 9 // 11:49 p.m.

THE TIMER WENT OFF, and Katie silenced it. Sweat dripped in her eyes and she swiped at it with the towel flung over her shoulder before grabbing the oven mitt and opening the oven. A blast of hot, meaty air stung her face, stabbing at her gag reflex. Carefully, she pulled the pot roast out of the oven. If she never saw another piece of meat, it would be too soon, she thought, setting it on the cooling rack.

Scratching at the rash on the back of her neck, she found her reflection in the blackened kitchen window and frowned. When had it gotten dark out? Turning to the living room, she saw Parker's sleeping form on the couch. She didn't remember putting the kids to bed. What time was it even? Her eyes widened as they found the clock on the wall. 11:50 p.m.? "Really?"

Turning back to the counter, she finally noticed the mess. Every surface was covered. Blanched tomatoes sat waiting for jars, which covered every surface. Some were full, some were empty, some were sealed and cooling. Bowls of cooked meat covered the kitchen table, waiting for the pressure canner that maddeningly only held *four* jars at a time, and took an hour and a half per batch. There were two large pots on the stove filled with boiling water for the tomatoes.

Miss Michelle had dropped the pressure canner off at the bar along with very specific instructions for Katie, which was lucky because if she had gone based on the instructions she found with the two cases of canning jars she'd found at the grocery, she probably would have probably killed them all with botulism. Pressing the heels of her hands into her eyes, she swayed with exhaustion. The timer on her phone went off quietly, and she pulled the four jars in the bath on the stove out and set them in the sink. Then she examined the rows of cooling jars on the counter.

All day she had worked, all *damn* day, sweating and scratching—she itched the red patchy skin on the inside of her arms—for thirty-one jars of tasteless meat, and twenty-three jars of tomatoes. It was heartbreaking. At the rate she was going, even the *cooked* meat would go bad before she could get it in the damn jars. Tears sprang to her eyes and her arms felt like lead as she swiped at them. If she stopped even for a minute to consider how little she'd accomplished, or the very real chances that she was doing it wrong, she'd never get going again.

Wiping her forehead again, she lined up the next batch of jars, poured the last of the peeled mushy tomatoes inside, and put them back into the boiling water.

Absently, she grabbed a jar from the sink, needing to get them out of the way, so she could do the dishes. Pain shot through her fingertips as it clattered back into the sink. "Shit," she hissed, flipping on the faucet and running her fingers under the cool water. "Fucking…*shit.*" The tears came again, and she swiped them away with her other hand, trying to steady her shaking breath. She was just tired. Everyone was. It was okay. She could do this. Just one thing at a time.

———

AN HOUR LATER, she heard JJ's truck. The kitchen was still a mess, but at least all the dishes were done and the meat was in jars, ready to go. Wiping her blistered hands on a towel, she waited for the guys to come in. A minute later, the front door opened.

Despite JJ's distant attitude, a wave of relief washed over her. She was glad he was home.

Sam turned the corner into the kitchen, and his eyes widened in surprise. "Holy shit. What happened—"

She shushed him as Parker shifted on the couch.

"Sorry," he said. "What—"

"Where's JJ?"

Sam shrugged, looking apologetic. "He stayed."

"Stayed?"

"Yeah, they had an extra truck, so he went back out."

Katie's face fell. "Wow. He really hates me that much?"

"It's not about you," Sam said.

Her eyebrow went up.

"Okay. It's not *only* about you. He talked to his mom today. He's just..." Sam pressed his fingers to his temples. "Hell, feeling how we all are. Helpless and...fucked."

Katie pulled a beer out of the fridge. "You want one?"

Sam's brows went up hopefully. "For real?"

She huffed a laugh as the corners of her mouth turned up. After what they'd lived through the past week, and the way he'd stepped up, he was more of a man than most men she knew. "In case you haven't noticed, you're not a kid anymore."

He reached for the beer. "Is it fucked up that I suddenly wish I was?"

She twisted the cap of her bottle. "No, it just means you're smart."

The top popped on his beer, and he tossed it in the trash. He took a long swig, then met her eyes, his full of tears. "Is it fucked up that I-I want to cry because I miss my mom?"

Katie's heart broke as she pulled him into her arms. Hot tears fell down her cheeks as he squeezed her and sobbed quietly against her shoulder. She pressed her hand to the back of his head comfortingly. "No. It's..." It was happening to all the kids, the same way. One minute they seemed okay, and the next they were inconsolable. Every time it happened, she didn't know what to say. It's okay? It will be alright? No, it probably wouldn't. And saying anything else was a lie. JJ was right. They didn't need to be lied to right now.

"Have you been able to get through to her?" she asked, pulling back a minute later.

Sam wiped his eyes, looking embarrassed. "Yeah, I talked to her this afternoon. She's the reason I'm back. I was gonna stay with JJ, but she made me promise to come back and get some rest."

"Smart woman. I wish JJ's mom would have made him make the same promise."

Sam shook his head with a small smile. "He's not afraid of his mama like I am."

Katie's timer went off, and she pulled the last of the tomatoes out of the bath and turned off the burner.

"You hungry?" she asked.

Sam shrugged.

"I've got some bland pot roast and cooked carrots?"

He shrugged again, and she made him a plate, and set it in front of him as she sat down. "Tell me about your mom. She sounds pretty amazing."

Sam scooped up some meat on his fork. "She is. Sweet as sugar, tough as nails, my grandfather used to say." He took a bite, then frowned. "Shit. You weren't kidding. This is awful."

"Hey!"

Getting up from his chair, he headed to the cabinet beside the stove. "Needs garlic salt or...something," he mumbled, rifling through the spices.

"I bet she's really proud of the man you're becoming." Katie said after he sat back down.

Unscrewing the cap of the garlic salt, he sprinkled some on. Then onion powder. He scooped up another forkful of meat and was about to put it in his mouth, then changed his mind and dropped it on the plate. "Fuck," he snapped, as fresh tears filled his eyes.

Katie blanched. "Is it that bad?"

"No, it's not the food." He shook his head, then thumped the table. "Damn it. I just miss her so much. And all I can think about is all the fucked-up shit I did to her over the years." He swiped at his tears. "You know what I kept thinking about all day?"

Katie shook her head.

"Since my dad passed, she and I have spent every Christmas morning together, just the two of us, watchin' old videos and stuff, to remember him. But last year..." He laughed bitterly. "Last year, I told her I wanted to spend Christmas morning with my *girlfriend*. We had only been together for a couple of weeks, we only lasted a month after that, and..." He shook his head. "What the hell? Why did I do that? What if I don't get another Christmas with her? How could I be so stupid?" he cried.

Katie squeezed his shoulder, recognizing the regret in his voice, remembering the self-hatred that came along with it. Matt popped into her head, followed by JJ and it occurred to her that maybe he was right to not trust her. After all, she'd blown it the last time.

Sam stared at his plate. "I'll tell you why. Because I was selfish." He pressed his palms to the sides of his head and doubled over. "Goddamn it."

Katie pulled him in for another hug, and he clung to her. "You were just being a kid, Sam. Your mom knows that." She wondered if JJ was having similar thoughts.

"She was right there. And I just left."

"Shh. Your mom knows you love her. She loves you, too. And the truth is... this whole thing, the Veil, the virus, not only is it taking lives, it's making it painfully obvious what a shitty job we were doing living them too. Myself, included. Myself foremost."

Taking him by the shoulders, she found his eyes and smiled sadly.

The timer on the pressure canner went off, and she jumped up and turned it off, flipped the valve to release the pressure. "I don't know if it's just human nature, or if it's because of the technology we've acquired, or what, but...It's like I look at my life now, and wonder what the hell I was *doing* with it. I spent ninety percent of my time trying to get people I didn't know or care about to like me. Who does that? *Why* do they do it? I don't know."

She leaned against the sink. "They say hindsight is twenty-twenty, but with what's happened, I think it's more like twenty-ten. This has been a wake-up call for all of us."

Sam met her eyes again. "Do you think it's too late? For all of us?"

She shrugged. "All I know is that we can't change the past, no matter how much we may want to."

Sam wiped his eyes with the back of his hand, and she wished she could think of something to say that would make him feel better. His mom would probably know exactly...

"Call your mom. Right now. And tell her how you feel."

"What?"

"Don't wait. Don't let another minute go by," she rushed. All they had was right now, and while she couldn't fix the past, or predict the future, she *could* do her best to make sure the kids didn't waste the present while they had it.

"But it's one in the morning."

She shrugged. "Who cares?"

Sam bit his lip, then nodded as Jinn appeared in the doorway. Her eyes were teary and red, and Kate realized she must have been eavesdropping for a while. "I'm gonna head outside and call my parents, and my best friend," she said before heading for the door.

Katie nodded, then looked at Sam. "I'm going to close my

eyes for a minute while the canner vents. You can sleep in JJ's room tonight. Can you wake me up before you head to bed?"

He nodded.

"Call your mom," she repeated, limping into the living room.

The recliner groaned as she dropped into it. She didn't dare lay down in the bed or she'd never get back up. Her foot, fingers and head throbbed in time with her heart.

Leaning her head back against the headrest, she sighed as Sam's voice whispered from the kitchen, "Hey, mama. No, everything is alright, I just wanted to–to talk…"

Katie didn't hear the rest.

Chapter Eighteen

Day 10 // 11:38 p.m.

HE WANTED to stay for a second night shift, but after he fell asleep behind the wheel and almost ran over a Coast Guard officer, they insisted he go home to sleep.

Pressing his head to the passenger's side window, JJ closed his eyes, only to open them a moment later and realize they were home.

Sam cut the engine, and they all just sat for a moment, not moving. "It's a hell of a thing," Mike said finally, from his seat in the middle. With tight lips, JJ nodded. That phrase had become but a eulogy of sorts, to acknowledge every one of the swollen, bug-infested bodies they'd uncovered, and an unspoken agreement to never speak of them again.

A minute later, JJ was in the kitchen and Sam was sitting at the table eating something. "You gonna eat or just stand there?"

JJ didn't remember opening the door of the truck or walking into the house. His eyes widened.

What the hell had happened to his kitchen? There was shit everywhere. Looking over his shoulder, he spied Parker asleep on the couch. Eat? Shaking his head, he turned for his bedroom. No, he was too tired to eat. Only when he reached the door and saw that Katie wasn't there did he finally wake up. Spinning around, he thumped back down the hall. Had she been thrown in jail again? Or worse, left? "Where is K—"

Sam pressed his finger to his lips and pointed at the recliner. JJ peered over the back and sighed in relief. She was curled on her side…His brows came together. Coming around in front, he leaned closer. Red splotches covered her face. *Heat rash.* She had it bad too. Crouching down, he carefully pushed the hair that had escaped her bun back. It was on her neck too and looked painful.

Then he noticed her hands curled on the arm of the chair. The polish was peeling off her nails, and turning her palm up, he gasped quietly as he ran his calloused fingers over the blisters and burns that covered her fingers. *What in the—*

The hair on the back of his neck went up in warning and he froze as his eyes met her wide-open ones in the dark. Dropping her hand, he stood as she struggled to sit up. She looked as delirious as he felt. "Did the timer go off?" she asked.

He looked into the kitchen, then back at her and shook his head.

She slumped back into the chair. "Okay."

"Why are you out here?" he whispered.

She didn't open her eyes. "So I can hear the timer."

"When is the last time you slept?"

She didn't answer, because she'd fallen back asleep.

He went into the kitchen and picked up a jar. It looked like chicken. He picked up another. Pears maybe? They covered the whole counter. There had to be over a hundred jars. "What is she doing?"

"Her and Barb and Ms. Michelle are trying to save the food from the grocery."

"Do you know when she last slept?"

Sam shook his head. "She insisted I sleep in your bed last night. Said the food was going bad, and she couldn't stop. And by the looks of all this, I'd say not since you have."

"What happened to her face? Why is her rash so bad?"

"It was like a hundred degrees when I came in here last night. She had pots on the stove and all kinds of shit everywhere."

JJ looked at the machine on the counter, then at the timer on the console in the middle of it. Eleven minutes. He made an executive decision. "When the timer goes off...turn it off."

"How—"

"I don't know. You're smart. You can figure it out. And if you can't, throw it out the fucking window. She needs to sleep." Without waiting for Sam to reply, he went back to the chair, scooped Katie up, and carried her down the hall. Her eyes fluttered open as she wrapped her arms around his neck, and again when he set her on the bed.

"What are you doing? I have to—"

"You're done for today," he said, sitting beside her, pushing her gently back onto the pillow.

She tried to sit up. "No, I have—" He took her hand, and maybe it was just because he was tired, but he pressed it to his chest and gave it a squeeze. "You did good today, Katie, but you need to sleep."

Tears leaked from her closed eyes. "No, I can't. Everything is going bad and..."

Folding her into his tired arms, he smoothed the hair back off her face. "Shh. It is time to sleep. Lay..." The words stuck in his throat, but remembering his conversation with his mom, he pushed through them. Katie was so tired, she wouldn't remember in the morning, anyway. "Lay by me and let's just rest for a little while. Okay?"

"O-okay."

Butterflies filled his stomach as she scooted over. Not even bothering to take his boots off, he lay down beside her and pulled her into his arms. With a heavy sigh, she rolled against him, resting her hand on his chest again, throwing her leg over his as if she'd been doing it forever.

JJ stared at the ceiling as she snuggled closer and wrapped her arm around his neck. His heart thumped loudly in his ears, but if Katie heard it, she didn't acknowledge it. What was it about exhaustion that made it so easy to conquer one's fears?

Before he could have second thoughts, he pressed his lips to the top of her head and said again, "You did good."

And then he fell asleep.

Chapter Nineteen

Day 11 // 8:22 a.m.

KATIE WOKE with a start to the sound of a far-off beeping. It vanished into the gasp that filled her throat at the sight of a man's arm draped over her hip. She recognized JJ's hand but... But how had she ended up lying beneath it? The last thing she remembered was peeling apples alone in the kitchen while the kids slept.

Slowly, she turned her head, inhaling sharply as tingling spread through her chest. JJ was fast asleep in his clothes behind her. She turned back on her side, careful not to wake him, as his hand slid from her hip, across her stomach, and around her ribs. Was she dreaming? When had he come home? Her eyes widened as he tucked his hand between the bed and the side of her breast, cupping it, and pulled her closer. Why were they snuggling in bed? She exhaled, trying not to move, and closed her eyes. *Why does it feel so good?*

He shifted, and his breath tickled the back of her neck, as he pulled her in closer for a moment, flexing his arm in a squeeze, before relaxing it again. She studied the bit of tattoo she could see over her shoulder, realizing it was part of a half sleeve. There was a clock with roman numerals, and some flowers, roses maybe, and...a heart...She leaned back into him so she could read the banner across it. *Fuck you.* Her brow went up. *Ouch.* Was that for Erica? Was that why he didn't want to get close to her, because he still wasn't over his ex? She frowned. That wasn't a pleasant thought. Or was it like Mr. Goebell said that JJ was scared? He'd admitted as much in his truck the day the Veil went up, hadn't he?

But why? What had she done? And how was she supposed to ease his fear when he wouldn't even get near her?

Pulling her head back, she turned and stared at him, resisting the temptation to run her blistered fingers through his scruffy beard. Some men looked like boys when they slept, but not JJ. Instead, it highlighted his masculinity, making him look both sexier and kinder at the same time. Both were always there, of course, below the surface. She felt them every time she looked at him, every time he came to her rescue. But when he was awake, he forced them into the shadow of his scowls. She smiled. But now they were free. And she was breathless.

His lips were parted just enough to breathe, and she marveled at how full they were when he wasn't pressing them into a seam. She bit hers. What would happen if she just leaned over and kissed him? Her eyes flicked to his. They were still closed. Should she try?

A soft bang came from the living room, and his eyes fluttered, stealing her nerve, before closing again.

Katie exhaled. And dear lord, his eyelashes were amazing. Were they even real? She paid two hundred and fifty dollars a month for hers, and they looked nothing like that. She had never seen lashes like that on a man before. No wonder his eyes were so captivating. Framed as they were, how could they be anything else?

The sound of glass shattering collapsed the little sanctuary JJ's arms had created around her and she turned toward the door as the hundred things she had to do rushed into her head at once. Lifting her head, she spied the clock. It was almost nine?

Falling back into the pillow, she pushed the loose strands of hair back off her forehead. "Shit."

She needed to get up. The kids needed breakfast, and both Barb and Ms. Michelle were expecting her, and she'd left the food out and hadn't turned off the pressure canner. "Shit." Lifting JJ's arm, she went to roll away, then stopped. Turning back, she stared at him as a dozen thoughts rolled in swift succession through her mind. Ignoring all but the first one, she pressed her lips to his as fireworks went off in her chest. And not the shitty ones they always set off in the middle of the show, either. No, these were the good ones.

She was about to pull away, when his hand slid around her waist, dragging her closer and his slightly minty mouth sleepily answered hers, taking the fireworks from pretty great, to a mind shattering fireball. Pressing her hand to his chest, she held her breath as their lips danced, afraid to wake him as lightning shot all the way to the tips of her toes.

His eyes remained closed, but there was a hint of a smile on his lips as he released her a moment later, fell against the pillow, and began to snore.

She lay still for a moment, staring at the ceiling, then lifted his arm again and scooted toward his side of the bed, her heart thumping like a drum. *Holy shit.*

Sitting up, she touched her lips as he rolled on his back and threw his arm over his face. The silly thought of watching him do that every morning for the rest of her life crossed her mind, making her feel... it was such a foreign sensation she didn't even know what to call it. It felt like hot cocoa and a warm blanket. Like curling up on the couch and watching a movie. Like... Christmas morning, the way it looked on TV, not the way it was when she was a little girl, like a warm bath with lavender bubbles and a glass of wine. Whatever it was, she wanted to crawl inside of it. Whatever it was, it had been missing from her life, and she craved it.

Voices from the other room drew her back to the crisis at hand, and she jumped up. She gasped at her reflection in the mirror as she hurried to the door. *Dear god.* Had JJ seen her like this? Splotchy neck, crazy hair, extra-large hobo bags under her eyes. Was that why he'd slept with her? Out of pity? Tugging at the bun that hung to the side of her head, she fled the bedroom for the bathroom, closing the door on the way out.

The counter was cool as she pressed her palms into it and hung her head over the sink. Turning the faucet on, she splashed water onto her burning cheeks, praying she didn't look as bad last night as she did this morning. Her fingers throbbed as she wiped her face with a towel. She brushed her teeth, then pulled the door open. Her eyes went to JJ's door and for a split second, she considered going back in, crawling back under his arm and going back to sleep. But then she imagined the awkward conversation that would follow when he woke up, assuming he didn't just leap out of the bed and run, and decided against it. She didn't want to kill whatever magic had brought them together last night.

Following the voices down the hall, Katie headed toward the kitchen mess she needed to clean.

To her surprise, Barb was at the sink squeezing out a rag, while Jinn swept up the remaining glass.

"Where are the kids?" she asked, sitting in the nearest chair, twisting her hair back up into a bun.

"At the bar, eating breakfast with Sam," Jinn said. Katie noticed she was wearing a tight, tie-dyed low-cut tank top in place of the short sleeve button-down shirt she'd been wearing before, and a pair of ripped jeans instead of her slacks, that looked very much like... Katie looked down at her jeans then back at Jinn. "Did you get new clothes?"

Jinn nodded. "Ms. Michelle. They're kids, but they fit. I did the jeans...like yours."

Katie forced a smile. That was obvious. So was the fact that combined Jinn and Barb probably weighed less than she did. *Let it be.* "It looks good."

"There's coffee in the microwave for you," Jinn said.

Katie pressed the button, and a minute later, pulled a steaming cup of coffee from the microwave and pressed it into her hands. She added to her silly fantasy of waking in JJ's arms and watching him sleep, heading into the kitchen afterward, for a hot cup of coffee, just like the one in her hands, and waiting for him to get up.

It was stupid, but the sight of the steaming mug filled her with the same feeling JJ had, and it made her want to cry. "Thanks," she said, taking a sip. It was nutty and dark, and delicious as always.

When she was younger, Katie had wanted so many things. Money. She'd wanted to travel and see the world. She wanted designer clothes, and an enviable body, and a tan, and invitations to fancy parties, and a place all her own with a view of the LA skyline. But now...

"Where do you guys get your coffee from? It's so good." Now all she wanted was—

"JJ." Barb said, reading her mind. The older woman wiped her hands on her apron and turned around.

Katie stared into her mug. Yeah. All she wanted now was JJ, and this simple life, and a hot cup of coffee. "Where does he get it from?"

Barb laughed. "He roasts it in his mom's garage next door."

Katie's jaw dropped open. "You're kidding."

"Nope. Orders the beans online from somewhere out in California." Barb paused for a minute, staring at her. "After you're done, go take a cool shower. It'll help with the rash."

Katie touched her neck. "That's okay. I've already wasted enough time. It will just come back anyway, when I get too hot," she explained, scratching the back of her neck. The kitchen was already sweltering. "It's no big deal."

"Maybe you ought to take a break from all of this," Barb said, still looking concerned.

Katie shook her head. "I'm praying we don't need any of this, but...my gut, and what I've seen on the news, is telling me we will. Besides, I need to do something. I can't just sit around and watch TV. It's so…"

"Depressing? Terrifying?" Jinn supplied. "I talked to my mom yesterday, and she said the police keep blocking off portions of the city, and that convoys of trucks have been going back and forth past the house for days now."

"Convoys of trucks? For what?"

"Some are delivering food, but others… She thinks they are disposing of bodies."

Katie drained her mug, shaking her head. "I don't get it. Why can't people just do what they're supposed to?"

"My mom says they are, but it's airborne, so maybe…it's just the air and it doesn't matter anymore? I mean, what other reason could there be for the numbers going up like they are when no one is out?"

It was a dire thought. But she was right. According to the local news, since the Veil went up, most of the drama had been on the outside, with the fires and thefts and missing persons. On the inside, only a handful of morons had tried to break the quarantine and had been quickly subdued. Otherwise it had been quiet, eerily so.

"But then, what was the point of quarantining at all?" Katie scratched at her chest, then at the base of her scalp.

Jinn shook her head. "Well, it seems to be working in other places, just not here. I saw on the news this morning, Detroit had its first outbreak. I mean… How did it survive there without spreading to everyone for almost two weeks?"

Katie shook her head, scratching again. "I don't know."

"Go take a long, cool shower." Barb said. "Jinn and I will hold the fort down."

Katie took the hint and got up. If Barb thought she was looking rough, then a shower was most certainly in order.

"Okay. Thanks." She made her way back down the hall into the bathroom and closed the door, wondering if the president and other world leaders had any idea what they were doing. It didn't seem like it. The shower curtain screeched as she pulled it back and turned on the water. Peeling out of her clothes, she sighed and reached under the sink for her toiletries, then climbed in the tub.

Barb was right. The cool water felt like heaven on her inflamed skin. She stood under the stream of water until her legs began to wobble, then collapsed on the floor of the tub, pulling her knees up to her chest as the coolness pushed her hair forward, and pattered against her neck.

She didn't remember going to bed with JJ last night, but it must have been late. And somehow, instead of giving her strength, the sleep had made her more tired. Again, she had the urge to crawl back in bed with him and ride out the rest of the nightmare asleep in his arms. Instead, she laid on her side, curling her arm under her head, and fell asleep.

***.

A hard rap on the door brought her back around, and she realized the cool water had turned to ice.

"You okay in there?" Sam asked.

Sloshing to her feet, she reached for her shampoo. "Yeah. Be out in a minute."

She washed her hair, then cut the water. Her clothes smelled like cooked meat, so she popped her head out the door and asked Jinn to grab her bag from JJ's room. A few moments later, she emerged from the bathroom feeling cleaner than she had in days. Why hadn't she even thought to change her clothes?

"Do we have any more coffee?" she asked, pulling her wet hair back into a bun at the base of her neck.

Jinn nodded at the thermos on the counter. "Between you and JJ, Barb thought you would need it."

"Is he up yet?"

Jinn shook her head as the girls came racing through the door. "Don't tell Parker where we are." They begged, disappearing down the hall.

Katie's brow went up as she poured another cup of coffee. Parker was playing hide and seek with the girls? What else had she missed in the handful of hours she'd been asleep? Dropping into the recliner, she flipped on the TV.

"...still no reported cases in Chicago, Miami or Vancouver." The news anchor, a pretty blond woman in her early-thirties said. *"Officials in Detroit had confirmed a single outbreak on the west side of this city, but so far, no further cases have been reported, while in Dallas the number of X-Virus related deaths soars as local residents refuse to obey the quarantine."* There was no good news anymore, she thought. *"In Atlanta, as the number of deaths mysteriously continues to climb, both the ICPH and CDC frantically search for a probable cause. The CDC has ruled out contamination of water, food sources and person-to-person transmission, claiming that there would be identifiable patterns in the virus's distribution if that were the case. There is speculation that one in three, possibly two, households within the Veil are already dead. According to a source inside the Veil, more than half the food and water rations delivered over the last week have remained unclaimed from doorsteps, and footage obtained by our crews this morning..."* A video taken through the Veil, zoomed in on a row of houses, and even through the sparkly interference, the boxes on three of the five stoops were clearly visible. *"...appears to confirm this. As you can see from the video, shot only hours ago, the majority of houses have not claimed their food rations. Atlanta, the source claimed to our reporter last night, '...looks like a ghost town, because it is one.'"*

Katie wondered if the news was as confusing to everyone else as it was to her? Patterns of distribution? What did that mean? And were they saying half of Atlanta was already *dead*? How could that be?

The little girls raced out the door squealing, and Katie smiled, their cheerful voices a welcome break from all the devastation, as they raced in the bedroom and slammed the door.

Katie muted the news as it switched to the international crisis in Dubai, where food supplies were running dangerously low. She sipped her coffee as they showed brief clips of Jakarta, Paris, and Amsterdam. It was easy to forget that the rest of the world was in the same boat, that there were children in China, Spain, Russia, separated from their families, just as there were here. A video clip eerily similar to the ones that had aired earlier last week of Atlanta, and the fires surrounding the city filled the screen as the ticker at the bottom of the screen read **"Fires ravage Italian countryside in wake of shift in Veil."** Shift in Veil, meant that someone had tried to take down a tower and failed. It must have sparked the fires, just as they had here.

The screen door creaked as Grace pulled it open. "Miss. Barb asked me to come get you," she said. "You have a phone call at the bar."

Katie frowned. Who could possibly be calling her? And why were they calling her at the *bar*?

Slipping her feet into her slippers, she followed Grace out the door, noticing the girl's blond hair as it shimmered in the sun.

"How's your head?" she asked.

"Fine." Grace said as they crossed JJ's mom's front lawn. "How's your foot?"

"Pretty good, actually." For the first time since she'd injured her foot, it did not ache as she walked, and she reminded herself that she needed to thank JJ for that. The slippers were just what she needed to protect her foot, but also give it air to heal.

A minute the bell jingled as Grace pushed the bar door open, and Katie was inside again. Blinking, she crossed the small dining room and made her way to the bar where Barb was talking on the phone.

"Hold on, she's right here," Barb said, placing her hand over the receiver. She handed the phone to Katie, with an expression on her face she couldn't quite read. "It's the mother of one of the kids you got over there."

"Hello?" Katie said, frowning.

Her eyes widened as the woman on the other end of the line introduced herself.

Chapter Twenty

JJ GROANED and tried to sit up. With one palm into the bed to keep the room from spinning, he squinted in the light, stabbing at his eyeballs. "Shit," he exhaled, rubbing his temples. He felt like he was waking from a coma and hung over at the same time.

Dragging himself to his feet, he stretched his back. His shoulder ached and as he massaged it, remembering why. The breath hissed out of his mouth at the memory of Katie curled up beside him, leg thrown over his. He rubbed the spot on his chest where her head had been for most of the night. Reaching for the doorknob, he pulled it open, listening. The house was quiet. Fishing his phone out of his pocket, he checked the time. "What the hell?" It was almost eight *at night*? He ran his fingers through his oily hair. He'd slept all day? "Shit."

Heading to the bathroom, he noticed he only had ten percent battery left, and went back in the bedroom to plug it in, then brushed his teeth and took a much-needed shower.

The sleep hadn't done much for his body, but his mind was clearer, he thought as he stood under the stream of hot water. He couldn't believe he'd fallen asleep in his work clothes, let alone his boots, but at least when he'd awoken in the middle of the night, he'd had the sense to get up and brush his teeth. He should burn all of it after what they'd witnessed, pretty sure the stink of death would never come out of them, but who knew how long it would be until stores were back up and running? The water splashed on his face as he rinsed the shampoo from his head and beard. He needed to trim his beard. It was too hot to have a full one. He should have done it before he got in the shower, he realized, turning off the water.

The curtain groaned as he pulled it back and grabbed the towel off the rack. It was still slightly damp, and it smelled like her. Feeling stupid, but unable to resist, he pressed it to his nose and inhaled. Even now, she smelled so damn good. He dragged it across his sternum, then swiped at the mirror, clearing the fog from the glass, and inspecting himself with a critical eye. He had his dad's jaw, wide shoulders and barrel chest, which meant that even if he lost twenty pounds, which he could certainly afford to do, he'd still never have a body like the guy he'd seen Katie draped over on a beach in Acapulco. He wanted to believe his mom, and the looks Katie kept giving him, but the fact of the matter was...

Meeting his eyes in the mirror, he sighed. Those he got from his mom. Everyone said so. The one time he'd seen his dad drunk, his father had leaned over, as they sat at the kitchen table watching her make dinner, and whispered conspiratorially in his ear, *'I love everything about your mother Jay, but I love her eyes the most. I remember the first time I saw her. She looked my way and those eyes just...burned me to the ground.'* If his eyes held that kind of power, it was lost in bloodshot exhaustion at the moment.

He dried his right arm, admiring the half sleeve of tattoos it bore. Then he dried his left, sliding the towel over the tattoos that spread from his arm to his chest. Katie's Instagram guys were ripped. But not a single one of them looked like they'd put in a hard day's work in their life. He did, though. And he had. He huffed a laugh. They were like brand-new work boots in a catalog, while he was more like the scuffed proven pair sitting beside the back door. Maybe that counted for something? Wrapping the towel around his waist, he opened the medicine cabinet and pulled the shaving cream down.

———

THE DOOR SWUNG CLOSED behind him and he made his way through the tables to the long one they'd pushed together and were sitting, eating at. Except for the devastating image on the muted TV behind the bar, it almost felt like a holiday. They were all there, their weird little quarantine family, Dave, Mike, Mr. Goebell, Ms. Michelle, Barb, and, of course, Katie and the kids. Everyone was talking over each other as they passed and piled the dirty dishes in the middle of the table. Someone even laughed.

Barb motioned him over. "There's still some grub left. I'll make you a plate." Ms. Michelle and Mike nodded at him, as Katie turned in her chair. He almost tripped over his own feet, as she took him in from head to toe and met his eyes, he thought, rather approvingly. Grabbing the back of the chair beside him, he regained his balance, feeling like he'd done that before, then went around the opposite side of the table and sat in the empty chair by Mike. Hunger finally caught up with him, and his stomach growled as Barb set a plate of greens and chicken in front of him. He couldn't remember the last time he ate. Maybe sometime yesterday morning? Avoiding her eyes, he shoveled food into his mouth, and then downed his beer with one giant swig, and asked for another plate.

———

HE WAS TRYING to avoid thinking about her, but it was impossible because every conversation he'd had in the past half hour began with her name. *Katie is amazing. Katie found boxes of canning jars in Mike's garage. Katie read me a story. Katie. Katie.* The voices at the table sounded like the ones in his head. And to his dismay, every time he lost track of thought, he'd blink and be staring right at her. He was doing it now. "Shit."

She smiled, and he looked away. He dreamed he kissed her last night, and he couldn't get that out of his head either. He could still feel it, the gentle pressure of her mouth on his. It made his pulse race even now. Once, when he was in high school, his mom had told him, *'You'll think all kissing is the same until you realize it isn't. When that day comes Jay, pay attention. Because that's the girl you want to hold on to.'* He shook his head, trying to clear it. Why was he remembering that now? The kiss wasn't even real.

But holding her was. Yes. And damn it, that felt almost as good. She'd fit against him like a glove, like a puzzle piece curved in all the right places, locked snuggly against him in the dark. Maybe that's why he remembered what his mom said about kissing. Because lying there beside her had been like that. He'd slept with women before, of course, but it had been a while since he just laid there afterward...And even then they did not drape themselves over him the way Katie had, wrap their arms around his neck, sigh into his chest as he pulled them closer. Instead, they moved to their 'side,' or straight up, *got* up, showered and left. It had been the same with Erica. He hadn't even known what he was missing. But he sure as hell did, now. And he wanted more.

Katie's rash, or whatever it was, was gone, and she was fresh-faced as she went to the carafe on the bar and poured herself more coffee. She was wearing her jeans, the ones she'd had on the day the Veil went up, and his mom's Braves t-shirt, which was about four sizes too small and looked fantastic, stretched across her chest.

"Earth to JJ." Sam laughed.

JJ met Katie's eyes *again*, and his cheeks burst into flames at the realization that she'd been watching him ogle her. Ducking his head, he scratched at the back of his neck. "Fuck," he muttered, before lifting his head again. "What? Sorry."

"I said you clean up nice," Sam repeated.

JJ looked down at his gray t-shirt and jeans. If this was 'nice,' he clearly had not set the bar too high over the last two weeks. He glanced at Katie out of the corner of his eye, but her chair was empty. She must have gone in the back with Barb, who had also disappeared.

"You want another beer?" Sam asked.

He nodded. The fact that half the world was trapped and dying and they still had ice cold draft beer on tap defied all logic. It just went to show how utterly absurd television was when depicting the end of the world. Instead of being buried by sand dunes or fighting off zombies, or wearing rags and eating each other, there they were, in jeans and t-shirts, sitting around a giant table having cocktails. Ms. Michelle spun the ice in her Old Fashioned, as Sam set a beer in front of him, and sat back down.

Mike held the remote up to the TV and a second later, the volume drowned out the motors of the coolers that lined the back of the bar.

"Several cities, including Dallas and Atlanta, have seen exponential upticks in deaths over the last forty-eight hours. Jakarta and Rome have also reported surges in X-Virus related deaths..."

The mood in the room deteriorated as the anchor went from one devastating piece of news to another. More reported cases of arson around Atlanta, more robberies. He watched footage of fires, very much like the ones that had happened in Atlanta burning the countryside somewhere in Europe. *"The ICPH continues to monitor the escalating crisis, and urges each nation to continue adhering to the quarantine guidelines, stating in a press conference earlier today that while cities within the Veil continue to struggle, not a single case of the Virus has been reported on the outside."* The video switched to a woman with dark hair in a gray suit standing at a podium. *"This is an extraordinary accomplishment, and the citizens of the world should be proud. But we are not out of the woods yet, and we must remain vigilant. Rome was not conquered in a day, and this virus is more powerful than all the world's armies combined. So we must remain strong, we must remain careful. The Virus, if it is out, has been crippled by our swift action. Let's keep it that way."*

The news segment switched back to the anchor. *"When asked about those suffering on the inside, the spokesperson for the ICPH said teams of virologists were working 'around the clock' to find a cure, and that the ICPH would not rest until it had. That assurance, however, perhaps paltry comfort for the millions of helpless people dying in their homes."*

JJ stared into his glass. Damn, they were lucky. He couldn't imagine being on the inside. He couldn't imagine what his mom and Sierra must be feeling.

A sniffle brought his head up, and he watched as Parker pulled his headphones out of his pocket. "Here." he said, putting them in Grace's ears as she wiped her eyes. "Don't listen to that shit."

"I want to listen too!" Amelia said.

Parker rolled his eyes. "I only have—"

Grace pulled one from her ear and handed it to the little girl, warming JJ's heart, as Parker scrolled through his phone. They certainly had become one weird little family over the last few days that he'd been gone. A minute later, a thin stream of music could be heard beneath the commentary. Grace and Amelia bent back to drawing on bar napkins, as Parker met his eyes. Barb told him he and Grace had become attached at the hip, and JJ wondered if the boy had any siblings. Then he realized he'd been so self absorbed in his own drama, he hadn't asked any of the kids who they had on the inside. What an ass. JJ leaned forward, resting his elbows on the table, and asked. "Parker, who do you have inside?"

"My mom, stepdad, and stepsister."

"I'm sor—"

"Don't be," he said.

Jinn appeared out of nowhere, looking a lot more grown up than she had the last time he'd seen her, and sat down next to Sam.

"How'd it go?" Sam asked, patting her leg.

JJ's brow shot up.

She wiped her eyes. "They're okay for now. But they said the Michaelson's, who live next door, got carted away in the middle of the night last night. My mom doesn't understand. She swears they never left their house."

"Maybe they caught it before the Veil?"

Jinn shook her head. "They would have been dead days ago." She swiped at the tears in her eyes, and JJ's brow went up higher as Sam put an arm around her shoulder and she leaned into him. "I'm scared they're going to die," she confessed.

"We're all scared," he said, brushing her hair back over her shoulder before squeezing it.

Katie came back out, holding a tray. On it were fresh-baked cookies. "Dessert!" she said, setting it down in the middle of the table. Her voice was cheerful, but the hollow ring to it gave her away, so did her worried glance at the TV.

Mike reached for a muffin. Then Parker grabbed one. No one said a word.

Katie sat down beside him, and he avoided her eyes.

"Sam is right. You clean up nice," she said finally, forcing him to turn.

But the way she was looking at him made him feel like he was naked. Resisting the urge to cover his junk, he nodded. "Thanks. You do too." The words came out before he could inform himself he'd sound like an idiot if he said them out loud.

His palm ached to slap itself against his forehead as she laughed. "Thanks, I guess."

He peeked at her. She was staring at his arm. "I didn't know you had so much ink."

His heart thumped. So much? When had she seen his tattoos? Had she woken up last night while he was asleep? "You didn't ask," he blurted. It was another asinine comment, and arguably even more stupid than the first thing he'd said, but he couldn't think.

"Can I see?" Tilting her head to the side, she met his eyes. He rolled his hand over on the table, exposing the inside of his arm as he pulled his sleeve up over his shoulder. While there was no six-pack hiding under his shirt, his arms were strong and muscular. Dragging chains, and doing all the heavy lifting at Mike's shop over the past five years had seen to that. He hoped she didn't ask him what they meant. Not that he was embarrassed, he just didn't want to go into it. The loss of his father, then losing Erica and then... He stared at the ornate clock that hid the title he'd briefly held beneath it. "Time heals" was the suggestion the sympathetic tattoo artist had made when JJ told her what he needed her to do.

Luckily, Katie didn't ask. Instead, she ran her fingers over the ink, as he tried not to shiver. *Rules, JJ*, he reminded himself.

"Oh, no." Ms. Michelle's voice dragged him from his thoughts and he tugged his sleeve down as he turned toward the TV.

"The President of India, Bahaar Anand, has confirmed death tolls in Delhi have exceeded six million, and the city is failing despite attempts to section off infected portions of the city. In a press conference she gave earlier today, President Anand said the madness associated with the virus has made the quarantine impossible, as millions of crazed, infected people continue to wreak havoc on the dying city."

Video footage of people shouting and wandering the streets was terrifying. Some were violent, kicking and screaming at the people they encountered. One man was sitting in the middle of the road, holding his head, just rocking back and forth. A half-naked little girl crossed in front of the camera, then wandered down the road by herself, climbing over bodies as if they were mounds of dirt. "Shit." JJ breathed, wondering where that girl's family was. Another vacant-eyed person walked by, blood running down their neck and disappeared. They weren't zombies, but they were close.

JJ looked at Amelia, sitting next to Grace, with her hair in fancy braids, clean and cared for. She smiled at him, and he smiled back. Then his eyes went back to the TV, and the dying city halfway around the world. He had known since he was a boy that life was not fair, but this...this was just cruel. He pushed his beer back toward the center of the table, as his guilt for being one of the lucky ones stabbed at his heart. The little girl vanished around a corner, and JJ wondered if she was still alive, or lying dead in a road somewhere.

Katie sighed behind him. Then she slapped her hand against the table, making him jump. "Fuck this," she whispered.

Before he could say anything, she'd already run out the door. He went to get up and follow her, but a little hand stopped him. "I made this for you." He turned back the other way. Amelia was standing beside him, holding out a napkin. He took it and smoothed it out. On it was a crudely drawn picture of two large stick people, holding hands, and a little stick person beneath them, surrounded by holes where the pen had torn through the paper. "Oh...Um thanks."

JJ looked back toward the door, wondering if he should go after her or give her space? Space was usually what women wanted from him, but she seemed pretty upset, and they needed to talk anyway about last night.

"That's me, and that's you and my mom."

JJ choked on his own breath, as all the eyes at the table, except Grace's, fell on him. He looked at the 'couple' holding hands. "Oh..."

"I thought you could be my dad if you want."

JJ felt hot and cold all at once, and a little like throwing up. "Oh, I... Don't you have a dad?"

"Nope. Just my mom and Nana, and Abuelita and Papa Chuy. Do you *want* to be my dad?" she asked, her big brown puppy eyes staring shamelessly into his.

"Oh. Um..." *Shit. Shit. Shit.* Sweat dripped from his armpits, down his sides. *No,* was what he *wanted* to say. He couldn't. He wasn't ready. But what came out was, "Um...sure I can do that. Just until you're back with your mom, though."

"No, after the Veil is done, too. I want you to marry my mom and live with us, and you can be my dad forever."

"Well, I'm not sure..."

"Don't worry, she's not like Ms. Katie," Amelia rushed on. "She's no trouble at *all*," she added for extra measure. "I promise. She is totally different. More like you. You will like her. She *is* the right kind of girl for you."

"Oh, shit..." Sam said, bringing JJ's head up. Katie was standing in the middle of the dining room, and by the look on her face, she'd heard everything.

Fuckity fuck.

Amelia squinted at Katie, inspecting her. "My mom is not as tall as her, and her hair is shorter. And she doesn't smell like candy but..." That made her frown, but then she brightened. "But she's grouchy like you and she speaks Spanish and her belly is more rounder, like yours—"

"Okay!" Sam intervened, tickling her sides, making her laugh. "We get the picture. He'll think about it. Go color."

JJ followed Katie with his eyes as she walked around the other side of the table, toward the bar, grasping at the words to explain what she'd just heard before it was too late.

With a sigh, he got up and went to the counter. "Katie, listen—"

Her jaw was tight as she ignored him, fumbling with something behind the bar.

"I can explain..." His voice trailed off as she met his eyes. His heart stuttered in his chest. She looked hurt. *Shit.* Instead of apologizing, he stood, frozen, rooted to the spot like an idiot as her eyes narrowed on him and she shook her head, like he'd disappointed her.

Well, that made two of them. He never meant for her to hear that. "*Fuck.* Listen, I..." the words died in his throat a second time as the corners of her mouth tilted up in a wicked—she met his eyes—calculating smile. The temperature in the room went up ten degrees as he stared. Had he been about to say something? Before he could remember, she turned and walked away, breaking the spell, and reminding him that yes, he had.

He hurried along the row of stools, tripping over the leg of one as she came around the corner of the bar.

"Katie, I can explain. You see what happened was—" he began, but she walked away before he could get the rest out.

Sweat popped out on his brow, and he swiped at it. If everything got fucked up because he'd confessed his confused feelings to a three-year-old... He ran his fingers through his hair. "Fuck."

Katie went over to Mike, took the remote out of his surprised hand, and flipped off the TV.

She spun around. "We've had enough doom and gloom for one day," she announced. "And I, for one, could really use a break from being sad, and—" she met JJ's eyes, "—*scared.*"

His brows came together. What exactly was that supposed to mean?

Looking back at everyone else, she continued. "And I'm tired of feeling guilty that I'm here while everyone else is... where they are." She started stacking the chairs in the middle of the room in a pile. "I'm tired of trying not to cry when that's all I truly want to do half the time," she said, dragging them out of the way. Grace pulled the headphones out of her ears, as JJ again tried not to stare at Katie's ass as she worked, and went on. "Ever since the Veil went up, I feel like I can't breathe and the other half of the time I feel like I'm losing my mind." The table she was moving screeched as she pushed it against the wall. "The world is f-ed," she said, glancing at Amelia. "We know that. But *we're* not." She pushed another table out of the way with a grunt. "Not yet, anyway." She asked over her shoulder. "And I just…I mean, what's the point of living if all we're going to do is sit here and wait to die?"

A neon light JJ hadn't seen lit up in years turned on as Katie pulled the cord behind it. A second and third one went on, as Sam and Jinn frowned at each other, then at him. Shaking his head, he shrugged.

"I know you're all hurting, and…" She met his eyes again. "…I know you all have loved ones on the inside…but…damn it, we are still alive, all of us and…" Her facade fell for a moment, before her resolve forced it back in place. "We will never be happy again, like we were before. But I just need a break from being miserable. I just need… an hour to pretend… to pretend that it's still *possible*, to pretend like maybe everything will work out and be okay. To laugh and not feel like… a horrible person for it."

Sam wiped his eyes as Mike smiled sadly, and Jinn and Barb nodded their heads in agreement.

Katie took a deep breath, regaining her composure, and headed straight toward him. "And on that note…" The ominous look returned to her eyes as she glared at him. Grabbing his shoulder, she pulled his ear down to her mouth. "You made a big mistake."

Fuck. For a second, he'd forgotten that he was in deep shit. "Yeah, I did. I'm—"

She didn't wait for him to finish. "And now you're going to pay for it."

Before he could ask her what she meant, she held up the remote, pointed it at the bar, and pushed the button.

Pay for it? A second later, the opening beats to a very

familiar song blared through the speaker, and the blood drained from his head. "Oh, shit." It was Kesha's top-ten hit *Die Young*, and he knew every word of this song—heat rushed heat rushed into his cheeks, and his ears burst into flames as Katie winked at him and grinned, grabbed the girls and went to the center of the little dance floor she'd created—because the album was his. *"Oh shit."* Had she found his box of old CDs? His Katy Perry album? He pinched the bridge of his nose. "Please god, no." He could not bear the humiliation.

When he looked up again, his mouth fell open, and he forgot about his collection of dance pop music.

Katie's hands were above her head and she was dancing. His brain turned to quicksand as she swayed her hips back and forth to the beat, swallowing up every disjointed question in his head. So she wasn't angry? Was that possible? Where had she found his CDs? Was she going to tell everyone they were his? Why was his throat so dry? Why was it so fucking hot in there all of the sudden?

Relief, mixed with razor sharp humiliation as Jinn asked, "Who is this?"

Sam shook his head. "I don't know. Sounds like nineties techno-pop."

They looked at him and he stilled his tapping toe, trying to look as confused as they did even though he'd bought the album the day it debuted in 2012.

Shrugging, Jinn said, "Oh, well," then dragged Sam to his feet, and they joined the party.

JJ didn't know what was more embarrassing, that Katie had discovered his collection, or that he still liked it.

A small smile crossed his lips as Amelia and Grace shrieked and jumped up and down in time to the music. Katie was doing a damn good job of jumping up and down herself, reminding him of girls at the concerts he used to sneak off to in Atlanta in his early twenties. JJ dragged his hands over his face as she twirled, and her hair flew over her shoulders. God, she was beautiful. Had he truly slept in the same bed with her last night? Was he insane to have spent the last ten days pushing her away? His mom seemed to think so.

JJ dropped into the nearest chair as the music thumped and the girls laughed, and Barb dragged Mike out of his chair.

His smile widened. Did Mike even know how to dance? JJ hadn't thought so, but as he took to the floor and twirled Barb around like they were at prom, Mike proved him wrong. Grace led Parker out to join her and Katie and Amelia, leaving him the only one on the sidelines.

Katie rolled her hips, and he lost his train of thought. She did it again, and a new one, involving his hands in her hair, her mouth on his, and *way* less clothing between the two of them, took its place and raced down the track in his mind straight toward his bedroom. "Shit," he hissed, realizing she had stopped dancing and was staring at him. How long had she been watching him watch her?

Holding up her hand, she gave him the 'come hither' finger.

He shook his head, unable to swallow past the lump in his throat. He might not be able to breathe either, he couldn't tell.

Her gaze, as she danced made her way around the table was so hot, it boiled the blood in his veins and turned it to ash, reminding him of his dad's comment about his mom's eyes and his mom's comment about what his dad would have done in this situation, with the woman he *knew* he belonged with. To his utter surprise, and in fulfillment of every boyhood fantasy he'd ever had, Katie threw her leg over his, and sat right down on his lap. It was just as wonderful as he'd imagined it would be. Yes, he definitely was having trouble breathing. He latched onto the edge of the table like it was a life raft, and did not let go as she laughed at what had to be a very confused expression on his face. Which made absolute sense, because he had no idea what was happening. But before he forgot completely, he had to explain about Amelia's comment, because that was exactly the kind of situation that fucked everything up in movies and came back to bite people in the ass later. "About what Amelia said—"

Katie pressed her finger to his lips. "Guess what?"

Sweat dripped from the back of his neck and down his sides as she put her hand on his shoulder and leaned closer. "W-what?" he choked, wishing he did more cardio so he could breathe right now without sounding like he was dying.

"I don't care what Amelia said."

He squeezed his eyes shut. *Thank god.*

"Guess what else?" Her lips only brushed his ear, but somehow he felt it everywhere else, too.

"What?"

"I found your box of CDs when I was cleaning the guest room."

That was obvious.

She continued. "It seems like you've been keeping a lot of things from me, JJ."

He swallowed hard, hands still latched to the table like clamps, wishing to god he'd thrown those damn CDs away when he'd cleared them out of his old truck. He hated to lie, but he would die before admitting the music blaring through the speakers was his. Shaking his head, he choked. "My sister..." His voice trailed off as she sat back, shaking her head, her finger moving back and forth like a ticking metronome in front of his face. Her eyes sparkled as they bore into his, and his head felt light enough to float away.

The way the hair hung over her shoulders, the feel of her ass pressed against his lap, the blaring music, and the goddamn beer swirling thought his veins were too much.

She leaned closer. "Don't lie to me."

"I'm not—" He absolutely was, because if she knew he knew every word to the album that was playing right now, he'd have to throw himself into the Veil.

Lifting herself off his lap, she leaned closer again. As her chest met his, JJ's heart banged against his ribs. Her breath tickled his ear. "I know the truth. About everything."

He shook his head again.

One of her hands closed over the opposite side of his head, trapping it. "I talked to your mom," she whispered.

His eyes widened, and he tried to push her back, but she wouldn't budge. *"What? When?"*

"Now, are you going to dance with me," she continued, ignoring his question, "or do I have to tell everyone here that a twenty-five-year-old *man* bought this CD, then dragged his little sister to the concert so it didn't look like he was the one who wanted to go?" Leaning back, she crossed her arms, and he stared at her with his mouth hanging open. First of all, he was going to have to kill his mom. Second, Katie was *blackmailing* him? His heart continued to thud as he stared at her lips, turned up in a smug smile. *Holy shit.* She was. His eyes narrowed. Why was that so goddamn hot?

She sat back down on his lap and hung her arms over his shoulders and—his hands flew to her hips and he tried to shove her up, as his teenage nightmare came springing to life in his pants. *Oh, please, god no.* Hadn't he suffered enough humiliation tonight? Pressing his fingers to her jeans, he tried to force her up, but she wouldn't budge. Looking down, he saw her feet wrapped around the legs of the chair on either side of him. *Goddamn it.*

"Dance with me," she said, rocking against his thighs.

"Katie," he warned.

"JJ," she said, mimicking his tone.

Dear god, he was going to die of embarrassment and lust in the same breath. Squeezing his eyes closed, he begged his body to listen to his brain. Follow the rule. *Follow the fucking rule.* "I *need* you to get off my lap."

"And I *need* you to dance with me," she said with a smile.

JJ shook his head. His 'need' was a little more pressing at the moment.

"We can do this the easy way. Or…" She ground her hips into his, and he almost fainted as he came to full attention beneath her. "The hard—"

The chair skidded out from behind him and toppled over as he jumped up.

Katie clung to his neck, laughing as he set her on her feet and tried to push her away. They both almost fell over the chair behind him as she clung to his neck and he stumbled out of the way. "You're trapped, Mr. Dayton."

His eyes darted around for an escape, but she was right. He was cornered on all sides, by her, the tent in his pants, the kids, and the longest song in the history of the world, which was still playing. *Fuck*, again. Thank god she was blocking him and no one was looking.

She stepped back and crossed her arms. "Not your kind of girl, huh?" Her eyes flicked to his crotch and then crinkled at the corners and met his again.

Wow. *Did she really just…* JJ dragged his hands over his face. "Please stop," he begged.

Wrapping her arm around his neck, she leaned against him, brushing her hips across his. "Dance with me, JJ."

"Oh, for fuck's sake." He took her by the wrist. Why was he trying to be a nice guy when she clearly wanted to play dirty?

Downing the rest of his beer, he turned her around, steering her around the table in front of him onto the dance floor. The kids cheered as he spun her around to face him. Draping one arm around his neck, he reached for the other one and pulled her close. It wasn't a slow song, but he'd have a coronary if he jumped up and down or tried to move his hips like she had. He pressed his palm into the small of her back. She wanted to play dirty? Fine. *Two can play at this game.* Exactly. He dragged her hips to his. *Fuck the rules.*

She came to him much more easily than he expected, and he had to take an extra step backward to keep from tumbling over. With a laugh, she fell against his chest, sliding her thigh between his legs, rubbing him in all the right ways. His knees almost buckled and fuck him. If they were playing a game, then she was winning.

Pressing her leg into his, her hips did that rolling thing that made him wonder if her bones were composed of rubber. Yes. He stifled a groan. She was definitely winning. The music thumped as she swayed in his arms. Releasing her hand, he pulled her even closer, and she gave him a blindingly beautiful smile, before sliding her other arm around his neck and pressing her cheek to his.

"I lied to Amelia." he whispered into her ear. It was a crappy apology, but it got the point across, and his brain really wasn't capable of stringing more than two words together at the moment.

"I know," she whispered back as the kids cheered again.

JJ tried not to pass out as Katie melted against him and the girls leaped around them like crazy little frogs. If there was a heaven, this was it. And she was right. They needed this. A break from the terror and fear and helplessness. A minute to feel human again, and not like an overstretched rubber band ready to snap or break, whichever came first.

The song ended abruptly, and he groaned. Of course, it would end the moment he convinced himself that he really was awake and not dreaming, and Katie really did like him. The universe must really hate him to fuck with him so—

"Again!"

Thankfully, little Amelia was not done, and as soon as the next song began, her sweet, but demanding little voice shouted, "Not that one. The other one. Again! Again!" until Katie extracted herself from his arms and went to appease her.

He quickly dropped into the nearest chair as she went back

behind the bar, wondering where his self-control had gone? Probably to the same place his rule had. Because after what just happened…goddamn it, he wanted her.

A second later, the song started again, and his heart pounded to the beat of the drum as Katie's body and the music video he had jerked off to a thousand times blended together before his eyes. Where in the *hell* had she learned to dance like that? The way her body moved, it was almost like she was liquid. She pulled him to his feet, and he practically jumped out of his chair, desperate to have her under his palms again.

His hand slid up her sweaty back under her shirt. "Take it easy, tiger," she whispered. "There are kids—"

He found the back of her neck and gently pressed her forehead to his, heaving like he'd run a marathon. To be fair, the last couple of weeks felt like one. "I can't…" 'Taking it easy' had taken a permanent vacation the moment she sat on his lap. "I can't do this anymore," he said, his tightly balled feelings unraveling so fast in his head it made him dizzy.

"What?" her breath was hot against his lips.

His fingers tangled in her hair as he clenched his fist. "Live with you, sleep beside you and not—" Jesus, was he really saying this? *Yes.*

"Just kiss me," she begged.

His ears were not the only part of him that heard that, and as he dragged her through the bar to the front door, it begged him to follow through this time.

The bell jingled as he threw the door open and pulled her outside. Bugs worked themselves into a frenzy around the light over the door as he pressed her back against the wall beside it and leaned in, his insides doing the same. His upbringing forced him to stop, just before he descended upon her. "Is this okay? Are you—"

She dragged his head to hers. "Yes."

His mouth closed over hers and he had about a tenth of a

second to enjoy it before Katie threw her hands up and turned her head away. He turned and did the same as a vehicle with high beams on, pulled to a stop at the curb. It was so bright he couldn't see a damn thing. The creak and bang of doors opening and closing was quickly followed by an unfamiliar voice. "Now, what do we have here?"

JJ spun around and shoved Katie behind him.

"Looks like a party to me. I think someone forgot the world is endin'."

Two men appeared, one shorter, the other about JJ's height. "Y'all got any booze in there?" The shorter guy nodded in the direction of the bar.

"It's closed." JJ said.

"Looks pretty open to me," the taller one said, taking a step toward the door.

JJ pushed Katie back as he stepped forward. The kids were in there, and there was no way he was letting either of those men anywhere near them. "I said it's closed. Get out of—"

The shorter one pulled a gun from behind his back. "I don't think so," he interrupted, as Katie peeked around him and gasped. "Now get the fuck out of my way before I—

When it came to *women*, JJ hesitated. He took a large step forward. But with assholes—he grabbed the guy's arm—he did not. Turning the gun away he yanked him forward, slamming his forehead right into his nose.

The man howled and his grip on the gun loosened as he raised his hand to his face. JJ yanked the gun away, spun around, and threw it as hard as he could. It clattered onto the roof of the grocery store.

"JJ!" Katie cried

He spun back around and threw his arm up, deflecting the taller guy's fist. It clipped his lip, but he didn't flinch. Above the music inside, he heard Amelia laugh. He was not afraid to die protecting Katie, or the kids. He lunged forward, his fist collided with the guy's chin. *But you're afraid to kiss her?* It was pretty much the stupidest thing he'd ever heard. His conversation with his mom echoed in his head. She was right. What in the hell was wrong with him? He needed to fix that ASAP. But first...

The first guy came at him, and he flung him off, but not before getting boxed in the ear. He swung at the second guy again as Katie screamed. JJ clocked him upside the head again, and he fell backward. Following him to the ground, he straddled him, punching him again. He was about to go for a third, when arms closed over his. He swung.

"Hey!" Sam shouted, jumping back. "It's me."

Leaping back to his feet, he surveyed the scene. The shorter guy was doubled over, holding his nose, blood everywhere, as the taller one struggled to get to his feet. Katie stood to the side, her hand over her mouth, while Mike and Sam stood on either side of him, ready to start swinging.

Wiping his bloody lip with the back of his hand, JJ stormed over to the shorter guy, grabbing him by the shirt and dragging him toward the headlights. Both of his eyes were already swelling shut. "Get the fuck out of here! Both of you!"

The second guy ran to the car, and as JJ pushed the first guy in, hopped in the driver's seat. Before he could close the door, the car was backing up. JJ jumped out of the way as it flew forward, and disappeared, plunging them back into darkness.

"You okay?" Mike asked, as JJ turned back toward the bar.

Jinn and Barb stood in the doorway. Katie was still under the light with her hand over her mouth.

"I'm fine," he said, although his lip stung like a bitch. "Come on, let's go inside."

"You think they'll be back?" Sam asked.

Shaking his head made it spin a little. "Nah. They were so drunk they probably won't even remember what happened tomorrow."

He was about to follow everyone into the bar when Katie's

hand closed over his wrist, holding him back.

"We're not done yet."

He pressed the back of his hand to his lip, the high from the fight, mixing with his lust as he turned. There was no mistaking the hunger in her eyes as his hand slid over her hip, pushing her away from the door. There was no hesitation on her part like there usually was for him in these situations. All he felt was straight up lust and god, it was the biggest turn on. "I'm not either," he said, sliding his hand along her jaw, as her arms came around his neck again.

The door jingled, and Grace's voice threw them apart as it pierced the night. "Amelia peed her pants again," she announced.

JJ turned away, squeezing his eyes shut. "Fuck."

Disappointed didn't come close to what he felt as Amelia said, "It's not my fault! You were the one that made me laugh."

He looked over his shoulder as Katie pushed her hair back. "Okay, just go home and change. There's a clean pair of pants in the pile on the kitchen table. Do you need me to—"

Please say no, JJ begged silently as Grace took Amelia's hand. "No, I got it."

He exhaled.

"Actually, it's getting pretty late," Katie said. "Why don't you girls get your pajamas on and brush your teeth? I'll be over in a few minutes to read stories." The door jingled again and Parker came out.

"I'm gonna head back, too. Come on." He gave JJ a nod as he ushered the girls toward the house. "Good night." He waved a hand over his head before disappearing into the night.

"Good night," she said, meeting JJ's eyes in the semi-darkness.

Neither of them spoke as he tried to gauge her mood, but the shadows on her face made it impossible to tell if she was disappointed or... over it. Not wanting to make an awkward moment worse, he said, "Let's go back inside."

As he turned, she grabbed his wrist. "Just so we're clear, I want this. I want you, JJ, whenever you're ready."

Oh, he was ready right now. Rules be damned. Took him fucking long enough, but he was.

"And I won't tell anyone you listen to tween pop." The laughter had returned to her voice, and even in the harsh light, with tiny buggy shadows dancing across her face, she was breathtaking. And that grin. He wanted nothing more than to wipe it off her lips with his, to feel her body against his and pick up right where they left off, with his hands in her hair.

Katie's brows came together. "What's the matter?"

"Nothing," he said before grabbing her head gently, but firmly, in his hands, and kissing her the way he'd wanted to since the day they met.

A breathy moan rushed over his lips as she flattened her palms against his chest. Her tongue flicked against his as she slid her arms around him, tugging until there was no space left between them. Fuck his fear, and Erica. He was done with both.

He pulled back, just far enough to speak, pushing her hair back off her face. "I want you too."

He was a breath away from claiming her mouth again when he was interrupted by the sound of an approaching vehicle. "Shit," he said, as Katie stiffened.

He squinted in the direction of the headlights, regretting having thrown the gun out of reach as they pulled to a stop right in front of them. Turning, he pushed Katie back behind him again. If this was it for him, at least he'd lived long enough to grow a pair of balls and kiss her. His old man would be proud. So would his mom.

The lights stayed and JJ heard the groan of a car door being pushed open. He was definitely going to die. "Stay behind me," he whispered over his shoulder. "And when I say go, run inside, lock the—"

"Is he bothering you?" Easton asked.

JJ's shoulders sagged in relief. "Goddamn it, Easton." He had never been so happy to hear Easton's fucking voice in his life. "Turn off the goddamn lights." He turned toward Katie, who shook her head, then buried it against his shoulder with what he thought sounded like a disappointed sigh. At least he wasn't the only one.

The lights went off and a moment later, Easton sauntered over to them. "What the hell happened to your face?" he asked through his mask. To Katie, he asked, "What's going on here? Is he—"

JJ ground his teeth together, setting a possessive hand on Katie's hip as she huffed a laugh and hid against him. "Exactly what it looks like," he said, as she squeezed him. "Now get the hell out of here."

Easton eyed him for a moment before shaking his head. "Goin' back to your roots, I see," he said, looking at Katie. "Slumming it with loser—"

Her head turned. "Shut up, Easton."

Easton laughed, and JJ wondered when exactly they'd become so familiar that he knew anything about her 'roots.' The thought of Easton alone with Katie made his blood boil for a lot of reasons. Namely, because of what Erica had called it his 'dark side.'

JJ looked down at the top of Katie's head, still pressed to his shirt, and remembered the incident on the day they'd met, when he was driving her back to Atlanta, how frightened she'd been. He pulled a protective arm around her shoulder and squeezed her back. "Get out of here, Easton." he repeated.

Eason laughed again. "Y'all have a good evening."

As the bell jingled, JJ released Katie. "He's gone."

Exhaling, she stepped back. The bugs continued to hover and dive around them, and she stared at her shoes and swatted at them.

"Fuck." It was all he could think to say.

She laughed shyly. "Yeah."

"Should we just give up or—"

Before he could finish, she grabbed his face in her hands and silenced him.

He winced as her mouth moved eagerly over his sore lips. But he didn't stop her. Instead, his hand found her waist and pulled. Fourth time had to be the charm, right? Bunching his shirt in her hand, her nails raked across his chest as her other hand slid up around his neck, pulling his head down harder against hers. He winced again as she pushed his lips apart with her tongue. Guess he would take that as a no.

His hands slid from her waist, over her hips, to her ass. His toes curled in his boots as he cupped it in his palms and lifted her off the ground. Goddamn it, she felt nice. He spun around, pinning her hips between his and the brick wall as she wrapped her legs around him. That did too. Rolling against him, she clung to him and kissed him like the world was ending. His free hands traveled up and down her sides, under her shirt, over her thighs as they gripped him like a vise. He groaned. *Holy shit.* He was going to—

"Katie?" Grace's voice brought their passionate embrace to a grinding halt. "Are you guys still out there?" she called through the darkness.

JJ pressed his head to her chest. "Son of a—" he whispered, as Katie laughed quietly, making his head bounce.

"Katie?" she called again from the house. "Are you guys out here?"

With a deep sigh, JJ retrieved his hand from under her shirt and lowered her to the ground.

"Um…Yeah." she called back, pulling the hem down.

"Amelia is getting cranky, and she wants you. I-I think she needs to go to bed. But she wants her story."

JJ sighed as Katie slumped against the wall between his arms and looked up at him. "It's the only thing she likes me to do for her," she whispered with a shrug. "Otherwise it's all *her* 'Beast'."

Yeah, he wasn't sure he liked that nickname. "Fine," he said. "Go."

"Thanks," she said before shouting into the dark. "I'll be right there!"

Pulling him close, she pressed her forehead to his chest again, and squeezed. "Okay, well, I'd better not keep *your daughter* waiting."

JJ huffed. "So you did hear all that, huh?"

"Yeah. It was nice of you to accept."

"Listen, about what she said about you—"

Katie lifted her head and brought her lips to his. "I don't care," she said against his mouth.

He kissed her, then leaned back. "Why aren't you upset? Every other woman I know would be."

She met his eyes. "Is it true?"

He shook his head, hoping that was crystal-fucking clear. "No."

She smiled. "That's why." Touching his lip, she added, "And thanks for looking out for all of us. Me. The kids. I've never had a hero before."

"I'm not—"

"Yes, you are. And it's nice."

He pulled her back into his arms for an extra second. Just because he could. Again, she came without hesitation, without... stiffness, or apprehension, and it gave him the confidence in the one area of his life where he lacked it. Bending his head toward her ear, he whispered, "You're nice, too. And we are not done."

She pulled back and gave him a playful wink. "I certainly hope not."

He watched her until she disappeared inside the house. Then, feeling more alive than he had in years, he went back into the bar for another beer.

Chapter Twenty-One

Day 12 // 2:30 a.m.

KATIE LIFTED the kitchen window with a grunt, letting in the breeze. Every other window in the house was open, but it was still hot. Her rash was back, and she'd scratched the insides of her elbows raw from the itching.

Amelia had been so amped up after their little dance party that Katie had to go through their little ABC story three times before she finally settled down. And then, Katie had fallen asleep too, somewhere between *'furry fox'* and *'great gorilla.'*

Katie looked at the timer on the canner, then pushed the flyaways back off her sticky forehead.

When her eyes had fluttered open only moments ago, and she realized she'd fallen asleep, she'd jumped out of bed and hurried to JJ's room. But he was already asleep.

The timer went off, and she turned it off quickly before it woke the kids, and vented it.

The wind picked up, and she stood in the cool breeze, fanning her neck as it filtered through the kitchen, rustling the pictures on the fridge. Katie turned and re-read the note JJ's mom had placed there sometime before the Veil.

There's meatloaf in the fridge. And I'm headed to Lincoln in the morning if you want me to drop off your water bill. Love you. Mom

When Katie had gone to answer the phone at Barb's yesterday and Mrs. Dayton had said who she was, Katie had almost dropped it, bracing herself for some kind of reprimand or warning about messing with her son. But instead, Mrs. Dayton had said how much she wished they could have met in person. And then she'd asked Katie to be patient with him. To give him time, and not to give up on him if he got "bull-brained," whatever that meant, although she could guess. Katie had tried to assure her nothing was going on between them, but Mrs. Dayton had put a stop to that with a tsk. *"I know my son. And while he might not know it, I do. He likes you...And if he likes you...then in my book you are worthy of liking.*

She blushed at that and tried to deny it, but again, Mrs. Dayton was having none of it.

"He does. Trust me. And it's terrifying him. You know how men are. Tough as nails, except when it comes to love or the common cold. Then they are worse than babies. His father was the same way. Jay's a good boy, and if you can hang in there long enough, you'll see it."

Katie hadn't known how to respond.

"The truth is, if I hadn't made the first move, we'd still be sitting in his pickup truck staring at each other, like love-sick fools and JJ wouldn't even be here."

Katie smiled.

"Be honest with him." Mrs. Dayton went on. "And be crystal clear about what you want. Because that boy won't take a hint if you smacked him upside the head with it. Another trait he got from his father." Her voice softened. "And then give him time to figure it out. Because he needs it."

"Figure out what?" she had asked.

"That you're not Erica, and that even if you were, she is not the evil person he thinks she is."

That had caught Katie's attention. "Who was she then?"

"Just a frightened girl who fell in love with the wrong kind of guy and became a mother before she was ready. She only did what most of us would."

Mother? Katie's mouth had gone dry at that.

Mrs. Dayton went on. "She followed her heart and did what she thought was best for her child."

Child? JJ had a child with Erica? She remembered the pictures that JJ had hidden. Oh god. Was that who he was hiding? Photos of his son? "Which was…?" she choked.

"Raising him with his father."

"Wait, JJ wasn't—?"

"No, but he wanted to be. He was trying to be. He loved her, he really did, but…her heart had always belonged to someone else. So, his broke twice when they left, and he's struggled ever since."

"Who was the—"

"Easton. Easton Barns. A boy Jay went to—"

Everything had slid into place then. "I know who he is." That was the reason JJ hated Easton so much, why he resisted the kids when he was clearly wonderful with them, why he didn't trust her.

Another cool gust of wind blew through the kitchen and the cabinet door creaked as she pulled it open and took a glass down.

It had been an enlightening conversation, and Mrs. Dayton's timing had been perfect. She had also been right about everything, because Katie had done just as she asked, and JJ had proved it last night.

A flash beyond the window caught her eye as she stared past Mrs. Dayton's dark house and downtown Hartford Creek, toward the horizon. Another pop of light followed. Lightning. A storm was coming. She could smell it on the wind. The rain would be welcome, especially in the areas where the fires were still burning.

Pouring a glass of water, she swallowed it in one gulp, then with oven mitts, swapped the jars and set the new jars in and timer again.

With a sigh, she set her glass in the sink and quietly made her way back to the bedroom, wondering if JJ thought she'd fallen asleep with the girls on purpose. But as she quietly slipped into bed beside him, he reached his arm around her and kissed her neck.

"I've been waiting for you," he mumbled against her head, as the trifecta worked its magic over her tired body.

Snuggling as close to him as she could, Katie closed her eyes and fell back asleep almost immediately.

Chapter Twenty-Two

Day 12 // 7:55 a.m.

KATIE'S EYES opened as thunder rumbled in the distance. JJ's side of the bed was empty when she rolled over. "Shit." She had wanted a minute to talk to him.

Pulling her hair into a bun, she shimmied into her jeans and headed into the living room.

JJ was sitting on the couch in the same jeans and T-shirt he'd had on the day before. His tattoos were even hotter in the daylight, as was the way his hair spiked up in the back from sleep. "Coffee's in the thermos."

Pouring herself a cup, she padded back into the living room, hesitating. He had been a little drunk last night, but *she* had been stone cold sober, and she wasn't sure about how he was feeling about what happened.... Chewing her lip, she tried to decide where to sit. By him on the couch, or the recliner?

Without looking away from the TV, he patted the couch next to him.

She sat down, leaving a couple of inches between them as the news anchor said,

"...still no cases of the virus in Miami or Chicago. Internationally, only Amsterdam remains unaffected. However, a new threat has befallen those inside the Veil, as outsiders, concerned by the possibility that they may disarm the Veils and free the virus, have made efforts to destroy the cities themselves. In the U.S. a domestic terrorist group calling themselves

the Army of Freedom, publicly threatened the president last week, claiming if he did not destroy the Veiled cities, they would. Since then, they have mounted several coordinated, but unsuccessful attempts to destroy the Veils in both Dallas and Atlanta where numbers continue to skyrocket. In a public statement made by the White House yesterday, President Rodriguez..."

"Where are the kids?" she asked.

He turned down the volume as she took a sip of her coffee. "At Ms. Michelle's getting eggs."

"I didn't know you roasted the coffee here. It's the best I've ever had. Seriously."

He gave her a sideways glance, and as the corner of his mouth went up. *Jesus Christ.* She nearly swooned as all the blood in her head rushed to...elsewhere.

His eyes went back to the TV, and she resisted the urge to crawl back on his lap. Why was she so horny? She wondered, studying his profile. Not even Matt had made her *this*...whatever this was.

"You're staring."

She blushed and hid it with a sip of coffee. "Sorry."

His hand closed over hers, and she sensed his nervousness as he laced their fingers together and set them on his thigh. He wouldn't look at her, but his thumb moved over the back of her hand causing a chain reaction that began with tingling in her special places, spread through her body like wildfire, and ended with her wanting to jump him right there on the couch.

Give him time, his mom had said. Katie groaned inwardly. She would. She would take it slow. Taking another sip of her coffee, she closed the space between them, resting her head on his shoulder. He lifted his arm, and she tucked herself against him as his heart hammered away beneath her ear as he turned up the volume. She would do whatever it took.

"...as deaths continue to climb in Dallas and Atlanta. According to the governor of Georgia however, the now dubbed–Atlantans–have been following the quarantine almost to the letter, yet the city continues to have the highest rate of infection in the country, leaving both the ICHP and CDC scratching their heads, and many people wondering if the president is hiding crucial information from the American people..."

"Goddamn it."

Katie bit her lip. She knew how worried JJ was for his mom and sister. She was worried about them, too. And the kid's parents that she'd gotten to know over the past several days now that the phones were working again... Just yesterday, after another tearful thank you for taking such good care of her daughter, Amelia's mom had told Katie that her parents would be on their way to get her as soon as they lifted the quarantine and obtained a permit to travel. Then she'd broken down and bawled like a baby, while Katie sat on the line and tried to think of something comforting to say.

Katie had been making sure all the kids called their parents every day. Even Parker, who only ever spoke for a minute before hanging up. Sometimes they couldn't get through, but most often they did. And the only thing more painful than talking to the parents herself was listening to the kids, the young girls especially, do it. Sometimes she sat on the other side of the wall and cried.

She squeezed JJ's hand, knowing how desperate he was to help them. They were all in the same boat...except her.

Because the truth that she could never admit to anyone was that the virus, and the Veil, had saved her. It had forced her to do what she should have done a long time ago, which was give up the meaningless, ridiculous life she'd been living. Abandon the facade of perfection that was so grueling and cruel to the woman buried beneath it. She didn't want to be perfect anymore. She didn't want everyone to like her. Instead, she just wanted to be happy, to do something meaningful and... She turned and looked at the disaster in JJ's gloomy kitchen, remembering her spotless, glistening, magazine-ready one in LA. She wanted a lived-in and messy house. Turning, she studied JJ's profile again. And she wanted love. Real, honest-to-god, love.

Thunder rumbled again, and she looked out the window at Mike's across the street, and the pond out back behind it. And all of that was right here. In Hartford Creek, Georgia of all places. The thought made her smile.

For the first time in her life, she truly felt like she belonged somewhere. And as impossible as it may have seemed two weeks ago, it was here. Not LA. Not New York, not on a yacht in the Caribbean with some young tech mogul. But right here, in this little house in the middle of nowhere. Because somewhere between Barb and Mr. Goebell and the kids and JJ, she'd found a world where people genuinely liked her for who she was, and not what she looked like. She found a small place where she felt needed and had purpose.

Heat rushed to her cheeks as she realized JJ was watching her. Her breath paused in her throat, forgetting which way to go as she stared. God, his eyes. They were like him, an irresistible contradiction. Gritty and sweet. Honey and mud, and she wanted to dive head-first into both, until every square inch of her body knew what it felt like to be seen by them. The flecks of amber flashed like fire, igniting her like a book of matches.

"What are you thinking?"

Slow, Katie. "I-I..." She couldn't answer with him looking at her like that. Tearing her gaze away, it landed on the TV. "I'm glad the fires have stopped." A news reporter in a blue blazer with dark brown hair pulled back in a ponytail was standing outside a small mansion in Dunwoody, the crumbling front of the house a magnificent example of the devastation they had caused.

"Thousands of families remain homeless in the wake of the wildfires that tore through the area earlier last week, contributing to the rapidly increasing number 'missing persons' reports. That is according to government officials, who addressed the mounting concerns of family members unable to locate their loved ones earlier today." The scene switched to a press conference with the Governor. Katie recognized him from the party she'd gone to in Savannah. *"Shelters are being set up as we speak, and as soon as possible, we will start compiling lists of families, similar to the ones we are doing for the displaced children, and get them out to the public. Until then, please hang tight and know we are working on it."* The scene switched back to the reporter in front of the collapsed house. A hole in the front exposed a charred couch and blackened piano.

"Not even the seclusion of Atlanta's premiere affluent neighborhood, Kirkland Estates, where homes range from one to twenty-five million dollars was spared.

"I still can't believe this is happening," JJ said. "I mean, I see it, and I *know* it is, but my brain just can't believe it." He huffed a laugh. "But if it's happening to rich people too, you know it's got to be real."

Katie nodded. "That was a hundred-thousand dollar piano."

JJ turned to her, looking surprised. "How do you know that?"

She tucked her hair back behind her ear and shrugged. "I've seen a lot of them over the years. At parties and… I went to this actress's house in Mexico City once, for a wrap party and she had a hand painted Steinway that she'd paid over three *million* dollars for."

JJ gave her a look she couldn't decipher. "That was really your life?" JJ interrupted.

Katie blinked. "What?"

"Parties, traveling, grand pianos, and beautiful actors?"

"Umm…" She shrugged. *Technically,* yes, it was. But it had

never felt like the way he made it sound. In truth, it was filled with the same things her career had been, a lot of stress and pressure and fear. It was no mystery to her why so many famous people struggled with drugs and alcohol. It was a beautiful, miserable life they all led. "Kind of. But it wasn't ever as glamorous as I made it look on my socials. At the end of the day, people are just people. They had nice *things*, expensive cars and fancy perfume but…There's more happiness in Hartford Creek than in most of the homes I've been to in LA."

The corner of JJ's mouth turned up. "They couldn't possibly smell as good as you do."

Why that made her blush, she didn't know, but it did. "It's custom. A perfumer in LA made it for me."

He sniffed her. "It smells like oatmeal cookies and mangoes—"

Katie burst out laughing as she leaned against him. "The mango is my shampoo. And oatmeal cookies? I think it's the bourbon vanilla you smell, which is usually reserved for men's cologne, a little oak, and coffee and orange blossom."

"Whatever it is, it's amazing."

The way he said that made her insides flutter as she stared at the graph on the TV and he laced their hands together again. "I don't understand how the numbers in Atlanta are still going up," she said, trying to ignore her amorous thoughts.

JJ sighed, dragging his hands through his hair, and she got another look at the tattoos on the inside of his arm as the spicy scent of his deodorant enveloped her, and she imagined his arm wrapped around her as it had been last night, cupping her breast while she slept. Heat flooded her cheeks. God, she wanted him in the worst way. And the best way too. And every other way in between, if she was being honest.

"I can't understand it either. My mom—" He released her hand and turned to face her, his brows drawn together. "Wait, a second. Yesterday you said you spoke with my mom. What exactly did you mean by that?"

Katie hesitated. "She called Barb yesterday. I was there, and I knew I might need to blackmail you at some point, so I... asked her about the CD's." That was true.

He laughed and blushed beneath his clipped beard. She just left out the beginning and middle part where Mrs. Dayton had called specifically to speak to Katie and the conversation they'd had about JJ.

"She confirmed everything, saying and I quote 'Oh yes. He used to blast it in the shower and when he was in the garage working'—"

JJ held up his hand. "Okay. Okay."

She gave him a serious look. "I don't know why you're so embarrassed about that—"

"Thanks."

Trying her best to keep the corners of her mouth down, she continued. "When you were twenty-five and still living with your mom."

JJ blanched. "Hey. I-I did move out. Eventually."

"Yeah, I noticed. Next door. Way to spread those wings, big boy."

JJ looked thoroughly mortified. "*What?*"

She broke into a grin.

"You're joking," he accused. Or maybe it was a question.

"Yes, I am." And enjoying his discomfort *way* too much.

"You have a sense of humor." Again, she couldn't tell if he was asking or stating a freshly gleaned fact.

"You finally noticed." She leaned closer and whispered. "I have a vagina, too. In case that sailed past your radar."

His eyes widened, then narrowed. "Exactly what did my mother say to you?"

She shrugged. "That you are a good man, like your dad, and

you've been taking care of her and your sister since he died." His jaw dropped open. "And that sometimes you're as dumb as a fence post and can't see what's right in front of you, so I ought to explain whatever I am trying to say to you as if I'm talking to a toddler."

His eyes widened, then narrowed again. "You're joking again."

"Yes, I am." She paused. "Mostly."

He studied her for a moment, chewing his lip. "Just so we're clear. My mom is the only one in the family with a sense of humor."

"I know," Katie said, matching his concerned expression, trying not to smile.

She bumped his shoulder. "Don't worry. I won't hold it against you." With a wink, she sat up and retrieved her coffee. "We all have our strong suits and our weaknesses."

JJ leaned forward on his elbows, giving her the side-eye. "It seems to me like all your suits are strong."

Katie shook her head. If only. "No. Not all of them."

JJ sighed and scratched his chin. "You really talked to my mom, huh?"

"Yeah. And kidding aside, she seems amazing." She nudged him again. "If she were my mother, I wouldn't have moved far either."

"I want to tell you about mine."

"Your what?" Katie asked.

"My... weaknesses. Why I've been..."

"An asshole?"

JJ shook his head, his mouth smiling beneath his scruff.

He'd smiled just like that at Barb that first day at the bar, and like then, it—*slow Katie*. Right.

"I don't know if I like you with a sense of humor," he said.

She smiled back. "Unfortunately, I don't come any other way."

"I was going to say *acting like a crazy person*, because that's what my mom called it."

She waited.

He dropped her hand and leaned forward, resting his elbows on his knees again. "I like you." He sounded like he had something stuck in his throat. "But I've been acting like a crazy person—"

"Wait," she interrupted. "So you've talked to her, your mom, about me?"

"Yeah." He gave her a guilty smile. "Of course I have. A lot too. And the reason I've been..."

"Difficult?"

"Yeah, it's because..." He took a deep breath. "...because I've been screwed over by a beautiful woman before and she um... Well, it's taken me an embarrassingly long time to get over it." He shook his head. "What I mean is..." His shoulders sagged, and he dropped his head into his hands. "Fuck. I don't know what I'm trying to say."

She sat up and leaned forward so she could see his face. "How about you just tell me what happened?"

"Her name is Erica. We were in high school together. She was a couple years behind me. She was *the* popular girl. The one all the other girls wanted to be. She was pretty, not beautiful like you, but cute...in her own way." He laughed. "She was a cheerleader, and always had her nails painted and wore a thong that somehow always managed to peek out of the top of her jeans, and all the guys, myself included, dreamed of doing...*anything* with her. Holding her hand, carrying her books... It was the same after she graduated. She was the 'it' girl in town, working at the drive-thru, going to community college."

Katie stared at her feet. In high school, she had been at the opposite end of that hierarchy. The invisible last stop before falling into nothing.

"Well, anyway, she got pregnant. No one knew who by, and

for a long time, I didn't think she even knew, because she partied a lot. But suddenly she wasn't popular anymore. People... Well, you know how young people are."

Katie sighed. Yes, she did.

"Between that and the small-town gossip, she was black-listed. Her friends abandoned her. Another girl, Ashleigh Green, took her place at the top of the food chain, and..." He laughed bitterly. "Poor Erica. That's what I thought, anyway. I wasn't popular, never had been, and I was out of school by then, so I had nothing to lose by befriending her. Once we became friends, she convinced me she'd been taken advantage of, that she was not the girl that everyone thought she was. She told me the same things you told me last night." JJ paused, meeting her eyes out of the corner of his eye. "Even then, I knew I shouldn't, but...I believed her. I ignored the fact that she was out of my league, and had never dated anyone that...I don't know, wasn't a sports star, didn't have a six-pack. But she said she'd changed, and I believed her." Smiling sadly, he scratched his beard, then went on. "For the first time in my life, a beautiful woman saw me." He laughed. "And I fell for it. Hard. Hook line and sinker and we started dating."

Katie sipped her coffee.

"She was eighteen, and her mom was a fucking waste of air, and her dad had been gone forever, so I got a job, and an apartment close to school and the hospital, and we moved in together. I went to every doctor's appointment." He twisted his hands together as he stared at them. "I was there when she picked out the crib and the sheets with the little elephants on them. And when she had a meltdown in the middle of Target over what kind of baby wipes to get." He laughed again. "I was in the car when she burst into tears over a dead raccoon mom and her babies on the side of the road. I was there when..." His voice broke, and Katie's heart broke along with it. "...when Brian was born. He was so small. And so damn cute. His tiny fingers latched onto mine, and I remember sitting there, holding him, thinking about how small his bones must be, how fragile, like little toothpicks, and how it was now my job to make sure they never broke. And it filled me with something..." He shook his head. "Powerful and meaningful. I had purpose, and god, I loved that boy as if he were my own."

Tears filled Katie's eyes.

"And he was. For one year and seven months."

She squeezed her eyes shut. *Oh, god.* "JJ."

"It turns out Erica *did* know who knocked her up. And after Brian was born, and the dust had settled, the father wanted back in on the action."

Easton. Katie pressed her fingers into her temples.

"He was tall, and handsome, heading into a respectable career as a prominent member of the community."

Katie reached for his hand, but he pulled it back into his lap. "When she told me who it was, I was surprised, but not really. Easton was good-looking. He played basketball, varsity football his freshmen year. And he'd always been a douche, ever since we were kids. Anyway, when she told me what he wanted, I thought..." He shook his head. "I thought we'd laugh about it, and she'd tell him to fuck off."

"But she didn't."

"No. And I know it's my fault but... When she said she was going to allow it, allow him to be a part of Brian's life...I felt betrayed. I felt like she was stripping my fatherhood away." He rubbed his arm. "I felt like everything I loved was slipping through my fingers and there was nothing I could do about it. I gave her an ultimatum. Again, my fault. Me or him." He laughed again. "I had been working at the quick lube for about a year then, and stocking shelves at the local grocery in the evenings. Basically, I was going nowhere, so it wasn't a hard decision for her to make."

"I'm sure that's not—"

J.N. SMITH

"A week later, she moved out of our apartment and in with him."

His mom's words echoed in her head. *Just a frightened girl who became a mother before she was ready. She was doing what she thought was best for her child.*

"Watching her take Brian, and know there was nothing I could do about it..." He shook his head again. "It's not *her* I haven't been able to get over. It's my fear of getting played again. Because she took my son, Katie." He met her eyes. "And she gave him to Easton."

Katie swallowed the lump that had formed in her throat. Her voice was a hoarse whisper as she asked. "But...they aren't together now, are they?"

JJ leaned back against the couch and rubbed his eyes with the heel of his hands. "Nope. They lasted six months, and at least half of that time, they hated each other. I think she left because he hit her, that son of a bitch."

"Where is she now?"

"Last I heard, she was living with her mom near Chattanooga."

"You don't keep in touch?"

He shook his head.

"Why not?"

"When she realized things weren't going to work out with Easton..."

"She wanted to come back?"

"Yeah."

"And you said no."

"Yeah. I couldn't." He shrugged. "I didn't trust her anymore, and I was too afraid she would," he rubbed his arm again, "...take him from me again, and I couldn't bear it. I still can't. Which is why it's so hard for me now with kids."

"And why you were so worried about getting in touch with their parents when the Veil went up?"

262

He nodded. "I-I know what it feels like to not know where your kids are... To wonder if they're safe. To wonder what they're doing."

Katie ran her hands over her face as JJ got up and disappeared down the hall. He returned a minute later, holding a photo, and handed it to her.

She barely recognized him. His face was rounder, and younger, but it was his smiling eyes that made him almost unrecognizable. The way they crinkled at the corners, and sparkled like they'd just heard a hilarious joke. She smiled at the boy in his arms. He had blue eyes and chubby cheeks, and was wearing a monster truck t-shirt. Maybe it was because she knew, but he looked just like Easton, same nose, and pronounced brow. He had his fingers curled around JJ's neck affectionately. The third person in the photograph had to be Erica. She was tiny and skinny and had blond hair. She was everything Katie had never been. Her face was heart-shaped, her features delicate and cute. She had a small heart-shaped mouth to match, and a button nose, and her blue eyes were slivers as she grinned at the camera. They'd made a beautiful family. "I—" She didn't know what to say.

Standing over her, JJ took the photo and stared at it. "I am trying really hard not to project any of my shit on you, but...I've got to be honest. Every time I get near you, half of me wants to wrap you in my arms and never let go, and the other half is screaming at me to run for my life before I get fucked all over again."

She wasn't anything like Erica, but she understood where he was coming from. She didn't blame him for being wary, especially if he'd seen her social media account. After all, she had spent most of her life *trying* to fake precisely what Erica had been naturally. Desirable, popular, beautiful, admired. None of that had come easily for her...Except maybe the desirable part. But that hadn't been in the way any woman would want, and it certainly had not worked out to her advantage. At least when she was young.

With a heavy breath, she stared into her empty mug. "I owe you an explanation too," she heard herself say. *Are you doing this?* Her heart thumped in her chest. *Are you really going to tell him?*

Yes, she was. Unfolding herself from the couch, she got up and went to the kitchen. She poured herself the rest of the coffee, and then, spying the whiskey, pulled the bottle off the top of the fridge and took a long pull.

"Hey." JJ's voice was soft from the doorway. "You don't have to... I didn't tell you about my situation because I wanted you to explain yours."

She held up her hand, and took another drink, then twisted the cap back on and set it back in its place. The coffee mug was comforting and hot in her hands as she went back to the couch and sat down. Instead of sitting down, JJ remained in the doorway to the kitchen, watching her.

She took a deep breath. "Despite what you may think, I was nothing like Erica in high school. I was the opposite, unpopular and—"

"I remember."

"Don't get me wrong. I-I *wanted* to be. Every girl does. I don't care who they are. And if they say they don't, then they're lying. Anyway, my parents are not like yours. They're..." How did she even begin to explain her parents? "Let's just say they gave white trash a bad name."

JJ smiled at her sad joke.

"I wanted attention. And the only kind I got at school was bad. So I started seeking it elsewhere. And I was so desperate to be noticed and feel ...*wanted,* I took whatever anyone would give me from *whoever* gave it to me. I started chatting online with guys. I was young and stupid, and..."

She squeezed her eyes shut and exhaled through her parted lips as her heart stuttered in her chest. *Tell him.* She'd never told anyone. Not even Matt knew. *Tell him.* She took another deep breath. She was trying. And she *wanted* JJ to know. "Anyway, my dad used to hang out at this bar." Coffee spilled out of her mug, so she set it down, pulling her shaking hands into her lap. "It was right around the corner from our house, and my mom used to send me to get him sometimes, and there were these guys there. The kind of shit guys you'd expect to be hanging around a shit bar in the middle of the afternoon. He called them friends, and maybe they were... I- I don't know."

JJ made a sound, and she looked up. The way he was looking at her almost made her stop, but she'd already come this far. And she wanted him to know. He was not the damaged one.

"There was this one guy. Lenny. He was..." She felt like she was going to have a heart attack saying his name out loud. "He started smiling at me when I came in. Then he started complimenting me, saying things like...How do you not have a boyfriend?" She swallowed hard as his face appeared. His greasy blond hair pulled back in a ponytail, his square jaw, and missing tooth. The lust in his eyes that she'd mistaken for desire. "He made me laugh. I felt...seen."

JJ's hands closed over hers, and she blinked in surprise to find him sitting in front of her, on the coffee table.

"And I liked being seen." She stared at JJ's hands. "One day after school, I went over there to get my dad, and he was outside smoking a cigarette. He pulled me aside before I could go in, and asked me how old I was. I had just turned eighteen the week before... he kissed me. Right there in broad daylight and I... I kissed him back. It was my first. Then he pulled me around the side of the building and..."

"Jesus."

"No." She shook her head. Unfortunately, they weren't to the worst part yet. "We just made out. Nothing else happened. He let me go, and I went in and got my dad, and we went home."

JJ exhaled. "Thank god."

Katie smiled sadly. "Not quite."

"How old was he?"

"In his mid-thirties, I think. I'm not sure. We didn't talk about *his* age much."

JJ squeezed her hands. "So neither of us had a great experience with—"

"I'm not done," she said, meeting his eyes and his face fell. "I started sneaking out to see him." She paused, remembering, "Sneaking is a strong word. My parents didn't care where I went, not enough to stop me, anyway. I started going to the bar and meeting up with him and his friends after my dad came home and passed out. They seemed cool. We played pool or darts. They joked with me, flirted. I was the only girl there, and it felt amazing to get all the attention. And the more I got, the more I wanted." She paused. "Even though I was eighteen then, I'd never had a boyfriend. And the men in my life treated me like crap, so... I ate it up." *It's time.*

Yes, it was. She took another deep breath, then exhaled, and began. "One night, we were all hanging out, and he asked me if I wanted to do a hit of ecstasy. I didn't but, all the guys were all doing it, and so..." She shrugged. What else could she do in the face of such stupidity? "Long story short, it wasn't ecstasy. I don't know what it was, maybe a roofie or something else... I have exactly two memories from that night. One, I'm in some hotel room, I don't know whose, and there are a bunch of older men I don't know there. Mostly in suits, but a few others and I'm sitting in a chair, just watching them."

"Is that why you prefer younger guys?" JJ asked.

She nodded. "Yeah. They're...safer. And the second...I was naked and on my knees on the bed and..." It hit her the same every time she thought about it. It was like waking up in a nightmare and knowing how it ends but still having to live through the terror. The men, her confusion, the pain and humiliation, the sweet, vile scent of expensive brandy on their breath.

She gasped, tugging at the collar of her t-shirt. Then gasped again, trying to get enough air in her lungs to get the rest of the story out, but they kept deflating before the words could come.

Gasp. Gasp.

She clutched her knees as JJ squeezed her shoulder.

Gasp. Gasp.

Oh, god, she couldn't breathe.

He put his hand on her back, as she leaned forward, rubbing giant circles over her shoulder blades. "Hey. Hey. It's okay. Breathe."

She shook her head. Gasp. She couldn't. And now she remembered why Easton scared her so much. He looked and acted just like one of the men at that party. A South Florida Sheriff's officer, blond, blue eyed and bruta—

JJ cupped her face in his hands, his eyes searing holes into hers as she clung to his arms. "Breathe Katie." She opened her mouth, and a whisper of air slipped into her lungs. He nodded. "That's it, breathe. You don't need to tell me more."

"But I want you to know the—" Gasp. Gasp.

"I know enough." The horror in his eyes confirmed it. Whatever he was imagining was close enough to the truth. Exhaling, she nodded.

"Just...take it easy," he soothed. "You're okay now."

She nodded again and took a deep breath. She'd done it. Tears filled her eyes. She'd finally told someone. And the shame of the burden she'd carried around for the last fifteen years dissolved as she disentangled herself from the past, let it roll down her cheeks, and brushed it away.

When her breath steadied, she released him and met his eyes. There was no judgment, despite her gross stupidity, only compassion and anger. The latter directed not at her, but at them, the ghosts of her past.

For the first time, JJ looked like a dangerous man, and the look in his eyes was deadly as he stared at her, looking like he wanted to do more than punch someone. "Did you ever press charges?" he asked, finally.

She shook her head. "It was my fault. I was the one sneaking out to hang out with them. Everyone knew that. And he never made me do anything...At least not that I remember. I voluntarily took that pill. And I wasn't a minor anymore." She pulled her hair back. "I think...I think they'd planned that on purpose. Just in case I tried to press charges."

"Fuck."

"I woke up the next morning in Lenny's bed, ass naked. He acted like nothing had happened out of the ordinary, and I was so groggy and hung over I thought maybe I'd imagined the whole thing. But then when I went to get up... I was *so* sore. He brushed it off when I asked him. He told me we'd just had a wild night. Told me how 'wonderful' I was and how I was the best lay of his life. And I wanted to believe him."

JJ groaned, burying his face in his hands.

"I hung out with him for a couple more weeks after that. I don't know why. I was so confused. And he seemed so sure of everything. He continued to flatter me. He bought me a ring, called me his girl... and in exchange, I slept with him, and he... taught me 'the way men like things done.' Anyway, one night we go to a party, to hang out with some new 'friends' he made. We get to this condo on the ocean... it smelled like booze and cigarettes, and it was just like before. Guys in business suits, but no other women. He handed me a shot of tequila, and offered me another pill, and I just... I knew he had lied. I knew it had happened, and I knew he wanted me to do it again, and I couldn't." She folded her hands together. "When I left, he followed me down the hall screaming all sorts of terrible things at me. Calling me a whore and a slut."

"At least you left."

"But it had already happened once. I got tested right away, and by some miracle I hadn't contracted anything, or gotten pregnant, But I was so ashamed, and felt so stupid and used. Then the videos surfaced. He'd taken two that night of the party, and they spread like wildfire on the internet. My dad found out and threw me out of his house, which was fine because I couldn't stay there anymore, anyway, but..." She met his eyes. "I've never watched them, but... just so you know, there are videos of me out there. Doing...things you might not like to see." Pressing her fingers to her forehead, she massaged her brow. "They fade away for a while, but every few years they pop back up and..."

"I'm sorry."

She shrugged. "Maybe with the internet down, they'll finally be gone for good."

JJ gave her a small smile.

"Anyway, I was in a hurry to leave south Florida but didn't have a car or anything at all except a suitcase full of clothes. My plan was to head up to New York, live with a guy I met on spring break, and get my GED, but I needed money first. There was this guy I'd been talking to online. His name was Ali... He went to The University of Florida, and was a vet major," she huffed a laugh. "AliGator0615 was his handle. He told me to come up to Gainesville, that I could stay with him until I got on my feet. I had nowhere else to go, so I went. When I got there, he was nice, pushy, but nice. He was cute, had an amazing apartment, and seemed to enjoy spending money on me. I wanted to move on, forget my past, but it haunted me. Every time I looked in the mirror, or pulled one of my old t-shirts over my head, it was there, reminding me of everything I was trying to forget."

The way JJ was looking at her made it clear he couldn't

imagine feeling that way about his home, and she was glad for that.

"That was why I decided to reinvent myself. I went on my first diet. I got my hair done, tanned, trashed all my clothes. Ali bought me new ones. I was depressed and living off cigarettes, so I lost fifteen pounds in less than a month. He told me I was beautiful. I learned how to do makeup and bought my first pair of high heels. I ended up sleeping with him, although he was quite a bit older than me. From my experience with Lenny, I knew what to do. But he 'taught' me more, and I did whatever he asked. I figured I owed him for everything he was doing for me, and besides, what was I holding out for? True love? Like that would ever happen. I mean, what respectable family man would want me after they found out about the videos?"

She unfolded, then refolded her hands. "It was great for about a month, but then he started talking about when we 'got married.' He took me to look at a house, and we fucked in the walk-in closet and as he pulled his pants up, he told me we were going to have three kids and he wanted me to get pregnant as soon as possible. He said once I was, he would buy me a house just like the one we were in and we'd live happily ever after. I freaked out." She paused, remembering just the way he said it. It hadn't been a hope or a request, but a demand. "The next day when he left for class, I grabbed my shit and took off, vowing I was done with older guys who thought they had something to teach me."

JJ snorted through his nose.

"In a weird twist of fate, the social media page I'd created to document my transformation, caught the eye of a minor celebrity in the fashion world. She reposted one of my posts and... Boom. Just like that, I was famous. I was an inspiration to girls everywhere. Guys, old and young, told me how beautiful I was and... all my dreams started coming true. I headed up the east coast, toward New York, and people started offering me things. I was in

Raleigh, staying at a seedy shit-hole hotel, when this famous plastic surgeon from L.A. called me and offered to fly me out and give me a free boob job." Her jitters had subsided, and she felt as incredulous as she had back then. "I didn't know what was happening. I mean...one minute, I'm high school trash and the next minute I'm flying first class across the country? What the *fuck*? But that's exactly what happened."

"What happened with Ali?"

"Nothing other than becoming my longest tenured stalker. But I've had a bunch over the years. There was Brayden, and Rick, Dylan, Pete...The list goes on. But as I've gotten older, Ali is the only one who's stuck with me."

"Are you serious?"

"Yep. It was pointless to block him from my social media accounts, because he would just create a new user name, and friend me again to see where I was, what I was up to. Usually, I post a day behind, so I'm not actually where it looks like I am, but if I'm advertising for an event...I can't avoid people knowing. So, he'd show up unannounced at venues I was at, trying to convince me to get back together with him. The way he spoke about us, you'd have thought we were together for years, not weeks. Matt, my ex, that's how we met. We were at the same charity event in L.A. He was on leave and spending a few days with his friend Gates. Ali turned up, and wouldn't leave me alone. Matt came up and asked me if he was bothering me. I said yes. Matt punched him in the face, just dropped him right there in front of everyone. He almost got arrested." She smiled. "Matt, not Ali."

"Then, when we started dating, and he had to head back overseas, he convinced me to press charges. Ali went to jail for nine months the first time, then two years because he broke his parole and the restraining order I had against him. He gets out again in August. But without the internet..."

"No one can find you."

She shook her head. "Not anymore."

"What happened with you and Matt?"

Katie reached for her mug as JJ sat back down beside her on the couch. "Are we just going to air it all out then?" she asked.

"You don't have to if you don't want to."

She did, and she didn't. "Matt was in the Army. Like I said, I met him on leave. He was...amazing." She smiled. "Like you. The complete package. As great on the inside as he was on the outside. Brave, loyal, kind of an asshole, but hilarious and good natured. Hot. But best of all, he was young, and less experienced than me."

"You were in control."

She nodded. "He was twenty-four, and I was thirty-two, and I didn't know what I wanted from our relationship, but he didn't pressure me, or try to mold me. He followed *my* lead. I liked that. And not that it mattered, but he was amazing for my social media. My female followers loved him. Surprisingly, my guy followers did too, because he was a hero. Everything was perfect. We were perfect and then..." Her hands stilled in her lap. "And then he asked me to marry him. And everything just fell apart in my head. The sweeter and kinder he was to me, the more suspicious I became. The less I trusted him. He knew that I was messed up, that my parents were dead beats, so he was patient with me. Incredibly so, but in my fucked-up brain, that *proved* to me he was after something... I started thinking he was trying to trap me, to trick me, or subdue me, otherwise why would he ask? Why did he want to change our relationship? I-I loved him. I really did, but I didn't *want* to because I was afraid he was going to hurt me. And I couldn't let that happen again. So, I found his weakness, and I hurt him first."

The rumble of Old Ray's engine brought her head around. Damn it. The kids were back, and she hadn't yet told JJ how much she regretted what she'd done, how she'd vowed to change, how with the help of therapy, she *had* changed, that she was different now, a better person.

Parker cut the engine and a second later climbed out, followed by Amelia.

"But I'm not that person anymore," she managed just before Grace pulled the door open. JJ met her eyes, looking uncertain, she thought. "I mean it. I'm not."

Chapter Twenty-Three

Day 12 // 10:33 p.m.

THEY HADN'T FINISHED their conversation, but Katie had given him plenty to think about for the next thirty-six hours. And that was a good thing, because when he, Sam and Mike had arrived at the Veil yesterday, he'd needed the distraction from the truck-loads of bodies that the authorities were disposing of. He still didn't know how it happened, but it was as if overnight, Atlanta had become the city media outlets and the numbers were saying it was. The virus was suddenly everywhere, and it didn't seem like there was much anyone could do to stop it. He, Mike, and Sam had gone from not being able to turn away from the bodies to not being able to look in less than a minute, and since then, it had only gotten worse.

He heard a zap and squinted through the dark. Something must have tried to pass through the Veil, a bird or squirrel or something. He turned and watched as several masked men loaded a forklift of 4x4's onto the truck. JJ stayed near the cab, and out of their way, and took a sip of his water.

Officials were calling the places where the bodies were being vaporized, sanitation points, and it seemed like every few hours, a new one popped up on the outskirts of town, where major roads intersected the Veil. He'd talked to his mom earlier, and she'd confirmed his worry. "More people are out and about. I don't know if they don't believe in the quarantine anymore, or if they've just given up. I mean, we did everything they asked and still... I saw a man and a woman going for a walk with their dog today, like nothing was wrong. It made me cry," she'd said.

The Coast Guard had put him to work with a salvage crew. They were the ones loading the truck while he was in charge of driving it. The president, or whoever, had decided to move the no-trespass boundary back a couple of miles and they were in the process of clearing out all the businesses and shops of their inventory. It seemed insane that the government could just take what it wanted, but that was exactly what they were doing. They'd set up huge depots, and for the past twenty-four hours, it had been one semi after another, dropping off trailers full of stuff, and heading back out to get more. Sam and Mike had gone back home in his truck, but JJ had stayed on to help. As soon as the crew finished loading, he'd be on his way again.

JJ rubbed his eyes. He was tired, but he didn't want to be far away from the city if his mom or sister called.

He heard another zap and turned. The Veil cut right through the home improvement store they were loading, and he was only twenty feet from the barricade that warned trespassers away, but it was dark behind the store, too dark to see whatever it was. He listened to the frogs in the pond somewhere behind him, wondering how the Veil dealt with that. Mike said he heard it sterilized the water, killing all the biological organisms in it, the same as it did on land. JJ couldn't even begin to understand how that worked.

Who he did understand better, though, was Katie. She said she wasn't like Erica, but their stories were similar enough. Teenage girl makes a mistake. Gets...fucked by guy. *Guys.* JJ squeezed his eyes shut, wishing he knew who they were so he could go smash their faces in. Then, girl meets someone who *actually* cares about them and...screws them over, because she's scared. The only difference was, Katie seemed to regret hurting Matt. The way she talked about him, like he was some kind of saint, made him wonder. Did she still love him? JJ knew her feelings for him were genuine, but he'd learned his lesson. Settling for second place was not a mistake he'd make again. He had to be first or not at all—

Another zap brought his head around. Then two more. Zap. Zap.

"What the hell?" Pulling his phone from his pocket, he headed toward the back of the lot and the sound. He could make out the tops of several pines as he pressed the button for the light and shined it around. He jumped back as a squirrel, on the other side, stopped just before colliding with the Veil. It stared at him with glittering black eyes. Pressing a hand to his chest, he turned back to the truck, glad his dad wasn't there to see him have a heart attack over a squirrel. "Jesus."

A second later, he heard the zap and knew his little friend had met its demise.

It was another twenty minutes before they finished loading the truck, then JJ climbed in and headed out.

An odd sound brought him and the truck to a stop. He looked up in time to see fireworks explode from somewhere near downtown. "What the hell?" He wouldn't have thought they could even go through the flat low ceiling of the Veil, but apparently they could. Another pop was followed by another display. Lifting his foot off the brake, he continued north along the Veil as more fireworks lit the sky, and quickly dialed his mom. "Hey, sweetie."

"What is happening in there?"

"Haven't you seen the news?"

"No. I'm working."

"It seems like the city's given up. After today and yesterday. They don't trust the President. They think it's some sort of experiment and he's trying to kill us. All day people were driving up and down the streets, shouting about some big party downtown."

"You're not going."

"No, of course not."

"Have you been outside at all?"

"No. But…I think people in the building are dying. We can smell them."

"Did you see anyone go out?"

"No. I've only seen a few dogs out, doing their business— oh, wait. I wanted to tell you I spoke with Katie."

JJ pressed the phone between his shoulder and his ear and shifted gears. "Yeah, I know." He huffed. "She told me. Thanks for selling me out."

"What?"

"My CD's?"

"Oh…" she paused. "Was that not okay?"

"Well, she used it to blackmail me, so you tell me."

His mom laughed, and he noticed for the first time how much he loved that sound. "I like her," she said.

"Yeah…You've mentioned that."

"Well, I'm sorry if I embarrassed you. I'll be sure to zip my lips about your music in the future."

"Alright. I gotta go. I love you, mom. Tell Sierra I love—"

"Sei! Your brother says he loves you."

"Shut up," his sister replied in the background, and he smiled. That's what she always said.

"Talk to you later, honey, and get some sleep. I worry about you on the road all night."

He hung up, feeling like his head was going to explode.

More fireworks lit up the sky, and he swore.

Movement up ahead, on the other side of the Veil, made him brake. He watched in surprise as a young woman in a black dress made her way down the front walk of an apartment complex just on the other side. Two other women trailed behind her, one in a tight green dress, and the other in what looked like a prom dress. They were maybe seventeen or eighteen.

He rolled to a stop in the middle of the street and rolled down his window.

"Hey! What are you guys doing?" he shouted.

They all turned, and the one in the black dress laughed, held up a bottle of champagne and shouted "Woohoo!"

The other girls joined in as they stumbled to a car parked on the street.

JJ threw the truck into park and jumped out. The Veil pricked at the hairs on his body, making his face feel almost numb as he hurried over to it. "Go back inside!" he shouted. "You need to go home."

The girl in the green dress hiccupped and took a swig from her own bottle as she stepped off the curb and almost fell. "No, I'm gonna go get laid before I die." She hiccupped again. "That's what I'm gonna do."

JJ stared helplessly as they got in the car, did a U-turn, and drove away.

The street fell silent, except for the rumbling of the engine of the truck behind him and the animals rustling in the trees.

Turning, he started back toward the truck, when out of nowhere a black cat ran past his feet. "Shit," he hissed, practically tripping over it as the creature looked back, its wide eyes flashing in the darkness, before it ran off.

That was when it hit him. With a gasp he spun around, every hair on his body on end, and not because of the Veil. Running to the truck, he cut the engine, then went back to the Veil, staring up into the trees, listening to the frantic chittering. He turned and looked behind him down the quiet boulevard.

Silence.

He turned back in time to see two squirrels race down the trunk of a tree and disappear into the Veil.

JJ stumbled back toward the truck.

The squirrels.

Spinning around, he ran for the truck

It was the goddamn fucking *squirrels*.

The truck roared to life, and JJ quickly shifted into gear. Pulling into the first parking lot he came to, he turned the truck around and headed for the nearest Coast Guard base.

Then he turned on the radio.

"...control here as more and more Atlantans join the festivities. I'm telling you, I've never seen anything like it. It's the biggest party I've ever seen. Free concerts are going on, Velvet Country, Davis Gordon, Elishea St. Cloud."

The DJ laughed. *"There are people here in everything from tuxes and ball gowns to body paint and fursuits. It's a free-for-all. There's booze, food. Games for the kids."* JJ could hear the party in the background. *"The authorities lost control of this crowd hours ago, yet there's been no violence to speak of. Instead, my fellow Atlantans are showing the world how it's done. How what's done? You might ask?"* He hiccupped, then laughed. *"Attending your own funeral. Since we are all going to die anyway, I'm going to skip the ads and go straight back to the music. Here's an oldie but goodie to get your grind on."* Ice, Ice, Baby began to blare through the speakers, and he turned the station. The next DJ wasn't having as much fun, and his voice was clipped and professional. *"...explanation for why the numbers in Atlanta continue to climb. If you go by the national news, it's because Atlantans have refused to quarantine. But that just isn't true, as most of us have witnessed first-hand. The mayor issued a statement last night urging residents to continue adhering to the mandates, but many in the city feel that they've been specifically targeted, and trapped, and what started as a right-wing Christian fellowship's attempt to welcome Jesus back to earth has evolved into what can only be described as a raging kegger. And the whole city has been invited. Despite the fact that law enforcement was overwhelmed hours ago, there have been no reports of violence. Unbelievably, the impromptu party, while certainly out of control, has maintained peace."*

JJ turned off the radio. What good was peace when they'd all be dead in forty-eight hours, anyway?

Up ahead, he saw the bright lights of the temporary Coast Guard base. They had taken over a large warehouse facility on the west side of the Veil between Vinings and Cumberland.

He knew he'd never be able to get the truck turned around inside, so he pulled over outside the gate and hopped out.

The guards were immediately on him, and he raised his arms in the air as they shouted for him to place his hands on the truck. The metal was hot under his palms, but he did what he was told, remembering the news reports about the vigilante groups threatening the Veil. They'd also been targeting the temporary Coast Guard and Army bases that were patrolling the Veils and keeping them safe.

"I'm part of the salvage crew. I helped you guys search for survivors after the Veil went up..." They patted him down, and satisfied he wasn't armed, backed away, guns still pointed at him.

"What are you doing here?" The first soldier asked.

He turned around. "I need to talk to someone in charge."

The second soldier laughed. "Not going to happen."

"Please," JJ begged, keeping his hand where they could see them. "It's important. I think I know how the virus is spreading."

That made them pause, and they looked at each other.

The first one shook his head. "Then you need to call the ICPH hotline—"

"I can't get through to them," JJ lied, shaking his head. "And by the time I get through, thousands more could be dead." He didn't know if that was an exaggeration or not. "Please. I just need five minutes. I just—"

The one guy, who looked a little more sympathetic, said something into the walkie-talkie hooked to the shoulder of his uniform. They waited a moment before a gruff voice replied through the speaker, "Let him in."

They quickly escorted JJ inside, and he had to sidestep

dozens of frantic men and women loading supplies onto trucks. A minute later, he was standing before the base commander whose office was set up in a Conex-style transport box, perched on the back of a flatbed truck. The man was short, in his mid-fifties. His eyes were tired behind his thick glasses—

"Let's hear it," he said, dropping everything from the top of his desk into a box on the floor.

"My name is JJ—"

"I don't care what your name is. You know something about the virus?"

"Well, not exactly. I just—"

The commander glared at him.

"There is something wrong with the squirrels inside the Veil," he blurted.

The commander stared at him for a moment before he burst out laughing. Shaking his head, he spoke to the armed soldier on the ground outside. "Get this guy out of—"

"No, wait! Hear me out. I think they are spreading the virus. Maybe to other animals who are infecting people, or just—I don't know how it works."

The commander held up his hand, waving the soldier back. "You're a truck driver, right?"

"I know. But I've seen them. Just tonight, I saw—"

"And you're a virologist too?"

"No. But my dad and I—when I was a kid, we hunted squirrels, lots of times and—"

The commander laughed again, giving JJ a once-over as he organized a stack of papers, and dropped them into the box. "Of course you did. So what?"

JJ tried to keep his anger in check. "We hunted them during the *day,* usually in the morning, because they sleep at night. Or they are supposed to, anyway. That's why their eyes don't reflect, like a cat's or a raccoon."

The Commander looked about a breath away from throwing him out.

JJ rushed on. "But the ones in the Veil." He pointed. "They're not asleep. They're wide awake in there. You must have heard them. Come outside. I'll show you."

The Commander rolled his eyes. "Oh, for Christ's sake, I don't have time for this."

"I'm—" JJ finally remembered a news report he'd seen earlier that spring. He'd been sitting in his mom's kitchen, having coffee, when the segment came on. It was about the surge in the squirrel, chipmunk and vole populations in northern Georgia. It had something to do with a mild winter and a bumper crop of acorns. "Fuck." That had to be it.

"Get out of my office." The commander growled.

"No! Listen." JJ cried. "I'm serious. It's the squirrels, maybe mice and…I don't know. Whatever the fuck eats nuts. *They* are the ones spreading the virus, getting into homes, passing it onto the people." JJ insisted.

"I've got more important things to do than worry about birds and squirrels."

JJ shook his head. He hadn't heard birds. Did that mean something? Were birds immune? "Not birds, I don't think." JJ pulled his hat off his head. "I need you to get in touch with the CDC or the ICP-whatever and let them know before—"

"Listen, son, there are people on this. Okay? People who, unlike you, have advanced degrees and know what they are doing."

"Please," JJ's stomach sank. "Just tell them—"

The commander held up his hand. "I'm sure if this theory of yours made any sense, the ICPH would have chased it down a week ago."

JJ's anger flared. "Would they? Because it doesn't look to me like they are doing anything at all to help the people inside."

The commander put the lid on the box he'd packed and

shoved it under his desk. "It's time for you to go."

"They are doing everything you've asked them to do, and somehow they are still being infected. They are losing hope. And this makes sense. Help them! Just call—"

"My job is to follow orders. And right now, we are needed in D.C."

JJ's jaw dropped. "What?" He looked over his shoulder at the door. "You are *leaving*? Who will protect the Veil from the assholes who want to take it down?"

"I'm following—"

"Which are what?"

"None of your business. This conversation is over."

The hell it was. "Fuck you. You're gonna leave all those people inside—"

"My job is to follow—"

"Fuck your job!" JJ slammed his fist onto the empty desk.

A second later, he was being dragged from the truck. "You need to help them!" He twisted his body, trying to get away. "My mom is in there! And my sister. And they have done every goddamn thing you asked them to! You owe them!" He screamed as they dragged him through the busy parking lot.

"What do we do with him?" The man holding his left arm asked as he tried to break free. If they weren't going to help him, then *he* had to do it himself. Call the radio station or...try the ICPH, and pray he could get through.

"Put him in the brig," someone said

The *what*? JJ stopped and spun around, breaking free. "You can't arrest me! I'm a civilian! I need to—"

"Please come with me, sir," said a boy that was no older than Sam.

He was being *arrested* for trying to help? No. He needed to warn people. Turning toward the entrance and his truck, he said. "Fuck you. I'm out of here."

A hand closed over his arm, and without thinking, he took a

swing, connecting with a face. Then he took another as shouting erupted around him. The next thing he knew, he was lying on the ground, his head spinning. A few seconds after *that*, he was back on his feet in handcuffs, being led to a convoy truck. "You need to help them!" he pleaded. "Please!"

The kid helped him into the back of the truck and onto the bench inside.

Tears filled JJ's eyes. "*Please. They are going to die if we* don't do something."

The kid unlocked his cuffs while his partner stood armed beside the door to make sure JJ didn't make a run for it. "We are trying," he said, before stepping back onto the ground.

"Well, try hard—"

The door slammed and locked, and JJ was alone. Reaching into his pocket, he pulled out his phone. Maybe he could still get through to the ICPH. Then he realized he didn't have the number. Or the one to the radio station. Damn it. He'd never written either down. Jumping up, he kicked the bench, then pounded on the door. But no one came. He tried to dial 911, but it rang busy.

"Damn it, damn it, *damn it*!" He knew he needed to think, but it was so *hard* to do through the panic. Pacing the small, dark box, he inhaled deeply through his nose. He could fix this. Yes, he was a stupid truck driver, but he could figure this out. There was still time. Maybe if he called his mom, she could get a hold of someone, make them listen. *Yes.*

He sat down and tried his mom again. The line rang busy as more fireworks popped in the distance. Hanging up, he tried again.

Busy.

JJ tried again.

It took several tries, but on the fifth attempt, she finally picked up. "Oh, thank god. Mom. I need you to do something for me." And then he explained.

Chapter Twenty-Four

Day 13 // 7:33 a.m.

KATIE WAS WIPING sleep from her eyes and refilling the pressure canner when she heard it. A far away clap that rattled the windows. Turning, she met Jinn's eyes in the living room. She heard it too. Before Katie could make it to the front door to look outside, the TV went off, and the house fell eerily still.

A rock formed in her stomach as she stepped out onto the front porch. No, it was more like a boulder, rooting her to the spot as she listened. She looked west, toward Atlanta, scanning the horizon. Would she be able to see it if—Jinn and Sam came out and stood beside her, squinting in the same direction. There was nothing else, no sound other than the wind, and the girls— who always woke up early—playing on the tire-swing. Katie looked up into the branches of the oak, then toward the trees behind Mike's. The birds that were usually so loud in the morning had fallen silent, confirming her suspicion. Something had happened.

Her fingers closed around the post beside the front steps, and she fell against it. *Something bad.*

Jinn said something that she couldn't make out, and Sam's voice responded. Amelia squealed with laughter from the swing as Katie stared up the road, afraid to move, to even think, because if she did, her brain would tell her things she didn't want to know, things she didn't want to hear. It would ask her questions with terrible, *terrible* answers, like *what was that?*

She clung to the post as Jinn's panic-filled voice reached her ears. "Why aren't they answering?" She cried over and over. "Why aren't they answering? Why aren't they answering?"

Katie turned. Both she and Sam had their phones pressed to their ears, their faces slack with shock. They were thinking the same thing she was.

"Look!" Amelia called, and Katie's head flew up. "Look at me! I'm as high as a bird." The breath she'd been holding punched from her lungs. Oh, for a second she'd thought...

"Katie!"

Still clutching the rail of the porch, she turned. Barb was standing on the sidewalk, out in front of the bar. She'd only said her name, but somehow it conveyed everything. Katie pulled her phone out and dialed JJ as she crossed his mom's yard, feeling like she was moving through a dream. It went straight to voice-mail. She hung up and dialed again as she floated toward Barb, her internal clock counting down the remaining seconds of blessed ignorance like a timer on a bomb that was about to go... It was a poor analogy. She stopped in front of the older woman, and Barb's watery blue eyes met hers.

"It's gone," she said.

Katie's arm fell to her side, as JJ's voice asked her to leave a message after the tone. "How—how do you know?"

"The radio."

Katie stared at her. Atlanta was gone?

She turned and looked at their makeshift family across the lawn. Their families were gone. Shielding her eyes, she looked down the forlorn road in the direction JJ had driven off in yester-day, but instead of feeling sadness, all she felt was a burst of energy and the intense need to take control of something.

She turned back to Barb. "Do you have a generator?"

Barb's brows came together. "A what?"

Katie looked over her shoulder towards Goebell's. "The food. It's all going to go bad now. We need to cook what we can immediately."

"Did you hear me?" Barb asked, sounding confused. "Atlanta is—"

Katie pulled her hair up into a bun, then pulled the elastic from her wrist and secured it on top of her head as her brain kicked into overdrive. "I know. The gas still works though, right? So the stoves will still light?"

"Katie..."

She couldn't think about Atlanta right now. "Just answer the question!"

"Yes. We run on propane out here."

"Good. We need to cook everything. Now."

"We need to tell the kids."

Bile rose in Katie's throat at the thought. No. She was not telling the kids that their parents were dead. "We don't know anything for sure yet. They might be fine—"

Barb shook her head. "They're saying it was like New York."

Katie ran her hands over her eyes and face. She didn't need to know that.

"I'm sorry," Barb said.

Kate stared at her. What was she sorry for? The fact that there was a deadly virus on the loose? Or the fact that—Katie turned as Grace continued to push Amelia on the swing—those girls were now orphans? Or was it that JJ hadn't come back and was probably—

"Start your oven," she blurted. "I'm going to make the girls some oatmeal and then I'll be over."

The wind picked up, blowing Barb's frizzy hair in her face. "You can't avoid this," she said, tucking it back behind her ears.

Maybe not, but she was going to try for as long as humanly possible. "Girls!" she shouted, her voice weirdly normal. "Ten more minutes, then come inside and get some breakfast."

"Katie..."

"I have work to do." Her body floated back across the lawn, up the steps past Jinn, who was sobbing in Sam's arms, and into the house. Pulling the pot out of the sink, she got the measuring cup and measured out the oatmeal and water. With the lighter she found in the drawer, she lit the stove.

"Hey, Katie?" Sam's voice wobbled behind her.

She turned, swallowing hard. "You hungry?"

His eyes went from hers to the pot. They were red-rimmed and full of tears. "N-no. Thanks." The look in his eyes sliced a hole in her facade and she had to look away.

Tears filled her eyes, and she blinked them back as she stared at the ceiling. She was not doing this. She could not cry. If she did, she'd never be able to stop, and she had to be strong for the kids. "What's up?"

"I-I...I can't breathe."

She turned just as he collapsed. Grabbing him around the waist, she lowered him into the nearest chair and pressed his head between his knees. "Try not to think. Just relax your body. Let every thought go. Don't—"

A wail erupted from his down turned head as his long fingers clawed at his hair.

"Shh..." she said, sitting in the chair beside him, rubbing her hand on his back. She was not ready for this. To comfort these kids. She squeezed her eyes shut. To *raise* them.

Another wail erupted, and he grabbed at her like he was drowning, and she almost fell off the chair. "I'm here," was all she could think to say. It was a sorry consolation, but she wasn't going to tell him it would be alright. Fuck that.

Jinn appeared in the doorway, her eyes red, mouth pressed in a wobbling line. A hiss from the stove made Katie turn, as oatmeal bubbled out of the small pot onto the burner. She jumped up and turned it off.

When she turned back around, they were both staring at her, their eyes begging for help.

"I'm so sorry." Crossing the room, she dragged Jinn into her arms. "I don't know what to do. What to say," she confessed. "I—"

Jinn's shoulders slumped as she clung to Katie and cried. Katie held her until she turned down the hall, toward the bedroom. Katie met Sam's eyes apologetically. "Anything you need from me. I'm here."

The door flew open, and the girls ran in. Sam jumped up and headed out the kitchen door before they saw him crying. For the first time all morning, Katie realized Parker was gone.

Wiping her eyes, she turned back to the stove. "Are you girls ready for breakfast?"

"Yeah." They sounded breathless and happy, and she wondered if it was for the last time.

"Go wash your hands," she said, feeling like there was a hand around her neck squeezing her throat. It was one thing, feeling sorry for herself, but hurting for someone else who was suffering and not being able to do anything about it... It was her first time, and it was a thousand times more painful.

Scooping overcooked oatmeal into bowls, she set them on the counter, then pulled the brown sugar out of the cabinet, as the thoughts she was trying to hold at bay swarmed her like angry bees. What would happen to the kids now? What was she supposed to tell the girls? Where was JJ? Was he dead? Or trapped under a collapsed overpass? He had to be, didn't he? Otherwise, he would have answered his phone. He would have called her back, at least. A weird shrieking sound filled her ears, reminding her of the day the Veil went up.

"Ready!" Amelia pulled out the chair and climbed onto it, sitting on her knees. But Katie couldn't hear her over the noise. The sound grew louder as she placed the bowls in front of the girls and a tingling—not the good kind—quickly spread up her arms.

Grace gave her an odd look, and the girls jumped as she shouted, "I have to go help Barb. I'll be back in a little bit." She didn't know what was happening to her, but she had to get out of there. Now.

Without waiting, she rushed to the kitchen door, flung it open, and ran out as it slammed against the kitchen counter. Stumbling across the yard, she swiped at her eyes, terrified that if she stopped moving, even for a second, she'd never be able to start again. And the kids needed her. Even though she didn't know what she was doing. Even though she was on her own. They needed her, and she couldn't fall apart in the middle of the kitchen, or the yard, or…anywhere. She needed to keep going. Forward. Don't look back. Don't think. Just move. Her legs steadied under her as she made her way to Barb's, and a list organized itself in her head. Coolers. They needed to find coolers for the meat. That would give them an extra day on it, maybe. And they needed to figure out who had generators and how to work them. Someone would have to go over to Michelle's and check on her. They had to figure out lighting before it got dark. Find batteries, and a way to charge their phones. She needed to call Matt too, just to make sure he was okay.

Just as she arrived at Barb's, Easton pulled up in his cruiser, screeching to a halt, before jumping out. "I need Jay."

"He's not here."

"Where the fuck—"

"He didn't come back—"

"What? Why not?"

Her shoulders sagged as she raised her arms.

Easton kicked the ground. "Fuck! Is Mike around?"

"I think—"

He turned and headed across the street to the garage. She followed him. "Wait! Where…What's going on?"

"What do you think's going on? Everything is *fucked*! That's what's—It's all fucked—" He pulled his hands through his clipped hair, the armpits of his shirt soaked with sweat. "People are panicking. And I don't blame them—Mike!" he shouted, then continued. "There are accidents everywhere." He banged on the door. "Mike! I need you!" He turned back to her. "The goddamn phone won't stop ringing. It is chaos everywhere, people trying to run. The fucking president should have just let us all die."

The sound of rapidly approaching jet engines filled the air, and they paused as two fighter jets raced across the sky toward Atlanta, then disappeared. Easton turned back to the door, as his radio on his belt crackled, spouting something Katie couldn't understand. "Mike, goddamn it! Open the fucking door!" He looked back at Katie. "We're all fucked. We're all as good as—"

The door opened, and a sleepy-looking Mike stood in the middle of it in his boxers.

Easton scowled. "What in the hell's the matter with you? Get some clothes on. I need you to drive Jay's truck."

"What? Why?"

Easton huffed an incredulous laugh. "Shit. You don't know."

Mike scratched his head. "Know? What?"

"Atlanta. It's gone."

"Wh-what? When?"

"About thirty minutes ago."

Mike found Katie's eyes. "JJ?"

She shook her head.

Mike stumbled backward. "Oh, Jesus."

"Yeah, fuck Jesus." Easton spat. "Get your pants on. We need to roll."

Without waiting for an answer, he headed back across the street.

"I can help," Katie offered.

Easton shook his head. "You got your hands full with the Brady Bunch."

"Jinn can watch them," she said, following him into the bar.

"No. There's all kinds of crazy on the roads now, I don't want to have to worry about you on top of—" Pressing the button on the side of the radio hooked to the shoulder of his shirt, he said "Ten-four, I'm on my way with a wrecker, ETA about thirty minutes, if he can get his goddamn pants on."

"But I can—" Katie began.

"Copy that," his radio interrupted. "Paramedics are on their way, ETA twelve minutes."

"Easton—"

He glared at her. "Sergeant."

"Sorry, Sarg—"

"Barbie! I need something to eat," he shouted, "Fast. I don't care what."

"Let me help," she begged, desperate for the distraction.

"Fine, get me some coffee. Between the missing persons and trying to get every country asshole tagged, I haven't slept in forty-eight hours."

"I can do more than—"

"Barbie!" he shouted, heading for the kitchen.

Katie blinked back tears as she hurried around the counter and filled a styrofoam cup with coffee.

A minute later, Easton reemerged with their last box of crackers and a jar of chicken.

"Here," she said, handing him the cup.

He nodded, his jaw tight, as he headed for the door.

She followed him back outside. "I want to help. I need to do—"

"Where we headed?" Mike hollered from across the street as Easton set his coffee on the roof of his car and pulled the door open.

"Please."

He looked at her feet and scowled. Damn it. She was barefoot. "If you see my brother, tell him to call me," he said. "I've been trying to get a hold of his ass for a couple days now." Over her shoulder, he yelled. "Mount up. We're headed to Loganville. You got gas?"

Katie turned as Mike nodded and climbed up into JJ's truck.

JJ. Tears flooded her eyes, and she wiped them away.

"Hold up!" Sam shouted as he ran down the front walk of the house. "I'm coming with you!"

Easton thought about that for a moment, then nodded. "Yeah. Good. Ride with Mike." Grabbing his coffee, he climbed in his cruiser, and met her eyes, giving her a sympathetic look. "I'm sorry about JJ." Then he pulled it closed.

Katie backed up as the engine turned over and her head pounded. It wasn't that she didn't know. But why did he have to say it out loud? She watched as Easton threw his car into reverse, and peeled out, pausing only for a fraction of a second beneath the dead light over the intersection before punching the gas and turning left. A second later, JJ's truck followed, with Sam in the driver's seat. And then they were gone, and she was left standing alone, on the decaying sidewalk, in the sun.

Move, Katie. She blinked, realizing she had stopped. Spinning around, she raced into the bar. "Coolers. I need coolers, and…"

———

TWO COOLERS WERE all they were able to find. It was heartbreaking, but in light of everything else, she didn't even shed a tear as she and Jinn dug a hole out back and buried what could not be saved. She went through all the produce, too. Salvaging what she could for the next few days, and tossing the rest on top of the spoiling meat. The crows watched with interest, tilting their heads from one side to the other, cawing and flapping about as Katie piled dry, red dirt on top of everything and then dragged an old car hood, someone had 'left' out back, on top of it.

Then she helped Barb get her generator up and running. Unsurprisingly, there was no local news, since all the stations had been destroyed along with the city, but there was national coverage. They spewed lies and made it sound like everyone in Atlanta thought the virus was a joke. Katie paused just long enough to down a cup of coffee, and then she went back to the house to grab the canner.

When the girls asked why nothing in the house was working, Katie paused a beat, knowing she needed to tell them, but not sure how.

Parker saved her the trouble. "Atlanta is gone," he said simply.

"What about my mom and dad?" Grace asked with a quivering jaw, as the choking feeling returned, rendering Katie speechless.

"Do you believe in God?" Parker asked her.

The girl nodded. "Then they are waiting for you in heaven. Until then…" He cast a glance toward Katie. "They asked us to be your family. And we said yes."

Katie had nodded, as Grace dropped onto the couch, clutching Amelia's hand. "Like a real family?"

Parker sat down beside her and hugged her, unrecognizable as the boy she'd met two weeks ago as he said, "As real as they come. We won't leave you. I promise."

"Why are you crying?" Amelia asked, not really understanding.

"Because our parents are dead, stupid!" Grace shot back, before burying her head in Parker's shoulder.

Amelia frowned. "Is *Abuelita* and Abba Chuy dead too?"

"No sweetie, they are still coming to get you," Katie said, finally finding her voice.

"So I'm not in your family, then?" Amelia asked, rushing over to her, wrapping her little arms around her leg, looking like she was going to cry.

"Of course you are. "Katie wiped her eyes and pressed the girl's head gently against her thigh. "You'll just have two families, where the rest of us only have one."

Amelia brightened at that and pulled away. "JJ is gonna be in our family too, right?"

Katie knew she should tell them, but she wasn't ready to face it yet herself, so she just nodded.

"Okay," she turned to Grace. "Want to go back out to the swing?"

Grace shook her head.

"We're here for you. Whatever you need," Parker said, taking Grace by the shoulders.

He turned to Amelia. "You too."

"Well, I need someone to push me on the swing," she said, putting her hands on her hips.

Reluctantly, Parker nodded and got up. Grace laid down on the couch, as he followed Amelia out the door, and Katie got back to distracting herself from the terrible reality that surrounded them all.

They were alone, and things were only going to get worse.

———

SHE WAS SITTING on the front porch, in the dark, when Sam and Mike returned. She knew she needed to sleep, but she couldn't face her thoughts, let alone JJ's room. So she sat up, drinking water and trying to think of all the things that needed to be done that she could actually do something about.

The kids came first, obviously. She'd told Amelia her grandparents were coming, but the truth was, she didn't know that anymore. The phones were back to what they had been on the first day. It was impossible to get through to anyone. Whether it was the towers or the sheer volume of people trying to figure out where their loved ones were, no one knew. Amelia still didn't understand what had happened. Just before bed, she had asked Katie to call her mom and tell her the news about her 'two' families. And Katie had tried to explain...

The thought trailed off as a familiar shadow made its way up the walk toward her. Her surprise paralyzed her until he was practically on top of her.

"JJ?" she whispered.

He stopped, but didn't say anything as Sam's lanky shadow came up behind him.

Was she hallucinating? She stumbled to her feet. "JJ?" She cried, sounding like she was being strangled.

He just stood there, in the dark, staring at her.

"JJ!" she cried, throwing her arms around him as the sobs she'd been holding back all day wracked her body. It was like the sheriff's office all over again, except a hundred times stronger. Every fear she'd been keeping at bay shook itself free of her nerves as she clutched at him, shaking and dizzy with relief. His palm landed on the middle of her back, but otherwise he didn't touch her or move. Finally noticing, she pulled back. "JJ?"

"We found him walking on the side of the road about twenty miles back. The Coast Guard let him out on their way to some emergency in D.C. I guess..."

Katie grabbed JJ's face in her hands. "Are you alright? What happened? What—"

He pulled away, and without saying a word, climbed the steps and went into the dark house.

She turned to Sam. "What happened?"

"He was there when it happened. He saw it go..."

"Oh, no." Katie's shoulders slumped.

"It's a fucking... mess out there. People are panicking. We pulled a minivan out of a pileup on the highway up north...three kids dead in the back seat. But the parents survived." Sam shook his head in the darkness as Katie groped for him and pulled him in for a hug.

"I'm so sorry," she said. "About everything. I... I keep wanting to say something that will make you feel better, but...I can't think of anything."

Sam squeezed her back. "I know. I felt the same way this morning with Jinn. Where is she? Is she okay?"

Katie pulled back. "Not really, but she finally fell asleep about a half hour ago." She squeezed his shoulder. "Are you hungry?"

"Naw."

"Okay. There's no power inside." Pulling a flashlight she'd taken from Goebell's out of her back pocket, she said. "Here's a flashlight, so you don't have to waste the battery on your phone."

"Keep it. I don't have anyone to call anymore, anyway." He sat down on the step. "And I don't think I'm ready for bed yet."

The moon was just illuminating the horizon to the east, casting faint shadows over the lawn, while the croaks and chirps of the frogs and crickets carried on as if nothing had happened.

"Do you want company?" Katie asked, looking through the screen as a door inside closed.

"That's okay. I don't really feel like talking."

Katie sat down beside him. "Who says we have to talk?"

Chapter Twenty-Five

Day 15 // 1:17 p.m.

EVEN IF HE'D wanted to, and he didn't, his body wouldn't have allowed him to get up. Every time he surfaced from the darkness and the nightmares, it was as if he, the bed, the floor and the whole damn world were glued together, and he was helpless to do anything but take a breath and go back under.

He had vague memories of Katie asking him to drink, and Amelia crying, and the thwack of the screen door, but other than that, he occupied a hell of ash and the distant screams of his mom and Sierra. He had failed them.

He blinked as the pressure in his bladder grew. Shit. If he didn't get up, he'd piss the bed. His head throbbed as he rolled to his side. The thud of his feet landing on the floor boomed in his ears and he pressed his palm into the bed and tried to sit up. Heat and nausea swept through his body as he gasped at the cramp in the back of his leg.

He looked on the nightstand for his phone and grabbed it, but it didn't go on. It wasn't plugged in. Then he remembered there was no power to charge it, anyway.

His mouth burned for water, and his breath was toxic as he pried his lips apart and tried to moisten them. Then he saw the glass of water. *Please, just drink.* Katie's voice echoed in his head as he pressed his palm to the side of it. Picking up the glass, he downed the whole thing in one gulp. The urge to pee returned, and he dragged himself to his feet, leaning against the closet door for support, as he made his way to the hall.

Whatever time it was, it was still daylight, he noted as he leaned against the jamb and dragged his feet into the bathroom. Quickly he did his business, noticed it was the color of whiskey and flushed. Avoiding his eyes, he fumbled in the drawer for his toothbrush, then went through the motions of brushing his teeth. Twice.

The house was quiet as he opened the door. Making his way down the hall, he heard the chitter of a squirrel through the open screen door.

It had to be the squirrels. The goddamn fucking squirrels. Not that it mattered now. They were dead. He'd never hear his mom's voice again. His sister wouldn't graduate college and become a filmmaker like she'd planned. He'd failed them. His father would be so disappointed. Especially because his last words to his son were, *take care of them for me.*

Turning the corner into the kitchen, he paused, as Katie, her back turned to him, unloaded the dry dishes from the rack into the cabinets. All the canning shit she'd had everywhere was gone, and the kitchen had gone back to the way it used to be. No, actually it was neater, and—his brows converged as he studied his glistening stove—way cleaner. He hadn't even realized it was white like the fridge, always assuming it was more of a cream color.

She turned and dropped the pot she was holding, her hand flying to her chest as it clattered to the ground, pounding in JJ's head like a steel drum. "Jesus. You scared me." Her hair was pulled back in a ponytail that looked like it had been slept in. Wisps of hair hovered around her face like a halo, and he noticed the red splotches on her neck again as she scratched them. He met her tired, bloodshot eyes, and then they fell to her chest and the shirt she was wearing. He recognized it immediately. His frown turned into an angry scowl. That didn't belong to her. That was his mom—

"Yoo-hoo! Katie? You got that there filter cleaned yet?" The front door flew open and JJ turned in time to see Mike stumble in with a heavy container of gasoline. "Oh. Yer finally up."

Katie bent down and picked up the pot and set it on the stove, then wiped her hands on a towel. "Yeah. It's out back, by the generator. I didn't know where to put it..." Her eyes went to JJ again as he continued to glower at her.

"Out back is just fine. Do you mind runnin' to the shop to grab my Phillips screwdriver? It's the red one on the workbench by the coffeemaker."

Her eyes went from JJ's to Mike's, then back again, as she nodded, and scooted by him, and out the door.

"Whatever yer thinkin' of saying, you'd best keep it to yerself, you hear?" Mike said.

"She's wearing my mom's—"

"Yeah. I know. She's been over to the house, too."

"What the *hell?*"

Mike pushed the back door open and set the container of gasoline on the small deck outside. "Yer mom asked her to."

"What?"

"Yer mom asked her and Barb to go take care of the house if somethin' happened. Didn't want you havin' to do it."

JJ headed for the door. "They better not have touched—"

Mike put his arm up, blocking the way. He smelled like he hadn't showered in days.... Wait, no. JJ pulled at his shirt. *Christ.* It was him.

"Hold yer goddamn horses, you thick headed lout."

Lout? *Lout?* What the fuck was a—

"They just cleaned out the fridge. And the clothes Katie took, they was in a box in the garage to donate. Saw 'em myself when we went to get the generator. She didn't touch your mom's things."

"Still."

"Still what? That poor girl has been killin' herself with worry for you, bustin' her hump to help those poor kids. You're not the only one who lost someone, Jenson. At least you got to grow up with parents. These poor kids… They need you."

"I can't. I failed—"

"Well, now you're failing them, too. And they're still here. If your head wasn't so far up your own asshole of self-pity you'd see that."

The corner of JJ's mouth turned up on its own at that colorful phrasing. He pulled it back down. "And what happened to yer mom and Sierra that weren't your fault, Jay. No matter what you think."

"My dad—"

"If yer dad was here, he wouldn't be sleepin' his sorrows away while there were children and a woman who loved him right there, needin' him to be strong."

That hit a little close to home. "I can't."

Mike huffed a laugh. "It ain't about you anymore, moron."

JJ stared at him.

"Get yer act together Jay, or git gone."

"It's my house."

The front door opened.

"Mind me, boy," Mike said as Katie entered the kitchen, holding the screwdriver. Katie followed Mike out back as JJ went to the sink and got another glass of water. A minute later, Sam walked across the backyard with Jinn holding a basket that looked like it was full of wet clothes. He watched as they began to hang clothes on a line that hadn't been there the last time he looked out the window. He saw Mike's coveralls and one of Barb's aprons.

"JJ!" He turned around in time for Amelia, in pig-tails and a sundress to throw her arms around his legs. "You sure were tired!"

Grace met his eyes from the doorway. She looked less excited to see him, and tired, but her hair was braided neatly, and she was dressed. He absently noticed her nails were pink. He looked down at Amelia, who was now hanging from his legs like he was a eucalyptus and she was a koala. "Your nails look nice," he noted as she began to slide to the floor.

"Miss…I mean Katie–she said to just call her that now—did it! She got polish from the nice lady next door."

"What lady?"

"The one who used to live there. She told Katie that she wanted us to have all her polishes—"

"Amelia." Katie's voice came through the screen.

JJ looked at Katie, then at Amelia. "That *lady* was my mom," he said. *Was.* Never had a single word made him feel so sick. Disentangling himself from Amelia, he turned, grabbed the bottle of whiskey off the top of the fridge and hurried back into his bedroom.

Chapter Twenty-Six

Day 18 // 11:48 a.m.

STORM CLOUDS LOOMED OVERHEAD, as Katie kicked the laundry basket and unclipped another sheet, dropping it in. She kicked it again, and moved on to the next one, praying the deluge held off just a little longer, so she could get the clothes off the line. Except for when Amelia's grandparents had called to say their departure was delayed, the last several days—since the fall of Atlanta—had blurred together.

Every morning she got up at five after barely having slept, went for a quick run, then came back and made coffee. Then she sat on the front porch praying today would be the day that JJ finally emerged from his room. After the girls woke up, she made breakfast for the kids, then it was off to Barb's to decide on an evening meal. Then she took the bike she'd found in JJ's mom's garage, and checked on Mr. Goebell, who'd fallen and bruised his hip, and Ms. Michelle.

After *that* it was fill the gas cans with gas they were siphoning from the tanks under the Gas-n-Go, do dishes, and laundry. God, why was there so much laundry?

She moved the basket again, tucking the wisps of hair back behind her ears, and unclipped a pillowcase.

Then, if she still had any time left, she cleaned. One bathroom for seven people was a lot. At least for her, and it was always a mess. Her apartment in LA had been small, but she'd had a whole counter in the bathroom for her makeup and skin care products. Here she had half a drawer and all of her things were covered in toothpaste.

She did all of that while caring for the kids. School, of any kind, was out of the question, since she didn't have books, or the book learning required to teach them. But Miss Michelle was teaching Grace how to sew and knit, and the girl seemed to enjoy that. Parker read a lot. Katie had never been much of a reader, but there was a weird peacefulness that settled over her like a blanket when Amelia climbed onto her lap and they opened a book together.

After she'd cleaned JJ's house, Katie had moved to his garage, which was hidden behind the house, then to his mom's, leaving everything where it was, just dusting and sweeping around Mrs. Dayton's things. Then she cleaned the bar from top to bottom, even taking the time to glue down 'new' squares of vinyl flooring that had been in the cleaning closet since before she was born, probably. She washed windows, organized drawers, folded clothes, and wiped little butts. Holy hell. She was a regular June Cleaver.

And while she did all that, JJ slept. Or drank. But mostly, he slept. Every once in a while, he stumbled out of the bedroom to use the bathroom or get a glass of water. He wouldn't look at her or the kids. He barely ate.

She'd moved into the bedroom with Grace, Jinn, and Amelia, and was sleeping on the floor, which was why she got up so early. She was much too old to comfortably sleep on the floor anymore, unlike Amelia, who crawled out of bed every night and ended up curled by her side in the morning, but she made do.

Mike had tried to talk to JJ, Sam too, but it was no use. He either didn't want to be, or couldn't be, helped.

A sound, like a slamming car door, came from out front and she brought her head around. She pulled the last of the clothes off the line, grabbed the basket, and hurried inside. Setting it on the kitchen table, she went to the front door and peered out.

A camouflage painted jeep was parked across the street at Mike's. A man in fatigues hopped out and headed into the garage.

Katie stared, remembering her first day at Mike's. It seemed like a decade, no, a lifetime ago. She looked down at her chipped nails, and the callus forming on the outside of her index finger, then at her stained jeans. Yikes. Self consciously, she twisted her hair in her fingers. She hadn't gone this long without maintenance, or thinking about what she ate, since she was eighteen years old. It was liberating... and terrifying. She caught her reflection in the door window beside her. Her eyes were bloodshot and tired. Her long lashes were almost gone, just a couple, hanging on by a thread, and since she barely bothered with makeup anymore, she looked like she'd aged a decade. She actually looked thirty-six. The weird thing was, except for JJ, and the obvious devastation of the world, she was actually *happier* than she'd been in a long time. Which maybe wasn't saying much, but it said something. And the feeling had only grown over the past couple of weeks. She'd gone from 2 million followers to nine, but she knew their faces, their laugh, and they knew hers.

And follow her, they did. All of them—Barb, Mike, Dave, Ms. Michelle, Mr. Goebell and the kids had become a tighter family than she'd ever known, and more than made up for the lack of power and running water. While inconvenient, the hardships they now faced did not devastate her the way she'd expected them to.

The fatigue-clad man reappeared, hopped into his truck and drove off.

On the contrary, they had challenged her, allowed her to see how tough she really was. They had given her purpose, as they whiled away the quiet summer days in Hartford Creek, and the rest of the world continued to crumble and die.

Delhi had gone the day after Atlanta. It took two days for the news to reach them. Then, just over the weekend, a city she had never heard of in China and San Diego went in quick succession. It looked like Dubai—where people were starving to death—Cairo, and Phoenix were going to be the next to go. It was unbelievable. And the most terrifying thing was that many of those cities, like Phoenix, were thought to be virus free until a week ago. Then it just exploded. It happened that fast.

A door opened behind her and she turned in time to see JJ stumble out in the same clothes he'd worn for a week and lock himself in the bathroom. Knowing it was her only opportunity, she scooped up the set of sheets on the coffee table and ran into the room. Opening the window, she stripped the bed, trying to ignore the stale smell of sweat in the dirty sheets, then pulled the new ones over the mattress. Quickly, she lay fresh clothes on top of the comforter, hoping JJ would take the hint, and hurried into the kitchen to get him a fresh glass of water. She turned the corner just in time to see the bedroom door close behind him.

Pressing her knuckles to it, she knocked. She was trying not to judge him, because she didn't know what it was like to lose someone to the Veil. The closest she'd come was thinking she'd lost Matt. But he'd somehow made it home to his parent's house in the country and was fine, although still not speaking to her. But she knew it wasn't the same. And she was trying to be patient, because it had practically been his mom's dying wish. But he was slipping farther and farther away every day, and she didn't know what to do.

"JJ?" When he didn't answer, she pushed the door open and peeked inside. He was sprawled on the bed, on top of his clean clothes, with a pillow pulled over his head. Quietly, she set the water on the nightstand and left. At least he'd left the window open.

Chapter Twenty-Seven

Day 19 // 8:32 a.m.

JJ GROANED. Why in the hell was someone hammering a nail into a wall above his bed? Scowling, he pulled the pillow off his head. Sunlight streamed through the window, burning his eyes as the banging continued. It wasn't a hammer. Someone was at the front door.

"Katie!" He coughed, sounding like he had laryngitis. Rubbing his throat, he took a long pull from the bottomless glass of water beside his bed, as another round of banging thumped against the back of his aching eyeballs.

"Goddamn fucking…" he mumbled, dragging himself to his feet and flinging the bedroom door open.

Another hard round of banging erupted, rattling the front window.

"Hey!" he snapped, sliding his hands along the wall in the hall, trying to stay upright. "Jesus Christ." Dragging his hand over his face, he pulled the door open. "What the hell do—"

"JJ Dayton?" an unfamiliar voice asked as he tried to focus on the man in his doorway.

"Yeah." The other man's fatigues finally came into focus.

The guy was dressed in fatigues. "We require your assistance."

JJ huffed a laugh and went to shut the door. "Yeah, no."

The soldier threw his hand out. "This is not a request."

He didn't care what it was. "I don't give a fuck."

"Sir—"

"Get off my property."

"JJ…" Katie's voice came from behind him.

He didn't bother to turn around. "Stay out of this." To the soldier, he said, "I'm not interested."

"Then we're taking your truck."

"Like hell you are."

Katie put a gentle but firm hand on his arm as he punched the screen, and the soldier stepped back with a scowl.

Mike appeared out of nowhere, rushing up the front walk. "I'm sure we can work something out here."

JJ stepped onto the porch, trailing Katie behind him. He just wanted to deck the guy and go back to bed.

"We have orders to—"

"I don't care about your fucking orders!" He yanked his arm free and Katie stumbled making him feel like an asshole. His hand shot out to steady her. What was he doing? She was only trying to help. He turned. "Fuck. I'm sorry. I didn't mean to—"

"He just woke up. Can you give us an hour?" she asked the soldier sweetly.

"Thirty minutes and then we have to hit the pavement," the soldier counter offered.

"Okay," she said, pulling JJ toward the door and giving Mike a nod. He nodded back, agreeing to whatever unspoken thing had just passed between them.

"What's going on?" he demanded.

"We're trying to save your truck." Her voice was low. "Now shut up and come inside."

She pushed him through the door, and if he weren't so dead inside, he might have enjoyed the feel of her hands splayed across his chest. But he was dead. Or he should be, and…

"You need to take a shower or you'll kill poor Mike," she said, urging him down the hall.

Feeling obstinate and more than a little disoriented, he stood in the doorway of the bathroom, arms folded across his chest, glowering at her. That had been getting her to back off so far. His brows went up as her expression darkened, and she crossed her arms. *Not anymore.* Fuck.

Katie shoved him. "Get in the goddamn shower, JJ," she snapped, lifting the hem of his shirt as he stumbled backward. "Or they're going to take your truck."

He huffed, swatting her hands away. "I don't give a fuck about my—"

She didn't wait for him to finish. "Well, I do."

She reached for his shirt again, and he grabbed her wrists, pulling them down to her sides, dragging her forward until they were chest to chest. The thought of kissing her briefly crossed his mind, but when she turned her head away at his apparent stink, he decided against it, and let her go.

Stepping around him, she bent over and turned the water and him on at the same time. JJ looked down at his pants. "Fucking hell." Apparently, only his *soul* was dead. How comforting.

Not wanting her to see, he turned away and finally met his own eyes in the mirror. "Shit." He was a sight, looking like he'd crawled out from under a bridge after exacting tolls from frightened travelers.

Katie scooted past him, her hips touching his ass as she slid by. Also, a turn-on. "Take a shower. I'll make coffee."

She closed the door before he could argue, leaving him alone with Grizzly Adams' twin brother.

———

WHEN HE'D EMERGED from the bathroom, Katie had shoved him into his bedroom like he was a five-year-old who didn't want to go to school, and demanded he get dressed. She'd set a cup of coffee on his dresser as he pulled a crisp t-shirt, smelling like laundry detergent and sunshine, over his head, and stuffed his feet into his boots.

On his way to the front door, she'd pushed a bottle of water and a wrapped sandwich into his hand, then stood back as the door thwacked shut behind him, and he stomped down the front walk. He hadn't said goodbye, and neither had she.

Now he and Mike were headed back to Atlanta, or what was left of it, trailing behind the asshole in the Army Jeep.

JJ took another bite of his sandwich, as the hot air from the open window dried his hair and they barreled down the road. Now that he was conscious, he was *starving*.

He glanced at Mike out of the corner of his eye. The old man had been boring holes into the side of his head since they left. JJ tore off another bite of his sandwich and sighed. "*What* is your problem?"

"I'm disappointed in you, Jensen."

JJ rolled his eyes. Hadn't they already had this conversation? Or—he shoved the rest of the sandwich in his mouth—had that been a dream?

"If your mother was here—"

"Well, she's not," he reminded him, his tone less than polite.

"It's a good thing, too. She'd be so disappointed by the lout you've become."

Lout? His brows furrowed together beneath his sunglasses. They'd definitely had this conversation before. And once was enough.

"You know I'm right, Jay. If your mom saw how you've been behaving since…" He let the sentence hang, leaving JJ to fill in the blank himself. If she'd seen the way he'd been acting, she would have dragged him out of bed by the ear days ago, and told him to stop feeling sorry for himself. Mike was right. Katie was right. The ghost of his mom in his head was right. The thing was, self pity was easier to deal with than the possibility that if he'd noticed sooner about the squirrels and taken the information to someone who would actually use it, his mom and Sierra, and greater Atlanta for that matter, might still be alive.

"It's over. It's done. They're gone, and there is not a thing in the world that will bring them back. The quicker you accept that, the quicker..."

"What?" JJ threw his hand up, then thumped them on the steering wheel. "Then what?"

"You act like it's all over, Jay! The world hasn't vanished yet. There's still a few of us left."

A bug flew into the windshield, squirting yellow juice across the glass. JJ flipped the windshield wipers on, not sure if he felt sympathy for it or envy.

"You're gonna lose her." Mike said, shaking his head.

JJ didn't ask who. "I've got more important—"

"Like hell you do!" Mike smacked the dashboard in a rare display of emotion. "Haven't you learnt anything from this mess? Get your head outta your ass, boy! I mean it. Or—"

"Or what?"

Mike turned as another bug collided with the windshield. "You remember the day she showed up? In her fancy clothes, smelling like a million bucks, smilin' and talkin' to herself on her phone?"

Of course he did. Katie walking through the door of the bar would live rent free in his brain for the rest of his mortal life. It was the first thing he saw every time he closed his eyes. Or it had been until Atlanta had erupted in a cloud like Hiroshima, anyway. Since then, his mom and Sierra's startled faces just before the blast... He swallowed hard. *Katie.* Katie, with her long, curled hair and sunglasses pressed back on top of her head, and her smokey eyes, was a much better image.

"I'm an old fool, and dumb as a turd on the sidewalk, but even *I* can see yer actin' like an idiot. She's sleepin' in your bed, for Christ's sake."

Well, actually she wasn't. He didn't know where she'd been sleeping, but it wasn't with him. But he got the point. And when Mike said it like that...

"But I guarantee you she won't be there for much longer if you don't shape up. I'm surprised she hasn't left you already. Lord knows Easton's been layin' it on thick since she got here."

JJ's jaw tightened. Typical Easton. It was always a competition with him. He didn't care for Katie any more than he'd cared for Erica and Brian. He just liked to win. Sighing, JJ scooted his shades down and pinched the bridge of his nose.

Mike was right. He was blowing it with Katie. If there was even anything left to blow. He squeezed his eyes shut briefly before setting them back on the Jeep ahead. But there wasn't nearly enough caffeine in his body to be trying to sort all of it out. "Can we please just ride in silence? I haven't had nearly enough coffee to—"

Mike reached behind his seat and pulled out a thermos, dropping it rather firmly into JJ's lap. A grunt whooshed from his mouth. "What the—"

"She thought of that, too," Mike said.

Gripping the wheel with one hand, he rescued his junk from the anvil of coffee resting on top of it. "What's the matter with you?"

"What? It's not like you're using it for anything," the older man retorted.

"Ha ha. Fuck you."

"Funny you should mention it, because that's exactly what you're doin' to yerself."

JJ glanced at him out of the corner of his eye, wondering why Mike was so worked up before. "What's gotten into you, old man?"

The corner of Mike's eyes crinkled as he took the thermos from JJ's hand and untwisted the cap. The scent of hot coffee filled the cab. "Yer lucky I'm an old man, or I'd be after Katie myself. And that's a fact." JJ huffed, trying to imagine Mike going after *anyone*. "She can't cook for shit—" The corner of

JJ's mouth tipped up despite his attempt to keep it in a line. "—but other 'n that, that girl's damn near perfect."

JJ glanced at him over the top of his glasses. "I've never seen you like this before."

"I ain't never met someone like her before, and you neither. She's perfect for you, Jay." He handed JJ a lidless cup of piping hot coffee. "Don't blow it. Now drink yer damn coffee. There's three more sandwiches back there, too."

The corner of JJ's mouth flipped up again, despite himself, and his stomach growled as he dragged it back down. What Mike said made sense, but... he just couldn't take any more heartache now, and something told him, after his conversation with Katie about her ex, heartache followed her around like a goddamn puppy.

———

AN HOUR LATER, JJ wished he'd held off on that second sandwich. Gray ash covered everything, making the area around the remains of Atlanta look like it was covered in dirty snow. A post-apocalyptic Christmas in July. Rooftops, cars, lawns. He tried not to think too hard about what the ash was composed of, but it was almost impossible. The memory of the explosion played over and over in his head, as it had for weeks when he slept. The flash of light through the back window of the truck he'd been in, then the sound he heard through his whole body, as the shockwave passed through the vehicle, then the ash, as it shot into the sky like a fountain, before the top took on the familiar mushroom shaped cloud of devastation in the darkness.

As they came into the suburbs, he slowed. People were out and about, not mingling with each other, but on the road, in their yards. The quarantine had been lifted several days earlier, although the curfew was still in effect. Except for the ash, everything looked more or less... normal. A couple of stop lights were even working. The sign at the gas station was lit, offering one gallon of gas, per household, per week, for necessary transportation.

"It's incredible," Mike said.

It was. It really was. "How is all this still here?" They were less than ten miles from where the edge of the Veil had been, and all the buildings were still upright and intact, although many of the windows facing the city were broken and boarded up.

"I dunno. You saw it, right?"

JJ nodded. "I saw it shoot up into the sky. We were too far away to see what was happening on the ground. But, the size of it, I would have thought everything for fifty miles would have been taken out." He was no bomb expert, though. "But maybe not. New York was the same, wasn't it?"

"You think they're connected? What happened in New York and here? I thought New York went because they tried to take the Veil down?"

The light in front of him turned red, and he rolled to a stop. "That's what they *want* us to think. But I was there, and I promise you, no one was trying to take the Veil down in Atlanta that night."

Mike shrugged. "So..." There was a long pause as he seemed to sort out what JJ was saying in his head. "So you think our own government is dropping nukes on us?"

JJ consulted the paper he'd been given, showing the location of the first accident, and signaled left, as the light turned green. "I didn't see or hear anything fall from the sky before the blast, and I was watching."

"So what then?"

It was a crazy idea, but so was the Veil. And he was almost sure they were connected. "I think every major city is sitting on a nuclear warhead, and I think they were put there by whoever made the Veil."

"*What?*"

"What I don't get though is how, or why. I mean, someone would notice a fucking bomb being buried in Central Park, right?" Before Mike could answer, he went on. "Why bombs in the first place? The Veil kills everything. Why the hell bother blowing it up?"

"Well, no one *really* knows yet what happened, Jay. They're sayin' maybe the mob that gathered downtown tried to mount an attack on them there towers and…"

"Nope." JJ shook his head, bile rising up his throat like it did every time he thought about what the news was saying about Atlanta. He'd been there. *Right* there. "I told you! I was there, Mike." He slammed his fists on the steering wheel again. "Nothing like that was going on."

"Then what happened? Why do you think it was destroyed?"

"I don't know. But…" Several things gnawed at him. The first was, it was an odd coincidence that the Coast Guard *and* Army had been called away at almost the exact moment that Atlanta fell. Then there was the fact that he'd spent the previous several days clearing out the area immediately adjacent to it… "I think it was intentional. Both times, no matter what the media says about New York."

Mike looked truly scandalized. "What?"

"And I think it was the president."

"Why?"

That was the million-dollar question wasn't it? "I don't know."

"Why wouldn't he just take down the towers and wipe everyone out on the inside, like you said? Why make all this mess?"

"I don't know." But someone somewhere did, and JJ didn't want to think about the kind of reason that made incinerating an entire city full of people a worthwhile one.

Chapter Twenty-Eight

Day 21 // 12:58 p.m.

THE GOOD NEWS WAS, JJ was back on his feet. The bad news was, he was never there, and in the small pockets of time they had alone together, he was so tired he could barely stay awake. He was being a little nicer to her, though. Or at least she thought he was. It could have just been the exhaustion. At any rate, things certainly were not like they'd been before Atlanta fell. Every time she tried to get close to him, he made some excuse and backed away. She'd remained in the girls' room, not sure if she should move back into his room or not. If he noticed, he said nothing, and she took it as a sign to stay where she was.

He'd told her about his theory, about how the squirrels might be infecting the people. It made sense. Not that she was an expert by any means. But it did. He'd also said it didn't appear the birds had it, which was interesting because that would mean it only affected mammals. At least that's what her recollection of high school biology before she dropped out told her. Whether that meant something or not didn't matter though, because Atlanta was gone. Besides, there had to be a million scientists who knew all of that already. At least she hoped so.

The power being out was taking its toll on everyone. It was hot as hell inside during the day and almost nowhere in the small town was equipped with the right shade to be outside. She worried about Ms. Michelle and Mr. Goebell. Ms. Michelle at least had a deep porch to sit on. That's where she was on most days when Katie bicycled over to check on her.

Jinn was Katie's right-hand woman, and together with Barb they managed everything from meals to doling out bandages.

She made her way over the now familiar decrepit sidewalk. The door to the bar was open to allow air to flow through.

Katie twisted her hair into a bun at the base of her neck and looped an elastic around it as she passed inside. The window she had cleaned for the first time in a decade provided plenty of light to see during the day.

She recognized Easton's uniformed broad shoulders sitting at the bar immediately. Warily, she came up beside him.

His eyes were tired and bloodshot as they met hers, his jaw covered in several days' worth of stubble. He took another long pull from his mug of coffee.

"Hey," she offered. He was a jerk, but he was also stuck in the same mess they all were. The least she could do was be polite.

"Ma'am." He nodded formally.

"Is Barb getting you something to eat?"

He nodded again.

She reached over the counter for a mug, then set it under the carafe and dispensed herself a half a cup. "Did you know JJ roasts the coffee?"

Easton huffed. "Yeah."

She sat on the stool beside him, sweat dripping down her back. Even in the T-shirt and cut-off shorts she'd made out of an old pair of Mrs. Dayton's discarded jeans, she was melting. Easton must be dying in his uniform.

"How are things out there?" She asked.

He huffed again. "It's fucking chaos. Nobody is doing what they're supposed to. Hell, I don't even blame them, even though they're creating a bigger mess than they're solving. But we can't possibly arrest them all, so basically we've lost their respect and they don't give a shit. The president really dicked us over."

It seemed like the president had done that to everyone. "Well, don't go feeling special. I think he's done it to everyone."

The corner of Easton's mouth turned up as he took another sip from his cup. "Humph. The main thing now is making sure everyone is fitted with a tracker. It's mandatory. No exceptions. But folks around here, they get caught up in conspiracy theories and nonsense, and think…" He sighed. "I honestly don't know what they think. That the government is trying to spy on them, or whatever, and as soon as I get 'em tagged, they go home, take bolt cutters and take them off. There's one guy up in Maxwell I've personally tagged three times. Fucker—"

"Here you go." Barb shoved a plate of pasta and sauce with fresh sourdough under his nose. He dug in like he hadn't eaten in days.

"I'm sorry. I can't imagine being in law enforcement right now," Katie said.

"Excuse me?" an unfamiliar female voice asked from the front door.

They both turned. In it stood a woman and a man in their thirties, with two small boys. "We were just passing through and wondering… We were headed to my folks, but they're gone, and the kids…they haven't eaten since yesterday."

"This is exactly why everyone is supposed to stay put." Easton said, turning back to his food.

"Come on in, sweetie." Barb said, waving them in. "Sit over there. I'll fix y'all up a plate of pasta."

Katie got up and got four glasses of water as they sat down. "Where are you guys from?" She asked, noticing they all wore trackers.

"Dunwoody."

Katie didn't know where that was.

"They have distribution centers set up all throughout there." Easton grumbled. "You'd have been better off staying home."

"We know, but we were planning on moving in with my

folks," the man said. "They live out in Gunfreid and they were older...Only when we got there..." His voice trailed off and his wife patted his hand, looking like she might cry. "Do you know what happened out there?" the man asked.

"What?" Easton turned around.

"The town was completely destroyed. It looks like a fire and maybe possibly a tornado went through?"

Katie's brow furrowed as Barb came out of the kitchen balancing four plates on her arms. "Tornado?" She hadn't heard anything on the radio about it.

Her husband shook his head. "We should have gone sooner!"

"Then you'd be dead too. Did you find their bodies?" Easton asked, wiping his mouth on a napkin and getting up.

"Easton!" Katie said, tilting her head toward the two boys, who were devouring their plates of pasta.

"No. I looked through the...wreckage, but... I didn't find anything. I don't know if the wind swept them away, or if animals got to 'em and dragged them off."

"Wait. There wasn't *one* survivor?" Easton asked. That surprised Katie, too. Surely *someone* had survived.

"If you saw it, you'd understand. There was nowhere for anyone to live. The town was burnt to a crisp. Every building, not a tree left standing, not that there was much to begin with, but still."

"How many people live in Gunfreid?" Katie asked.

"Less than five hundred. It's a small community like this," Easton said.

Katie met the wife's eyes. "Where are you headed now?"

"Home," the woman said, sounding worried.

"It's the best place for you." Easton snapped. "That is where they are focusing all the relief efforts. Out here, it's everyone for themselves. And there's no gas. You're better off at home unless you own property that can sustain you."

"Let's let them eat." Barb said, waving Easton back to his seat.

The woman nodded. "Thank you."

Katie followed Easton back to the bar. "Hey, you haven't seen my brother recently, have you?" he asked, sitting back down.

"No." She shook her head. "Not since…I honestly don't remember the last time I saw him. You still haven't heard from him?"

"Nope. And now Green is MIA. She didn't show up for work yesterday or today, and isn't answering her phone. And I've been so damn busy, I haven't had a chance to check on him, or her."

"Where does he live?"

"In Oakdale. It's not that far, but all my calls have been back toward the city and—"

A voice crackled over the radio attached to his shoulder. Katie couldn't make it out, but apparently Easton could. Pulling it off his belt, he got up and pushed the button on the side and said, "On it." He turned to her with a sigh. "I guess Wes will have to wait a little longer."

Katie felt a burst of sympathy for him. "You want me to go? There's gas in Old Ray."

He smiled at her, possibly his first genuine smile ever, and shook his head. "I'm sure he's fine. Thanks, though. He's probably on a bender. He goes on one every now and then." Easton's laugh was bitter. "He's probably up at the cabin, drunk as a skunk, and float on' in the lake while I'm here sweating my balls off babysitting the whole goddamn countryside by myself."

Katie's sympathy grew. "Want a coffee for the road? Barb has an extra travel mug around here somewhere."

He nodded. "That would be helpful."

She went around the bar and got it, then filled it for him. "Sorry, no milk. You want sugar?"

He shook his head. "Black is fine."

She brought it around the bar. "You sure you don't want me to go check on Wes?"

Easton put a hand on her arm. "I'm sure." He looked over his shoulder at the family finishing their meal, and his eyes clouded. He leaned closer. "Just keep an eye on things here. Let me know if you see or hear anything...strange."

She caught on right away. "Like if people start disappearing?"

"Yeah."

"That's weird, right? That the whole town is gone?"

"Very. And it's not the first around here. So... watch your back. All kinds of people are on the move now. Keep an eye out for... trouble."

Katie nodded, biting her lip. It hadn't occurred to her to even worry about...What were they even called? Vagabonds? Thieves? Serial arsonists? And if they came, what exactly could she do about it, anyway?

Easton gave her arm a quick squeeze and then reached around and swatted her ass.

Her mouth fell open, and an incredulous laugh tumbled out. "Are you serious right now?" Katie shook her head. "I thought we were making such strides today."

He winked at her. "You're lucky that's all you got," His words joked, but something in his voice made her pause and she was glad Barb and the family of strangers were there.

"Jesus. You're such a redneck," she said, brushing him off.

He tilted his head, and his eyes narrowed. "I bet you'd like a little redneck in you, wouldn't you?"

Katie winced. No, she would not.

"I got a farmer's tan." Easton's tone was playful, but again laced with something darker. "...and a sweat-stained t-shirt, if that's what turns you on. Is that what turns you on?"

Another joke that felt like a threat. Hell would freeze over before she would answer that question. But she didn't want to pick a fight either. Turning his shoulders, she pushed him toward the door. "Get out of here before I—"

He laughed and spun around. "Arrest me?" He winked. "Handcuffs turn me on. You too, as I recall." Katie's fake smile faded as he leaned closer. "I've watched that video a dozen times," he confessed, as a weird mixture of embarrassment and fear settled in her belly. Why was he purposely trying to make her uncomfortable?

His eyes bore into hers, and the tension between them grew. "I ain't ever seen anything like what you let those boys do to you."

She didn't let them do anything. At least she didn't think so. "I was young and stupid."

A bang in the kitchen of a pot being dropped on the floor broke the spell Easton was under and he turned toward the back blinking, then looked back at her. "Weren't we all," he said with a laugh. "Barbie, y'allright back there?"

"I'm alright!" Barb called.

Easton's eyes grew lusty again as Katie stepped back. "I'll see you around."

She hoped not. Lesson learned. She and Easton would never be friends.

"In the meantime, I'll be 'watching' you. Ms. Newman."

Had he recorded the video? "You don't scare me."

He laughed. "Who says I'm trying to?"

He left, and she stood at the counter watching him go, wondering how the south had survived so long with men like him in charge.

Chapter Twenty-Nine

Day 21 // 1:15 p.m.

HE'D BEEN on for sixteen hours, helping clear the roads around the northeast side of the city. It was still a clusterfuck, but at least emergency vehicles could get in and out of most places if needed. Now if only they could only find people qualified to drive them.

But that wasn't JJ's problem. He wasn't smart enough for medical shit anyway, and the sight of needles made his knees buckle in the most unmanly way.

Pulling up in front of Mikes, he cut the engine and sighed.

"It's a hell of a thing." Mike said, like always.

JJ nodded.

"I'm gonna wash up, then grab a bite."

JJ nodded again, spying Easton's cruiser and a car he didn't recognize in front of Barb's. Hopping out, he headed across the street. He was passing in front of the window when something inside drew him to a stop; Easton leaning way too close to Katie.

He stared as they appeared to be whispering to each other. Then Easton reached around her and grabbed her ass. JJ's jaw tightened. "That son of a—" To his surprise, she laughed, and the rest of the words died in his throat. Shaking her head, but not looking angry, she grabbed his arm and pushed him playfully toward the door. JJ stepped back. *What the fuck?* A part of him knew he had no right to feel jealous after the way he'd been acting, but he didn't feel like listening to that part just then.

Storming into the bar, he almost collided with the bastard. "Hey, Jay." Easton said, pulling his sunglasses over his eyes.

"Leave her alone," JJ growled, noticing that Katie had disappeared. Had she gone into the kitchen? Or out the back door to avoid him?

Easton looked over his shoulder. "Relax," he said with an easy laugh. "We're old friends now." Then he brushed past JJ and headed out to his car.

Old friends? What the hell did that mean? JJ took in the family, finishing up their meal, then met Barb's eyes as she peeked out from the kitchen and nodded.

He went behind the bar. The keg beer was skunked, but the bottles were still good. Warm as shit, but good. He grabbed one out of the stale cooler and popped the top. Going around the front, he pulled his cap from his head and slumped onto a stool, his mood suddenly foul.

"What's got your face all screwed up?" Barb asked.

"Nothing." *Everything.* Was Katie talking to Easton? Since when? Last he remembered, she hated his guts, but that was not the impression he just got.

Barb let out a short, clipped laugh. "I've known you all yer life, JJ."

He glanced out the window at Easton pulling away. "Nothing."

"Oh hell, what did he do now?"

"Nothing."

A boy at the table behind them laughed, and his scowl deepened. He drained his beer, almost gagging on the fizziness.

Barb sighed. "So no one is allowed to laugh anymore, is that it? Is that what's got you riled?"

"What's there to laugh about? The entire world is either dead or dying."

"Not the whole world. There's still a couple of us left."

Hadn't Mike said the same thing to him recently? "And what

am I supposed to feel, exactly? Grateful for that?" JJ got up, went back behind the bar and got himself another beer out of the frig, wondering if everything between him and Katie was...bullshit? Was he doing it again? Being stupid and naïve to think someone like her would—

"Don't you?" Barb countered.

He went to close the door, then thought better and grabbed a second one before heading back to his seat. God, why did that thought make him so angry? "No."

"Then maybe they should have just let the virus kill us all."

"Maybe they should have," he agreed, popping the top off and taking another swig. At least then he could have been with his mom and sister. Who knew? Maybe they would have found a way to fight the virus off. Maybe they could have...hopped in his truck and driven to Canada and outrun it.

It was Barb's turn to scowl. "Might want to eat something first."

When he didn't answer, she shook her head. "I'm getting you some food. Is Mike coming?"

He nodded.

A few minutes later, Katie returned with the kids. His insides flipped as she strolled in wearing jean shorts and some kind of tank top she'd made out of one of his old t-shirts. She'd given up on her fancy outfits weeks ago, but she still dressed nice every day and her underwear...*holy fuck*. He'd seen them drying on the line on more than one occasion. He'd stared at one particular black, strappy set for almost fifteen minutes yesterday, first trying to figure out exactly what went where, then trying *not* to imagine it on her. He'd failed miserably and had been forced to take a *very* cold shower.

He recognized it peeking out from the low arm holes at her sides. At least she hadn't been wearing that when Easton was here. But even that was little consolation for his shitty mood.

"Hey." Her smile was warm and friendly as she sat down

beside him. For some reason, that pissed him off more. "So I just found out Grace's birthday was yesterday. She told Parker this morning. When I asked her about it, she said she didn't feel like celebrating."

He took a drink of his beer. She wasn't the only one.

"But I think we should. I think we *need* to. So, I'm going to run to Michelle's, pick her up for lunch and grab some eggs, so I can make a cake. But I want it to be a surprise. Would you mind taking Mr. Goebell his lunch? He can't walk, and I'm worried about him and the heat."

———

THREE HOURS later JJ was back on his stool at the bar, way more drunk than he should have been. They'd just sang happy birthday to Grace, and everyone seemed to be having a good time. Except him.

Grace opened a present, from who the hell knew where. It was a book, some kind of diary or something and markers.

And then Katie had turned the music on, and she and the kids danced again, to some country shit Barb had. And now...

"Come on. It's more fun with more players," Katie said, looking up from the game.

He swallowed his beer, feeling twice as thirsty as when he started, and possibly on the verge of throwing up. Reaching in his pocket, he extracted his last stick of gum and unwrapped it. "No," he said, shoving it into his mouth.

Katie got up, placed a hand on his arm, and her eyes, goddamn her eyes... He forgot where he was heading with that thought.

"Please?" she begged. "For—"

He slammed his palm on the bar, not understanding why he was so angry, or why his head felt like it was going to explode, or why he couldn't explain any of this to her. Something inside him needed to lash out, and he was trying really hard *not* to make her the target. "Damn it Katie! I said no!"

"What is the matter with you?" She leaned toward him like she had earlier with Easton. "Can't you put your self pity aside for a minute to just play a game with the girls?"

He *wanted* to. He wanted to get whatever poison had infected him out of his soul, but he didn't know how! It was rotting from the inside out and... He turned to face her. "Fuck you!"

Oh no.

The words just came out of his mouth, and worse, there were more on the way as he jabbed his finger at her. "You have no idea what it's like! *You* are the only one here that hasn't lost somebody! So don't lecture me—"

She slapped him. Honest to god, slapped him across the face, in front of everyone. He was so stunned he just stared at her as she yelled. "You *fucking* idiot. You don't think I've lost someone?"

His brows came together, and he blinked. Was he missing something? *Shit.* "Who?"

"I lost you, JJ." Her voice broke, as his anger returned.

He rolled his eyes. "Oh, please—"

"But unlike the Veil, I've been watching you die one minute at a time for the last two weeks, and it's *killing* me." She waved her arm around. "All of us. So how *dare* you say I don't know what it's like."

He knew everyone was watching him, listening, but he was beyond caring. "I'm warning you. Stay away from me."

"Or what?" She threw her arms up, looking genuinely hurt. "Did something happen when you were in the city? Why are you doing this?"

Because if he didn't, he'd—his stool slid back with a screech, as he shoved his fists in his pockets and headed for the door. He needed to get out of there. Now. He didn't care where he went, but he couldn't be there any longer or he'd explode like Atlanta had, and take them all with him.

"Where do you think you're going?" Katie demanded as he pushed the door open. It was pitch black out without the light from the lamp that normally illuminated the sidewalk in front of the bar. He tripped over the curb as it appeared beneath his feet sooner than he expected and stumbled into the street.

"Don't walk away from me, JJ Dayton." Katie said, sounding like a perfect blend of his mom and dad at the same time. Well, actually, his dad usually went for his *full* name. *'Jensen James Dayton, get your butt over—'*

Suddenly, she was standing in front of him, blocking his path to his truck, and he ran into her outstretched hands as he fumbled for his keys. "I said don't walk away from me," she repeated.

Should you be driving? some annoyingly sober part of him asked. He spit his gum on the ground. Probably not, but there was no one on the road anymore anyway, and he knew the sheriff, so he'd take his chances. "Get out of my way," he growled.

She crossed her arms. "Or what?"

It was too dark to see her, so he just imagined her instead. Her smile. Those fucking eyes. That body, in daisy-dukes and his old t-shirt. The zig-zag of black lace and straps beneath that crisscrossing her skin like a goddamn roadmap.

She was so beautiful. He hiccupped. No, not beautiful. What was it called when sunbeams shot out around something and blinded you? *Radiant?* Yeah. That was it. She was so fucking radiant he could hear angels singing from whatever corner of the universe they'd fled to every time he looked at her.

His mouth went dry and his hands suddenly ached to touch her. Or maybe it wasn't so sudden. Maybe that urge had been there from the moment she walked into Barb's, threw her Mary Poppins bag on the counter and he spun around on his barstool and almost fell off it. Yes, the want to touch her, to feel the smooth skin of her neck beneath his fingers, to tangle them in her hair and pull her head back as he looked into her eyes, had been there since—

"Or what?" she repeated.

"You don't want to know," he growled.

"Yes. I do," she replied evenly.

Clenching his fists at his sides, he stumbled backward. "No."

She didn't know what she was asking for. Couldn't see the snapping, angry, *needy* monster that had taken over his body. Couldn't she sense what he wanted to do to her? "Get out of here, Katie. *Now.*"

"Or what, JJ?"

"Please." He couldn't contain it any longer.

She touched his cheek and whispered. "Or what?"

Barely had the words come out before his mouth collided with hers. To his surprise, she grabbed his face in her hands, and answered him hungrily as his hands evolved a mind of their own and slid from her face, down her neck, along her sides to her ass.

Lifting her off the ground, they stumbled into the door of his truck, which was again much closer than he expected. The air rushed from her lungs as her back collided with it, and she threw her head skyward, grasping at a breath as his mouth found her neck and one of his hands found its way under her shirt. She moaned as his fingertips brushed over the straps of her bra and he squeezed her.

It was like when he'd opened his mouth inside. Some part of him knew what he was doing was wrong, but... the rest of him wanted to, no, *needed*...

Her tongue dipped into his mouth, tasting like cake and frosting, releasing something inside him he could not control.

Pressing his hips into hers, he wedged her against the truck, freeing his hands to pull her shirt over her head. He bit her neck, and she arched against him, groaning, her hips bucking into his in all the right places. Jesus, he would not last long if she kept doing that.

He squeezed her sides, her sweaty skin cool against his fingers, as he lowered her to the ground and reached for the door handle. He pulled her and the door back at the same time. "Get in," he demanded, in a voice he didn't recognize.

She climbed up onto the seat, and he followed like a crazed animal on the scent of its prey.

Laying her back on the seat, he slid his hand under the small of her back, lifting her farther inside as he climbed on top of her. He needed something, or he was going to disappear and— following her panting breath, he found her mouth again in the dark. His hand slid over her shoulder, searching for the strap of her bra, until he found it. Bringing his hips into hers, he yanked it down, and she cried out against his mouth as he squeezed her.

It wasn't much more than a yelp, but it was enough to make him realize what he was doing, which was—he had pinned her down, and she couldn't move.

"Oh, god." He scrambled back, dropping one foot on the floor of the cab to release her from the weight of his body. His wild hands anchored themselves in his hair and pulled. "Shit." He'd been too rough, too angry.

"JJ?"

In all his life, he'd never touched a woman the way he'd just touched her. "I'm sorry." He turned, groping for the door handle. "I'm so..." Who had he become? His anger and need to flee returned. "I'm so sorr—" He frantically slid his hand over the door.

She sat up. "What's the matter? What happened?"

"I'm sorry." He felt along the vinyl. Where in the hell was the handle?

"JJ." Her hands found his cheek and turned him back around to face her. He could barely see her in the dark, and that was good because he'd never survive the shame otherwise. "I'm—"

Suddenly, her mouth was on his again. Hot and heavy.

He fell into the door, banging his head in the window as she pressed her hand to his chest and followed him. Her other hand found his jaw, and she whispered two words that sent his self-control flying again.

"I'm not." Wrapping her hand around his neck, she pulled him back down on top of her as she lay back on the seat and pressed her hips into his.

"I can't!" JJ insisted against her mouth, in a last-ditch effort to back up. "I'm not in the right mind—"

Her hand slid down to his pants. "You need to get out of your fucking mind."

"No, I—"

"And I need you inside me," she said before biting his lip.

His eyes rolled back, and he groaned. Oh god, she was not making this easy. And his heart was beating so fast, and something was about to happen, and he was scared out of his goddamn mind.

"I want this, JJ. I *want* you like this. To be in control, to... rule me." Katie wrapped her hand around the back of his neck, dragging his mouth back to hers, the other fumbling with the button on his pants. "I promise you, the only way you can hurt me now is if you walk away."

What if she was wrong? What if he couldn't—

She popped the button, then anchored both of her hands in his hair and pulled, driving away all thought and filling him with glorious anticipation.

After one more brief moment of hesitation, he grabbed her hip and squeezed, pressing her against him. Her back arched, as her chest collided with his. "Yes." The pleasure in her voice made him do it again.

Shoving her hand under his shirt, she raked her nails across his skin, making him gasp. "Now, stop holding back, and give me what I want."

A switch flipped inside JJ as the monster inside of him reared its head and roared. He leaned back, popped the glove compartment open for a condom, and heard himself say, "Then get on your knees."

The truck rocked as she hastily complied and he reached for the button of her jeans.

Then he descended upon her, issuing command after command, hands groping, squeezing, pulling, reveling in the sounds she made as she did whatever he asked. His heart tore free of its prison, of its past, and it was born again into the moment, beating for the first time in *years* without fear. All of his thoughts fled save one, and he repeated it over and over as she ground against him, urging him on. *I can stop if she asks me to.*

But instead of stopping him, she met him at every turn, then begged for more. He'd never been with anyone like Katie, and the awful beast he'd unleashed that sought to overpower her, control her, was no match for the magnificent one beneath him that possessed his soul and drove him to earth-shattering pleasure in the cab of his truck.

Chapter Thirty

Day 21 // 10:30 p.m.

"DON'T STOP." Tears leaked from her eyes as she squeezed them shut and clung to him, perfectly suspended between pleasure and pain. Her nails dug into the back of his neck.

JJ growled above her in answer as the cab rocked like a boat. *Finally,* she had him. Heart, body and soul. He'd tried to keep all three from her, but the dam had finally burst, and he was holding *nothing* back now.

She groaned as their bodies came together faster, rougher, but not violently. And that was exactly what she wanted, what she *needed.* Because sex for her was complicated. At least the kind that *meant* anything. Romance, candles, flowers, flattery, all of those things confused her. What turned her on—she was quickly realizing—was darker, edgier. It involved pain, and giving up the one thing she never did. Control.

Plenty of men would have been more than happy to dominate her over the years if she had let them. But she hadn't trusted a single one of them enough to relinquish control, because she'd been too afraid of what might happen if she did. For her submission was the *ultimate* form of intimacy, and up until now, she had been as afraid to share it as JJ was afraid to accept it.

And he needed to. He needed to control her as much as she wanted him to, because it was the only way to set him free from the prison he'd put himself in. The one that made him feel unlovable and helpless. It was the only way for her to prove to him that she really wanted him, trusted him, and desired *him,* and she did, with every fiber of her being and ounce of her soul.

As he whispered dirty things to her, the don't-give-a-shit man he was in the daylight, merged with the one he was in the dark, and a need that had *never* been met grew in Katie's core. She wanted his rawness, because it allowed her to free her own, and she'd been holding it back, hiding what she truly wanted for *so* long.

"Harder," she choked.

She wanted to feel the sting of a trustworthy palm against her skin, to give herself over to the dark desires of a man who, with every word and stroke and pull, made her feel safer.

And the harder he came at her—she groaned—the more cherished she felt, because she knew, if she asked him to, he would stop.

Dipping her tongue into his mouth again, she wrapped her legs around him. "Give me what I want, JJ."

He jerked her head back by her hair, bringing more tears, and bit her neck as she cried out and the truck rocked.

"Fuck. Fuck…" He panted against her ear.

"Don't. Stop," she moaned, blinded nearly as much by the *pain* as by the pleasure that was rapidly filling her body. He was coming undone too, losing control, poised on the edge again. She could feel it, and she wanted nothing more than to fall with him. Because he would catch her before she hit the bottom. Because even though he had disarmed and unraveled her, he would never let her hit the ground.

"Don't—" Pleasure wound up through her body like a corkscrew as she dug her nails into his neck.

JJ's mouth swallowed her scream as he rocked into her again and it exploded.

"That's it," his voice was a rough whisper against her mouth. "That's my good… Oh, god… oh…"

A moan vibrated against her neck as he buried his head against it, and found his own release.

More tears fell as she clung to him, riding out his pleasure and the remnants of her own, and for the first time in her life, Katie felt whole.

———

HIS FINGERS TICKLED her cheek as he brushed her hair back off her face. Lying half across his naked body, swallowed in darkness, her heart slowed to a satisfied thump in her chest as she bit her lip, not entirely sure what had just happened.

She'd had sex plenty of times… Okay, more than plenty, but this—JJ shifted his arm beneath her and she groaned—this was something entirely different that made all her other sexual encounters feel like a chaste peck on the cheek. She didn't know what surprised her more, that *she* initiated it with a man she'd only met a month ago, or that she enjoyed it so damn much.

Tears filled her eyes, and she swiped at them, trying to understand why she suddenly felt like crying. She wasn't sad. In fact, she'd never been happier. Never felt safer, never felt—

"I'm so sorry." JJ's voice was hoarse with regret, and she realized he was misinterpreting her tears.

"No." Propping herself up on her elbow, she squinted at him, finding his scratchy jaw and holding it in her hand. "Don't even think that. That's not why I'm… I-I loved it, actually."

He was silent.

"I mean it JJ. I'm not…" She suddenly wondered if she'd scared *him*. After all, what kind of woman liked getting her ass slapped and hair—

"You *liked* it, really?" He sounded almost boyish, and she smiled.

"Yeah, I did." She dropped her head back into his shoulder. "Did…you?"

"Um…I… I mean, *yes*. But…" He made a sound like he was dragging his hand over his face. "Jesus Christ. I've never done *anything* like that before."

She exhaled through her nose. "Me either."

He shifted, trying to get a better look at her. "You mean that's not how you normally…" He seemed to regret starting that sentence and let it drop.

"No."

He shifted again, his warm palm sliding from her waist to her hip. "I see," he said, sounding like he didn't at all. "Did I do something that made you think that was what *I* wanted?"

"That is what you wanted."

He didn't answer.

"It was what I needed too."

"I don't understand."

"You needed control and… I think this is the first time I've been honest with myself in… *the* moment. I think this is the first time I've felt safe enough to allow what I want to happen, *happen*." Her insides ached and her limbs felt like jelly floating in the remnants of her pleasure. That had never happened to her before either, and made her feel vulnerable. A thought occurred to her, perhaps a little too late. "Do you like me JJ?" She thought so, but sometimes he was so hard to read. And while she *trusted* him with her body, his heart—

"Do you really think I could do what we just did if I didn't?"

"I don't know. Maybe?" Every other guy she knew could have. Half of them had slept with her, not even knowing her name. "You wouldn't be the first, I guess, which is why I'm asking."

He took a deep breath and sighed. His voice wobbled as he spoke. "I…" He swallowed again. "Shit."

Sensing she'd asked him a question he wasn't ready to answer, she tried to sit up, feeling confused and self conscious.

Had she totally misread what was happening between them? "It's okay if you don't—"

"I've been in love with you since the moment I saw you." The words rushed from his mouth as he pulled her back down on his chest and his fingers found her cheek.

"I—" His hands anchored in her hair again, but they were gentle as he pulled her forehead to his. "I love you Katie, and I want every… every part of you, and you have no idea how much that scares me. Every time you walk into the room, I want to run."

Katie smiled through her tears.

"But the longer we're together, the more I feel like running *to* you. The more I want nothing more than to…crush you in my arms and…and never let you go. Because I'm afraid you will. Go. And I don't want—" He sounded like he was on the verge of tears. "I'm sorry if I hurt you just now. I—"

"I told you."

"My dad would be so ashamed of the way I spoke to you. The things—"

"Hey, I told you. I know you didn't mean them. And I like it."

"But—"

"I never met your dad, but your mom told me a little about him, and you are every bit as good as he was, or I never would have let you do what we just did. Do you understand?"

"Not really. And no, I'm not."

"Yes, you are."

"No, if I was, then…"

"Then what? Erica wouldn't have left you?"

JJ was silent.

Katie shook her head. "Don't confuse her stupidity for your lack of character, JJ. And don't let anyone tell you what kind of person you are, not even the ghost of your father. Trust me, that never ends well."

"I just—I don't want to fuck this up…anymore than I already have." He added.

She sighed. "I care about you, too. A lot. And I want to say I love you back, because we both know it's what's in my heart, but just like you, I'm afraid."

"Afraid of what?"

"That you'll let me down. Or that I'll let you down."

"Yeah, I'm kinda worried about that too," he said before blurting, "Do you still have feelings for your ex?"

Katie's eyebrows went up. "Matt?" Then she remembered. They hadn't finished their conversation, and she was glad, because up until this moment, she wasn't a hundred percent sure. But she was now.

Whatever this was between her and JJ was so much deeper and vulnerable, and *honest* than what she'd shared with Matt. She had loved him. But she'd been too scared to fall *in* love with him. "No. I care about him, but—"

"You just said the same thing about me. And I need more than a vague…"

She met his eyes in the dark and hoped he could see them enough to see the truth. "JJ, you are not my second *choice*." She kissed him, softly. "But you *are* my second chance," she whispered against his mouth. His body responded beneath her. "And I never want a third. Is that enough for now? Until I can say the words?"

He sucked in a sharp breath, nodding slightly.

"Good." She lay back down, as he trailed his fingers up and down her side, leaving goosebumps in their wake. "How many girls have been in this truck?" she asked, trying to lighten the mood for a moment before things got hot and heavy again. Because they were going to. How could they not after he'd just satisfied her every desire *and* told her he loved her? No, she wasn't done yet. Not nearly.

"A lot. I'm a tow—"

She laughed as she climbed on top of him, straddling his hips. "No, I mean for sex," she said, as his hands paused against her thighs and he gasped.

"*What?*" he sounded truly appalled. "No. I've never—"

"Relax." She smiled as she pressed herself down into him and he swore under his breath. "It was a joke." Kind of. Mostly. Okay, she was suddenly a possessive bitch and didn't want to share JJ or his truck with anyone else.

"Relaxing around you is damn near impossible," he choked, sliding his hands over her waist and digging his fingers in.

"It is?" She leaned down and bit his ear, making him yelp. "Well then, how about we do the opposite of relaxing, then?"

He sucked in another harsh breath as she reached for him.

"What are you doing?" he asked, sounding scandalized.

"I want you again. Right here. Right now. The same way as before."

"Are you sure?" His voice was rough. "You don't want to go to bed?"

Another small laugh burst from her throat, before her desire climbed back in the driver's seat. "I'm not even close to being done with you…" She dug her nails gently into his most sensitive skin and he jumped. "Mr. Dayton."

Bolting upright, he grabbed her around the waist and flipped her over. As her back hit the seat, Katie felt freer than she had since she was six years old, flying on a swing with her feet touching the sky.

"Is that so?" JJ's voice was rough.

"Yes," she said breathlessly.

"God, I love you," he growled, pinning her wrists above her head.

"Prove it," she whispered, her insides already coiling in anticipation.

"Oh, I will." He nipped her ear back. "Now, be a good girl, and do exactly what you're told."

***

Several wildly blissful moments later, they were still again and panting.

As Katie lay nestled in JJ's arms, his fingers brushing her shoulder, she wondered if maybe she was dreaming.

"I want to take you somewhere," he said gently, his voice cutting the quiet.

Because what she felt lying beside him was so foreign, and so... surreal.

His chest rose and fell beneath her palm, as his heart thudded beneath her ear, and she knew there was nowhere on earth, nowhere in time even, she would rather be than right where she was. Was that what love was? God, if so, it hurt and felt wonderful at the same time. She smiled. Just like sex with—

JJ went on. "I'm not trying to... I don't mean to... Shit. What I mean is, I'm not trying to contradict or counteract what just happened between us. I just...want to take you somewhere, and show you something. Is that okay?"

"Now?"

"Yeah. Now."

She looked down. "Do I need clothes?"

He laughed, and something that had been missing from his voice for the last few weeks returned. "Just a shirt."

"I think mine is on the road somewhere."

He laughed again, and it made her heart light. "Here," he said, pressing his shirt to her chest as he sat up and fumbled for his pants. "I'll be back in a minute." There was a pause and then shuffling and the drag of a zipper. "Don't go anywhere," he said, pushing the door open.

She smiled in the darkness. He need not worry. "I'll be right here."

TWENTY MINUTES LATER, JJ cut the engine of his dad's old pickup. They sat for a long moment staring at the gap in the pines where the river ran, before he spoke.

"I…I liked that, what we just did. But I also feel other things for you and I just… I was in control back there, but you are in control here, Katie." There was a pause and then he laughed. "You don't need me to tell you that. But I just…I was being honest with you before. I want to be honest with you now, too. But I don't want you to freak out."

"Why would I freak out?"

"Because I know you've never let anyone make love to you before. And that's what I want to do."

Her heart stopped in her chest, making her feel lightheaded and tingly in the strangest places. Like the corners of her mouth, the creases of her elbows, the palms of her hands. She rolled them over in her lap as they shook, and she wasn't sure if it was with desire or—

JJ's hands closed over hers, and the tingling spread down her arms, across her chest. "I don't want you to be afraid of me," he said, touching her cheek, making her gasp. "And I know you said I can't hurt you, but I think I can. And…" He pushed her chin up, meeting her eyes in the dashboard lights. "You trust me enough to be rough with you. Do you trust me enough to love you too? Will you let me do that?"

She stared at him as the tingling rushed through her body again. Was this really happening? And was she going to let it? "I-I don't know what to do," she confessed, realizing that yes, she was.

His smile was kind and confident, and she was sure she'd never seen a more beautiful man in her life. "I know," he said. "But I do."

"I'm sorry about Erica," she blurted, instantly regretting it. Now was not the time to bring up his ex, but she was so damn nervous.

His expression changed, but the smile remained. "I'm not. Not anymore. Come on." He grabbed the handle and pushed his door open.

Katie did the same, and by the time she made it around the back of the truck, he'd dropped the tailgate and spread a blanket in the back.

He stood on one side of the bed, shirtless. She stood on the other with only his shirt on, and she was suddenly terrified. Of making a mistake, of not doing it right. The shaking in her hands spread quickly through her body and she suddenly couldn't breathe.

"Did I ever tell you about my granddad and my grandma, how they met?" he asked, hopping onto the tailgate.

She shook her head as he stood up on the back of the truck and extended his hand to her. She took it, and he pulled her up, sliding his hand around her waist as butterflies took flight in her stomach, making her feel like she was going to throw up. He brushed the hair out of her eyes, and she looked down at his chest, reminding herself she'd had sex before—less than an hour ago, as a matter of fact, and there was no need to be nervous. *But not like this, you haven't.* She pressed her head to his ink-covered chest and exhaled. No, not like this.

"It's a good story," JJ went on, taking her hand, then leading her down onto the bed of the truck.

"Does it have a happy ending?" she asked as he pulled her into his arms, and she looked up at the cloudless sky full of stars.

The sound of rushing water and JJ's gentle laugh soothed her nerves. "Yes, but boy did they have a rough start."

She nestled against him as he pushed his arm under his head, pulling her close. "Sounds familiar. Did she compliment his dad-bod?" Katie asked, unable to help herself.

JJ laughed again, the sound rumbling against her ear. "No, thank god. Otherwise, I probably wouldn't be here."

Katie smiled at his joke, but sobered quickly. "When I said that, what I meant was—"

"I know what you meant, Katie," he said, lacing their fingers together.

"Are you sure?"

It was a moment before he answered. "I am now."

Then he told her the endearing and funny story, and she laughed, half convinced that the Veil and the virus were nothing more than a dream, because how could anything so horrible exist in the most beautiful moment of her life?

Then when she was ready, he made love to her-and if she'd lost herself in the cab of his truck, she was a thousand times more gone beneath the stars and his gentle touch.

As the sun came up over the pines, and the sparrows took flight in the cloudless blue sky, Katie fell asleep completely exposed and fully surrendered JJ's arms.

Chapter Thirty-One

Day 22 // 11:11 a.m.

SAM STOOD at the edge of the crater beside JJ, probably thinking the same thing he was. Where was his mom in all that mess? The answer was probably both nowhere and everywhere at once.

It was otherworldly, like they'd stepped off a spaceship and landed on a planet punched with holes. The bottom had to be almost a quarter mile deep at the center and filled with rubble, mostly rock except for the occasional pool of water, or shiny glint of metal that hinted at the city that had once been there.

"This isn't how this is supposed to look," Sam said.

JJ turned. "What do you mean?"

"Well, I'm no…bomb expert, but in high school, I saw a documentary on Hiroshima and Nagasaki, and…It didn't look like this. At all. There was no hole like there is here. The people were all gone, but there were still buildings and cars. The *ground* was still there. And it went on for miles. This is so, I dunno." He shook his head. "Precise. I mean, shit. Look at it. It's like…giant fucking hole in the ground and then…" He turned around to face the shopping center behind them. "…a Save Smart with grocery carts still lined up outside the door a hundred feet away."

It *was* odd. But JJ guessed a lot had changed in the interceding years since World War II, although *whose* technology it was still had to be determined.

"Why blow it up?" Sam asked, his composure cracking as he threw his hands in the air, reminding JJ of his conversation with

Mike. "They were already inside. And it's not like they could get out. They were gonna fucking die, anyway." Dragging his hands through his growing, curly hair, he pulled at it as he doubled over and turned away. "Jesus—" His voice broke, and a sob followed it. "Why? What kind of narcissistic fuck blows up people who are already dying? How could the president let this happen to his people?"

JJ kept his theories about the president to himself. They'd only add fuel to Sam's fire, one which, until last night, had been raging out of control in JJ's own chest since the fall of Atlanta. But not anymore. Katie had extinguished it. Not by blowing it out, but by stoking it in the cab of his truck until all the helplessness and hatred had been sucked out of his soul and lit on fire. And then... And then she'd held him while it burned, moved with him until they used up all the oxygen and then it had snuffed itself out.

He still wasn't sure *exactly* how it all started. Or why? He'd been pretty drunk at first. Angry too. He remembered that much. He'd been feeling all the things he shouldn't, and tried to stop her. But then... JJ dragged his hands through his hair. But then Katie had stripped away everything his propriety and his parents had ever taught him about women with her touch and words, and when he climbed down from the truck an hour later, he barely recognized the half-dressed, incredibly happy man who had done and said the things he had in the darkness of that cab.

And while Katie hadn't been gentle, nor had she said 'I love you' back, she'd done something far better. She'd shown him. By *trusting* him. By being honest and *vulnerable* with him, and if that wasn't love, he didn't know what was. He'd felt it, in his heart, down his back, in his bones, as she clung to him and cried out, and it was the most breathtakingly intimate experience of his life, to be loved like that. To *feel* her rawness and answer it. And he had decided right then and there, he was done hiding behind his excuses. Done being hung up on Erica. Done with rules and feeling unworthy inside. His heart had been broken. So fucking what? Life went on. He was a grown man. And if he was even half the one Katie seemed to think he was, he needed to stop being such an annoying jackass, and get over himself. He needed to take control of his heart again, just like he'd taken control of her in his truck, and quit acting like a moron, for fuck's sake. And he was ready. He'd been ready since their first kiss. So goddamn ready. And he'd wanted to make that clear. Prove to her he was *completely* over it, himself, his past, and that if anything, he was glad Erica left him, because if she hadn't... He wouldn't have been free when Katie came storming into his life. And he could not bear that thought.

That was why he'd taken her to the river after. Not to make up for what they'd just done in the cab, but to return her vulnerability, to make sure there was no lingering doubt in her mind he was holding back any part of himself. He wanted more from her than a casual fuck, or even a hot one in his truck. He *loved* her with his whole heart, mind and soul, and hopefully, that was obvious to her now.

"Earth to JJ?" Sam asked with a raised brow.

It took him a second to remember what they had been talking about. "I don't know." JJ said, taking Sam by the shoulder and pushing his thought of Katie aside.

He had a theory, though. He'd come up with it after asking himself a very simple question. Why do people dig holes? *To bury things.* He'd never be able to prove it, but he was almost sure there was something buried under that city that someone didn't want found. Again, the question was whose secret lay beneath the millions of tons of rubble? The president's? The 'undisclosed third-party' that had constructed the Veil? Or someone else? "Come on, let's go. The faster we unload this fencing and get it up, the faster we can get the fuck out of here."

Sam wiped his eyes, a hint of a smile returning to his face. "Why? Got something special waiting for you back home?"

JJ's cheeks burned beneath his beard as he pulled his cap off and ran his fingers through his hair. Jesus. Did someone see them last night? In his truck? He shook his head. "No."

Sam's brow went up. "The teeth marks on your neck would suggest otherwise."

The corner of JJ's mouth turned up. Yes, they did. But he had told the truth. He didn't have some*thing;* he had *someone.*

Chapter Thirty-Two

Day 22 // 12:05 p.m.

"I'M HUNGRY."

Katie's eyes flew open, and she realized she'd fallen asleep in the recliner. Amelia stood before her in a long t-shirt, holding Beaver, waiting while she sat up. Katie rubbed her sleepy eyes as the little girl climbed onto her lap and rested her head on her shoulder. She smiled and smoothed her hair.

Amelia had been doing that a lot lately. Well, since Atlanta fell. Whether it was because she missed her mom or JJ, Katie couldn't tell, but the girl was extra cuddly and she enjoyed the time immensely while they waited for word from her grandparents.

"You're hungry?" Katie asked, pushing the tangly hair back off Amelia's face.

"Yeah."

"You ready for some lunch?"

She nodded.

"Okay, come on." Katie said, sliding the girl off her lap.

"I'm *super* hungry," Amelia clarified.

Amelia had the appetite of a grown woman and yet was still as thin as a rail, whereas... Katie looked down at her stomach, pressing her finger into her slightly squishy middle, and sighed. Her pants were fitting a little tighter than they should, too.

"What's the matter?" Amelia asked, tilting her head like a puppy.

Katie sighed heading to the kitchen for a glass of water. Of course, *she* would be the only one to gain weight during a world crisis. She ought to be grateful, because it meant they had food when so many others didn't. But it was hard to let go of what she'd held on to for so long. "I think you need to eat more and I need to eat less."

Parker appeared in the doorway. "No. You're both just eating the right amount and look great."

It was an odd compliment and one that normally made her uncomfortable when coming from a young man, unless he was…

A major piece of the Parker puzzle slid into place. She gasped, not believing she hadn't caught on sooner.

"Go get dressed and ask Grace if she wants to come with us for breakfast," she said to Amelia, who ran off down the hall.

Looking up, she studied Parker, seeing him clearly for the first time. "Thanks for the compliment. I've been meaning to ask you, how did you end up at Carlton Christian school?"

He gave her a look that said he knew *she* knew. "My parents were desperate."

"Why?"

He shrugged. "Because they thought I was going to hell."

"For being gay?"

He nodded, carefully watching for her reaction. When she didn't react at all, he went on. "Pray the gay away," he said with a weary smile. "Or pressure it away, whatever works."

"I wish I could pray away assholes and period cramps."

He laughed, but she saw the pain in his eyes.

"I'm sorry. I didn't mean to joke about—"

"It's okay."

"No, it's not. You are an incredible young man, Parker. You deserve love and respect, just as you are."

Tears filled his eyes, and he pressed his hand to his mouth as a sob exploded from it.

That was not the reaction she'd expected. Had she said something wrong? "What's the matter?"

His face contorted as he tried to get himself under control. "Why couldn't *they* say that?"

Katie's heart broke. "Your parents?"

"Why did they have to believe that stupid shit they believed?" he demanded. "Why couldn't they just—I don't know, not care?" He swiped at his eyes. "And now they are fucking gone, and I don't know what to feel. I don't want to be angry anymore, but it's not my fault I wasn't inside the Veil with them. *They* did this. But I feel guilty anyway. Why do I feel so bad, Katie?" He sounded like a hurt little boy.

Her eyes filled with tears. And in a way, he was.

"Why do I feel like it's my fault?" His voice wobbled. "Why do I *miss* them and wish they were here when they've been like strangers to me for the past three years?"

Tears spilled down her cheeks as Katie pulled him in for a hug. "Because you are stronger than most of us, and your love is unconditional, and that is so..." She squeezed him. "...so beautiful. You should be proud. You have such a big heart, Parker. I've seen you with Grace. You are her anchor." She took his face in her hands. "And you respect yourself enough to be angry when others don't respect *you*. That's a strength, not a weakness." Shaking her head, she dropped into one of the dining room chairs, pulling him into the one beside her. "I wish I'd had half the self respect you do when I was your age. It would have saved me a lot of heartache."

Wiping his eyes, he shook his head.

"I can't tell you what to feel. If you want to forgive them, then do. If you are not ready, then don't. And if your feelings change over time, that's okay too. I support your truth, no matter what it is, and you can talk to me about anything."

"I want to forgive them," he said quietly.

Katie smiled sadly. "Well then, for what it's worth, my parents never once tried to "fix" me. Most of the time, they didn't even notice I was there. So..."

Parker was silent for a moment. "Is that why you chose social media? So people would notice you?"

Katie huffed a laugh. Well, if that didn't make a hell of a lot of sense. And where was her therapist Hunter with that astute observation? She wondered, massaging her temples. "Have you ever thought about going into therapy?"

A genuine smile spread across his face, and Katie's heart grew. "Have you ever thought about being a mom?" He asked with a raised brow.

A warmth she'd never felt before spread through her chest to her cheeks, rendering her speechless as Parker laughed. "Apparently not. But you'd make a good mother. You *will* make a good one." His eyes went to the hall, and she knew he meant Grace. Then he added, "For me too, maybe?"

Katie's heart nearly exploded with joy, and she wondered if that was what true mothers felt when they gazed upon their babies for the first time. Unable to see through her tears, she dragged him into her arms. "Of course. Oh, my god." *Fuck.*

He laughed, and she realized she might have said that last part out loud.

He wrapped his arms around her. "Don't worry, I won't call you mom, or anything. I don't want to...replace my parents even though..." His voice trailed off. "You guys will still be Katie and JJ... just *our* Katie and JJ."

"I would love that," she whispered, and his assumption that JJ would be his father-figure brought even more tears. He would not disappoint the boy. Of that, she was sure.

"Do you think he will care?" Parker asked against her shoulder.

"Who? JJ?" She smoothed out his hair, as one wonderful new feeling after another rolled through her.

"Yeah."

Katy pushed him back, meeting his eyes. "No. Absolutely not."

He still looked worried. "Are you sure?"

She squeezed his shoulders. "I am positive. Like you and Sam, JJ is one of the best men I've ever met." She blinked back tears. The Veil had brought *all* of them into her life. "I feel bad sometimes that the virus and the Veil have caused so much suffering." She shrugged. "Because for me, it's brought only good things."

Parker rolled his eyes.

"No, really. I'm being serious. Except for one man, I've never met better men than you guys. And I've known a *lot* of them."

The corner of Parker's mouth turned up. "I know. I've followed your Instagram for the last three years."

Katie's mouth fell open. *"You what?"*

Parker tried not to smile. "When you got on the bus the day the Veil went up, I couldn't believe it." His brows came together. "FYI, I almost had a heart attack when you split with Matt. That's the other guy you meant, yeah?"

She sighed. "Yeah." Dropping her head in her hands, she groaned. "Ugh. I did, too. Until quite recently, I thought that was the biggest mistake of my life, and let me tell you..." She looked up. "...that's saying something because I've fucked up a *lot.*"

"But you don't anymore?" Parker asked. "Think it was a mistake?"

She blushed, remembering he'd seen her and JJ out in front of the bar. "No, not anymore."

His brows went up. "Because of JJ?"

She laughed. "Yeah. Because of JJ."

"I don't need to point out that they are very different people, do I?" he asked seriously.

She laughed again. "No. Matt was...is a great person, but I wasn't ready. And the truth is, I didn't love him like I should have."

"But JJ?"

Was he asking if she loved JJ? Yes, she did. Was she ready to confess it to the world? Taking a deep breath, she sighed. "Can I be honest with you?"

Parker gave her a conspiratorial grin. "Sure."

"I think I do. But I don't know if I'm ready to admit it because it's only been a few weeks since we met, and I know…" She sighed. "There's a part of me that thinks I'd be an idiot to fall in love so quickly. And JJ… I know he cares about me, deeply. But I also feel like… Like he's holding his breath, Parker, just waiting for me to let him down. He doesn't think so, but he is, and it scares me."

"Why?"

"Because it makes me feel like he doesn't trust me." She shrugged. "It makes me think I will."

"No—"

She shook her head. "I've done it before. And he's just so… complicated inside, you know?" With a sigh, she twisted her hair and tied it in a knot at the back of her head. "So to answer your question, I'm head over heels, and terrified out of my mind."

Parker laughed as Amelia came running in wearing another Avant-guard outfit of zebra print leggings, a cartoon sweatshirt, and her favorite orange tulle tutu with little witches embossed on it.

"What happened?" she asked, detecting the somber mood.

Parker stood up. "Your outfit happened." He said before Katie dragged him into her arms one more time. "I'm here for anything you're going through, okay?"

"Likewise." He squeezed her arm. "And about you and JJ. I think you guys are great together."

Grace appeared around the corner, and Katie smiled. "We'll see. You guys ready for breakfast?"

"Are you going?" Grace asked Parker.

"Yeah, come on." Draping his arm over her shoulder, he led her to the back door.

As Katie followed them across the yard, she couldn't help but notice that in addition to weight around her belly, the Veil had also surrounded her with the best group of people she'd ever known. JJ, Sam, Parker, Mike. Barb, Ms. Michelle. Even old Mr. Goebell. Every one of them was a kind, decent human being. It was the exact opposite of her childhood. Even Easton was turning out to be not *so* terrible.

Chapter Thirty-Three

Day 22 // 3:44 p.m.

THERE WERE dozens of men at the drop off point, and it only took them minutes to unload.

JJ pulled into a shady spot about a hundred yards from the edge of the crater and they got out. "As soon as Mike gets back here, we'll take off," he said.

Sam stretched his back. "Want to check out what all the fuss is about?" He nodded toward the crowd gathered in the middle of the intersection ahead. He recognized a familiar face. The governor.

"Sure."

Sam handed him a bottle of water as they made their way closer. There were military officials, too, which sent his hackles up. The Army and Coast Guard were back. How convenient. There were men and women with hard hats, loads of civilian volunteers like him and Sam, and an old man in a fancy suit. Everyone except the governor wore masks. Two camera crews were there as well, front and center, and about a dozen journalist-looking types with microphones and recorders.

JJ and Sam sidled up and listened in.

Governor Williams stood on the back of the work truck in a pair of khakis and a sweat-stained button-down white shirt and tie. He was pinching the bridge of his nose, looking like he hadn't slept in *weeks*.

"Ready in five, four, three…"

With a deep breath, he put on his game face, stared into the lenses of the waiting cameras, and began. "Good afternoon. As I've stated before, securing the debris field continues to be our number one priority. It is not safe to be anywhere near the crater. It's unstable and there are too many hazards to even list. We've got crews working around the clock trying to mitigate all the major ones, cap off all the gas leaks, etcetera, but they continue to be a problem, which is why we urge everyone to stay away. I'm sure many of you are aware of the accident last week down on the south side. I continue to pray for the families of the six teenagers lost in the explosion." He paused for a moment. "We don't want anyone else to get hurt, which is why we need to keep civilians out of the area until everything is buttoned up and secured. Please know we are doing everything we can to protect your homes and businesses from being vandalized. But anyone caught in the restricted zone will be arrested and prosecuted."

That made sense, JJ thought.

"For those of you who had to leave your homes, if you haven't already, please get your names on the waiting list for housing, as soon as possible. There are several places you can do this. Your local city offices and libraries should have a sign-up sheet, as well as all Home Construction hardware stores. Please only contact your local police and fire stations in cases of emergency, and to report crimes, as they are not staffed to help with the housing crisis. We have crews constructing temporary housing for displaced residents as we speak in local parks and open spaces surrounding the city. They are going up fast, and I am grateful to all the contractors, trades-workers, men, women, and the folks at Home Construction, who are making it possible. We are averaging *fifty* homes a day, which is incredible, but there are over a million displaced residents in the Atlanta area, still seeking shelter. If you'd like to host a family in need, or have a second home you are willing to loan out, please head to the mentioned locations, your local government offices, library, or Home Construction store, and put your name on the adopt-a-family list." He took another breath, and a quick sip of water, then continued. "I am sure many of you will recognize the man beside me from the ads you've seen on TV. This is Dennis Corvier, the owner of one of the largest RV manufacturing companies in the country, Corvier Cruisers. He has generously donated *all*, I repeat, all of his current inventory, to help with the housing shortage in Atlanta, and I thank him from the bottom of my heart."

The governor stepped back, and everyone clapped as Mr. Corvier took center stage. "First and foremost, my prayers go out to all of you who lost someone in Atlanta. My son Brayden was a casualty of this nightmare as well, and my heart aches for our nation, for the people of our great fallen cities, for the families and friends they left behind." He shook his head. "But over the past few weeks, I've also seen such beautiful things. I've seen strangers helping each other, entire neighborhoods popping up where there was nothing but fields or farmland the day before. I've seen old and young alike volunteering side by side to distribute food and clothes to families in need." He smiled. "I saw an entire playground go up in an hour, and then I watched dozens of children descend upon it with joy-filled laughter. You all have inspired me, and I am honored to stand beside you as a Georgia resident, and give back to our people and our community in our time of need. Thank you."

There was more clapping, and the governor stepped forward again. "As stated previously, priority will be given to families with children, and then we will go from there. In the meantime, temporary shelters have been set up at all Vacation Inn, Rest Easy Inn, and Peachtree Hotel locations around the city, and everyone is welcome there for respite, a hot meal, and a safe place to rest."

"This is so crazy," Sam whispered in JJ's ear.

It was true. Back in Hartford Creek, almost nothing had changed. Even without electricity. But here, trying to relocate thousands of families, the immediate dangers of exposure and starvation... JJ was glad he was not the governor.

"As mentioned in previous statements, all stores and businesses are to remain closed for the interim. While food is being brought in, everything else must be procured locally and rationed. To that end, inventory from nationally recognized chains has been seized by the federal government, with compensation for these companies coming at a later date as outlined by President Rodriguez. The local grocery stores have been turned into distribution centers, and that is where all families, *with trackers*, will continue to go for food and supplies. As you know, the trackers are mandatory, and necessary both to assist with monitoring ration distribution and in curbing the increasing reports of missing persons. To participate in any relief effort, you must be fitted with a tracker. For those of you on medications, we have tasked special teams with collecting and inventorying the local pharmacies, and their work is almost complete. Once we have a repository set up, we will then begin to fill and deliver medical prescriptions to those that require them." He paused, sighing heavily. "I know it has taken a lot longer than anticipated to get organized, and a lot of you are struggling, but we are doing our best to get you what you need *very* soon."

He stood to the side, lifting his arm toward the Veil. "The devastation behind me is our past." He turned back to the camera. "But our future rests with you, the people of this great state. Who you choose to be in this time of crisis, *how* you chose to live, will determine what comes next. So be kind to your neighbors, help those around you, follow the rules, and most of all pray for those around the country who are still trapped behind the Veil. Thank you."

The camera man dropped his camera, and the governor dropped the act, his shoulders slumping, his confident resolve evaporating into tired obligation, as Mr. Corvier patted his shoulder and told him to 'hang in there' before walking away.

Then he addressed the men and women standing in front of him. "You are all here because you'll be team leaders. The Coast Guard and Army have cleared most of the essentials out of the uninhabitable zone, but that leaves thousands of other retailers with much needed supplies. We have been given the go-ahead to clear out all the national *chain* stores. An agreement has been hammered out between the president and the CEOs of those companies to take what we need. What we cannot do is take anything from privately owned businesses. Those are the livelihoods of a lot of people, and they are counting on us to protect them until they can return. Once the area is cleared and people can begin collecting their things, they are going to need their inventory to start again. So we can't touch it. Understand?"

There were nods and murmurs from the crowd.

"The depots are still in the same locations, and that's where you'll make deliveries to. Keep nothing for yourselves. If you do, and get caught, you will be charged with theft. I know you might feel you need something, but I guarantee you, there is someone out there who needs it more. So, don't steal from them. The Red Cross is doing its best to take care of the people. It's our job to make sure they have what they need to do it." He ran his hands over his face. "Look. This is a difficult time for all of us, unprecedented in world history, and I'm not going to lie, the most chaotic, unorganized shit-show I've ever seen."

There were chuckles from the crowd.

"But I am doing my best. My staff is doing its best. The hundreds of local government officials, law enforcement officers, health care providers, contractors I've met, they're all doing their best. And I know right now, it doesn't seem like it's helping. It doesn't seem like it's good enough. But everyday it's getting better. Every day we are helping more and more people. And we all just have to hang in there long enough to get a system up and running. And we're going to make mistakes and have setbacks, but we all just have to keep at it. Keep moving forward. The faster we do that, the faster we can establish a new normal for the traumatized people around us, and hopefully move on with our lives. We can't change the past. But we can shape the future. One person at a time. God bless."

He hopped off the truck and was immediately swarmed by people who wanted to shake his hand or ask a question. It appeared everyone there had empathy for the governor and was on his side.

JJ turned to Sam. "Let's get our orders and head out. I don't want to be here any longer than we have to."

Sam's mouth turned up in a smirk. "Again, I have to ask, what is making you so anxious to get—"

"Shut up," JJ interrupted as his cheeks burst into flames again.

"You guys hooked up!"

"No—"

"You're a liar! A—" Sam leaned in, and slapped his knee, "—fucking liar!"

JJ broke into a grin and shook his head.

"It's about damn time," Sam muttered, following him to the woman in charge of handing out their assignment, as JJ's smile widened. Yes, it was about time.

Ten minutes later, they were in their freshly sanitized delivery truck and heading out.

They rode for a few minutes down the empty, ash covered road.

"I ate there once." Sam said as they passed an Olive Branch Italian restaurant. "With my mom and dad. I think it was for their anniversary. But I don't remember. I acted up, and they ended up having to take their food to go, and putting me to bed early without dessert."

JJ smiled.

"I was such a pain in the ass." The regret in Sam's voice was sharp.

"All kids are a pain in the ass."

Sam thumped the window sill. "I was worse than most."

"Why do you think that is?"

"I keep asking myself that, man. I go over it again and again in my head. All the stupid shit I did and I just don't know."

He felt the same way. All the times he should have been grateful to his mom, or kinder to Sierra. But It was like the governor said. There was nothing they could do about the past. JJ decided to change the subject. "How are things with you and Jinn?"

"What things?" Sam asked slowly.

"I've seen you guys sneak off together."

"Nothin—"

JJ laughed. "Now it's my turn to call bullshit."

Sam was quiet for a minute, then he sighed. "Can I tell you something? And you promise not to laugh?"

JJ's brow went up. "Uh, sure."

"*She* wants things to happen, but I'm the one...See, I've never..." He made an 'o' with his thumb and index finger and then pumped his other finger through it.

JJ's mouth fell open in surprise. "You're a *virgin*?"

"I know what you're thinking. How could I keep this fine-ass body to myself but..." Sam's joking facade fell. "But the truth is, my mama told me I had to feel something *for* a girl for it to be right, not just want something *from* her, and up until now...that hasn't been the case. I mean, sure, I've fooled around or what-ever, but..."

JJ waited with the feeling that he'd just been roped into his first fatherly birds and bees conversation, and he was neither mentally prepared nor particularly qualified to undergo such a task. Because, as Katie vividly illustrated several times last night, he clearly did not know as much about women as he thought.

"I don't know um..." Sam cleared his throat. "...what to do, *exactly.*" He gestured his hands in front of him, like he was shaping a ball of invisible clay. "I mean, I know the main part." He made the 'o' again.

JJ swatted his hand down. "Stop doing that. It's gross."

"Sorry, I…"

He exhaled heavily, not sure who was more nervous; Sam, or him. "Well, first of all, it's Jinn. So I don't think *she* knows what she's doing either."

Sam rolled his eyes. "Great. Thanks."

"No, I'm being serious. That means you can learn together, which is good. Look, every woman is gonna be different. There's no sure bet. So I don't want to tell you what to *do*. The main thing is to practice safety and respect. Don't get a girl pregnant before she's ready to be a mother, and be respectful, always. Women are not objects to be owned, or claimed, or tamed or dominated…" He paused, now feeling compelled to add, "Even if they enjoy some of those roles behind closed doors."

Sam's brow went up, and JJ rushed on before he could ask questions. "They are *human beings* and they deserve respect in and out of the bedroom." It was the talk he'd rehearsed to give to Brian one day when he was grown up. At least it wouldn't go to waste now.

"How do I know what that is? I mean, if we're doing the deed…"

"Ask her. Ask her what she wants, what she likes, and if she doesn't know, then help her figure it out." This part of the lecture was new, because up until last night, he would have said being respectful equaled being gentle and romantic. Taking things slow. "It might surprise you, or it might not, but whatever it is, respect it, and create a safe place for it to thrive. That's what intimacy is. It's being honest, it's asking, it's respecting, and it's communicating. Before and after."

"You're telling me to tell her that I don't know what the fuck to do? Won't that kinda kill the mood?"

"No. I'm telling you to ask her what *she* wants, do it to the best of your ability, and play the rest by ear. I guarantee she won't get mad if you ask her what she likes and then give it to her."

Sam thought about that, nodding his head subtly at first and then harder as a smile appeared on his face. "I gotcha. I gotcha. Yeah. I like that."

JJ sighed again, thinking of Katie, counting the minutes until he was home and they could... "If Jinn is anything like Katie, she's gonna surprise the hell out of you, so be ready."

Sam sighed. "Why do you gotta go and make it sound so scary?"

JJ laughed. "No, not scary. Just...I think men assume we know what women like in the bedroom, and what they don't. But I've recently become aware of the very real possibility that we have no fucking clue what turns them on."

"What?" Sam turned. "You mean like kinky stuff, BDSM shit? Is that how you got all those scratch marks and—"

"I mean like anything. Women have suffered through a lot of judgment about their sexuality, been shamed into conformity by threat of punishment, by titles like slut and whore for centuries. They have never been free to express themselves the way we have." He remembered many conversations he'd had with his mom about inequality. "It fucking sucks."

She'd made him promise to be a good example for Sierra, in his father's place, so she'd know the difference between a real man and sexist pricks when she grew up. There was a sharp pang in his heart for his sister and the future she'd never have. "You ever notice there's no man-shaming equivalent titles?"

"Well, player."

"Yeah, but have you ever heard of a guy that was ashamed of being called a player?"

Sam huffed. "No."

"Exactly. Society has bullied and repressed women for too

long. We've got to stop assuming shit that we just don't know. We need to *ask* them what they want, and normalize whatever that is."

"Did you ask Katie?"

JJ swallowed hard. "No." He paused. "But lucky for me, she told me anyway, and I learned a *very* important lesson."

"Which was what?"

JJ huffed a laugh. "Assume *nothing*."

Sam laughed.

"Also, I feel like I should inform you I don't have a lot of experience with women."

"Yeah, I definitely got that vibe when I first met you."

JJ huffed again. "Thanks."

Sam shrugged. "But, I dunno. Now, I actually think you might know more than most."

"And that is really fucking sad."

"Yes, it is."

Sam leaned back in his seat, apparently satisfied. "Well, thanks for this… chat."

"You're welcome."

"Any chance you're gonna tell me what went down between you and Katie the other night?"

"Nope. Absolutely not."

"You're just gonna leave it to my imagination?"

JJ shook his head. "First, *again*, that's gross. Second, no matter how hard you try, believe me, you won't even come close."

Chapter Thirty-Four

Day 23 // 2:55 p.m.

SAM AND JINN were off together in Old Ray again. Katie absolutely did not want to think about what they may or may not be doing in her car. Out the window, she studied JJ's truck parked across the street, remembering all too vividly their weirdly liberating and magical night.

Mike and Sam had returned the evening before, but JJ was still in Atlanta. They'd asked him to stay because he was one of the few that knew how to drive the big trucks. To say she was disappointed would be an understatement.

Katie pulled her hair up into a messy bun and secured it with a rubber band, fanning her neck as she glanced up at the TV.

"...insider claims that the domestic terrorist group Army For Freedom is responsible for the recent surge in arson and robberies across the state. A memo issued from the Office of the President to government and law enforcement officials, claims to have unearthed evidence that the AFF are in the process of recruiting and gathering financing to launch an attack on the cities that are still standing. While the president has described them as nothing more than modern-day pirates and thieves, the AFF leaders deny any involvement in the fires or the thefts, preferring to think of themselves as unsung heroes of the American people, saying 'We would never harm small-town folks. Those are exactly the people we are trying to protect. Think of us as post-apocalyptic Robin Hoods, exposing the corrupt government for what it is, and taking it back for the

people that are left. That's all we're trying to do.'" The anchor paused. *"Implying, of course, that President Rodriguez is the fabled, notoriously self-serving Prince John. And as for the 'people' they are referring to, their answer is simple. 'Those inside the Veil are lost. If we are to survive, our energies must be focused on preserving, at whatever cost necessary, those that remain on the outside."*

Amelia colored at the table. There was no regular programming anymore, no cartoons, much to her disappointment. Just around the clock news and most of it was the same.

"Anything new?" Barb asked, leaning against the bar top.

Katie shrugged. There was always something new. But it was never good. Dallas was the hot spot for the virus now that Atlanta was gone, and most of the major cities that still had Veil's around them were experiencing mass exoduses from the suburbs surrounding them because everyone was afraid of being vaporized, or killed by the explosion. That or being attacked by the Army of Freedom. No one, it seemed, whether they agreed with the AFF or not, trusted the president anymore, and Katie wondered if they were like her, not wanting to suspect him of foul play, but unable to think of a better explanation for the strange things that were happening on the outside.

"Look," Barb said, turning up the volume.

"Prominent Atlanta businessman Jeffery Goodalls, and his family, reported missing one week ago by concerned family members, has been found at a family cabin outside of Louisville, Kentucky, supporting the claim of local authorities who insist that the escalating number of missing persons are just temporary, urging people to remain calm, not jump to conclusions, and be patient."

"Well, that's good news," Barb said.

But as the segment switched, listing not only the names of displaced children, but missing families too, Katie wasn't so sure.

The news anchor continued. *"Still the number of unaccounted loved ones remains a problem for some, and protesters outside of the Duluth City Hall, like Patricia Concklin of Lawrenceville, Georgia, insist that there is more going on than meets the eye, claiming her son, daughter-in-law and their children would never abandon their home and flee without telling her, nor would they join the AFF, as the president suggests is happening across the country. She is quote 'certain they have been abducted,' although to what end, remains unclear, and is demanding law enforcement to take action on these cases before it is too late."* The scene switched from protesters with signs to a sixty-year-old-woman with dyed red hair, and a Grand 'ole Opry t-shirt on. *"The police aren't doing their job. And someone needs to hold them accountable. My son is missing. My daughter-in-law and my grandchildren are missing. And I promise you they didn't join the damn Army for Freedom. Someone needs to find my family before they are found in a shallow grave somewhere."* The segment switched back to the newsroom. *"In other news, the outbreak in Los Angeles has…"*

Barb turned the volume back down.

Patrica Conklin's family sounded like Wes. "It's weird, isn't it? People going missing?"

Barb turned off the TV. "Not really. Back when I was a kid, before cell phones and GPS and all that shit, this is how it was. Neighbors gets a bloody nose in the driveway, then goes on vacation and don't tell anyone, and by the time they get back from Pensacola all relaxed and sunburned, half the state is lookin' for em."

Katie's brow went up. It was an oddly specific example.

"That actually happened. In South Atlanta when I was seventeen."

"So, you just think people are moving without telling anyone?"

"Or joinin' up with vigilante groups."

"You believe that?"

Barb shrugged. "Maybe."

"What about their trackers?"

"Well, even with the quarantine lifted, we ain't really supposed to be movin' around. So it makes sense, they'd take 'em off if they're goin' somewhere." She chewed her lip. "You know, a lot of folks around here think these trackers are part of some kinda conspiracy." She looked down at her wrist.

"The AFF thinks the whole Veil is."

"I'm inclined to agree."

That surprised Katie. "Really? Why?"

"I don't know why, but I've got a good sense about when I'm being lied to." She gave Katie a look she couldn't quite interpret. "And I sense a lie, somewhere—shit."

Katie turned and froze.

Out front, two men got out of a very familiar truck. Even if their faces weren't healed, she would have recognized them. *Shit.* The men JJ had fought on the night of their first kiss. "Get Amelia," Barb said, before turning and rushing toward the back.

"Amelia!" Katie's legs wobbled as she ran around the bar and dragged the little girl off her chair, scouring the room for a hiding place. Amelia struggled to get away. "You're hurting me," she complained.

The closet.

"Shh." Katie snatched Beaver off the table, grabbed Amelia around the waist, lifting her off the ground, and hurried over to it as something metal slammed into the front glass-paneled door.

Katie dragged the door open and shoved her inside, beside the mop bucket. "There are dangerous men here who will hurt you. Do not move or make a sound. Do you under—"

Another bang on the door.

She winced, and her heart lurched into her throat. "Do you

understand? You stay here until I tell you!" Not waiting for an answer, she slammed the door shut and spun back around.

One of the men had his nose pressed to the glass. The other was missing. Katie's eyes flew around the room again. She needed a weapon. *A knife.*

She ran into the kitchen, flinging plastic containers aside as she dug through the pile of clean dishes for a—

"I wouldn't do that if I were you." A deep voice warned.

Katie froze.

"Turn around slow. Hands where I can see them."

She lifted her hands and slowly turned around, ready to give him whatever he wanted to get him gone. "Take whatever you —" The last word died in her throat, as a terror unlike any she'd ever felt before crashed over her like a wave. *Oh god.*

"Sorry, Katie," Grace apologized as if it were her fault the smaller man had his arm across her throat and was squeezing it. In the other hand was a gun. They were in the hall. The door to the closet where Amelia was hidden only a foot behind them. Katie willed the little girl to stay silent with every fiber of her being.

Grace whimpered and her heart lurched into her throat and she tried to speak around it. "Please. Don't hurt...h-her." She held up her hands in a sign of peace, or surrender, or whatever he wanted. "Please. You can—"

"Shut up." His eyes were red rimmed, his pupils dilated. Neither was a good sign. Best case scenario, he was drunk or high, worst case, he had the virus.

The sound of shattering glass interrupted her thoughts.

The man holding Grace hostage looked to the front. "You give us what we want and no one gets hurt."

Katie nodded. "W-what do you want?"

"All the booze you got left in this place."

They could have it all. She'd personally carry it out to the truck for them. "You can—"

A shot rang out.

Followed by a raspy scream from the front of the bar.

Katie lunged for Grace as the man dragged her toward the door. "No!"

A shot whizzed by her head as she ducked behind the bar where Barb was huddled with her shotgun.

The next thirty seconds were the most helpless of Katie's life as she hid, one man bleeding to death on the floor beside her while the other screaming obscenities and firing at will dragged Grace, crying, toward the shattered front door.

The moment the shooting stopped, she peeked over the bar top. "Wait! Stop!"

Another shot from Barb made her duck. *Damn it!* "No!"

Katie shoved the gun down. She couldn't let him take Grace. He'd kill her. Or worse.

"We surrender!" She cried as the bells jingled and they disappeared. "Come back! We're putting the gun down!" She turned to Barb. "Throw it up on the bar. So he can—"

Barb shook her head. "He'll…kill us all if I do that," she wheezed, sounding how Katie felt. Like all the air had been sucked from the room and she couldn't breathe.

Katie tried to wrestle it free. "He will kill Grace if you—"

Another shot fired, rocking Katie's brain as a row of bottles behind the bar exploded and Barb yanked the gun away.

A second later, the rumble of an engine replaced the ringing in her ears, and Katie jumped up in time to see the truck lurch backward.

Grace was in the front passenger seat.

"No!" Katie leaped over the dead man and ran to the door, sliding on the bits of tempered glass as she skidded into the bar and pushed the door open. The bells jingled again as the truck sped away in the direction of Ms. Michelle's and Atlanta with a terrified looking Grace sitting in the front seat.

For a moment, the shock that he'd actually taken Grace

rooted her to the spot. Something so terrible couldn't actually happen, could it? It reminded her of the day the Veil went up.

Katie found her voice. "Watch Amelia!" she yelled over her shoulder.

She started running toward the house, then remembered Sam and Jinn had her car. "Shit." She spun around, spying JJ's truck. "Mike!" She couldn't drive it but he could. "Mike!" She banged on the door. He didn't answer. "Mike!" She pressed her hand to the window, but couldn't make out anything inside. Where in the hell was he? "Mike!" The hot Georgia sun baked her back and head as she yanked on the door handle. It didn't budge. "Mike!"

Katie jumped backward as Barb materialized beside her with a brick in her hand. Before she could say anything, Barb threw it into the door. It shattered the same as the one at the bar had. "There. And take this." She pressed the shotgun into Katie's hand. "It's got one shell left."

Katie couldn't breathe, and Barb looked like she was still struggling, too.

She shook her head. "I can't. And I don't know where Mike—"

"There's no time, Katie." Barb's voice was thick with the truth.

Katie stared at her. But she couldn't go after Grace alone. Could she?

"Katie?"

"Okay." *Holy shit.* Yes, she abso-fucking-lutely could. The ease with which she answered that question, without all the normal laborious fanfare, was dizzying. Or maybe that was the adrenaline?

More glass crunched beneath her feet as she reached into the dark shop, unlocked the door, pushed it open, and grabbed the keys to JJ's truck off the hook.

"I'm sorry. I-I didn't mean for any of this to happen," Barb said.

Katie squeezed her arm as she hurried past. "I know." She unlocked the door to JJ's truck and hoisted herself onto the running board. "Call Easton. Tell him what's happened."

Barb pressed her hand to her chest. "I will. Go. Be safe."

Katie hopped in and dropped the gun on the seat beside her. The last time she tried to drive JJ's truck, Sam had appeared out of nowhere shouting for her to stop. He'd proceeded to rescue her. Where was he now? She scanned the vacant horizon. Where was anyone besides Barb who looked like she was suffering from heat stroke.

Katie's heart thumped painfully against her ribs as she cranked the engine and pushed her hair back off her sweaty forehead. To her relief, the truck had a full tank of gas. Probably because it was part of the salvage/rescue team in the city and the Coast Guard, or whoever was in charge, wanted JJ to come back.

She pressed her foot down on the clutch. "I can do this," she whispered before throwing the truck into first gear.

The truck groaned and lurched. Katie gave Barb one last nod as the truck bucked and she made a U-turn in the middle of the road.

It stuttered again as she accelerated and tried to shift into second gear, but once she got to third, things smoothed out, and by fourth gear, she had gotten the hang of it.

The hot summer wind blew past her as she flew down the empty road.

She inhaled through her nose, then pushed the breath out of her mouth. She needed to calm down so she could think.

Inhale. Exhale.

She had to catch up with them before they turned, and from what she remembered, the next major intersection was a little less than five miles away.

Katie bit her lip, pressing the pedal down as far as it would go. But then what would she do once she did? Grace was in the truck. She couldn't just drive them off the road. And what if he saw her and shot Grace while they were still on the highway?

Katie took another deep breath as sweat dripped down her back. She scratched at the hives popping out on the back of her neck. Maybe she should just tail them, wait until he stopped and then try to rescue Grace? She scratched her neck again. Yes. That was the best thing to do, the safest thing for Grace.

But first she had to catch them.

The sign for the intersection came up fast, and she spotted a vehicle just before it disappeared over the horizon.

The tow truck skidded as she turned right. Something flew off the back as she sped north and she glanced at it in the rearview as it bounced to a stop in the middle of the road. The vehicle ahead appeared again over the horizon and she squinted, praying it was them. If it wasn't, Grace was gone.

Eyes darting between the road and the gear shifter, she switched gears and accelerated again.

And she needed to let JJ know what was happening. Because she needed backup. Because—she eyed the gun pressed against her leg and shook her head—she didn't have a clue how to use a gun or how to save Grace.

Once the pointer on the speedometer passed eighty-five again, she reached for her phone, her fingers freezing on her empty back pocket.

Switching hands on the steering wheel, she frantically felt the other side. It was empty except for the lighter she kept there to light the stove. "No…" Had she forgotten her phone?

Pressing her feet to the floor, she lifted her butt off the seat, sliding her hand around, and then turned and chanced a look. The seat was empty. "No. no…no…no." Where was her phone? She looked on the floor, then at the well between the seat and the door. Where was her goddamn phone? "Fuck!" Katie slammed her hands on the steering wheel. "Fuck! Fuck! *Fuck!*"

Wherever it was, it was not there. How could she be so

stupid? So careless? Pulling her hands through her hair, she looked in the rearview, tears blurring her eyes, as the panic she'd been staving off flooded her veins.

The truck veered onto the shoulder, and she jerked it back into the lane.

Her foot came off the gas as she glanced in the rearview, back toward Hartford Creek, and the truck slowed. Should she go back for it? She swiped at her eyes with the back of her hand. How would anyone find them without her phone? What if she needed help?

Up ahead, red tail lights flashed before the truck turned and disappeared behind a stand of trees.

Katie pressed her foot back down. No, if she lost them now, they might never find Grace. She had to keep going.

Pressing the clutch, she shifted gears, and met her frantic eyes in the rearview. *She* had to get Grace back. Her foot came down on the clutch and she shifted again.

Katie pressed her lips together as the gas pedal hit the floor. And she would.

The stop sign came up quickly, and she spotted the retreating truck as it disappeared around another bend. "Thank god." It was them.

Katie redoubled her grip on the steering wheel and punched the brake.

Because all the kids—she yanked the wheel—Jinn, Sam, Parker, Amelia—the truck slid around the corner, more stuff flying off the back—*and* Grace, were hers now. Not to own, but to protect and care for.

Katie grabbed the gear shifter and popped the clutch, as her old self—the one that smiled for cameras, wore designer shoes and feared for her future—faded away for good.

As the truck flew around the bend a new self, one that didn't give a shit about shoes or herself appeared in her place, and by the time the road straightened back out into a line, Katie's transformation was complete.

She adjusted the mirror as she popped the clutch and the wind whipped through the open window. "I'm a mother now." She met her eyes in the mirror. "And nobody takes my kids."

Chapter Thirty-Five

Day 23 // 4:02 p.m.

JJ SQUEEZED HIS EYES SHUT, then flung them back open as he pulled the semi truck into the depot. He'd been awake for twenty-two hours and he desperately needed a nap. Hopefully, this would be his last run, and he could catch a quick snooze. Otherwise, he'd probably fall asleep behind the wheel and kill himself.

One of the men pointed to an empty bay, and JJ brought the truck around.

Hopefully, they'd let him go home tomorrow, even if only for a day.

A shrill beep filled the cab as he found the bay door in his side-view mirror and backed toward it.

He missed Katie and the kids.

The man nearest the door held his fist up, signaling stop and JJ pressed his foot over the brake and turned the truck off. Voices drifted into the cab as he tilted his head back against the seat and finally let his eyes close. Damn, that felt good. He dragged his hat down over his eyes and sighed.

The truck rocked as the men unloaded, lulling him to sleep. He'd just rest for fifteen minutes and then—

His phone rang, and he jumped. "Shit." He pushed his hat back and fished it out of his pocket. "Parker?" Activating the call, he pressed the phone to his ear as another truck backed into the bay beside him. "Hey, Parker, what's—"

"Barb is dead." Parker's voice wobbled. "And Katie… Grace…gone and…. I found …there's a–a guy. I can't—"

JJ sat up. "Wait. Hold up." He pulled the phone away from his ear and upped the volume. It sounded like he said Barb was dead, which wasn't possible. "Sorry I couldn't—"

"W-what do I do?"

"About what?" JJ turned the key and rolled the window up. "Say it again, I'm sorry I couldn't hear—"

"Barb is dead!"

JJ's finger slipped off the button and the window stopped just before reaching the top. *"What?"*

"And there's a guy here. He's been shot."

JJ jammed his finger into the seatbelt release and flung the door open. *"What?* What happened?"

"I-I don't know! She was just laying on the ground in front of Mike's when I got back from Ms. Michelle's! I tried to… Oh, god. And everything is all busted up! I don't know what to do!"

Adrenaline rushed through his veins as JJ headed for his truck, parked along the fence at the back of the lot. "Okay. Parker, I need you to calm down. Where is Katie? Where is—"

"I don't know! I don't know where Sam or Mike are and—JJ, I'm scared."

"Hey! Where are you going?" A voice called.

JJ spun around and covered the phone. "Family emergency. I have to go."

He pulled the phone back to his ear. "I know you're scared." He switched the phone to the other hand and ear as he dug into his pocket for his keys and sweat dripped into his eyes. "But I need you to tell me exactly what happened."

"I wasn't here!"

Someone else yelled something at him, but JJ ignored them. He was going home. Now. "Is anyone else there?"

"Only Amelia. She was in the closet at the bar. She said a 'dangerous man' came and Katie told her to stay there—" JJ broke into a dead run as Parker's words bounced against his ear. "...shots and a dead man...truck missing...broken glass...Amelia crying...God JJ...scared...help..."

He jammed the key into the lock and almost ripped the door off the hinges as he flung it open and leaped inside. "Are you and Amelia safe?"

"We're at the house. I locked the door."

"Okay." JJ pressed the phone between his shoulder and ear, cranked the engine, and threw the truck in reverse. "Hang up and call the sheriff." He backed up and threw it into drive. "Do you have his number?" The tires squealed.

"Yeah. Katie made me—"

The truck lurched forward, and he slammed his palm into the horn as he steered toward the gated entrance. "Tell him everything. Then call me back right away."

"But—"

JJ laid into the horn again as the guard scrambled out of his way and he burst through the half-closed gate onto the street. He would probably go to jail for that. "Call Easton!" JJ shouted, slamming his foot on the gas. *If* they could catch him. "And then call me back. I'm on my way. I'll be there in—" *Two hours.* That was how long it took to get home. "I'll be there as soon as I can. Call Easton. Now."

There was a pause. "Okay."

He tried to dial Katie, but it just rang and went to voicemail. "Call me as soon as you get this," he said before hanging up.

JJ dropped his phone between his legs and scanned the rearview. Empty.

He rolled the windows down, and the wind immediately sucked the sweltering air out of the cab as JJ's teeth ground together inside of his mouth. *Damn it.* He should have never left town. What was he thinking? *You were trying to help.* "Damn it!" He slammed his fists into the steering wheel. He'd failed again.

First his mom and Sierra and now them. He should have never left them there all alone!

His phone rang and he practically drove off the road answering it. He didn't recognize the number. "Hello?" He checked the rearview again before he took the ramp that curved onto the freeway that would take him home. "Parker?"

"No," an unfamiliar voice answered.

JJ pressed the phone between his shoulder and ear as he rolled the window up again. "Hello? Who is this?"

"You were right."

JJ pulled the phone away from his ear again. Was this the person who killed Barb? "Who the hell—"

"The virus. It got into the animals. That's why Atlanta fell."

He finally recognized the voice. The Coast Guard commander he'd spoken to the night Atlanta fell. *"What?"* JJ laid on the horn as he swerved around a car so crammed full of stuff the driver couldn't see out any windows but the front. *Oh god.* Now was not the time for this conversation.

"They sent us away on purpose. The President...he *knew* it was going to go. He knows everything. He's been lying to—"

The commander stopped.

"Hello?" Sweat dripped into JJ's eyes. "Hello?" He yanked his phone back and checked the connection. It was still good. "Are you—"

"I just wanted to say I'm sorry. About your family. I thought I was doing the right thing. I thought I was one of the good guys."

JJ swerved around another car and punched the gas. It appeared he wasn't the only one making mistakes. "There are no good guys anymore,"

he said before ending the call and dropping the phone on his lap.

He didn't have time for that bullshit now. He needed to focus. He needed to figure out where in the hell his family was.

Chapter Thirty-Six

Day 23 // 9:00 p.m.

KATIE SWATTED at the bugs as she crouched beside the truck and watched the men in the small, dilapidated cottage. There were three of them huddled around a battery-operated lamp inside. The man that had taken Grace, and two others. They had locked Grace in a bedroom in the back—by herself, thank god—and were now pacing the room, waving their arms around and shouting at each other.

Another mosquito bit her neck, and she slapped it. They were eating her alive, but she didn't move.

Luckily, the roads had been mostly clear except for a few utility trucks, and Grace's kidnapper hadn't been driving that fast. Once she caught up, it had actually been surprisingly easy to follow them.

She swatted at another bug as Grace's captor took a long pull from a bottle of vodka and stumbled into a chair. And now, it was obvious why. Whether to call it good fortune was debatable, but he was so drunk he could barely walk, and it had kept his pace on the road slow enough that Katie could catch up.

She bit her lip as the yelling resumed. His gun lay on an end table beside the couch.

A mosquito whined in her ear, and she shooed it away as a gust of wind, heavy with rain, blew past. God, she hoped it didn't start raining. Her plan wouldn't work if it did.

If he were the only one there, she'd have taken her chances one on one and gone in after Grace. But—she swatted at another bug. His friends were not so drunk, and as much as she wanted to, she was smart enough to know there was no way she could fight off three men—or shoot them because she only had one bullet left—*and* rescue Grace *and* escape at the same time. She looked up at the clouds and rapidly darkening sky. So she had to wait.

Another bug bit her knee, and she scratched at her itchy legs, fingering the lighter in her hand, going over the plan one more time. It was a terrible one probably, if it even worked, but...

The gun in her lap shifted, as she scrunched her toes together in her shoe, trying to return circulation to her right foot.

But unless Easton or JJ showed up with a better one, it was all she had. And it wouldn't work until *all* the daylight was gone and the darkness could hide them.

Katie looked over her shoulder toward the road. She'd parked JJ's truck about a half mile back. In just a moment, she would create her "diversion" to draw the men away, grab Grace while they were distracted and head through the woods behind the house back to the truck, hopefully avoiding any direct conflict with them at all as they escaped.

With any luck, she and Grace would be on the road before they even knew Grace was missing.

Katie chewed on her lip. How to get back to Hartford Creek was another story. Maybe she could find her way back during the day, but at night, it would be nearly impossible, because she hadn't paid attention to where she was going until it was too late.

She swatted at another bug as a candy wrapper from the overflowing garbage bin beside the house joined the rest of the trash blowing through the yard.

She'd just have to cross that bridge later. One thing at a time. She had to get Grace out of that house, and she needed to do it without anyone seeing her.

She looked up. The sky above had turned an inky blue. Time to get into position.

She bit her lip again as an empty can of energy drink rolled across the open expanse of driveway she had to cross to get to the trees. It was probably only fifteen feet, but she'd be exposed for a moment and if they happened to look her way, they'd certainly see her and the whole thing would be off.

Katie scrunched her toes again, hesitating.

Beside the truck was the only place that afforded her a clear view into the house, so she could see what was happening. Once she got to the trees, she'd no longer have a line of sight to the door Grace was hidden behind. If they went in before she was able to create her distraction or moved her—Katie shook her head. No. She couldn't think like that. Not now.

She scooted back behind the truck, swatting at the bugs as she got to her feet. Needles stabbed at her right leg as she twirled her ankle. It would only be a few minutes more. Grace would be fine.

Keeping her eyes on the front door, Katie gathered her supplies, an empty bag of kettle potato chips, a rock about the size of her palm, the shotgun and the lighter she'd found in JJ's glove compartment, and ran across the gravel into the trees that framed the small isolated lot.

She'd had all afternoon to decide on the best position, and it was there, behind a large tree, just on the edge of the overgrown drive where she would make her move and pray the volunteer fireman she'd dated—well, went to one movie with and slept with just to shut him up—wasn't as full of shit as the plot of the movie they'd gone to see. If not, they were screwed.

The yard was quiet except for the crickets, whining mosquitoes, and occasional bit of rustling trash.

More yelling came from the house as Katie peeked around the tree, hardly able to believe what she was about to do. It was insane. All of it. A month ago, almost to the day, she'd been drinking champagne on a *yacht,* her greatest fear; growing old. Now she was huddled in the dark, by herself, clutching a *shotgun*, afraid of everything *but* that. "Focus, Katie."

She rolled back against the tree, the bark digging into her itchy shoulders as she clutched the gun to her chest. A month ago, the bugs alone probably would have done her in. And if she hadn't met Ken, the fireman, she probably would have tried shooting her last precious bullets at the truck, praying it hit the gas tank and exploded. But she *had* met Ken and as they sat in the movie theater and that very scenario played out on screen, he'd waved his hand and said, "That's bullshit. They've made gas tanks out of plastic since the mid-eighties. You want to start a car fire? You need a rag and a lighter. Hell, a bag of chips will work too." She'd laughed. Then, to the annoyance of everyone around them, he'd spent the rest of the movie explaining in hushed tones the ins and outs of how to properly start a vehicle fire and only stopped when she'd propositioned him for sex.

She wasn't laughing now.

Propping the gun against the tree, she quickly flipped the Frito Lay bag inside out, dropped the rock in, and twisted it closed. The noise was deafening, but unavoidable. There was no rag, or anything else she could get to without being seen. It was that or nothing.

She peeked around the trunk and scanned the yard, heart thumping, cheeks burning like her head was on fire.

Thankfully, it was still quiet.

And so dark she could barely see. Perfect.

She had to hurry now. Assuming it actually worked, she couldn't miss her mark, or she'd have to go back and light it herself, and then they'd see her, defeating the whole purpose of the diversion.

Katie leaned back behind the tree. One more deep breath in and out and then she would do it.

The sharp scent of pine and gasoline filling her nostrils as she inhaled and did what she told Sam to do after Atlanta fell, when his brain couldn't possibly handle what it faced. "Try not to think," she whispered. It was the only way she could go through with it. The only way she could do what she needed to get Grace. *This is it.* The air rushed from her lips in a shaky whoosh as she pushed away from the tree and another mosquito bit the back of her knee. "This is it."

Taking the lighter, she flicked it, the orange glow oddly comforting in the darkness. With the other hand, she held up the bag, twisted around the rock, and took one more wobbly breath.

One chance. She had to make it.

She peeked out from behind the tree and waited until all the men were looking away. Then she brought her hands together.

As soon as the flames hit the grease coated bag, it ignited. Her courage bolstered. *Thank you, Ken.* So far, so good.

In slow motion, Katie took aim and lobbed the small fireball across the open driveway. It looked like a shooting star against the navy background as it sailed through the air.

To her utter amazement, it landed right where it was supposed to, under the truck.

Fire whooshed to life beneath it from the gas line she had conveniently spotted as she sat huddled beside it, trying to figure out what in the hell to do. That was what sparked her memory of Ken and their conversation. In a world full of things gone wrong, she'd simply had a single moment of luck when she needed it most. A bad date and disappointing sex suddenly redeemed.

The fire spread quickly to everything she had sprinkled and rubbed gas on earlier, as the front door opened and the two sober men ran out with the lamp.

It spread to the puddle of gas beneath their car, parked beside the truck, where she'd done the same thing. "What the hell?" The one shouted as Katie ducked back into the trees. "Shit! Shit!" the other cried as she started toward the back of the house. It was followed by another whoosh. "Where's the fucking hose?" The first man shouted

Katie waited until the drunk man finally joined his companions. "I don't got one, dude!"

More cursing and another whoosh followed, and then something in the back of the truck exploded with a sharp pop!

They all ducked.

Now.

Armed with the cumbersome shotgun, Katie ran across the open lawn toward the back door, scooping up a brick from the pile next to the deck.

She tested the knob as the men on the other side of the house shouted. Locked. She smashed the window beside it, the breaking glass ten times louder than the crumpling chip bag had been. But like the bag, she had no choice. Hopefully, all commotion out front masked the sound. She had to move fast now, because there hadn't been much gas in either vehicle and if they didn't properly catch on fire, her diversion wouldn't last long.

Carefully, she reached in, feeling around for the lock, and flipped it.

Thunder rumbled in the distance as she pushed the door open and listened. The house was shrouded in darkness except for the light from the fire outside and the men still out front. She could hear their voices.

The gun banged into the counter as she made her way through the dark kitchen, and she knew she had to let it go. It was too big, too heavy. But what was she supposed to do with it now? She couldn't just leave it on the kitchen table.

Her heart thumped in her throat, making it hard to swallow, and for one awful moment Katie's legs became jelly beneath her. She grabbed the back of a dining chair to keep from falling as dizziness rushed through her head. "Shit." But then Grace's tear-stained face appeared in her mind and both she and her knees found their strength again. *They asked us to be your family, and we said yes.* That was what Parker had promised. That was what *she* had promised.

Katie peeked into the living room. Empty.

And not a shitty family like she'd had. No. Katie meant a real family, filled with love and trust. She thought about Grace's mother, and the promise she'd made to her as firelight from the burning vehicles danced across the walls and she ducked as best she could below the giant picture window in the living room and headed for the hall.

Sharpness replaced panic in her head as she grabbed the smaller gun off the table on her way and shoved the heavy shotgun under the couch where it hopefully wouldn't be found.

She clutched the smaller gun, sweat dripped down her back, tickling her sides. "That's better." She glanced over her shoulder as she pushed the bedroom door open. "Grace?" she called, her voice so loud it made her jump.

There was no answer.

Katie stepped into the darkened room. Had they moved her? "Grace?" she called again, spinning around. Where was she? "Grace!" They had to get out before the men knew she was there or she'd never be able to fight them off.

"Katie?" a muffled voice called from the shadows.

"Grace!" Katie rushed toward her voice, tripping over the bed. "Where are you?" It was so dark she could barely see.

A door appeared out of the darkness and Katie flung it open. Grace threw herself into her arms sobbing and she stumbled back. The springs groaned as Katie landed on the bed behind her. "Are you okay?" she asked, pushing Grace back, trying to read her face in the dark. "Did he hurt you? Did they…"

Grace shook her head. "I'm okay."

"Are you sure?" She shoved the girl's sweaty hair off her face and smelled urine. "He didn't hit you or…." She didn't know how to ask the question that worried her the most. It was unlikely, but he could have done something to her in the truck on the way there.

"He yelled at me," Grace cried, clinging to her. "And I peed m-my pants."

"But he didn't... they didn't touch you?"

"No. B-but he said he'd k-kill me if I didn't listen. He said he was going to kill all of us."

"The guy who took you?"

She nodded. "His name is C-carson."

"It's okay. I've got you now. And we're going to get—"

The sound of tires on gravel brought Katie's head up as a beam of light flashed across the trees outside the bedroom window. Someone else was there. Hopefully it was Easton, but they couldn't stick around to find out.

"Shit." Grabbing Grace's arm, Katie dragged her to her feet. "Come on! We've got to go." She snatched the gun off the bed and pulled Grace into the hall.

The knob on the front door twisted as they rushed past the couch. "Hurry," she whispered.

"What the fuck..." Carson's voice carried over her shoulder as they rounded the corner into the kitchen.

She pushed Grace around the table toward the back door. "Go!" she said, as his footsteps thudded across the living room.

"Hey!" he shouted, sounding like he was just behind her as their feet crunched on broken glass as she shoved Grace out onto the deck. "Run!" she yelled, as he crashed into the kitchen table.

"Hey!" he shouted again as they both took off into the dark, across the lawn. "Hey! Get back here, you stupid bitch!"

Heavy footfalls thumped across the wooden deck as they ran for the trees.

Without even bothering to aim, Katie fired the gun in the direction of the house.

"Go! Go!" she urged Grace as they stumbled over the uneven lawn. More shots rang out, and Katie ducked as she followed Grace into the trees. Either Carson had found another gun or the one she'd taken was not his.

As soon as they were in the woods, the terrain changed. It was much hillier than she expected, and she realized too late, there would be no "straight" path back to the truck.

Heading in what she hoped was the right direction, she urged Grace up the low rise as Carson shouted obscenities, assuring them he was going to kill them as soon as he found them. "That way." Katie pointed to her right.

Grace almost glowed in her white t-shirt as they darted between saplings and scraggly, scratchy pines. Hopefully, Carson couldn't see her as clearly as Katie could. Her muscles screamed for oxygen. "Don't stop," she urged, waiting for the inevitable moment when she was either shot or Carson caught up to them and dragged her to the ground. "Whatever happens to me, keep running."

But neither happened as they continued up and down through the hilly forest.

They came into a road and Katie raced onto it, praying that JJ's truck was nearby. But as they passed several small gravel turnouts, she realized they were in some sort of campground. "Shit!" They'd gone the wrong way. She retreated back into the trees in what she prayed was the right direction. "Come on." A moment later, she skidded to a stop at the edge of a small cliff that descended into an enormous lake. *Lake?* Katie pressed her hands to the sides of her head, trying to catch her breath. "Shit."

A strange crackling sound brought her head around, and Katie scanned the trees behind them.

"Are you okay?" Grace asked, voice wobbling.

"Shh," she whispered. If Carson was out there, he'd hear them before he saw them.

"What?"

Katie held up her hand. Her breath paused in her throat as she listened. But the only sounds were the insects, and the water as it gently lapped against the shore.

"Did we make it?" Grace asked, reading her mind.

Katie dropped her hands to her knees, gasping as quietly as she could. *Holy shit.* She pressed her fingers to her heart. *Yes.* They'd made it. She'd found Grace, and they'd escaped! Katie laughed and looked up, head spinning. "Yeah."

"Are you sure you're okay?" Grace whispered.

Katie pressed her finger to her lips, and nodded. She was a little out of shape maybe, but she'd been running for years. She'd be fine.

"But…"

Katie frowned. "But what?" She blinked, trying to see Grace's face in the dark. "Are *you* okay?"

"Yeah. But…" Katie finally found her eyes. No, she wasn't. She was *terrified.*

A sharp pain shot through her chest as she turned and looked over her shoulder, expecting to find Carson standing directly behind them. "What's the matter?"

Grace didn't answer.

"Grace, what—"

"I think you were shot."

It took a moment for the words to register. *"What?"* Katie squinted at her chest, running her hands over her torso. "Where?"

A snapping twig brought her head around, and she pulled Grace behind her as she raised the gun. She would worry about being shot later. Her body, knowing her breath would give them away, thankfully clamped her throat shut. Maybe she'd spoken too soon about having made it.

There was another snap, closer than the first, and she pushed Grace back. She swung the gun back and forth. Not knowing if someone was there was almost more frightening than knowing they were. If Carson *was* there, she probably wouldn't see him until he was on top of them. A bright flash to her right brought her head up. It was quickly followed by the crackling sound.

"What was that?" Grace whispered in her ear.

"Shh…" Katie's voice trailed off as the hairs on her arms stood on end and her lips began to tingle.

From about fifty feet in front of them, Carson's voice cut through the quiet night. "What in the hell?"

"Oh, god," Katie choked, squinting through the trees. *It can't be.*

"What?" Grace asked.

Katie couldn't see it, but she knew it was there. "Oh, no," she said as the frantic snapping of branches and Carson's voice echoed through the darkness.

"Oh shit!" he cried. "Oh shit! Oh shit! *Oh sh*—" A scream split the night then ended abruptly. The wood immediately fell ominously silent again.

"What happened?" Grace asked again, as Katie nudged her backward with her elbow. A twig popped beneath her own foot.

"The Veil," she whispered, grabbing Grace by the wrist, dragging her away from it. *Why is there a Veil here?*

"What? Where?" the girl asked, stumbling after her.

"Run!" Katie said, praying they were on the right side of it as they darted through the trees. She was grateful for the adrenaline pumping through her body. Because if it wasn't for that, she would have fainted by now.

Something crashed through the trees behind them and Katie threw her arm back, and fired a shot in its direction, urging Grace on.

A second later an animal—raccoon maybe—scurried past them as another crackle and flash of light popped behind them.

"What was that?" Grace cried as they ran and something else scurried past them on the ground.

"I don't know! Keep going!"

If things weren't bad enough, it began to pour rain as they scrambled up and down, over rises and valleys that quickly became slick with wet leaves and earth.

It felt like an hour, but it was probably closer to only ten minutes before Grace slowed, clutching her stomach. "I can't—I need to stop," she gasped, as Katie looked over her shoulder. Had the Veil gotten Carson? It had sure sounded like it. Was it still coming for them? She couldn't take the chance.

"Just a little further," she said, going first. "Come on Grace," she encouraged over her shoulder. "Just a little farther and then we'll—" The rest of her words were swallowed up as the ground disappeared from under her feet and she fell.

Chapter Thirty-Seven

Day 24 // 6:05 a.m.

"SO THE DUDE just called you and confessed?" Sam asked.

JJ shrugged. "Yeah. He said I was right, that the President pulled everyone out because he knew Atlanta was gonna go."

"Shit." Sam said, as they bounced down the road

"I heard on the news that the Army for Freedom thinks the virus escaped. Do you think it really got out?" Parker asked, splitting the candy bar and handing half to Sam. They were all crammed in the cab of his dad's truck and it was pouring rain. And they'd been at it all night, too. Driving up and down country roads. Like breadcrumbs, he'd found debris at two turns on the road from his truck early, but then the trail had gone cold, and they'd been left to wander wander backroads until Easton called saying someone had spotted his truck.

"No," Sam said, shoving his whole half into his mouth. "Well, I mean not out from behind the Veil anyway," he mumbled around a mouthful of chocolate. "But the virus itself is almost certainly out."

"*What?*" JJ glanced at Sam as fresh drops of rain smacked into the windshield. Switching hands on the wheel, he rolled up his window.

Sam rolled his eyes. "Come on. Are you serious? Did you even graduate high school, man? Tell me the truth. Did you? Because sometimes—"

"Sam." He was not in the mood.

Sam sighed. "Fine. I don't know who came up with the Veil

or how they made it…" He glanced at JJ out of the corner of his eye. "Nor am I an expert on infectious diseases. But I do know it's statistically impossible to contain it."

JJ had no idea what that meant. "Meaning?"

"Meaning somewhere, somehow it got out. Or more likely, it was never completely in to begin with. Which means…" Sam waved his hand in a circular motion in front of his chest, urging JJ to use his own brain to sort out the rest.

It took a good long minute, but he finally caught on. "The president, or the government or whoever, they knew that too?"

"Bingo."

"You really think so?" Parker asked.

Sam nodded. "I guarantee it."

JJ scratched his head. It was consistent with what the commander had told him. "But if they knew they couldn't contain it, why even bother with the Veils?"

"Well, I don't know. And frankly, I prefer calculations that solve the mysteries of the universe, rather than predict deaths, so I can't say for sure, but if you held a gun to my head…" He stopped and JJ briefly thought about the dead man in the bar with a shotgun sized hole in his head that poor Mike had been left to clean up. "Sorry, bad choice of words. If you asked me to come up with a theory…" He shrugged. "Odds, man."

"Meaning what?"

Sam turned, leaning his back against the passenger's side door, as more drops splattered on the windshield. "Well, if they didn't veil the cities, we'd all be dead now. Too many people, and not enough manpower to contain it." He paused, thinking. "Now, they could have blown everyone up from the get-go, and I'm guessing if it wasn't for the Veil, that's exactly what would have happened. But luckily, someone did invent it, and now… Well, at least some of the Veiled cities are still standing." He paused again. "Maybe *that* is the reason they were put up. Not to save the cities that already had the virus. But to save the ones they thought had it but didn't. If the Virus can't get out, it can't get in either."

JJ was lost. "I don't—"

"Think about it," Sam said. "Right now, it seems like the Veils are traps for the virus. But if it *did* get out, then all of us on the *outside* are screwed too, and only the safe place will be…"

"The non-infected cities."

"Yep. They'd be like islands in the middle of a viral ocean, safe and sound while the rest of us drown."

"Holy shit," Parker said. "You think that's why they are everywhere?"

"Yeah. I think someone told the powers that be this was their only shot."

The cab fell silent for a moment, as JJ tried to wrap his brain around that. Could all the world leaders be in on it together? "But that's impossible. They never agree on anything."

"Well, if the argument they were presented with was compelling enough, they would," Sam said. "Which means…"

JJ finished for him again. "It must be *really* bad."

Sam nodded.

"So maybe the Prez is not the asshole everyone thinks he is?" Parker asked.

"Maybe, maybe not. All I know is that they apparently had to move fast on a complicated problem." Sam turned back in his seat and looked out the window over the mostly dark suburbs. "And maybe it's working. Look, most of us outsiders are still here."

JJ huffed. "But not for long if the virus is out."

Sam shrugged again. "But it's more manageable out here than in there. There's zero chance they'd be able to stop the spread in the cities. But out in the country, in the smaller towns, the population is lower, the playing field larger. They have a shot. Maybe not a great one, but it's more than nothing. The people are isolated, spread thin, and most everyone is tagged now."

"So they're just going to keep vaporizing people until they stop it?" That seemed like a really shitty plan.

"Oh, no," Sam said, shaking his head. "They can't stop it."

"But then why—" Parker began.

"They're just trying to slow it down enough to track it."

Parker looked as confused as JJ felt. "But what does that do?"

"It buys time," Sam said with way too much confidence.

JJ shook his head, not understanding. If they couldn't contain it and they couldn't stop it, what was any of this for? "Buys time for what?"

Sam gave JJ another exasperated look. "To find a fucking cure, man. That's the *only* way we're gonna stop this thing. You can't quarantine it out of the population."

Even though JJ knew next to nothing, something about what Sam said rang true. "So you think the Veils were just to...take out 'most' of the infected people, so the government could focus its energy and manpower on tracking down the... stragglers that made it out of the cities?"

"Why not?"

The clouds opened up, dumping rain on them and JJ flipped the lights on as the wipers swiped frantically at the bug smeared windshield and Sam rolled his window closed.

"It's brilliant, really. Because worst-case-scenario—which is they don't find the cure—then the Veils become their own fail-safe and protect the people in cities that aren't infected from the rest of us."

JJ couldn't believe it. But it made sense. It made *perfect* sense. "But..." he began. If that was the best idea anyone had come up with—

"We're screwed," Parker said, reading his mind.

Sam nodded. "Probably. Because again, I'm pretty sure all of this is a long shot. But look at it this way. If the chances of survival without the Veil is a million to one, and the chances with it are a million to two. Which would you pick?"

The cab fell silent as JJ barreled down the highway. He'd witnessed the Veil first hand and the destruction and chaos it caused. At the time, he'd been unable to imagine anything that would justify that devastation. But if Sam was right, and they were really talking about the human *race,* then the Veil, the destruction, all of it made *perfect* sense.

But right now, that wasn't his problem. At least it wasn't until they found Grace and Katie. "You're definitely smarter than the average college kid," he noted, turning left on the rain-splattered country road.

"Yeah, I agree." Parker said.

The corner of Sam's mouth went up. "Technically, I'm a genius."

JJ huffed.

"No really. I've got an IQ of 134, baby."

JJ rolled his eyes as Parker huffed a laugh. "Despite that," he began, "I'm really glad you're with us, both of you, because I'm clearly dumber than a rock. And if we are going to survive this, I'm going to need all the help I can get."

Sam laughed. "Pfft. Naw. You're not *that* dumb. You're just a different kinda guy."

Parker spoke up. "He's right. You're the kind of guy that hears a scream and runs into a burning building without a second thought. You're the kind of guy that steps into a fight instead of backing away from it. I've seen you."

JJ laughed. That was true. "Yeah, like I said, stupid."

"Man, he's tryin' to tell you, you're a hero." Sam shook his head. "Can't take a damn hint...I swear." Parker gave JJ a steady look. "And it's not stupid. Not to the people you save."

Was he talking about himself? JJ shook his head. "Back at the Veil, that was all Katie."

"No, it was half Katie, half you."

JJ flipped the switch and turned the vent on to cool his reddening cheeks. He wasn't used to compliments like that. Especially not ones that meant as much to him as that one did, and it made him uncomfortable. "No. I didn't want to—"

Sam pfft again, silencing him. "Just like I know that you probably failed history, I also know you wouldn't have left the kids there if Katie hadn't been there. You might have *wanted* to—"

"I did." JJ interrupted. "Believe me."

Parker laughed. "Oh my god, me too. The lice..." he shivered.

Sam raised his hand. "Same. I still get the heebie jeebies thinking about those infested little...scalawags."

Parker laughed again, and so did JJ, despite everything.

Sam went on. "But we hung in there. All of us, like we're doing now. And we did it because you and Katie were there to lead us."

The cab fell silent again as the minerally scent from outside mixed with exhaust and blasted them with moist air.

"I miss them." Parker's voice wobbled. "Do you think—"

Whatever question he was about to ask, JJ wasn't ready to answer, so he slung his arm around the boy and gave him a comforting squeeze. "I miss them too. We're gonna find them."

"Oh my god, you smell," Parker said, gagging.

They all erupted in much-needed laughter again as JJ scratched at his beard. He had changed his shirt, but yes, he did smell.

He sobered quickly as his tow truck came into view, abandoned on the side of the road, just as Easton had said. A fire crew spotted it earlier on their way back from a nearby wildfire, although how anything could catch fire in all the rain was a mystery. Now they just had to find the right house.

"What's the plan?" Parker asked, all the humor gone from his voice.

JJ's grip tightened on the steering wheel. "The plan is to get our girls back."

———

"KATIE!" JJ called, trying not to panic, as he ran past the burnt-out vehicles toward the front door. He recognized the truck, what was left of it, anyway. This was the right place.

"Katie! Grace! Katie!" He threw the front door open, rushing into the unfamiliar living room. "Grace! Are you here?" He ran down the hall as heat rushed up his neck into his head. He checked the two small bedrooms. "Katie! He flung open the last door. It was a bathroom, and it was empty.

"Shit." There was no sign of them anywhere.

"JJ!" Parker called from the other room.

Spinning around, he hurried into the kitchen with his heart in his throat. "What?"

"Look..." he followed Parker's eyes to the broken window beside the door and remembered Katie's confession the night after the Veil went up. '*I broke a window...*' It had to be her. He pictured her creeping up to the house alone, in the dark. He should have been there instead. "Fuck."

"And the door was wide open."

He stared at the knob. That meant she probably made it inside, but the question was, had she made it *out* in time?

"Hey!" Sam said from the backyard. "Over here!"

JJ's head snapped up, and flinging the door open, he rushed out into the eerily silent morning. "What?"

"A footprint."

JJ looked down at the non-descript shoe print in the wet soil, wishing he'd paid more attention to those forensics shows his mom used to watch. All he could tell was it looked too big to be either Katie's or Grace's.

JJ looked off in the direction it pointed. "Do you think this means she had escaped and someone tried to follow her?" he asked.

"I dunno." Sam said doubtfully. "I mean, this could have been made a week ago, from someone standing on the edge of the woods taking a piss."

Parker hurried past them into the trees. "Let's look for more."

They spread out, but if there were more footprints on the small rise that led away from the backyard, the rain had washed them away.

JJ kicked the dirt. "Goddamn it!" he yelled, dragging his hands over his face.

"What do we do now?" Parker asked, scanning the horizon.

JJ climbed to the top of the tiny ridge. "I'm not giving up until we find them."

"And how are we going to do that?" Sam said, asking the obvious question.

JJ didn't care how. He would do it. "I won't lose anyone else." The trees were eerily silent as he made his way back down to his truck. "You guys coming?"

Chapter Thirty-Eight

Day 24 // 8:08 a.m.

"KATIE?" Grace asked, bringing her around.

Groaning, Katie tried to sit up, but collapsed almost immediately as pain shot through her shoulder and fire ripped down her side. She cried out, which only brought to her attention the searing pain on the side of her head.

"Katie?" She could tell by Grace's voice she was terrified.

"I'm okay," she reassured the girl, reaching a hand out in her direction. She probably wasn't, but why worry her? "Wh-what happened?" She couldn't see out of her right eye, and could only make out blurry shadows with her left.

Grace found her hand and squeezed. "You... You went over the rocks."

Katie squinted at the twenty-foot-tall shadow looming over them. That made sense, because that's exactly what she felt like had happened.

"There's a road close by, though. Just over there," Grace said.

Katie rolled to her side and tried to sit up. Heat rushed to her head as the rest of her body went cold, as if to freeze out the pain.

"What do I do?" Grace asked, as Katie tried to survey the damage. But her eyes just wouldn't focus. Bile filled her throat as she brought herself up to sit. Leave it to her to escape a crazed gunman, only to fall off a fucking cliff a minute later. "You haven't seen Carson?" she whispered. "Heard anything?"

"No. Not since you fell."

Katie groaned and tried to inhale. A sharp pain shot through her ribs, pushing the breath back out. Carefully, she felt her arms and legs for broken bones. She hurt like she'd been snapped in half, but nothing seemed to be out of place. Her eyes burned as she blinked up at the blurry cliff again. Maybe the silver lining of her little tumble was that it had thrown Carson off their scent. Something warm and wet dripped down her neck, and she wiped at it. Her right breast ached and her face—she lifted her blood smeared hand.

"Don't touch it," Grace whispered, shaking her head.

Katie stared at her for a moment, then put it down. Maybe Grace was right. Maybe it was better that she didn't know. "Help me get up. Where is the road?"

Grace sniffled. "It's over there."

Katie's vision went black as Grace tried to help her to her feet. "Wait! Stop," she gasped, clinging to Grace's shoulders. "Give me a minute to…" Slowly, the darkness and dizziness passed. "Okay," she said, straightening out the rest of the way. "I'm okay."

"Are you going to die?" Grace asked.

The corner of Katie's mouth turned up. "I look that bad, huh?"

Grace didn't answer.

Kate straightened out her t-shirt as she took a wobbly step. She'd made it this far. She wasn't quitting now. "No," she said, leaning against the nearest tree as the ground swayed, and her left eye tried to focus. "I'm fine."

"Are you sure?" Grace asked as she stumbled to the next tree.

"It's just a scratch."

And Katie Newman never gives up.

Up ahead, she made out something that resembled blacktop.

"Okay, let's go. But we have to be careful. Stay hidden in the trees, okay? And tell me if you see anything."

Grace didn't answer.

A nauseating wave of dizziness washed over Katie as she turned. "Grace? What is it? What—"

"Nothing. I just…" Her voice wobbled. "I'm scared."

"I know." Katie gripped the nearest tree. "But the worst part is over now." She prayed that was true, because she didn't know how much more she could take.

"How do you know?"

A game she'd played once as a kid popped into her head. Rather than answer the question truthfully or lie, she said, "How about we play *'would you rather…?'* Do you know that game?"

Grace sniffed. "No."

Katie stumbled to the next tree, tripping through god only knew what kind of underbrush. Hopefully, it wasn't poison ivy. "I give you two terrible choices and you have to pick the least awful one. Ready?"

"O-okay."

Swallowing the vomit lurching up her throat, Katie dragged herself forward another step. "Would you rather…eat ice cream with ketchup on it, or a-a hot dog with…hot—" She took a shallow breath, and took another step. "…a hot dog with chocolate sauce on it?"

Grace laughed. "Hot dog, for sure."

Katie's face ached as she smiled. "Me too. Your turn."

Chapter Thirty-Nine

Day 24 // 9:17 a.m.

THEY HAD BEEN DRIVING for over an hour, but there was no sign of Katie or Grace. But they hadn't found any bodies back at the house, so it was *possible* that they had made it. Now, the question was, if they had, where would they go? His truck was his first thought, but it had been empty, keys still in the ignition when they found it.

As they drove up and down the hilly roads, calling for her, JJ kept checking the rearview, his guilt over leaving Katie mixing with his growing fear that—

"Oh, shit," Sam said.

JJ's eyes flew back to the empty rearview mirror, then he turned. "What?"

"Look…"

JJ followed Sam's gaze to the dash, and the little gas pump shaped light illuminated beside the odometer.

"Are you kidding me?" That meant even if they found Katie… "Fuck!" He slammed his palms into the steering wheel. Even if they found her, they were stranded. "Fuck!" Why couldn't *one* thing go right? "Shit! Shit! *Shit!*" He beat his hands against the steering wheel. Why did it have to be so hard? Couldn't they just find them and go home and live happily ever after?

"Wait!" Parker shouted in his ear.

JJ slammed on the brakes, and they all flew forward as the truck skidded to a stop. "Shit, Parker. What the—"

"Look!"

His head flew up, eyes settling on the road ahead, and a woman stumbling out of the trees.

"Holy shit." Sam said. "Is that…?"

JJ just stared. *No, it couldn't be.*

"Move!" Parker said, shoving his arm as sat paralyzed, staring at Katie, or what was left of her, as she waved her hand over her head saying something he couldn't hear through the windshield.

She was almost unrecognizable, covered in blood and dirt, the side of her face cut open and swollen. If it wasn't for his mom's old Brave's T-shirt, he would have doubted it was even her. His shoulders rocked as Parker shoved him again. "JJ, move!"

He went through the motions of parking and pushing the door open. Clinging to it, so he didn't fall, he leaned out of Parker's way as he scanned the empty road behind her.

Dear god, what had they done to her? And where was Grace?

Chapter Forty

"WAIT HERE," Katie said as she slipped and slid through the wet leaves onto the gravel that lined the side of the road. "Do not come out until I say it's safe."

With her better eye, Katie saw Grace's shadow nod from her hiding spot. Then she turned toward the road and stepped out onto it.

"Help!" she cried, waving her arms as she stumbled down the highway toward the vehicle that was heading toward them. "Help! Help! Help me!"

A second later, it stopped, and a couple of men jumped out. Hopefully, they were friends, not foes, because she didn't think she could run or defend either of them now, and the gun was gone. She'd lost it in the fall.

"Help! Help me! Help!" Her entire body shook as she pitched herself forward on wobbling legs. "Help!" What was wrong with her feet? Looking down, she finally noticed the angry red slashes that crossed her legs. She lifted her head, trying to keep her balance. "Help! Hel—"

"Katie?"

She stopped in the middle of the road and tried to make out his face through her swollen eye. "Parker?"

Was she dreaming? She touched her head. Or hallucinating?

"Oh, my god." The man behind him said.

She recognized his broad shoulders immediately. "JJ?"

She made out Sam's lanky form beside the truck. They were

all staring at her like…like…Katie looked down. Well, she didn't look great, but all things considered…

JJ rushed toward her as Parker came into focus. "Katie!"

She touched the right side of her face where it hurt and winced. Now she knew why Grace told her to leave it alone. The flesh was actually hanging from her cheek. "Oh…"

JJ stopped beside Parker and held his hand out like she was a frightened kitten he was trying to catch. "It's okay." That was a lie. She could hear it in his voice. It wasn't okay. She touched her shoulder. Grace was right, she *had* been shot. In the shoulder. The adrenaline had masked it at first, but now she felt it every time she inhaled. And she had lost a lot of blood. For the first time, Katie wondered if she'd truly make it or if she might die. She tried to lick her lips, but her tongue was dry. That couldn't be good, could it?

"Parker!" Grace rushed past Katie into his arms, bawling.

"Hey, hey…" Parker squeezed and rocked her. "I got you. Are you okay?"

But Grace was crying too hard to answer, so Katie did for her. "She's okay." Then her weary shoulders slumped, tears burning her own eyes like fire as she smiled at Grace's blurry form tucked safely in Parker's arms. If she died now, it was okay, she supposed. Grace was safe. She'd got their girl back, and that was all that mattered.

"Katie?"

Sniffling, she turned back to JJ, squinting, unable to see him clearly enough to read his expression. Was he angry that she'd taken his truck and gone after Grace on her own? She couldn't tell. "I'm sorry I took your truck," she managed before the earth shifted beneath her feet and she fell again. Darkness closed in promising relief, and knowing Grace was safe, she let it take her.

Chapter Forty-One

Day 24 // 10:00 a.m.

"IT'S OKAY. I've got you," JJ said, as he, Katie, Parker and Grace huddled in the back of the truck and Sam sped down the road.

It was Parker who pointed out that Katie and Grace might have been exposed to the virus. Thinking about Jinn and Amelia, JJ had insisted Sam keep his distance, just in case. If by some horrible chance they'd contracted it, Jinn would need someone to help her with Amelia, and he was the only one who hadn't touched the girls.

Huddled beneath the blanket they'd made love on, JJ held her, trying to quell her shivering body, while she came in and out of consciousness, praying they had enough gas to a hospital. When she'd collapsed on the road in front of him, mid-apology for taking his truck, he'd almost had a heart attack thinking she'd died. But she was still breathing.

"Everything will be okay," he said, kissing her hair. They hit a bump, and she moaned.

"It's okay," he said, pressing the left side of her head to his chest. "It's okay. We've got you now. You're okay." He looked at Parker over the top of her head, as she moaned against him. "Shh. You're okay, Katie." Her head rolled back and her eye opened briefly before closing again. She was not okay. There was a gruesome gash under her right eye that was caked shut with blood and she was covered in scrapes and bruises. Grace said she fell from a 'cliff.' And that was *after* she had been shot. They hit another bump, and she cried out.

"Sorry!" Sam's muffled voice apologized from inside the cab, as JJ held her, wishing he could bury his head in his hands and hide. This was all his fault.

A minute later, his truck came into view. They hit another bump and Katie cried out again. "Shh. Almost there." That was a lie, but why tell the truth? They were driving on fumes, going the wrong way because they needed gas. And his tow- truck was the only thing for miles that might have any. He turned to Parker. "I need you to hold her while I siphon the gas out of the truck."

Grace huddled under the blanket, shivering, while Parker awkwardly traded places with JJ.

JJ tapped on the back window separating them from Sam. "Turn it around. Stay in the truck," he shouted through the glass before grabbing the hose and hopping out.

Sam turned the truck around and pulled up alongside as JJ stuck the short hose into his gas tank and placed his mouth over the other end. Less than a minute later, the tank was filling with gas as JJ gagged and tried to rinse the taste from his mouth with bottle of water he'd found in the cab. He'd also grabbed the first aid kit from under the seat of his truck and threw it in the back. A minute after that pulling the hose from the tanks, he threw it back in the truck and replaced the gas cap.

"Ready?" he asked, tapping the driver's side window. Sam nodded from inside. "Then let's get out of here." Quickly he hopped in the back, and he and Parker switched places again.

He sat back down as the truck rolled forward and picked up speed. "Help me lay her down," he said, thinking that might help with the pain in her shoulder. "Push her feet... Yeah," he said, as she moaned and Parker slid her feet toward the tailgate and laid her out.

They were about forty minutes away from Hartford Creek and the nearest hospital was in Athens, about twenty miles the other way. The entire drive to his truck, JJ had wrestled with whether to confess when they arrived, they might have been exposed to the virus. If he told the truth, they'd probably be turned away. But if he didn't and exposed everyone in that hospital to the virus... Could he live with himself?

Pulling his t-shirt over his head, JJ soaked the corner with water from his bottle and dabbed at Katie's face, trying to clear away the blood from her eyes. She cried out, but didn't open them as she turned away. "Katie. It's me. I'm trying to clean your—"

"It hurts," she whimpered, breaking his heart.

"I know, but we have to get it clean. I'll be gentle. Okay?" She stilled as he wiped the blood away from her eyes and the wound on her face. Once it was gone, he pushed the skin back over her cheek.

Fumbling with the first-aid box, he pulled out several bandages. His fingers shook, whether from the road or his own nerves, he couldn't tell, as he peeled the papers back. Katie gasped as he tried to press the bandage down, but fresh blood was already running over her cheek and it wouldn't stick. "Damn it!" he said, blinking back tears. Now was not the time to lose it.

"Hey, relax," Parker said, leaning over, putting his hand over JJ's. "Give me the shirt."

Carefully, Parker cleared away the blood as JJ quickly covered the edge of the cut with fresh bandages. It wouldn't stop the wound from getting infected, but at least it wasn't hanging open anymore. Her face was so swollen he didn't even recognize her. Grace said it was a fall that caused it. Not the man Carson, as he'd first suspected. A discarded wrapper took flight and sailed out of the back of the truck onto the road behind them.

If it were only the cut, he'd just take her home, but... He pulled the neck of her t-shirt down and peered at the hole in her shoulder. Not that he'd ever seen a bullet hole in a person before, but it didn't look *that* bad. Her face looked much worse. But he knew looks could be deceiving. He noted the rusty brown stain on her shirt. She could have internal bleeding or broken bones or an infection, and he didn't know how to treat any of those things, which is why they should go to a hospital. But that brought him full circle, back to his guilty conscience. If Sam was right and the virus was out... The ICPH was not messing around. If they found out the hospital had been exposed... "Shit." He smoothed Katie's grimy hair back. They were fucked. Either way, they were screwed.

"What?" Parker shouted over the wind.

"I don't think we can't take her to the hospital."

Parker frowned. "Why not?"

"Because if we tell them the truth, that we've all possibly been exposed, they'll contact the ICPH, and you know what Sam said. They'll probably nuke the whole hospital."

"Well, then we don't tell them."

"And risk exposing everyone there?"

Parker shook his head. "The chance they came in contact with it is small. I think it's worth—"

"But we don't know that," JJ interrupted.

Parker rolled his eyes. "Well, we can't just let her die either!"

"I know!" He snapped. "And she's not going to die." At least he hoped not. And he *wanted* to take her! *Damn it.* He wanted to lie. But... "But, there could be kids there, mothers having babies."

"Are you willing to take that chance?" Parker demanded.

JJ looked down at Katie, more tears blurring his eyes. Was he? Willing to risk losing her? He couldn't imagine the next minute without her, much less the rest of his life—however long that was, but...

"What if she gets an infection? It's your fault she's in this mess in the first place!" Parker accused. "You should have been there! You should have been there, JJ! We all should have!"

The words stung, but Parker was right.

"I know. I should have. And I'm sorry. I'm sorry I let you all down, but—"

Katie's hand slid over his and squeezed. Her left eye sought his as she whispered something he couldn't hear over the wind.

"What?" he asked, bending over her. "What's the matter?"

"Take me home," she said.

JJ blinked back tears. "It's just—"

"I know. Take me home, JJ."

"But—" Her hand fell, and her eyes rolled back before he could finish, and his heart leaped into his throat, choking him. "Katie?" He shook her. "Katie!" Her brows came together slightly—his only indication she was still alive—as he wrestled his phone from his pocket and dialed Easton.

Easton's voice was barely audible over the noise of the road. "What do you—"

"What do you know about gunshot wounds?" JJ asked, cutting him off.

There was a pause. "Christ. What did you do?"

"Not me. Katie's been shot."

There was another pause, then a huff. "Well, take her to a fucking hosp—"

"She might have been exposed to the virus," he said, not waiting for Easton to finish.

Katie winced again as they hit another bump.

Easton didn't answer.

Pulling the phone away from his ear, JJ checked to make sure they were still connected and pressed it back into place. "Hello?"

"Well, what in the fuck do you want me to do about it?" Easton said finally.

"I don't know! But you're all I have, and—aren't you required to take first aid classes or something?"

"Yeah, but not—"

"Goddamn it, Easton," JJ growled. "Help me."

There was a loud sigh. "Fine," Easton said, sounding bored. "Did it go out the other side?"

"Wh-what?" JJ looked down at Katie.

"Did the bullet go clear through, or is it stuck inside her? Where was she shot anyway?"

"Her shoulder. Um…" JJ looked at Parker. "Help me roll her."

They rolled Katie over and he peered down the back of her t-shirt as she groaned. "Sorry," he said, spying the exit wound. It looked the same and not worse than the front one did. "Yes, it went out."

"And how long ago did it happen?"

JJ looked at Grace. "When was Katie shot?"

"I-I don't know."

Of course, she didn't. "Was it right before we found you or —"

"No," Grace shook her head. "It was more like in the middle of the night, I think?"

Into the phone he said, "We don't know exactly, but it's been a few hours, at least."

"Well, then it must not have hit anything important, other-wise she'd be dead already."

JJ pushed Katie's hair off her face, smearing the blood running down her cheek into her hair with his fingers. "So that's good?"

"Maybe. Is the wound still bleeding?"

He shook his head. "I don't think so."

Easton paused again. "Well, then…my best guess is she'll survive until she's out of quarantine and can go to a hospital."

JJ exhaled, never more relieved to hear Easton's opinion on anything.

"Just make sure to disinfect it, keep her hydrated and watch out for fevers. If it goes over 103, you're in trouble."

"Okay. Water. 103," he repeated. "Got it. Thanks, man."

"Yeah."

JJ hung up, then tapped on the glass, meeting Sam's eyes in

the rearview. "We're not going to the hospital," he shouted above the wind.

Sam glanced at him over his shoulder. "What?" he shouted through the glass.

"We can't take her to the hospital until we know we don't have the virus." JJ chanced a glance at Parker, who looked like he wanted to kill him. "She'll be alright. I promise."

Parker only shook his head, blinking his own tears back as he rocked Grace in his arms.

To Sam, JJ shouted. "Take us home!"

The truck slowed. *"What?"*

Katie jerked as JJ repeated himself.

"I hope you know what you're doing," Parker said, as Sam did a U-turn in the middle of the road.

"She's going to be fine."

Chapter Forty-Two

Day 27 // 1:01 p.m.

KATIE'S DREAMS WERE WILD. First she was flying through the forest, like a dove, then she was a little girl again back in her yard on that sweltering Florida day, so hot she was practically melting. Her eyes burned with sweat, her chest ached—then she was in JJ's kitchen, and they were all together. JJ, Parker, the girls, even Amelia's Beaver, and they were eating donuts and JJ said—

"Katie?" the voice startled her, and she gasped.

Turning her head away, she blinked fiercely in the bright light

"It's okay. You're okay." An unfamiliar voice said as she pressed her back into something soft and tried to see past the black spot in her vision. Her entire body ached. A hand closed over hers and she pulled it away as Parker's voice said, "We're here. You're in the hospital."

Her forehead ached as she drew her brows together in a frown. She recognized the IV and the pulse oximeter on her middle finger as she raised her arm and felt her forehead. "The hospital?" she croaked.

Parker came into focus, and then Sam, and her eyes widened. They looked like they hadn't slept in weeks.

"Are you okay?" she asked, trying to remember what she had been doing that had landed her in the hospital. "You guys look terrible."

The corners of their mouths turned up briefly before they forced them back down into a frown.

"What?" she asked, as someone hit the button on her bed and brought her up to sit.

"How do you feel?" the doctor asked, as Sam slipped from the room.

She tried to sit up more, and pain shot through her shoulder. "Like shit. What happened?"

Parker's eyes widened. "You don't remember."

She looked between them. The last thing she remembered was driving in JJ's truck, trying to find—she gasped again, gripping the rails of the bed. "Grace! We need to find…"

The words died in her throat as Grace appeared in the doorway. Sam stood behind her with his hand on her shoulder.

Grace was safe?

"How? When?" Tears filled Katie's eyes as she waved the girl over, and Grace rushed into her arms. "You're okay?" Katie cried as someone lowered the bar on her bed, allowing Grace to climb up beside her. Katie's insides turned to jelly as Grace wrapped her arms around her neck, and a dam burst inside her.

"Oh, thank god," she repeated and her body shook as she sobbed.

"Take it easy," the doctor said. "Everything is okay now. Everyone is fine."

Katie laughed against Grace's head, making her ribs hurt. "How…"

"You don't remember anything?" The doctor asked, as she shook her head.

Pushing Grace back, she studied her face. "Are you okay? Is everything…?" A memory of her asking Grace that very question flashed into her consciousness, and she frowned.

"I'm fine." Grace nodded.

"Are you sure?" Katie asked, her smile returning. Somehow

this was the happiest moment of her life, which maybe wasn't saying much, but... God, it felt good.

"Yes. You don't remember saving me?" Grace asked shyly.

More tears filled Katie's eyes as she shook her head. "I did?"

"Uh-huh. That's why Carson shot at you."

Katie glanced at the doctor. "What exactly happened?"

"Well, as your daughter said, you were shot."

Katie's brow went up. *Daughter?*

"And you took a fall and you have a concussion. So it might take a few days for the memories to come back. But they will, and everything will go back to normal, and you'll be just fine."

Katie looked down at the gown she was wearing, at the bandage across her shoulder.

"You were lucky. It was a through and through and there was no serious damage, although it will be sore for a while." Kate smiled at Grace, then at Parker and Sam. Who cared about her shoulder? Everyone was alright.

"Where are Jinn, Amelia and JJ?" she asked.

"They're at home. JJ was just here. He will be back soon."

Smiling made her face ache, and she finally noticed the bandage on her right cheek. Squinting down, she touched it. "What is this from?"

"When you fell off the cliff," Grace said.

Katie jerked as the memory of the ground falling out from under her surfaced. "Oh!" *Shit.* Yes, she remembered that.

"You remember?" the doctor asked.

She nodded. "Yeah, it was dark." She tried to roll her eyes, but it made her headache. "But still, leave it to me to fall off a mountain. And *that* is why I've never been a hiker."

Grace laughed, and the doctor smiled. "You have some bruised ribs, and a nasty gash on your cheek that, I'm not gonna lie, is going to leave a scar, and a few other bumps and scratches. But to be honest, if the outcrop you fell from really was as high as Grace here says it is, you're in pretty good shape."

"So, what you're saying is I look like hell, but I'm going to be fine?"

The doctor smiled again at her attempt at humor. "Exactly."

She hugged Grace again. "Great! So can I go home?"

He nodded. "I just need you to sign a few papers, then you can have your husband bring the car around." Katie glanced at Parker, then at Grace. One of them must have told him that, because there was no way that JJ would have said he was her husband.

"Where is he?" she asked.

The doctor laughed. "He's barely left your side for the last twenty-four hours."

Katie frowned. *Twenty-four hours?*

"I'm sure he'll be back in a minute. I'm going to go grab those papers," he said. "If you'd like to get dressed, he brought you some clothes from home over there. One of the nurses will help you button your shirt if you need."

"Where did he go?" she asked Parker as soon as the doctor was gone.

"I don't know," he said. "But he'll be back soon."

Chapter Forty-Three

Day 27 // 2:00 p.m.

JJ LEANED against the wall of the bathroom stall he was hiding in. The boys and Grace were in with Katie, but he wasn't ready to face her yet. Now that he knew she was okay—the doctor insisted she would make a full recovery—the weight of the last three days was catching up with him.

When they'd gotten home, per Easton's instructions, he'd doused her wounds with alcohol, and given her some painkillers he'd found at his mom's house, and watched her, like a psycho, sleep for the better part of two days, checking for a temperature every five minutes it seemed.

Easton had stopped by to tell him that Erica was back in town with Brian, and reminded him to keep Katie hydrated, so he'd poured glasses of water down her throat every hour while they all waited to see whether any of them were infected with the Virus. As soon as the forty-eight hours were up, they'd rushed her here and all they'd done since was give her a few scans, fluids, and a total of thirty-three stitches, fourteen on her cheek, and the rest closing up the holes on the front and back of her shoulder. According to the doctor, the bullet had gone in her back and out the front. And that was it. Dr. Forrester said that JJ's 'wife' would be 'like new' in no time.

Parker was the one that started the lie. He was afraid that the doctors wouldn't let them see Katie, and concerned that they might try to take Grace away if they knew she and JJ weren't her real parents. Neither happened though, whether it was because everyone thought they were a family or not, he didn't know.

It's your fault she's in this mess! Despite his tearful apology to JJ for speaking them, Parker's words hung heavy in JJ's mind. He hadn't meant for any of it to happen, of course, But Parker was right. He should have been there, and he wasn't. His grief-addled brain had tricked him into thinking the thousands of people struggling on the outskirts of Atlanta needed him more than the handful of people he left at home, and he'd gone, possibly to redeem himself for his failure to help his mom and sister, and left them all vulnerable. How could he? *Katie is fine.*

JJ leaned against the sink and hung his head between his arms. Thank god. He hadn't lost her, or Grace. They were still a family. One that in less than a month had become more impor-tant to him than anything else in the world. He looked up, meeting his eyes in the mirror, hardly recognizing the man staring back at him. And he'd be damned if he'd ever leave them, or Hartford Creek, unprotected again.

But he still had to face Katie. To apologize for being such a goddamn idiot and—what if she didn't forgive him? The bath-room door opened and Sam slipped in. He leaned against the wall behind him. "She wants to see you."

JJ hung his head again. It wasn't that he didn't want to see her. He did. It was just his guilt—what if she blamed him like Parker did? He couldn't stand the thought that he'd let her down.

He loved Katie and the kids…god so much it hurt. Ever since the night in his truck, just the sight of her overwhelmed him so damn much he could barely think. He loved *all* them, completely and helplessly, and it scared the shit out of him because he was afraid he'd betrayed it, and she wouldn't forgive him.

"Come on, man, let's go. The doc is discharging her."

JJ pushed back from the counter and straightened his shoul-ders. Pulling his cap off, he pushed his shaggy hair back, so it wasn't sticking out everywhere, and flipped his hat around as he dropped it back on his head. He looked like a caveman. But at least he was showered and in clean clothes.

"Do you think she's upset that I wasn't there?" JJ asked, desperate for reassurance.

Sam winced. "None of us were. But…all we can do is apologize, right?" He shrugged. "If she's mad—and I don't think she is—she'll forgive you."

It was a lovely, albeit possibly misguided, thought. "How do you know that?"

Sam patted his shoulder. "Because that's what family does. *You* fuck up, and apologize." He pointed to the door. "*They* forgive you."

JJ huffed. "Your pep talks could use a little work, and…I'm not sure Katie and I are family like that." He wanted to be. *He* was like that, but she hadn't pulled the trigger on the 'L' word yet and after this...

"Sure you are. Come on," Sam said. "You don't want to be late to your own funeral."

"You're a dick," JJ said, shaking his head.

Sam laughed. "I guess some things never change."

And some do in a blink.

"Come on," Sam said in the mirror, waving him toward the door.

JJ ran his hands over his beard, took one last look at himself, and turned.

"I was just playing," Sam assured him as he pushed the door open and led him down the hall toward Katie's room.

JJ shook his head. "I don't know that you were."

"Of course I was," he said, having the nerve to laugh *again*, slinging his arm over JJ's shoulder and giving him a rough hug.

"How do you know?"

Sam stopped in front of Katie's door and stood back. "You really are as dumb as a stump, aren't you?"

JJ scowled.

"Because she loves you, stupid." Sam shook his head. "Man, I've always got to explain every damn thing..." He waved JJ off, still mumbling to himself as he headed for the waiting room.

JJ stood in the hall and dragged his hands over his face. It was the moment of truth. It was time to face the woman of his dreams, the one that filled his heart, the one he almost lost but didn't, and apologize for not being there when she needed him most. What was the worst that could happen? *Don't.* Right. He squared his shoulders. *Whatever you do, don't cry.* He wiped his eye. Right again. He was a grown man. He could do this.

"Hello?" His knuckles rapped against the door before stepping into the room.

Katie turned, her wide hazel eyes looking exactly as they had the first day they met.

Instead of stilettos and a halter top, though, she wore a faded blue hospital gown, fuzzy socks, and her hair was gently braided at the back of her neck. But she was as beautiful as ever, even with her cheek bandaged. She took his breath away in just the same way she had the first time he saw her at Barb's.

"Hey, how are you feeling?" he asked, standing just inside the doorway.

She searched his eyes for a moment before answering, and he wondered what she saw when she looked at him. "You can come in," she said. "I don't bite."

That brought up all kinds of memories, and the corner of his mouth tipped up. "Yes, you do," he said like an ass before he could stop himself.

She smiled, and again his breath caught in his throat. "You're right, I do."

He dragged his gaze out the window, to where the sun shined brilliantly between puffy white clouds as his guilt crashed over him like a wave. Even if *she* didn't blame him, he'd never forgive—

"Is it *that* hard for you to look at me?" she asked quietly.

He raised his eyes skyward. Yes. Oh god, yes, suddenly it was. But not for the reason she thought. *Tell her.* The voice in his head sounded like his mom. "It is hard to stand myself when I look at you," he said, glancing at her out of the corner of his eye.

Her expression changed completely at those words. "What? Why?"

He shook his head.

"Come, sit." She pointed at the chair beside her bed.

He crossed the room, slumping into it. The pressure behind his eyes exploded as she held out her hand, and he took it. "I'm so—" his voice was a wobbly whisper. *So much for not crying.*

"Can you look at me for just a minute?" she asked.

His breath was ragged as he met her eyes.

"I'm going to tell you what I told Parker and Sam."

He held his breath.

She smiled. "I am fine. And me being here is not your fault, no matter what you think. I went after Grace on my own."

He squeezed his eyes closed. "I should have been there."

She shook her head. "No. If you would have been there when Carson and his friends came, he probably would have killed you. Sam and Parker too. He almost killed Grace, and she's just a little girl."

"But—"

"No buts. That's the truth. If you had tried to stop him, there is a good chance you wouldn't be here now."

He shook his head.

"And I can't do this without you, JJ."

"But if—"

Tears filled her eyes as she shook her head. "I-I'm a mother now, to *five* kids who need a family. And in case you haven't noticed, the world is ending." She laughed and wiped a tear. "You're not going to be able to save us all the time. You might not be able to save us at all. I just...all I need you to do is get out of bed every morning, do your best, and be there with us for whatever comes next."

He could do that.

"And this," she waved her hand over her body, and then around the hospital room. "This is not your fault. I'm here because of the choices I made and I'm glad I made them, because it made it very clear to me who I am, and what I'm capable of. And it's a *lot* more than I thought."

"But—"

"I promised myself a long time ago that I would never be a victim again. But since the Veil went up, I've felt like one. And for a while there, I wasn't so sure I'd kept my promise to myself. But I am now."

He stared at her, not understanding.

"It wasn't your "job" to rescue Grace. It was *both* of ours." She squeezed his hand. "And it turns out I can be just as brave as you when I have to be. It turns out I am just as capable of protecting *our* kids as you are. And... you don't know how *good* that feels, JJ. To be my own hero."

He shook his head. "But if I would have been there..."

"Then what? Maybe you'd be sitting here instead of me?"

"But—"

She sat up further, wincing as she reached behind her to adjust the pillow. He jumped up and straightened it out behind her. "Does getting shot hurt men less—" she gave him a look over her brows as she grunted and scooted back, "—than it does women?"

He wasn't the sharpest tool in the shed, but he was smart enough to keep his mouth shut.

Her expression lightened. "It's not your 'job' to protect me, JJ. I love it when you do, but I am an adult. And I am responsible for myself." She held up her hand. "Which I'll admit, I didn't do a *great* job of, since I fell off a freaking cliff. But..." She shrugged. "I survived. I'm here."

He shook his head as the corners of his mouth tipped up. "But—"

"But nothing. I told you. I don't need you to save me or protect me. Save that energy for the kids. Just respect me and love me. *Trust* me. Wake up every morning beside me because you *want* to be there. That's all. If you can do that, then...I can handle the rest myself."

JJ searched Katie's eyes, a new side of her that either hadn't been there before, or he had missed, transforming the helpless injured woman he should have protected into a badass *warrior* that looked like she'd gone five rounds in a cage fight with a bear and won.

His eyes widened. And it was the most beautiful, awe-inspiring, sexy thing he'd ever seen. "I swear to god, I will happily do every one of those things for the rest of my life," he said, his voice hoarse.

"Good."

She still hadn't said she loved him, but he was too far gone to care. And he was done hiding from love. Now, in whatever time he had left, JJ Dayton would embrace it full, head-on even if it left him hurting in the end.

He got up from the chair and sat on the edge of the bed.

Tears filled Katie's eyes as he gently pulled her head to his chest. Her arms snaked around his waist as a sob vibrated against his sternum. He kissed her head, running his shaking palms over her hair and down her good shoulder, rubbing across her back.

"I know it was only a couple of hours, but...goddamn it, I missed you so much. You and Grace." Pushing her back, he brushed the tears off her cheeks. "And I've never been so..." With his mom and Sierra, some part of him had known that it wasn't his fault, but with Katie, it had been different. He'd been so afraid she and Grace would die *because* of him. "Oh, god. I've never been so scared." She smiled as he stumbled over himself. "Luckily, you are the bravest, most beautiful woman I have ever met." He pressed his forehead gently to hers, stroking her cheeks, wiping her tears. "Not all of us are as strong as you are, you know. I'm not." He shook his head, smiling ruefully. "But I promise I will get out of bed for you and the kids every morning. Until the Veils come down or we all fucking die, I swear I will. And I'll crawl into it each night for *you,* and you alone...." Her eyes sparkled at that. "If you will have me." Her lips silenced him. And more tears came as she took his face in her hands. Her mouth was soft and full of wanting.

Cupping her jaw gently in his hands, he kissed her back. "I love you," he whispered again. "For all of it. For everything—" Her lips brushed his again "—that you are." She made a sound, half sob, half sigh. "And I will spend the rest of my life— however long that is— proving it to you, if you just give me a chance to."

Pressing her finger to his lips, she smiled. A real smile, one that reached her eyes and shot like lightning straight into his heart. "I told you before," she said, staring into his eyes. "You are my second chance. And I don't want a third." Her brow went up. "Do you?"

Her words were like pressure on a valve and as soon as she said them, something inside him loosened, and the tears came like goddamn water works. If he wasn't so fucking happy, he would have died of embarrassment to be bawling like a baby. But he was happy. He dragged her back into his arms and shook his head. "No. Never."

"Good." She pressed her uninjured cheek to his chest. "You get all my chances from now on...if you want them."

"I love you," he whispered against her hair.

Katie clung to him. "I love you too."

His heart exploded like fireworks in his chest.

"Now let's get our kids and go home," she said.

Chapter Forty-Four

Day 89 // 5:44 p.m.

KATIE TUCKED her hair behind her ears, staring at the lumpy blobs on the tray. They were no donuts like her dream, but they would have to do. She rubbed her shoulder. Maybe she should have added some chocolate chips? Or less peanut butter?

"Can I have a cookie?" Amelia asked, with big puppy dog eyes.

Katie shook her head. "That only works on JJ, and your *abuelito*."

A few weeks after she was out of the hospital, they'd received the sad news that Amelia's grandmother had passed away, and her grandfather was too overwhelmed to take her on his own. So she and JJ had invited him to stay in Hartford Creek so he could be close to Amelia. He was currently living at Mrs. Dayton's house with Parker and was a wonderful addition to their strange little family. He regaled Amelia daily with stories of her mother and grandmother, and got along famously with Old Mr. Goebbel.

Amelia frowned. "What only works on JJ and Abba? And when is Brian going to get here?"

"Nothing. Never mind. And no cookies until after dinner."

Poor Brian, Erica's and Easton's son, was her new obsession, much to his seven-year-old dismay. Amelia followed him around like a devoted puppy. "Brian will be here in about an hour."

"But that's too long!" Amelia complained.

Katie shook her head. "Sorry, kiddo. You know Mr. Easton

has to work, and he and Ms. Erica like to wait for him to get home before they come."

Amelia rolled her eyes like a seasoned professional and huffed as she turned toward the hall and called for Grace.

Things were still awkward between JJ and Easton, but much better between Easton and everyone else since Erica had him speak to a doctor about his mood fluctuations. Sure enough, they diagnosed him with something called antisocial personality disorder. Once he'd gotten on a psychotherapy regime—the small, country hospitals like the one she had visited, were bearing the majority of the medical care caused by the Veil crisis spectacularly—and properly medicated, Katie's confusion over the kind of man he was, disappeared. Astonishment replaced it as he tried his damndest to be a good father to Brian and partner to Erica. He still had his moods, and was an asshole much of the time, but his sharp edges and the darkness in him were gone. It was a welcome change. Erica and JJ had talked too. She confessed the truth about everything, including the fact that Easton never had really abused her. She apologized for what she'd done, saying *there's just no excuse other than the fact I was young and stupid.* JJ had forgiven her on the spot, and as far as Katie could tell, there were no more painful feelings between them.

Since then, he had become 'Uncle JJ' to Brian, and Erica had become a welcome addition to their lives. Katie rubbed her sore shoulder again.

That was what the Veil and virus did. It took people you loved away and gave you new ones that you weren't expecting. Some were bad, like Carson and his friends. Some you only thought were bad, but ended up being better than you expected. That was Easton. It turned out that was Erica, too. Before the Veil, she had been a social worker for child welfare, but now she acted like a counselor, a therapist for their tiny community, and was instrumental in helping Katie and JJ navigate the difficult task of helping the kids process the loss of their parents and the new stresses that appeared every other day on the news as city after city continued to fall.

Katie remembered her therapist Hunter and wondered if he was still alive in LA? He'd been right. Counseling was an amazing tool. She'd always thought of it as a weakness, but it wasn't. It was a test of strength. And she was stronger now than she ever was, because instead of hiding from them, she met her demons head on and dealt with them as they came. *Let it be.* They all did. It was the only way to survive.

———

"GRACE?" she called, peeking into the living room.

Grace's head appeared in the doorway of her and Amelia's room.

"I'm headed over to the bar to get dinner started."

The girl nodded, and Katie noticed the notebook in her hand.

"What are you doing?"

Grace shrugged. "Just reading my mom's letters. Getting my memory ready for tonight."

Every Friday they had "Memory Night," where each person recited a memory of someone they lost to the Veil. It was hard at first, but Erica insisted it was important to keep talk about those that were gone out in the open, not hidden away. Katie came down the hall and drew her in for a hug. "Which one?"

Grace squeezed her. "The one about my first birthday, when I climbed out of my high chair and got blue icing all over the carpet."

Katie laughed. "Yeah, that was a good one." She pushed Grace back. "You know, it will always be alright to miss your parents. Always. And like Ms. Erica said, it's good for you to talk about them and remember. That's why we do this."

"I know. I've been writing things down. Everything I can

think of. And I'm glad my mom told you these stories about when I was little."

They had been very hard for Katie to hear over the phone and copy. But... "Me too. Do you want to come with me to the diner?" They'd stopped calling Barb's the bar and had completely rearranged the inside to look more like a banquet hall. "You can sit at the counter—"

Grace shook her head. "I'll stay here with Amelia until dinner."

Katie nodded, locked the front door and headed out the back door. As she made her way through Mrs. Dayton's yard, she thought about all the people who were gone. There were so many. And in every case, it was tragic. The lives snuffed out. And by what? Little specks that were light enough to float on air? It seemed impossible.

She looked up into the window of Barb's apartment where Jinn and Sam now lived. Jinn waved, then met her at the back door a minute later.

"Hey."

Katie smiled. "Ready to tackle another dinner for fifteen?"

Jinn nodded. She'd gone back to her classic style, and wore the white polo shirt she'd had on the first day the Veil went up and a floral skirt that must have come from Ms. Michelle's garbage-bags of clothes she's saved for quilt material. They were a happy couple, Jinn and Sam, and they'd finally slept together if the glow on Jinn's cheeks were any indication.

"I just spoke to Sam. He and JJ will be here any minute. They were able to get flour and baking soda. So I think we'll be able to make bread again next week."

Katie grinned. Her days of starving herself were over and the thought of freshly baked bread made her mouth water.

"Are we doing stew again?" Jinn asked, grabbing Barb's old apron off the hook on the wall.

"Yeah." It was all they had at the moment.

Katie flipped on the rechargeable emergency light in the kitchen, got her lucky lighter, the one that had saved Grace, and lit the stove.

The garden out back behind JJ's was only just starting to produce, so they were scraping the bottom of the barrel. Luckily, his house was on a well to keep it watered because it was turning out to be a very dry summer, and there had been lots more wildfires. At least that was what the news was reporting, but after her incident in the woods with Grace, Katie wasn't so sure that's what it was. But she'd kept her mouth shut, only telling JJ her theory, because the President couldn't possibly be stupid enough to think he could sweep the countryside with portable Veils and then blow-torch away the evidence, could he?

"Hey!" JJ's voice boomed.

Katie's heart lit up, as it did every time he returned from a trip to Atlanta. Since her accident, he refused to go back to work in the city. Especially after the Army Commander he had spoken to about the squirrels called up and confirmed his suspicions. He and Sam only made the trip once a month to get supplies from the depot. The rest of the time, unless he was on a call with Easton, who had deputized him to help out in emergencies, JJ was home working on the house and yard, helping the neighbors, or playing with the girls. He was turning out to be a wonderful father.

"We're in here!" She called back.

He rounded the doorway with a box, dropped it on the stainless-steel table, and drew her in, locking his hands together around her back. His eyes were the same as always, deep, smoldering and filled with perpetual amazement, like he *still* couldn't quite believe she was real. It always made her laugh.

"What are you smiling about?" he asked, leaning in.

Flipping his hat around on his head, she tilted hers back and met him halfway for a kiss. It was that gaze that had gotten her through adjusting to her scarred face and changing body.

Because a person could fake a lot of things, but not desire. Half of it was the look, the other half was the trifecta, how it made the person being looked at feel. Every time JJ looked at her, she felt it all the way down to her toes. Her grown-out roots, limited wardrobe, and softer body had not changed that, and it was breathtaking to be so free.

"Mmm. I've been waiting all day for that," he said against her mouth.

She smiled. "Me—" She stopped, sniffing his breath. *Is that...* "Hey!" She pulled back, pressing her hands to his scruffy cheeks as her eyes narrowed. "Did you have a coffee?"

He broke into a grin beneath his beard. "I did."

She hadn't had coffee since the hospital. "Did you save me some?"

He shook his head, still smiling.

Her brows came together. "Why not?"

"What is..." Jinn's voice made her turn.

She held two giant bags of green peas. No wait, not peas. They were *beans*.

Katie's eyes widened. "Oh, my god. Is that what I think it is?"

"Someone brought them into the depot, and no one wanted them because they thought they were peas, so..."

"Oh, my god. Yippee!" Katie jumped up and down as Sam came in with another box. "I see you told her about the coffee?" He asked, rolling his eyes, setting it down next to JJ.

JJ looked at Sam, then Jinn, who nodded almost imperceptibly. It reminded her of the first day after the Veil went up when they were all conspiring against her.

Katie turned around. "What?"

JJ took her hand and pulled. "I've got a little surprise for you."

She grinned. Oh. Surprises were good. "Okay."

"But you have to come with me." He pulled her toward the door.

"Will it take long because I have to—"

"We got dinner tonight, and the kids," Sam said behind her. "You youngsters go do whatever…"

His voice faded as JJ led her out the back door. Instead of his dad's truck, they headed for the tow truck. They'd dragged it back to Hartford Creek, and it had taken months, but they finally found a new computer for it, and it was up and running again. That was just another indication that a mini-Veil had gone through that night. There was no other explanation that made sense.

Climbing up, she eyed him suspiciously.

He didn't look at her as he did a U-turn in the middle of the road, and headed left at the light.

"Where are you taking me?" she asked.

"You'll see."

"Why are you taking me?"

The corner of his mouth turned up. "You'll see."

Scooting across the bench, she snuggled beside him as he draped his arm over her shoulder. "How was Atlanta?" she asked.

"Better now. The depots are up and running. And they have most people set up in housing and the electricity is running on a schedule now, and they have six hospitals I think, set up. It's hard to believe they've done everything so quickly, but they have.

"The government dumping all our military resources at it helps." She paused, again thinking of the mini-Veil, and the fires and all the missing persons. "Well, some of them." Did it make sense to help some people and hurt others at the same time?

"Yeah. I think the worst is over for them. I hope."

"Me too. And did Jinn tell you about the report we heard on the news? Your commander was right. *You* were right about the squirrels. They're saying the virus has jumped species, like it did with HIV and Ebola. It came from animals and now we've given it back to them and we are all spreading it. That's why Delhi and New York fell so quickly. It was rats."

"Too little too late." JJ said sadly.

"For Atlanta, yes, but maybe not the remaining cities. The ICPH is working on an eradication plan. That's good news."

He didn't say anything.

"Did you hear San Antonio is gone?" she asked.

"Yeah."

"And Buenos Aires. And Johannesburg is falling."

"Yeah. It's not over yet. Not by a long shot."

Katie pulled her hair out of her eyes. "Do you think we'll make it? Survive the virus?"

"We've made it this far."

"Yeah, but more people on the outside are dying every day, and since the president was exposed, nobody believes it's the Army of Freedom anymore, killing everyone."

"No, they don't." JJ shook his head.

"I think Sam's right. All the top people have been in on it from the start. And they've been lying to keep people from panicking. I mean, if we were inside, don't you think we'd feel a little better knowing he was, too?"

"I guess. But it was so elaborate. I mean, it's hard to imagine the Veils went up, and by six o'clock someone had thrown together a replica of the Oval office for him to sit in and address the nation."

"There is a lot more going on that we are not seeing," Katie said, glad she wasn't the president. "A *lot* more. And maybe... maybe it's for the best?"

"Yeah," he agreed.

"Every time they mention anything suspicious on the news now, I think it's us, though. The fires, the...missing people. The abandoned towns. I think it's a coverup for one of those...mini-Veil instances Grace and I felt in the woods that night. It's the ICPH "cleaning" up another mess."

"It probably is. But maybe they are doing what they have to. Maybe everybody is. The president, the people who made the Veil. Just like we are."

"You really still believe that? After everything?"

"Yes. I do. Don't you?"

"I don't know anymore. Maybe."

JJ took her hand and wove their fingers together.

"I mean, what if it ends up being us tomorrow?" she asked.

He squeezed her. "Then we'd better enjoy the hell out of today."

———

TEN MINUTES LATER, they turned down the road that led to the river.

JJ stopped just before the bank dipped down toward the water. The sun shot through the trees on the other side of the river, casting an orange glow over the windshield.

"What are we—"

He turned in his seat. "I love you."

Heat crawled up her cheeks, and her toes tingled. So did other places. She smiled. "I love you too."

"And... I don't know how you feel about...about..." He scratched the back of his neck. "What I mean is..." He opened his mouth, then closed it.

"JJ?" she asked, nervous all of the sudden.

If she hadn't been sitting down, the look in his eyes would have dragged her to her knees as he took her hand and kissed it. "Without a doubt, I fell for you the moment I saw you. But...it was here, in this truck, when shit was blowing up everywhere, and you'd just told me I had a dad-bod—I still don't know what the fuck that is by the way—that... I knew."

Katie laughed, tears filling her eyes, even though she didn't know why.

He smiled and rubbed his jaw. "My mom knew before then, though. I don't know how she could, but…she did. I think that's why she asked me to take her to Sierra's. So I'd have an excuse to… to come get you."

Katie's smile fell. "Oh, no…"

He shook his head, reaching for her hand. "No. It's okay. It's —I just… All I meant was, if it wasn't for her, I wouldn't be here with you, and—" He pulled his hat off his head, and ran his fingers through his spiky hair. "Fuck. Why is this so hard?"

"Why is what—?"

"She gave me this." He opened his hand, and in the center of his palm was a small gold band with a single tiny ruby embedded within it. "It's my mom's wedding band." Katie's mouth fell open as she stared. The side opposite the stone was so worn it was almost threadbare. JJ continued. "I was in shock. I'd never seen her take it off before, but she just slid it off her finger and…" He met her eyes. "She gave it to me that morning. Just before we left. Said she wanted me to have it. Said it was time for it to bring someone else joy."

"Oh…"

"So, what I'm trying to say, *ask,* I mean is…" He inhaled deeply. "I don't need you to promise me anything. And I don't want to own you, or steal your last name… But I… Will you wear it? As a symbol of the joy that I feel…" He blinked hard, and Katie did, too. "…sharing my life with you, because I swear to god, that is what fills me *every* morning when I wake up beside you, every time I look at you, every time I touch you."

Tears spilled down her cheeks as she nodded.

He slid the ring on her finger, then tucked the wispy hairs that had escaped her ponytail behind her ear. "You are the bravest—" he touched her cheek, and she looked up into his muddy brown eyes, "—*strongest* person I have ever known, and the only thing that amazes me more than that is your bottomless love and your endless forgiveness. I cannot believe that you put up with me and all my shit and didn't—didn't give up on me before." He leaned over, pressed a chaste, gentle kiss to her lips, and sat back.

Katie sniffled. His mom had been instrumental in that too, and she wondered if that was how the universe justified her own mother by creating someone like Mrs. Dayton to balance the scales.

Katie met JJ's eyes and sensed his hesitation. "It was the same for me."

"What was?"

"There was something about you. The first time I saw you, I felt it. The trifecta."

"Tri-what?"

"Shortness of breath." Turning, she got to her knees and dragged his hand to her chest as her heart hammered beneath it. She met his eyes in the dying daylight. "Thumping heart."

She climbed on his lap and pulled his cap off as he leaned back. "And tingling…" She leaned close to his ear as she dug her fingernails into his neck. "…everywhere I like to be touched." Gently, she bit his ear as he exhaled against her sternum, and his hand found her hip. "Thinking about you was all I did that week in Atlanta." She sat back on his lap, and his body answered.

His voice was husky as he spoke. "Well, this dad-bod is all yours."

The corner of her mouth turned up. "And this…" She glanced down at her chipped fingernails and thickening thighs. She also had a jagged scar on her cheek that Grace said made her look cool and Amelia said made her look like an alien.

"Incredible woman?" JJ supplied.

Her smile returned. "…is all yours." She kissed him. "And she…would like you to stop talking and—"

Katie squealed as he threw her on her back and climbed on top of her. Dragging his shirt over his head, she revealed his slightly leaner chest and the collage of tattoos that covered it.

Then she dragged her nails down his back as she pulled his head down to hers. "Don't be gentle. Because I won't."

He groaned as she covered his lips with hers, and suddenly his hands were everywhere, and Katie gave herself over to him, to the sting of his palm and the pull of his heart as they collided with her body, while the lust and fever that built up inside of her broke and the truck rocked.

Chapter Forty-Five

Day 89 // 8:38 p.m.

KATIE LAY IN HIS ARMS, under the blanket he'd brought, sipping her coffee, as the last rays of daylight faded through the trees.

"Mmm." She sighed, taking another sip. "Oh god, this is so good."

He'd brought it in his thermos from Atlanta to surprise her.

"I'm glad we had sex first," she said, a hint of laughter in her voice. "Because this would have been a tough act to follow."

JJ laughed, knowing that wasn't true in the least. This was the first time he'd agreed to being unrestrained with her since she'd been shot, and if the sounds she made were any indication, well, he'd given her *exactly* what she wanted. He looked down as she snuggled against him, hands wrapped around her mug, his mom's ring glistening on the middle finger of her left hand, remembering the day he'd picked her up in Atlanta, watching her climb up into his truck in her skin-tight jeans and ass-ugly shoes. Never in a million years would he have thought that it would lead to this.

Oh god, was he a lucky man.

He'd known it since the hospital, when, to his amazement, she forgave him for being such a dumb ass. *Just respect me and love me.* And he did with every fiber of his being. *Trust me.* And it was such a wonderful feeling to be free of the doubt that had plagued him since he split up with Erica. *Be there in the morning because you want to be.* There was nothing he wanted more in life than that. To roll over and see her there, as Amelia climbed on top of him and demanded breakfast. *If you can do that, then... I can handle the rest.* And she had. She had handled *everything*. From the kids to the garden, to taking care of the folks in town, she made sure everyone had what they needed. And because of her, their little oasis, in the middle of the crisis that still reigned over the rest of the world, was *thriving*. She made everything she touched beautiful and fun, and although the kids missed their families, they knew, unequivocally, they were loved. And there was nothing children needed more than that.

Katie took another sip of her coffee and groaned, making him smile.

And her lovemaking was just the same as before her injuries; passionate, powerful, and full of trust. He rubbed his calloused thumb over her bare shoulder. She defied his reality and rocked his world in the same breath and—she swallowed the rest of her coffee and laughed, interrupting his thoughts. "What?" he asked.

She turned. "Can you believe my tag line used to be *'Keep living your perfect life, whatever that is. As you can see, I'm living mine'*?"

"And?"

"That was a lie. All I knew was I *wasn't* living it. But I am now. It's this." Setting the cup on the dash, she wove her fingers through his. "I don't mean the Veil, or the virus, or all the people we have lost—"

"I know."

"But you, the kids. If you would have asked me a year ago what I wanted, I don't know what I would have said. But somehow, our weird, wonderful little family, and Hartford Creek—Jesus, I can't believe I'm saying that." She shook her head, and he laughed. "Somehow it's all... maybe perfect isn't the right word but..."

JJ remembered something his mom had said to him when he was thirteen. "It doesn't have to be perfect to be beautiful."

Katie smiled and pressed her hand to his cheek. "Yeah, exactly. And you are the most beautiful man I have ever met, JJ Dayton."

He rolled his eyes. "Great, thanks."

She gasped, sitting up. "Wait, no! That came out wrong. I didn't mean it like that. You're perfect, too." Her brows came together. "Well, most of the time, anyway. You do have your moments. What I meant was—"

He pulled her onto his lap, sliding his hands across her bare hips, before clasping them together behind her back. "I know what you meant. And you aren't so bad yourself, Ms. Newman."

Her frown disappeared as one gathered across his forehead and he went on. "Now *please*, for the love of god, don't ever compliment me again." The corner of her mouth tipped up, and he tried not to smile. "Because you're really, *really* bad at it, and my ego is too fragile to take any more of your flattery."

She laughed as he pulled her head down, pressing their foreheads together. "Let's stick with what we're good at," he said.

She licked her lips, eyes flickering. "Which is what?"

"This." He kissed her, and she kissed him back, laughing deep and happily against his mouth.

Afterword

Did you enjoy Atlanta: The Veil Book Two?
Give it a star rating or review to help other readers find it!
You can review at these helpful places.
Amazon
Goodreads
BookBub

Acknowledgments

A big thank you to all my alpha, beta and ARC readers (E, J, Melissa, Cindy, Esther to name a few) Thank you to my editor, Penny White, for taking the time to edit yet another book, and a HUGE thank you to Esther for proofreading it for me. I owe you. Thank you to Laura Martinez of The Indie Author's Advocate for formatting the manuscript and for all the beautiful ads and for keeping me in line.

Another huge thank you to my cover designer Esther Bokhorst-Beentjes of Meraki Cover design, for another fantastic cover. I don't know how you put up with me, but I'm so glad you do. From the first concept to the last detail, you never let me down.

A big thank you to my kids for trying their best to give me time to work. It's not easy juggling a writing career and family, but we are making it work and I am forever grateful.

And finally, as always, thank you to my husband for his encouragement, and honesty and companionship. These books are as much yours as they are mine. I love you. Space needle (seven) woohoo!

Also by J.N. Smith

Song Series

Barn Song

Maggie Dubois is on a collision course with a midlife crisis. A slight detour leads her to a singles' retreat in Michigan's gorgeous lake country. Instead of finding love, Maggie gets drunk and buys an abandoned, foreclosed farm. When she uproots her life and moves there, she discovers it is haunted by William Morgan, a farmer whose spirit cannot leave the land that killed him. Has she purchased a nightmare, or the beginning of a dream come true?

Available Now

War Song

One minute thirty-four-year-old Army Air Force pilot Matthew Morgan is plummeting to his death over eastern France, the next he wakes in a field, back home in the States. *His* field, to be exact.

Elegant eighty-four-year-old spinster and French expat, Camille Lamaire goes into the kitchen to make a cup of tea. When she returns, there is a dripping wet pilot falling over the chair in her living room, babbling in broken French about a war that ended seventy years ago.

As he and Camille search for answers to the questions surrounding his return, the extraordinary happens. Something neither is expecting.

Available Now

Field Song

Nineteen-year-old Claire Morgan, born in 1906, wakes up in a field in a soiled party dress and snagged stockings with no memory of how she got there.

Twenty-two-year-old Daige Johnson is a modern-day major league football player relegated to the bench for a bruised shoulder and his third concussion.

While recuperating at his cabin in the bleak Michigan countryside, their paths collide and they become unlikely companions on the search for the truth about Claire's existence.

Releases November 7, 2023

The Veil Series

Book 1: **DETROIT**

Between her first cup of coffee and her daily dose of Xanax, Jane receives a cryptic warning from a trusted friend.

Get out of the city. Now!

Narrowly escaping with her children, she watches in horror as Detroit, along with dozens of cities across the globe, become trapped behind "Veils".

As Jane navigates the modern-day dystopia she meets Army veteran Matt Patterson. Together they fight for her children's survival, and a future neither expected.

Available Now

Book 2: **ATLANTA**

Social influencer Katie Newman and tow-truck driver JJ Dayton have nothing in common until a mysterious 'Veil' surrounds the city of Atlanta and they find themselves in the midst of chaos, in possession of a school bus full of kids with no idea what the hell is going on.

As the days turn to weeks and unspeakable tragedies unfold, they must band together to survive, or risk losing it all.

Available Now

The Keepers of Samsara Series

Josephine and the Lighthouse Keeper

A woman washes ashore during a horrific storm, injured and alone, with only a whisper of name for a past. She doesn't know where she came from, or where she was going.

Awaiting rescue, Josephine makes herself at home in a small cottage nestled beside a candy-cane striped lighthouse perched on the edge of the sea.

As the storm rages on and the days of isolation grow, she is drawn into an enchanting world of monsters and magic, where anything can happen and nothing is too good to be true, including Josh, the ghost of the lighthouse keeper who used to live there. Or is he?

Available Now

Kiss of the Siren

Joshua Cahill is living his dream life until a chance encounter with Josephine Walsh. As soon as he touches her, he knows two things. One, he has crossed a line, and two, he doesn't ever want to stop.

Torn between his guilty conscience, the rules of society, and a woman he cannot forget, Josh must decide what he truly wants.

Doing the 'right' thing will cost him her.

Doing the 'wrong' thing will cost him everything else.

Available Now

A Light in the Lantern Room

It was all a lie. Everything.

As Josephine learns the truth of her harrowing ordeal, she must come to terms with the coward she was, the Self she's lost, and the broken woman she has become.

Releases November 28, 2023

———

The Roberts Creek Hauntings Duet
The Bend

Tristan wakes up in a ditch on the side of a country road. In need of medical attention, he stumbles to the nearest farmhouse, looking for help. Instead, he finds Anna Boyd, the skittish ghost with a hole in her chest, who steals his heart the minute she tucks her hair behind her ear and says "Don't be afraid."

But the longer it takes for help to arrive, the more he suspects he should be.

Available Now

The Clearing - Coming FALL 2024

About J.N. Smith

J.N. Smith is a scientist, turned mother of two amazing kids, turned writer. She enjoys reading and writing stories that bring people of all walks of life together. Her hobbies include watching her kids play on the shores of the Great Lakes and running. She lives with her husband, kids, and three chickens, in rural Michigan.

Connect with J.N. Smith

Hi there! Did you enjoy reading Atlanta? Want to be the first to know about new books, sales, giveaways, and other exclusive fun stuff? Make sure to join my **newsletter**!

I'm always posting book news and reviews, pictures of Lake Huron, bugs (LOL), and sneak peeks of upcoming projects on my social media too. So, let's chat!

Want to join my ARC team? Fill out this **form** and someone from the team will be in touch!

Find all important links about me at https://linktr.ee/authorjnsmith

Made in the USA
Monee, IL
23 January 2025

10780901R00267